ANGEL

Belle Grey

CENTURY
LONDON SYDNEY AUCKLAND JOHANNESBURG

First published in Great Britain in 1990 by
Random Century Group
20 Vauxhall Bridge Road, London SW1V 2SA

Century Hutchinson South Africa (Pty) Ltd
PO Box 337, Bergvlei 2012, South Africa

Random Century Australia Pty Ltd
20 Alfred Street, Milsons Point, Sydney, NSW 2061
Australia

Random Century New Zealand Ltd
PO Box 40-086, Glenfield, Auckland 10
New Zealand

British Library Cataloguing in Publication Data
Grey, Belle
Angel.
I. Title
823.914 [F]

ISBN 0-7126-3831-8

Phototypeset by Input Typesetting Ltd, London

Printed in Great Britain by Mackays of Chatham PLC,
Chatham, Kent

CHAPTER ONE

Heads generally turned when Count Rudi Lazar took his seven-year-old daughter, Sylvie, to Kugler's in the Gizela ter for her favourite flavoured ice. It was not only the fact that Count Lazar was not married to the child's glamorous American mother that made the stiff Hungarian matrons glance in scandalized disapproval over their tiny cups of sweet coffee, but that the incongruous pair took such obvious pleasure in each other's company. There Sylvie would sit, her thin legs dangling from the balloon-back chair, her chin almost touching the marble top of the little round table, spoon suspended in mid-air as she looked in wonder at the sparkling chandeliers high up in the white and gilt stucco ceiling, while Rudi sat opposite, eating his own ice with boyish relish. Through the windows, the cab horses shifted restlessly in the square, twitching as the spring flies bit into their shanks. Budapest, too, seemed almost twitchy this spring. Change was in the air; the city was expanding; new thoughts, feelings and loyalties were beating at the door, and the sleepy cobbled streets and elegant little squares, with their bronze statues of well-remembered patriots, seemed to be waiting for the winds of progress to blow in from the west.

Sylvie and Rudi were indeed an unlikely couple, he the handsome Magyar aristocrat in his frock coat and cravat, with his raven-black hair and moustache, the little girl somberly dressed in a dark blue coat and hat, with clumsy boots on her delicate feet, her huge grey eyes ringed with pale purplish shadows.

'You promised you'd finish telling me about the wolf, Papa!' she now demanded imperiously.

Rudi had just returned from a month's absence on his country estate, overseeing modifications to the family's sugar refinery, and Sylvie, who had sorely missed her dashing, if unreliable, father, was eager for more of his stories of derring-do. He had adamantly refused her pleas the night before that he finish the story as he tucked her into bed, on the grounds that it would give her nightmares; in reality, he had needed time to think up a suitably stirring end to his tale.

Rudi gave his spoon a final lick, pushed his sundae glass away from him and leant conspiratorially over the little table towards her. 'Well,' he began, as she wriggled closer on her chair, 'there I was, going along the edge of the forest. It was getting dark and I knew I still had an hour's hard riding before me. My horse, Taltos, was tired, so I dismounted to walk beside him for a while. The forest was tangled with brambles and thicket and, in the dusk, I could only see a few yards into the trees. Taltos kept shivering and pricking up his ears, and I could feel him becoming more and more restive. I blew into his nostrils to calm him. Then the birds fell silent, and I knew that we were being stalked!'

Sylvie's mouth was open in horror, her eyes like silver moons. She held her long-handled spoon poised over her blackcurrant ice, forgotten.

'Suddenly I heard a rushing noise like the wind, and Taltos screamed and bolted. I don't know if you've ever heard a horse scream?' he asked, as he might a fellow connoisseur of horseflesh.

Sylvie shook her head seriously. 'No,' she whispered.

Rudi struggled to keep a straight face. 'Well, it's a terrible, terrible sound, I can tell you.'

'Oh Papa!'

'I looked behind me, and there, low on the ground, like a grey mist, was the wolf. It ran like a greyhound, but was the size of a man. Its teeth were yellow and its long tongue flapped about its jaw. My pistols were in the saddle holsters, so all I could do was draw my sword, kneel down so that I could brace the guard against the earth, and wait for the wolf to leap at me. The next thing I knew, I could feel the beast's hot breath on my cheek and feel its heart's blood pumping out onto my hands where I gripped the sword. I had a devil of a job removing the blade, for the animal was heavy, despite its speed.'

The little girl closed her mouth at last and, blinking as the ordinary sounds of the confectioner's impinged upon her once more, came back from that imaginary world where her father's story had briefly transported her.

'And what happened next?' she piped.

Rudi laughed and leant across the table to stroke a wisp of red-gold hair gently from his daughter's cheek back under the hat from whence it had escaped. 'That will do for today, my angel,' he said indulgently. 'Eat up your ice. We mustn't be late or your mother will be cross.'

At the mention of Rosa, the spell was broken, and Sylvie was once again fully conscious of the mirrored room in which they sat, with its lace-covered windows and satin curtains looped back against the wall to divide the restaurant from the shop itself, and of the noise of chatter and crockery. She was sharply aware, too, of the cold looks of the women who queued up, waiting for their exquisitely tissue-wrapped parcels of cake. She slipped her hand into her father's as they walked towards the door, leaning in towards him, awkward in her heavy boots. He looked down at her and smiled, a smile full of comradeship and pride.

They set off together hand-in-hand towards the Ferencz Jozsef rakpart. Rudi adored Sylvie, his only child, and basked in the glow of the image of himself reflected in her shining eyes. He knew that he was essentially a weak man, but Sylvie made room for him to experience the effortless strength he wanted to possess, and she shared with him the ardent sentiment he wanted from life. As they walked across the Chain Bridge, he lifted her up to look over the parapet, out across the wide expanse of the Danube below. The river was smoky and thick with steamers and barges, heading north, past the Margaret Island, to Vienna, and south towards Bucharest and the Black Sea. Rudi looked up briefly at the great iron chains of the bridge bowed above them. Moved by the bigness of the scene, he closed his eyes and rubbed his nose into her hair, inhaling her clean, soft smell. He hugged her closer and she giggled, pushing him away: 'You're squeezing me too tight.'

'You just ate too much ice cream!' he laughed, putting her down.

He encouraged her to chatter as they climbed up the hill to Buda through the narrow winding streets of the Water Town. Sylvie always loved the glimpses into the little old houses with their open yards, planted with blossoming cherry and plum trees. 'Can we go to the summer house again this year, Papa?' she asked. 'I want to play with the chickens like last time, and bring you a fresh egg for your breakfast!'

The simple request cut him like a knife. 'I think your Mamma has set her sights on Bad Ischl this year, Sylvie,' he answered carefully, but he saw her disappointment at once. The depth of her gaze upon him soothed the turbulence that once more threatened to disturb them, and he squeezed her hand. 'But we can go for a drive in Obuda, if you like,' he continued, making the everyday treat sound crammed with possibility. 'Or I'll take you to hear the gypsy music in the Vigado park one evening.' She smiled up at him gratefully, and pretended to push him up the last stretch of the hill.

They emerged laughing and breathless into the wide

cobbled square of Buda. From here, the streets were narrow and low compared to the squares and avenues of Pest, their painted stucco fronts adorned with old-fashioned decoration and intricate wrought-iron balconies. The Lazar family house was in a street where Magyar nobility still rubbed shoulders with wealthy merchant families. Painted green, with three storeys of elegant windows facing those of the house directly opposite, it had a wide entrance through double wooden doors into a cool vaulted passage that led to a central courtyard beyond, more like a farmhouse than a palace.

Sylvie and Rudi opened the glazed door that gave access from the passageway to the wide stone staircase running up to the glazed-in first-floor gallery that looked down into the courtyard. Sylvie's mother hated the place, and constantly nagged Rudi to take one of the smart new apartments in Pest, but Rudi loved the old house where he had grown up, and laughingly ignored her pleas. 'This may not be the most fashionable part of town any more,' he said, 'but our household's irregularity demands a certain degree of discretion, don't you think?' Sylvie listened with anxiety, knowing that, in most things, Rosa eventually got her way; for she, too, loved the house, especially her bedroom, high up at the back from where she could look through the branches of the chestnut trees down over the stone and brick ramparts of the old city to the prosperous villas and gardens on the road that wound back down around Castle Hill to the river. Taught by her father, she revered the old values, though she did not wholly comprehend their full significance, but she felt that the cool, echoing courtyard and inconvenient arrangement of the rooms with their comfortable ceramic stoves were somehow central to their philosophy.

As they climbed the stairs, they could hear voices

issuing from the open door of the main salon: they were late.

'You'd better go and change, sweetheart,' whispered Rudi in Sylvie's ear, as they paused in the stairwell. 'Go to Kati, and I'll go straight in for tea.'

Sylvie nodded, and kissed him on the cheek. Although apprehensive of her mother's moods, she was excited, for that morning Rosa had, unaccountably, told her that she might join the company. When Rosa Lapham was 'at home' on Friday afternoons, there were few among the glitterati of Budapest who did not pay their respects. Rosa did not think of herself as a woman of pleasure, but there was no place in the social scheme of things for a woman who was neither a wife nor a whore. Diligently, she had set about creating a centre around herself for that half-life that exists in any city where a royal court sets the boundaries to social movement, and her beauty and cleverness meant that word had soon spread amongst the opera singers, musicians and more adventurous members of Budapest's aristocracy that, at *l'Américaine*'s, there would always be interesting people to meet and richly-spiced gossip worth hearing. The rigid etiquette of other salons was relaxed; people seated themselves comfortably or lounged by the tall windows, laughter and music were encouraged and several regulars stayed considerably longer than the ten to fifteen minutes properly allotted to an afternoon call.

Sylvie treasured those afternoons when she was permitted to join the guests, although she seldom took her eager eyes off her shiningly beautiful mother in her wide, flowing crinolines. She would sit, quiet and awestruck, breathless with pleasure when Rosa's remarks were greeted with particular merriment, or when, as the guests were leaving, they lingered over their adieux, holding Rosa's hand, their whispers making her blush prettily. As a small child, Sylvie had soon learned not to reach out for her mother's dangling earrings or spangled shawls and became content to worship from afar. She sensed that her mother was different from other women – not just because she spoke English to her, but because people treated her in a special way. Sylvie suspected sometimes that her mother had fairy blood, like the princesses her father told her about at bedtime, for Rudi had said that her mother came from a faraway place, across a huge ocean, far bigger even than Lake Balaton, and she adored her unreservedly. If not affectionate, Rosa was always consistent in her attitude to her child; Sylvie made few demands, and Rosa returned that consideration with unfailing indifference.

Tea had already been served when Sylvie entered the drawing room, dressed by Kati her nurse in a fresh white lace frock and white shoes and stockings, her hair newly brushed and tied with a yellow ribbon. Rudi turned from where he stood by the open window to smile at her. He watched as the child straightened her shoulders, looked directly at her magnificent mother and went over to where she sat by the tea table, ready to perform her part in the charade of Rosa's perfect motherhood, drawing compliments from all present with her pretty ways. Side by side, it was only the mass of Sylvie's hair that bore any resemblance to Rosa, although it was of a much deeper gold than her mother's fluffy blonde curls, for Sylvie's small features seemed pinched and sharp beside Rosa's glossy abundance. At twenty-seven, Rosa's hands, feet and the bones of her face were fine and delicate, her skin was a flawless confection of peaches and rose petals, and youth lent a softness to her face that hinted misleadingly at vulnerability. Normally, Rosa appeared to indulge her child, but today she and her guests were discussing a new arrival in the capital. She paid Sylvie scant attention, hurriedly put a small cake on a plate and handed it to her daughter with a slight push that Sylvie knew meant she should get out of the limelight.

Rudi witnessed Rosa's action, and understood how sensitive Sylvie was to her mother's appreciation of her attempts to please her by being the 'child full of wonder'. He saw his daughter sit on a chair against the wall, the untouched plate in her hands and her legs straight before her like a doll, responding automatically to the repertoire of silent glances and shrugs with which her mother reproved and controlled her. Rudi was only too aware that Sylvie would never resent Rosa for such disdain, blaming herself instead for having caused it by some trivial oversight or neglect of her own. He clenched his fists and turned away.

'But who is he?' asked Rosa, who had not yet met this stranger they were discussing. 'Who first introduced him?'

'Well, that's the odd thing,' answered Maria Zichy, a smart young matron who had lately modelled herself on Rosa. 'No one can actually remember when he first appeared, and now that he's in, no one can be found who knows quite where he came from in the first place, although he's so striking – quite small, you know, but dark and sleek – that I can't imagine how we missed him.'

'I'd like to know how he came by his wealth,' added her husband. 'It's certainly not from banking – although he talks creditably enough about the new steel and railway stocks – despite these American bonds he's placing.'

'And he's not the kind of man I'd like to question too closely, either. There's something about him: he's desperately charming and was terribly funny about poor Mimi's hat the other evening, but I still wouldn't like to say the wrong thing to him, if you know what I mean.'

'Yes,' added Henrietta Fischl, 'I know. I was introduced to him at Count Tisza's, and he seemed so courteous and spoke of himself in such a light way that I found I was on the verge of treating him as easily as any of my dearest friends. He seemed to enter a conversation in the middle, just plucking the topic in mid-air with a sardonic comment. Yet when he moved away, I found I was almost trembling, though I couldn't think why I should be anxious – it was such a nice party.'

'I thought perhaps there was a Slavic tilt to the outer corners of his eyes,' continued Maria Zichy, glancing flirtatiously at her husband. 'Some mingling of Genghis Khan's invaders among his forebears, but perhaps it was just the way he crinkled his eyes when he smiled.' The company laughed, as she pretended to blush behind her tea cup.

Sandor Zichy turned aside to where Rudi stood, staring moodily out of the window. 'Have you heard anything about him, Count Lazar?' he asked quietly. 'There have been rumours about this young man that he made his money supplying both sides during this recent Civil War in America.'

'What, Nye? Yes, I daresay he's just another of these young Americans who saw the Civil War for exactly what it was, a magnificent opportunity for profit. Isn't that how you bankers see war?' Rudi spoke too loudly, and the women around the tea table paused to listen, looking a little apprehensively towards Rosa. Rudi saw the look, and lifted his head stubbornly.

'The word I've heard is that he's a buccaneer and maybe worse. There's a story that he killed a man. Another that his partner in America committed suicide, but then no one knows what business they were in nor where it was. He's just one of many tumbling over themselves to get in on the ground floor of peace-time expansion. And where better to sell American bonds than here, now we've made our peace with Austria and are set for expansion ourselves? Oh,' continued Rudi, holding up his hand as Sandor Zichy was about to interrupt him, 'I know that most of you financiers see the compromise with Austria as a victory for Hungary, but, King or Kaiser, I still see Franz-Josef as a yoke around our necks, a yoke that I for one am too proud to wear!'

Rudi, bored, and not a little sore that Rosa constantly surrounded herself with people who had little time for him, was too tired after his walk and the wine he had drunk at lunch to put himself out for her friends, whom he considered superficial and disloyal to their country. 'So I'm sure that if he continues to be so witty about Mimi's hats, you can introduce him safely to your daughters. After all, there's no end to the opportunities for a young man with no old-fashioned scruples or childish beliefs in honour!'

Rosa bit her tongue. She had no wish to throw Rudi to the wolves, but really! His constant harking on about patriotism and loyalty was just dull, and she hated him to bore her friends, especially when she worked so hard to cultivate the smartest set in town. As it was, Rudi had left her last night to host a welcome-home dinner party for him alone while he had stayed carousing God knows where, no doubt drinking toasts to Magyar nationalism and other stupid ideals. It was too much!

'I'm surprised to find that your friends are so articulate, let alone accurate in their information.' She said it lightly, hoping to provoke a laugh and ease the moment by, and turned pointedly away, but Rudi coloured in fury and clenched his hands: he was no match for these people and knew better than to try.

'I'm sure you'll excuse me. I daresay I'm needed in the stables,' he said with clumsy irony. As he moved from the window, he saw from Sylvie's eyes that she instantly comprehended the by now familiar scene of conflict between her parents, and tears came to his own. He slammed the door, hard.

Sylvie started from her chair, as if to follow him, but caught sight of her mother's eyes brimming with tears, as it seemed to her, but in fact smarting with anger. Besides, as if with one movement, all the guests began to drink their last mouthfuls of tea, place their delicate green and white Herend cups back upon the tea table in front of Rosa and make their rustling adieux. Rosa made the best of it: in truth, it was getting late and her friends would probably have begun to leave soon anyway, but she knew that they were embarrassed at being witness to her crumbling romance.

'Will we see you at Count Karolyi's tomorrow night?' asked Henrietta Fischl solicitously as she kissed Rosa's cheek.

'Of course!' replied Rosa. 'After all, I promised the Count!' she added, smiling archly, trying to win back the light atmosphere for which her salons were famed.

But Henrietta leaned forward once more and whispered: 'Rudi's probably just tired after his journey.' She patted Rosa's arm and went out through the door. She could still be heard chattering as she reached the courtyard below.

'How is Rudi's mother, by the way?' asked Sandor Zichy. He and Maria were the last to leave. 'She must have been pleased to have his company. She no longer comes to town, I suppose?'

Rosa stared at him as if suspecting impertinence, but his face was perfectly respectful.

'Countess Lazar and my mother-in-law were great friends, you know,' explained Maria hurriedly, knowing Rosa's touchiness on the subject of Rudi's family. 'They were both widowed at the same time,' she went on, to forestall her husband pursuing the topic. 'May I call on you tomorrow, Rosa?'

Rosa squeezed her friend's arm as she kissed her.

'Yes, please do.' And she ushered the couple out onto the gallery that overlooked the courtyard. The windows had been opened and the spring freshness was noticeable in the air. Rosa breathed it in. 'How lovely!' she said, playfully taking Sandor Zichy's arm and proceeding with him down the stairs. 'Soon the lilac will be in bloom again. What a long dreary winter this has been, don't you think, Sandor?'

Maria, behind them, turned and popped her head back in through the door to the salon. 'Goodbye, Sylvie,' she called to where the child still sat quietly in the empty room.

Sylvie looked up and smiled gratefully, then stood politely, her hands folded correctly before her as she had been taught. 'Goodbye, Frau Zichy.'

Maria followed the others, shaking her head thoughtfully at the image of the abandoned little girl.

Sylvie had picked up her mother's shawl from where it had fallen to the floor behind her chair, and was folding it, caressing the soft fabric, as Rosa returned to the room. Her good humour was gone. 'Did you ever see such behaviour?' she demanded angrily. 'What is it with your father? Why does he have to behave like such a buffoon in front of my friends?'

Sylvie's lip trembled. It had been such a lovely day, and now it was all spoiled. She didn't know why her father had got so cross. She didn't understand why her parents had to fight. She felt somehow that it was all her fault. Perhaps it was because they were late home. Yes, it was all because she had made her Papa finish the story that they were late, and maybe that had upset her Mamma.

'I'm sorry, Mamma,' she said, beginning to cry.

'Mind my shawl!' exclaimed Rosa, snatching it from Sylvie's hands. 'Oh, for heaven's sake, don't cry! Everyone but me is out of sorts, it seems, today. Why don't you go and have a lie down? Or, better still, go and tell your father to sober up ready for the theatre tonight. I don't want him snoring next to me during the performance!'

Sylvie ran from the room in tears and went to look for the comforting figure of old Kati, her Czech nurse, leaving Rosa amid the debris of her tea party.

CHAPTER TWO

'Has Rudi ever been unfaithful to you?' enquired Maria Zichy late the following morning, helping herself to another cup of coffee. She and Rosa were sitting comfortably together in front of the open balcony windows of the salon. Rosa had her feet tucked under her, her striped yellow dress billowing out around the chair, while Maria, in a dark blue dress with a white lace collar, sat neatly resting her feet between the ornate ironwork of the balcony itself. The door to the salon was closed; they were too far above the avenue below for any observation other than the rudest stares; and they were gossiping hard.

Maria was the younger daughter of Budapest's leading newspaper proprietor. She had been married to Sandor Zichy, a wealthy banker, for five years, with no sign of children. A smart, determined young woman, she knew the social map of this corner of the Austro-Hungarian Empire better than anyone except her mother. She had lately decided that, if God did not intend her to raise a family, she would carve out other ambitions for herself.

Her first meeting with Rosa, six months before, had intrigued her. She herself was not naturally competitive and she had no desire to challenge Rosa's pre-eminence in the drawing room, realizing her own value lay in the information she possessed rather than in her wit and style. Rosa had quickly warmed to her, drawn by her openness and her quick understanding of the social nuances of the city, and they now made a formidable team. Sandor Zichy considered Rosa selfish and heartless, but Maria and her clever husband shared a sense of fun, and he thoroughly enjoyed the snippets of gossip that Maria exchanged during her regular visits with *l'Américaine* and had no objection to the friendship.

'Do you think he ever would betray you?' continued Maria candidly. She had a soft spot for Rudi. She was greatly taken with the cavalier manner in which he had, in most circles, assumed and ultimately gained acceptance for his relationship with Rosa, and admired his continuing loyalty to her. But she could hardly ignore the spats they were having lately, nor his drinking. She wondered privately if Sandor were right in his assumption that Rudi was trying to extricate himself from a situation that was all too obviously becoming increasingly trying. Although Maria found it hard to imagine that Rudi would jettison his daughter, he was a handsome man and would have no trouble finding consolation elsewhere, if that were what he wanted. His family – a branch, after all, of one of the noblest Magyar dynasties – must obviously be desperate for him to marry and produce a legal heir.

'No, I'm certain of it,' replied Rosa. 'He believes far too much in honour. Oddly, I think perhaps if we *had* been married, he might have strayed by now. But because we're not, he feels it all the more that he must behave correctly towards me – not take advantage of me, you know?'

Maria nodded, biting into one of the sweet cakes from the plate before her. 'I really don't see why you didn't just marry him, all the same. I can't see that anyone would ever have found out about your first marriage. If you hadn't told me, I'd have naturally assumed you were widowed. I'm sure that's what most people think.'

'It's my own fault, I know,' answered Rosa, also nibbling thoughtfully on a cake. 'When Rudi first brought me to Budapest, I was young and reckless and I thought the world was absolutely at my feet. In less than six months, remember, I'd gone from being an American schoolgirl who'd never left her home town, to a woman with two lovers who'd conquered Europe single-handed! Europe! I had it all at my fingertips. I thought it wild and daring to defy convention and be seen as a woman of passion. But you can't keep that up for years at a stretch, especially when you have a child! Now I'm just faintly disreputable!'

'Nonsense! But surely you could have just had it annulled or something? I mean, you were so young. How long were you with him?'

'Mr Lapham? Oh, only about three months,' answered Rosa gaily. 'Just as long as it took to get out of Saratoga Springs and off to Europe!'

'What on earth was so bad about Saratoga Springs?' laughed Maria.

'It wasn't so much the town. It could have been quite fun, really, especially in the summer season, when the hotels were full and the races were on. But my family would never have let me join in any of it.' Rosa's eyes darkened momentarily in anger at the memory. 'My brother used to go. He never minded them, even though my father whipped him once when he found he'd been betting on the horses! He was always wild. He never cared.' Rosa paused, a smile hovering about her lips. 'But it was like pressing your nose to a shop window and not being allowed inside to buy anything,' she continued, 'to see all the lovely dresses and carriages and handsome men. I don't think American men are as handsome as the Europeans, but they know how to look at a woman! And I know they used to look at me! I loved it!' Her laughter bubbled up once more.

'Rosa Lapham!' Maria laughed too, pretending to be shocked.

'So would you! I was only seventeen, but I used to feel like a queen when I walked down Broadway, the main street in Saratoga. They'd pass me on their way to the racecourse, or to the lake, and I could just feel their stares burning into my body.'

'Lucky you! I was still in the nursery at seventeen, waiting for my sister to find herself a husband.'

'But then in September all the people went off on the Hudson steamer, the orchestra playing, everyone on deck in their fine clothes. They never even looked back. And we were just left, my brother and I. . . . Well, I made up my mind to go too. It took me a week to persuade Onslow Lapham to elope with me!'

'But why him?'

'Simple. He mentioned he was going to Paris the following month! I wonder where he is now! Stupid man!'

Maria laughed heartily, her eyes shining at this delicious story. 'But why marry him?' she asked.

'I was only seventeen. I didn't dare refuse when he asked me.'

'Rosa!'

'No, seriously, I didn't. I had a hard enough time persuading him not to go and ask my father's permission! Which would have been the end of all my plans, naturally. Besides, when he proposed, he gave me a ring and matching earrings. Of course, they were nothing, really. I know that now. Only garnets. But I'd never been allowed any jewellery before. I thought that, if we were married, I'd be able to keep all the things he gave me. If we weren't, and I left him – as I fully intended to do – he might have said I'd stolen them, or something. I was just a bit scared, I suppose,' ended Rosa thoughtfully.

She looked in surprise at her friend, who was choking with laughter on her mouthful of cake.

'You'll get fat if you eat so many of those!' Rosa declared in a mock-pious voice. She waited while Maria wiped her mouth and took a sip of coffee to clear her throat.

'Do you never miss your family?' Maria asked seriously.

'I wonder sometimes what my brother is doing.' Suddenly, as the clock on the mantelpiece chimed the hour, Rosa uncurled herself from her chair, and stood up as if to brush the crumbs of cake from her skirt. 'Maria,' she continued as she busied herself, her voice almost drowned by the musical beat of the clock, 'you must never, never tell anyone any of this. You're the first person I've ever told in Budapest.' A look of distrust flickered over Rosa's face: she judged others by her own lights, and she herself was no respecter of confidences. But Maria was looking at her with wide eyes, obviously flattered by this distinction.

'You've got such style,' declared Maria admiringly. 'I can't imagine you being scared of anything.'

'I'm scared to death of being bored!' Rosa stretched her arms out wide, inhaling the breeze from the open windows.

'Well, there's always the mysterious Mr Nye,' said Maria promptly. This was the main topic she had intended to cover with Rosa that morning, and she plunged into it cheerfully. 'And I must say, if Mr Nye is anything to go by, I understand just what you mean about the way American men look at women. He's quite delicious!'

'Oh, I hope he is,' said Rosa, with a touch of real poignancy in her voice. She reached over and touched Maria's hand as she curled herself up once more in her chair. 'I can't tell you how awful it is with Rudi these days. He's so difficult.'

'Maybe if he saw you flirting with someone else, he'd appreciate you a bit more?'

'Maybe it's time for me to move on,' said Rosa pensively. This did succeed in shocking Maria.

'What, leave Rudi? You can't! What about Sylvie? No man would take on . . . ' She stopped in confusion.

'Another man's love-child?'

'Oh, no, Rosa, I didn't mean . . . '

'It's quite all right, Maria. I don't believe in deluding myself. And you're quite right. I mustn't lose Rudi's loyalty. But it's a shame. We had such fun when we first met. Well, for years, really. It's just since Sylvie was born, and then his father died, he's become so . . . so damned middle-aged!'

Maria pursed her lips: she felt sympathy for Rosa, yet championed Rudi for his constancy. He seldom denied Rosa anything she really wanted, and so obviously adored little Sylvie. But Maria's taste for intrigue got the better of her. 'Wait and have a look at Mr Nye at Count Karolyi's tonight,' she went on conspiratorially. 'He's bound to be there. A little intrigue won't hurt anyone, and you know you can rely on my discretion.'

Rosa laughed. The point of her tongue flew out and licked her top lip mischievously. 'Promise you won't be jealous?'

'Promise! On condition, of course, that you tell me everything!'

'Absolute candour, you have my word!' cried Rosa, rising and taking up the Herend pot to call for some fresh coffee. As she approached the door, it burst open, and in rushed Sylvie, still in her coat and bonnet, her hair escaping in all directions, followed at a more leisurely pace by Rudi.

'Good morning, Maria,' he greeted her courteously, and turned to kiss Rosa on the cheek. Maria felt a pang, seeing his smiling face and clear, dark eyes. With his elegant horseman's bearing and striking dark hair, he was a man that any woman would be lucky to have. 'Do excuse us,' he went on. 'Come, Sylvie, your Mamma has company.' He turned politely to leave the room, but Sylvie intervened.

'Oh no, Papa, let me tell her!' Without stopping, she

spun around to face Rosa, her eyes shining and her face flushed with excitement. 'Guess who we saw in Andrassy-ut? She stopped and talked to us, too!'

'I don't know. The Empress?'

Sylvie stamped her foot with impatient eagerness. 'No, Mamma,' she wailed. 'You've got to guess properly!'

Rudi saw the exasperation on Rosa's face, and, unsure of her reaction to the news, especially in front of Maria Zichy, stepped in to defuse the situation. 'We met my sister, Elizabeth. She was shopping and stopped to talk to us.' He tried to say it casually, to prevent Maria from picking up the truth of the matter, but Sylvie was not to be stopped.

'She kissed me, Mamma! She said that Papa should bring me to call on her. She said that . . . what was it she said about life being too short, Papa? What did she mean by that?'

Rudi saw that there was no hope for it, so explained with simple dignity to Maria. 'My parents, unfortunately, would not acknowledge Sylvie, or, according to their social code, Rosa. During my father's lifetime, my sister obeyed his wishes. Now she wants to know her niece, which is only as it should be.'

'And what about me?' asked Rosa coldly. 'Am I included in this cosy invitation?'

'One thing at a time, my dear,' answered Rudi gently, his eyes full of kindliness. He knew that Rosa had been hurt by the isolation she had suffered because of his family's attitude. 'We can talk all this over later.'

'You mean she still won't acknowledge me?' insisted Rosa, a note of hysteria in her voice. Sylvie looked inquisitively at her.

'Rosa, Rosa,' intervened Maria, laying a hand on Rudi's arm and signifying that he should leave this to her. 'You're an American. You forget how rigid the proprieties are here. Rudi's sister has just now done the unthinkable. It was a brave and courageous act. It was only right, of course, as Rudi says,' she went on hurriedly as Rosa opened her mouth to speak. 'But you're dealing with the habits of generations! These things just can't be rushed.'

Seeing that Rosa was prepared to be quelled by Maria's superior understanding of Budapest's unwritten laws, Rudi turned to Sylvie and saw the happiness on her face replaced now by confusion. 'Come, Sylvie, let's be civilized and take off our coats, then we can come back for some coffee.' He took the pot which Rosa still held forgotten in her hands and chivvied the little girl out of the room.

'Damn their arrogance!' burst out Rosa as the door closed. 'I left Saratoga because it was always "it's not done" or, "what would the neighbours think?". Cowards! I believed that in Europe there would be a wider sweep of things, that people who had seen a bit of life would have bigger ideas than a Sunday School picnic! For all their genealogy, those Lazars are as narrow-minded as my maiden aunts!'

'Hush, Rosa. Don't cry about it, please.'

'I'm just so angry at those mealy-mouthed hypocrites!'

'I know, I know,' soothed Maria, but Rosa shook herself free.

'I'll show them,' declared Rosa. She put up her hand to fluff out the blonde curls around her face, worn defiantly at variance with the prevailing fashion for smooth, straight hair, settled her earrings in place and shook out the creases in her wide skirts, then looked challengingly at her friend. 'You'll see,' she said, with a glint in her eye. 'You'll see.'

When Rudi came, as he usually did, to kiss Sylvie goodnight, she could smell the familiar tang of wine on his breath, mixed with the smell of his shaving soap, and saw that his eyes had that faraway look, even though he hugged her tight and brushed her cheek with his moustache to make her giggle.

'Tell me a story, Papa,' she insisted, refusing to let go of his coat sleeve.

'I told you one yesterday, about the wolf.' He pretended to be indignant. She responded by snaking her little arms up around his neck, kneeling on the bed in her long white nightgown.

'Tell it to me again, Papa,' she said, rubbing her nose against his cheek.

'I'll feed you to the wolves, if you're not careful.' And he began to tickle her, so that she loosened her hold on him. This was a familiar routine, but tonight it seemed to Sylvie that he wanted to hide his face against her as he pretended helplessness against the onslaught of her spidery hands, and that he stiffened when they heard, outside on the staircase, the luxurious rustle of Rosa's full skirts.

Rosa had refused to let Rudi even mention his meeting with his sister when they were alone together after Maria had been driven off in her barouche. 'Why don't you go back to your estates?' she'd taunted him. 'I've gotten along very nicely without you this past month. Now you're back, everything's gone wrong. You always spoil everything for me!'

Rudi burned with sympathy for her. He felt that her defiance hid her hurt. But her refusal to allow him near her, to comfort her, angered him, made him feel mad and miserable that they who had once clung to each other in such passion should now be so ugly together. And so he turned on her savagely, demanding to know why she had had to make such a scene in front of Sylvie, accusing her of being jealous of her own child, of Sylvie's ability to win love from her own flesh and blood. 'She's my child,' he'd shouted, hating himself for wanting to make Rosa acknowledge his power, even if it was only the power to wound her. 'Sylvie has a right to belong somewhere. You show her no more affection than my family do, so who are you to criticize my sister for wanting to change all that?' Afraid of saying more, he had flung out of the room and shut himself up in the library with a bottle of burgundy.

Rosa's twitching presence now in Sylvie's doorway was a timely reminder to Rudi that he was late in dressing to be ready to accompany her to Count Karolyi's reception. As he emerged from Sylvie's embrace, he stared hopelessly at Rosa: she looked stunning, with the clear, pale skin of her bare arms, neck and breast above the broad sweep of her pale, lilac silk gown glowing in the light from the hallway. Her swept-back skirts gave her an air of grandeur, and her face seemed to float above the cloud of spangled tulle draped low around her shoulders. She wore a wired spray of enamelled flowers in her white-blond hair that continued to bob languidly after she had stopped moving, and would shake with delight if she laughed. Her eyes were bright, it seemed with happiness, but in reality with hard determination not to let Rudi spoil her evening.

'Goodnight, Sylvie,' she called firmly from the doorway. 'Rudi, the carriage is already waiting for us.'

'Oh Mamma . . . ' started Sylvie.

'What, child?' Rosa spoke curtly, until she saw the open-mouthed admiration on Sylvie's face, then her own expression relaxed and she smiled and rustled over to Sylvie's bed. Sylvie looked at every detail of her hair, her jewellery, her dress: no one had such a creature for a mother!

'You look so beautiful, Mamma. Just like a fairy queen.'

Rosa stretched out a slim white hand and stroked Sylvie's cheek; the child caught the scent of violets on her mother's skin, but then, with a sweep of her skirts, she was gone.

'Goodnight, Mamma,' Sylvie called after the departing vision. Rudi, at the doorway, kissed his hand to her, before following Rosa down the stairs, but Sylvie's shining eyes barely saw him.

CHAPTER THREE

The heat in Count Karolyi's magnificent reception rooms was becoming uncomfortable. Hundreds of candles burned in the chandeliers high in the roof, and the brightly dressed throng below, chattering and fanning themselves, was flushed with wine and pleasure. This was one of the most sought-after parties of the season, and virtually everyone who had been invited was there. Rosa quickly joined her special group of friends, but Rudi chose to wander slowly among the crowd, absent-mindedly lifting flute after flute of champagne from the footmen who passed with trays of wine. Tonight he was content to greet acquaintances with a brief bow and 'how do you do?' and to enjoy the proceedings alone. Watching Rosa at the centre of her admiring circle, he felt she was quite simply the most beautiful creature in the room, with her translucent skin flushed with the heat and her spangled shawl sparkling in the candlelight.

With a pang, Rudi remembered the days in Paris when he had first met her, the child bride of a middle-aged dress salesman from New York. It had not taken him long to persuade her to return with him to Budapest. Tired of the salesman's talk of ribbons and buttons, she had not even bothered to leave him a note. How he had loved her then! She had answered life with an optimistic zest and sparkle that he found captivating, and he had seen only her craving for romance and the courage with which she pursued her independence.

Then there had been Sylvie, and his first sight of that perfect little rosebud face in Kati's arms had captured his heart in a totally new way. Ironically, it was Sylvie's birth that first made him question his devotion to Rosa, realizing that, although he held her in his arms, caressed and made love to her as though there were no tomorrow, he could never begin to love her with the same depth of passion and unquestioning loyalty with which he loved his new little daughter. But he admired her and was committed to her, and it was Rosa who now seemed trapped in the trails of their relationship, struggling, with sharp teeth, like some small suffering creature caught in the fine web of one of her own gossamer shawls.

He felt sick at heart at how badly things had gone since his return from his estates, and angry that she was forever surrounded by people, so that there was never a chance for them to regain what little sense of intimacy they had left. He heard her merry laugh ring out above the roar of voices: such pretty ways she had – ways that Sylvie had inherited. If only Rosa would let him love her as the child did! It was so easy, really. Rudi felt himself grow maudlin, and took another glass of champagne. As he raised his head to drink, he spotted Nye out of the corner of his eye, moving unobtrusively through the throng. Rudi guessed that Rosa had set her sights on adding this newcomer to her intimate circle, and surveyed him openly. Nye did not return his gaze. The young man was good-looking enough, he supposed, slight, but strong. His face was distinctive, urbane, civilized, yet with a wanton flash of some more ancient emotion – greed, cruelty, desire – that was subtle and hard to pinpoint. His character seemed to slide from under one's gaze. Rudi noted a small smile on his face, neither absent-minded nor polite, but a hunter's smile of pleasure in the chase, an appraisal of the trophy which still ran wild, beyond his gun. Well, if he were in any way a connoisseur of women, thought Rudi, he would not fail to pick up Rosa in his sights.

Count Karolyi himself, one of the Emperor Franz-Josef's closest ministers, had stopped to greet the circle of guests of which Rosa was a part. Rudi could not hear what was said, but he saw the statesman make his bow with an old-fashioned flourish over Rosa's hand, and Rosa blush becomingly while her friends stood around her smiling. She could look so fragile, so tender and appealing, that no one would ever suspect the grasping turmoil of need and acquisitiveness that lay beneath. No one and nothing would ever fill the emptiness beneath that beautiful shell. At that moment, Rudi realized that he had probably lost her.

Sure enough, as Count Karolyi moved on, Nye moved silently into a position where he could listen to what Rosa said and watch how she carried herself. Nye did not speak a word, merely reacted by the animation of his facial expressions to the others' conversation, his eyes resting on Rosa whenever he was not required to follow what was being said. Looking from one to the other, Rudi fancied he noticed a kinship in their two faces, as though she and Nye were long-lost twins. Eventually, curiosity got the better of Rudi, and he edged in closer to where Rosa stood beside Maria and Sandor Zichy, watching to see how she would manage to coax Nye to her. Maria smiled at him nervously, while her husband raised his eyebrows significantly, remembering their conversation the previous afternoon, and indicated Nye discreetly with his head. Rudi merely nodded carelessly in reply. When a break came in the conversation, Sandor performed the introductions.

'Mrs Lapham,' commented Nye: he spoke German well, with hardly a trace of any accent. 'That is an American name, is it not?'

'It is, sir,' assented Rosa. 'I believe that you, too, are an American?' she asked, making no attempt to hide her interest in him.

Nye smiled. 'You have the advantage over me, Mrs Lapham. I know nothing of you besides what the eye can learn – though that, as all must admit, should be sufficient.'

Rosa fanned herself delightedly. She was at her best, not only because she instinctively responded to Nye's quiet attention, but also because she was furious with Rudi, whom she felt was purposely ignoring her. And anger always made her strong.

'What part of America are you from, Mr Nye?' she enquired again.

'I sailed from New York, and have been in Europe for some time,' he answered, silver-tongued: his eyes teased Rosa, daring her to question him more closely.

'Ah, New York!' was all she said, ready and willing to play his game. But he called her bluff.

'You know it well?'

She was as quick as he. 'I was married there,' she responded readily, her eyes dancing.

'And Mr Lapham . . . ?' asked Nye vaguely, making as if to look around the room. The smile on his face broadened as he saw her head go up: he had her mettle!

Maria stood silently by, watching the exchange, and directing apprehensive glances at Rudi, whose attention was momentarily distracted by a passing tray of champagne-filled glasses.

Just then, Henrietta Fischl rustled up, apologizing to the people who hemmed them in as she squeezed past to take Rudi by the arm, almost spilling his drink.

'Rudi, dear! I thought you wouldn't come tonight. You seemed so cross with all of us yesterday! Oh no, I'm sorry,' she cried, as he pointedly moved his glass to the other hand, fastidiously shaking the few drips of wine off his fingers.

Rosa scowled at Henrietta's tactlessness, and Rudi caught a trace of humour on Nye's lips as he bowed slightly in acknowledgement of Henrietta's presence.

'Oh Mr Nye,' exclaimed Henrietta, blushing. 'I didn't see you there.'

Nye bent politely over her hand, but, as his lips brushed the air above her glove, he looked up, over her shoulder, directly at Rosa. She saw the glance, and her head rose triumphantly on her stem-like neck. Rudi also saw the silent but meaningful exchange. He knew, all too well, of Rosa's sensual nature, and saw the desire in her eyes. He saw, too, the look of ruthless possession in Nye's face, and resolved then and there that the other man should not have her. He would not be cast aside! His mind was fuddled with the wine, but the anger and self-hatred he had felt earlier rose again, and he turned on Henrietta.

'Do you really care whether or not you anger a man in his own house?' he asked challengingly. 'Or maybe you think it's funny to return hospitality in that way, laughing behind a man's back? I'm sure hospitality is just as *démodé* to you all as loyalty and honour!' He stood back slightly from the group, meaning to include them all in his contempt. He looked from one face to another. Maria, moving to comfort Henrietta, whose eyes registered shock at this outburst, shot Rudi a reproachful glance. But before anyone could speak, Rosa loudly and deliberately laughed. Poor, foolish Henrietta could not stifle the giggle that rose to her lips, and one or two others joined in nervously.

Suddenly, all the rancour Rudi felt at these people's patronizing tolerance, and the loathing he felt at his own confused emotions, boiled over, and he slashed about him, using words like sabre cuts.

'Honour! Honour is just words to you. You know nothing of genuine emotion!' He directed his words at Rosa, but it was only now that he seemed to see her. He knew only too well that, for Rosa, pity was a toxic substance, something to be urgently metabolized. He realized that he had charged too far, against an enemy he had no wish to harm, and he paused, confused and unable to retreat. Then he saw her glance quickly at Nye, and he felt a pang of distrust in himself like a wound. It was intolerable, and he moved to dash it away. He raised his arm as if to strike her, and froze, suddenly appalled by what he was doing. Slowly, as if waking from a dream, he lowered his arm. He looked at Rosa in anguished appeal. Words began to form on his lips.

'Blackguard!'

It was Nye. While the rest of the company stood staring and immobilized, the young man seized the moment. Rudi continued in desperate scrutiny of Rosa's face, but he could detect no softening, no hint of forgiveness. He paused a moment longer in his silent communion with Rosa to make some inner adjustment. Finally, he turned to face Nye, who, with his perpetual, icy sobriety, smiled at him dangerously.

The other guests scuttled out of the space between the two men, and heads turned in their direction from further off in the great room. Rosa, suddenly indisposed, was helped away through the crowd by Maria. Nye, slight in figure and compact in movement, in contrast to the strength and colour of the older man, stood unassumingly as Rudi pulled himself to attention and delivered his lines as if he were reciting a litany.

'Sir, you have referred to me before others in terms which no gentleman can honourably tolerate. Will you apologize?'

'Sir, you have behaved towards a lady in a way which no man may tolerate. You are a blackguard.'

Now that he knew who the enemy was, and would soon be coming under fire, Rudi's coolness matched Nye's. 'Then I demand satisfaction,' he said.

'It will be my pleasure. Your seconds should apply to Mr Racker.' Nye regarded him for a moment longer, then coolly left the room. Rudi followed him, avoiding the glances – both solicitous and sarcastic – of the people among whom he had spent his life. He went to appoint his seconds and secure a doctor before awaiting the agreed rendezvous.

It was the hour before dawn. Rudi had been sitting in a chair drawn up beside Sylvie's bed for several hours, watching as she lay with her hands thrown back on the pillow above her head, her hair spread out around her face. Her mouth was slightly open and he could smell the sweet tang of her breath on the air. He reached out and stroked her cheek gently, as he had often done before, cupping her sleeping head in his hand as if, momentarily, he held some essence of his daughter. As he sat beside her in the darkened room, sometimes looking down upon her, sometimes lost in the thoughts in his own mind, there was a stillness that sobered him and made the events of the glittering ballroom that evening seem far off, tinny and unreal.

He was not afraid for himself: he had fought in duels before, and occasionally been a second to one or other of his friends, but he felt afraid for the slumbering child beside him. He felt sadness at the notion that, if he died, she would have no one who loved her, and he was ashamed and angry with himself for the long chain of actions, most of them insignificant in themselves, which had led to this moment. He barely wondered why Nye had challenged him so swiftly, each of them speaking their lines as if the parts had been written for them, heedless of any legacy of revenge or retribution left as an inheritance for Sylvie.

Finally, he noticed the first light of dawn and heard the stirrings of the birds as they began to waken in the branches of the chestnut trees outside. From his finger he took the emerald ring that he always wore and which had belonged to his father, and put it in the case where Sylvie kept her pencils. If he lived, he could retrieve it later in the morning without her finding it, and if he died, Sylvie would find it for herself.

As he turned back towards the bed, he saw that her eyes were open and she was staring at him incuriously.

'Papa,' she said, extricating her hand from the covers and holding it out to him. He took it and kissed it. She smiled sleepily and lay still.

'What's the matter, Papa?' she asked suddenly in the silence. He shook his head, wondering how it could be that she did not guess more fully at his thoughts. He smiled at her, squeezing the little hot hand that lay in his.

Then he heard the sound of a horse's hooves on the cobbles below the window and, looking out, saw Stefan, one of his seconds, wrapped in his cloak against the morning chill, looking anxiously up at the blank house. Suddenly he guessed that he was to die. He looked again at Sylvie; she seemed so unaware of all the things that troubled her by day that he found it hard to believe that any harm could really come to her. The thought cheered him, and he kissed her on her warm face and again softly on the top of her head, smelling the fragrance of her hair. Then he whispered farewell.

'Night-night, Papa,' she answered, closing her eyes peacefully. She turned away from him and curled up so that only the top of her head showed above the quilt.

Within an hour of leaving his daughter's bedside, Rudi lay dead in a meadow by the Danube, the river low and fast-flowing. Nye's first shot had entered through Rudi's face, the soft-nosed lead bullet expanding on impact to tear off the back of his head, and throwing the body backwards. He fell as if he were beseeching, clutching desperately for the life that had left him, the white and red mess of his brain, skull and hair spread across the trampled grass, his eye sockets emptied and dull. As the rising sun dissipated the mist, bringing clarity to the scene, Nye's man Racker held open the case for the pistol as his master absent-mindedly replaced the heavy gun, glancing over his shoulder to where shrouded figures crouched over the corpse. Old Europe had clashed against the new order: dash had met expediency and was utterly destroyed.

CHAPTER FOUR

When Sylvie awoke in the morning, the house was quiet; the normal bustle of the household was stilled. She dimly remembered her father's strange presence in her bedroom during the night, but thought little of it, and chattered as usual to Kati, who came to get her dressed. Downstairs, in the breakfast room, her mother had pulled a chair up close to the huge ceramic stove in the corner of the room, though the morning was sunny and bright, and her coffee lay untouched on the table. She seemed startled by the door opening, and looked at Sylvie with large, frightened eyes. Quickly, she licked her dry lips and smoothed her morning gown with nervous hands.

'Sylvie! It's only you. Come in, child, and Kati will bring your hot chocolate.'

As Sylvie sat down at the table, she heard the sound of footsteps on the stairs from below, and looked up curiously. Normally, visitors rang the bell, and Kati, who acted also as concièrge, would announce them. Besides, few visitors called at this early hour. But the footsteps continued along the gallery outside and paused only to knock hesitantly on the breakfast room door. Rosa flew up from her chair, her hands at her mouth, but, seeing Sylvie watching her, strove to compose herself.

'Come in,' she called as normally as she could, staring at the door. It was Rudi's friend, Stefan. Sylvie smiled at him happily, expecting his usual greeting and ticklish bear-hug, but he seemed taken aback at seeing her there. Rosa instantly noticed his glance.

'Why, Stefan,' she said gaily. 'What on earth brings

you here at this hour? Rudi's out, you know. Come,' she hurried on, as he was about to speak, 'let's leave Sylvie to her breakfast. Let's talk in the next room.'

Stefan bowed politely, and allowed Rosa to precede him through the door.

Unconcerned, Sylvie waited as Kati fetched her breakfast.

'What are we going to do today?' she asked, as the nurse stood respectfully by the table.

'What did you have in mind?' Kati enquired dispassionately, as she pretended not to notice her charge dip her croissant into her foaming hot chocolate and munch on it with relish.

'I thought you might like to take me into town. You said you needed to buy yourself some new stockings.' Sylvie smiled sweetly up at her.

'I can buy those down the road.'

'Oh, but they do such lovely colours in that shop off Andrassy-ut.'

'You mean the one next door to the toy shop – the one with the big doll in the window!'

'Oh, is it?' asked Sylvie airily. 'I really hadn't noticed.' And they both burst out laughing together.

'Well, I suppose I could buy my stockings in town, if that's what you'd like to do,' Kati said indulgently. 'But you're not to start nagging your Papa again for that doll, mind.'

'But it's so lovely, Kati. It's got five petticoats, I counted, and . . . ' But her description was interrupted by Stefan's return, with Rosa leaning heavily on his arm, her hand hiding her eyes.

'Madame,' cried Kati, running to help Rosa to a chair. 'Madame Lapham, whatever can be the matter?'

Sylvie looked curiously at Stefan, not yet comprehending how her world was about to be shattered. Stefan held out his hands to her. Slowly, she slipped off her chair and went to him, putting her small hands in his and looking trustingly up at him. He bit his lip and looked angrily, as it seemed to Sylvie who stared up into his face, over at Rosa. 'It's your father, Sylvie,' he began in a quiet voice, but his words were drowned by a loud sob from Rosa. 'Your father,' he began again more resolutely, 'he's dead, Sylvie. He died this morning. I was with him.' He paused, again uncertain, looking once more at Rosa as if for permission. Kati, standing by her mistress, crossed herself devoutly, and began to mouth the words of a prayer, though her lips trembled.

'You tell her, Stefan,' said Rosa, speaking each word clearly and distinctly. 'You explain to Sylvie exactly what you just told me now, next door.'

Stefan's face was ashen as he wrenched his eyes from Rosa's gaze. He looked down at the child's puzzled face. She did not move a muscle, so he bent, resting on one knee, his face on a level with hers, and hugged her tightly to him, so that he did not have to look into those searing grey eyes. 'We were out riding,' he explained. 'Rudi's horse stumbled on a rabbit hole and threw him. His neck was broken. He died instantly.' He spoke between clenched teeth, as if it hurt him to say these words, and Sylvie felt the love Stefan had for her father flow into her. 'He loved you so much. Always remember that, Sylvie. He was forever talking about you.' She was hardly aware of weeping, yet her face was wet and her fists where she clung to the lapels of his coat were soaked, too.

'Where is he?' she cried plaintively. 'Where's my Papa?' She tugged angrily at the fabric of his coat, but Stefan hugged her closer, his arms encircling her thin frame, almost whispering into her hair. 'He loved you, Sylvie. More than anything.'

Further words were spoken over her head, then Kati came and gently disengaged her hands from Stefan's coat.

'Come, my little love. Kati will look after you. Come upstairs with Kati.' The old woman was crying openly now.

Stefan stood and placed one hand over Sylvie's head, as if in benediction, and seemed about to say something more, but his eyes glazed with tears and Kati led her away upstairs to her room. Almost immediately afterwards, she heard Stefan's footsteps clatter down the stairs and the glazed door below slam shut. She never saw him again, but this interview with his old friend's daughter haunted Stefan almost until his own death.

All that terrible day, Sylvie lay on her bed, with Kati sitting by her, stroking her hair and wiping away her tears. She felt fear as much as grief; fear that her life could prove to be so vulnerable, fear that this arbitrary force might strike at her again. What if Mamma were to die, also? And she clung to Kati, sobbing and wishing just once more for that familiar smell of her Papa's shaving soap and the brush of his moustache as he kissed her goodnight. Surely this was just a dream; come tomorrow, all this awful pain would be gone, and everything would be all right again?

But tomorrow came, and the next day, and Sylvie was inconsolable. As the first weeks passed, she was numb with grief, and even Rosa became alarmed by her wan appearance: she was almost mute and wandered the house silently or sat for hours on end by the window, looking down through the boughs of the chestnut trees to the street below. At night she crept out of bed and, in a ritual that she felt must be kept secret because of the way in which her father had left the sign for her, she took his ring from her pencil box and stared into the opaque colour of the flat-cut emerald.

No family came to comfort her, and Rosa's friends who called seemed oddly embarrassed by her presence and were happy to be closeted away privately with her mother after the child had received their strained condolences. Maria Zichy came regularly, and, once or twice, as she lingered on the gallery while making her adieux, Sylvie overheard snippets of conversation that drifted up the stairs to where she sat listlessly on the cool stone, too apathetic to return to her own room after her brief, polite appearance in the salon downstairs.

'Has he been seen?' Rosa's voice was low and urgent.

'Sandor says he was in Vienna, and then again in Linz, chasing some financial deal.'

'The authorities won't bother him, will they?'

'These things are best left to take care of themselves.'

And on another occasion, Maria asked anxiously: 'Has Count Tisza still not called on you yet?'

'Oh no,' Sylvie heard her mother answer bitterly. 'Don't you know I've been cut?'

'Give it time,' said Maria soothingly. 'Let the matter drop. People are in a bit of a quandary as to the proper emotions to display, but there'll soon be other exciting news to replace yours.'

'I don't think so. Not with Rudi gone. My position is no longer the same. I won't be so welcome now I'm a risk to other people's husbands.' Sylvie heard her mother laugh unhappily, but could hear no more as the women's speech was drowned by the noise of footsteps and rustling crinolines as they descended the stairs.

Only Kati encouraged Sylvie to talk of Rudi, to recall the happy times they had shared. Sylvie's favourite reverie, which brought tears to her eyes to remember his pride and faith in her, was of her last birthday, which had fallen in February. She had awoken early in the morning, before Kati came in to light her fire, to see a pair of white leather skating boots hanging by their laces around the bedpost. Shivering with cold, she pulled them on, gingerly removing the wooden guards to gloat over the sharp, gleaming blades. That afternoon, Rudi had taken her skating to the Varosligeti To, the great pond where the inhabitants of Budapest loved to sport each winter. She'd giggled nervously as she tied the laces of her new skates tightly about her thin ankles, then stood warily, wobbling as she clung to him. The lake was surrounded by willows; in between the trees were braziers where people grouped, warming themselves and munching roasted chestnuts. Horses and cabs came and went constantly, and she could smell the sulphur from the Szeczenyi Baths further off through the trees.

Something about Rudi's expression as he swathed her head with a white cashmere shawl to protect her ears from the bitter cold had made Sylvie pause.

'What is it, Papa?' she'd asked. 'You look sad.'

He had nodded. 'You remind me of my mother. You have her deep grey eyes. Though with your mane of autumn hair, you look more like one of the little Russian princesses in that shawl,' he'd declared, grinning broadly. 'I shall have to buy you a sable muff for your next birthday! Now let's try those skates!'

'I'll never be able to do it!' she had cried, watching the couples streaming over the ice, lost in the dreamlike sensation of effortless speed and grace.

'Give me your arm and hold tight. Keep your toes pointed outwards. That's it! Off we go!' And, supported almost entirely by her father's encircling arm, they had drifted off away from the bank. He had already taught her to ride, banishing her fears with his strong laugh, and now he held her steady until, gradually, she had relaxed and, unconsciously straightening her spine, balanced herself with her outspread arm. After several slow circuits, he let go of her waist and, just holding her hand, they skated slowly together.

'See! You can do it, you little angel. You can do anything!' shouted Rudi, touched by her childish grace and bravery, and she had laughed aloud, smiling joyously up at him, drawing her confidence from him, and tingling with cold and pleasure. Later, on the long drive home through the town, exhausted and hungry, she had relished his silent, contented presence beside her in the carriage.

All this had gone, she now told herself constantly, still finding it hard to believe the permanence of the silence that surrounded death: could he really have gone without a last word, he who had such faith in her? She felt almost angry at him that he could desert her. Was it really only weeks since he had last hugged her to him? Then, the first sticky buds were opening on the chestnut trees outside her window; now they spread their green canopy across the sky. So short a time! The pain of it hurt so! But then she remembered his presence in her room that night, and the ring he had left for her. She could not believe that he had any intuition of the accident that killed him, but, with her childish faith in miracles still intact, she accepted the ring as a talisman of his love and continuing protection.

It was with her mother that Sylvie found it hardest to express her grief. When Rosa found her mooning about the house, she merely told Sylvie tartly to stop being so sentimental.

'Rouse yourself, child!' she finally snapped at Sylvie one morning. 'Do you think it cheers me, when I have so many affairs to worry about, to find you lazing around here?'

Sylvie was immediately contrite. 'Oh I'm sorry, Mamma. Is there anything I can do to help you?'

Rosa was only slightly mollified. 'Perhaps if you spent less time dwelling on the past – on what can't be helped – and more on thinking how I feel. It's not easy for me on my own, you know.'

Sylvie fought back the tears, and went to her mother, silently taking her hand and squeezing it. 'You've still got me, Mamma,' she whispered humbly.

But Sylvie's sympathy was worse to Rosa than her openly expressed resentment. She felt that Sylvie's grief was a rebuke, exaggerated in order to fix the blame for Rudi's death firmly on her shoulders, as though Sylvie's sorrow contained an accusation she was determined to refute. Yet how could she openly voice her complaint against the girl, when she believed that Lazar had died in a simple riding accident? This sorrowful face looking up at her was more than Rosa could take, and she shook her hand free of Sylvie's gentle grasp. 'It's all too much! Oh, Rudi left us a little money in the bank, but if he was still here, I wouldn't have to deal with all these bills, and our friends would still visit us, and everything would be nice again, like it used to be!'

Rosa stamped her foot and rustled over to the windows that stood open to the narrow balcony overlooking the back of the house. Sylvie watched her neat, rounded figure, and saw that she was struggling to overcome her emotion. Instantly, she blamed herself for her selfishness in not being more sensitive to her mother's grief. She realized that her own sorrow merely made her mother bitter and angry, and resolved to pretend to a blitheness of spirit that she could never really feel.

From then on, Rudi's name was never mentioned between them, but, feeling an imaginative sympathy with her mother, Sylvie came to believe at last that she was of use to Rosa, convinced that, in their very silence on the subject of their common grief, they were growing closer than they had ever been in Rudi's lifetime. Sylvie treasured that belief.

One morning, about two months after Rudi's death, Kati announced a visitor.

'The Countess Karatsonyi.'

Sylvie, who was helping Rosa sort out her sheets of music on the floor by the piano, leapt up excitedly as Rudi's sister, Elizabeth, entered the room. She was tall and dark like Rudi, but seemed more fully conscious of the effect her regal beauty had on people. Her black hair, swept back into an elegant coil low on the nape of her neck, and her smooth, fitted walking dress, in the very latest Parisian style, contrasted strongly with Rosa's becoming fullness and obvious femininity. Rosa stared at her with a mixture of cunning and resentment, longing to sweep past her out of the room in protest at the way in which she and Sylvie had been completely brushed aside as Rudi's family had taken over his funeral and burial arrangements, but also avid to know what brought the Countess here. The thought crossed her mind that she would ask Rosa to vacate the house, but Rosa as quickly decided that, if that were the case, she would have sent a lawyer, not come in person.

'Countess.' Rosa acknowledged her curtly. 'You may go, Kati.'

Kati bobbed a curtsey as she left, grinning delightedly, for she had grown up in the service of Rudi's family, and had known the Countess all her life.

'Sylvie,' continued Rosa, 'please greet Countess Karatsonyi, then you may go to your room after picking up the rest of the music from the floor.'

Sylvie went gladly to her aunt, who kissed her on both cheeks and, still holding onto her arm, said, 'I would prefer Sylvie to stay and listen to what I have to say. The purpose of my visit concerns her.'

Again, Rosa struggled with conflicting emotions, but decided that the time had not yet come for open opposition. 'Very well,' she said. 'Leave the music where it is, Sylvie,' she added sharply, as the girl went to pick up the sheets. Rosa nodded towards a chair at the far side of the room and Sylvie sat down, licking her lips with excitement. 'Please,' Rosa continued, indicating a sofa for the Countess.

'Thank you.'

The two women sat silently for a few moments. This

was the first time that they had come openly face to face, and both were disconcerted to find that it was not as easy as they had expected to hate each other.

'Madame Lapham,' began the Countess, 'I regret the circumstances which have caused us never to meet before, though they were not of my making.' Although she spoke gently, she wore a determined look that as much as added – 'the fault lay with you' – but all she said was: 'And I fully share your grief in the loss of my brother.'

Rosa bowed her head with dignity.

'As I say, my visit concerns my niece.'

'My daughter Sylvie,' corrected Rosa, tight-lipped.

'Your daughter Sylvie,' conceded Elizabeth.

Sylvie sat breathlessly on her chair, looking from one woman to the other. What was going to happen?

Again, they sat silently regarding one another for a few moments, then the Countess removed her gaze and, smoothing the silk of her dress over her lap with both hands, went on resolutely. 'I should like to adopt Sylvie. To bring her up and educate her with my own daughters, who are a little younger than she. You have no family here in Hungary,' she continued hurriedly, hoping to placate the anger she could see rising in Rosa's face. 'You are unprotected. What would happen to Sylvie, if, Heaven forbid, anything should befall you? And, if you choose to return to America, Sylvie will leave the only country she has known. She belongs here. She is a Lazar.'

At that, Rosa openly snorted. 'You were not so keen to claim her as such during Rudi's lifetime!'

'Then she had Rudi's protection.'

'And what about me? Am I to lose all that is dear to me – first Rudi, then Sylvie?'

At that, Sylvie could bear it no longer. She left her chair and came to stand silently, protectively, by her mother. Rosa's head rose on her beautiful neck, and she put her arm around Sylvie's shoulders, aware of the touching vignette they must make.

'What do you want?' asked Elizabeth, simply and gently.

Rosa once again flushed with anger, and Elizabeth continued: 'I do not mean to insult you, Madame Lapham. I meant that I do not know what a woman like you wants from life. As you say, you have lost Rudi. What do you intend to do now?'

With the Countess's eyes upon her, so like Rudi's own, and Sylvie's curious gaze beside her, Rosa felt trapped, cheated, belittled. How could she answer such a question? What she wanted were the things that no woman was supposed to want – money, power, fun. Things that an ambitious woman could only obtain through her own disgrace in the eyes of someone such as the Countess Karatsonyi, who had been born with sufficient money and power not to have to think of finding other ways to get such commodities. How could she say to this aristocratic gentlewoman that she, Rosa, would do anything so long as it saved her from a life of boredom and propriety?

'Is there really a place for Sylvie in the life you want, my dear?' probed Elizabeth, leaning forward earnestly towards Rosa.

Sylvie edged in closer to her mother, putting her arm around Rosa's neck; yet she was fascinated by the vista of possibilities that had suddenly opened out before her. Never before had she dreamed that her life might be otherwise. Now there were two seemingly opposing claims on her: she could be her father's child, a Lazar, or she could join fortunes with her mother and perhaps even return with her to that unknown, mysterious region Rosa had inhabited before her own birth, before her parents met. Rosa had never told her much about her past, brushing Sylvie's questions off with vague answers, and Rudi had made a joke of it all, portraying

Rosa as a fairytale princess, born of sprites and fancies. For the first time, Sylvie now saw her mother as part of a wider chain, a chain to which she herself belonged, linked with a family of cousins, grandparents, aunts and uncles. She looked wide-eyed at her paternal aunt, and suddenly felt an urge to hurl herself at this woman who so closely resembled her father, to claim kinship and to bury her head in her bosom, as Rosa never allowed her to do, and cry her grief and longing dry. She felt instinctively that she would be safe with her.

But at this moment, Rosa shook herself free from Sylvie's clasp, and stood up. Sylvie looked up in surprise. Rosa's face was tight and hard and she was trembling. She walked unsteadily over to the window and stood, hugging herself with her arms. Before anyone could speak, Rosa, still with her back to the room, broke the ominous silence.

'He was probably drunk, you know.'

Sylvie and her aunt were shocked by the venom in her voice.

'Who was? I don't understand,' wailed Sylvie at last, her childish nature picking up the horror of what Rosa was about to do.

'Your sainted father.' Rosa swung around, her wide black skirts, already trimmed with the purple allowed to a lengthening period of mourning, sweeping after her. 'He was stiff and old, and he'd probably had too much to drink the night before. What was he doing out riding at that hour anyway? Tell me?' Her mouth worked, as if in anger, or to fight back sobs, and her eyes were dark and narrow, searching out Sylvie's frightened, uncomprehending gaze. 'It's all your father's fault. If he hadn't taken such stupid risks, showing off to Stefan on that horse of his! He drank too much. He should have known he was past it,' she went on, as if unable to stop, speaking lines she had obviously mentally rehearsed many times. For a full half minute she stood, locked in some inner battle, apparently unaware of the Countess's presence. 'It was over anyway,' she ended finally, as her shoulders sagged and the fight went out of her.

Sylvie was shaken and shocked by the incipient madness she saw lurking in her mother's eyes, and by the pain of what she'd said. She looked in hopeless confusion towards her aunt, as if beseeching her to do something. But her aunt shook her head sorrowfully. The Countess accepted that the child had been told a convenient story rather than the truth – sometimes the authorities could prove difficult over a duel – but Rosa's outburst hinted at far more dangerous waters. She went over to where Rosa stood, almost unconscious of her surroundings. The sheet music still lay scattered across the floor beside her. She touched Rosa softly on the arm.

'I'm sorry, my dear. Nevertheless, my request stands. If Sylvie would like to come.' She turned to go, and held out her hands to Sylvie.

'She just can't bear this sorrow,' gabbled the girl, pleading with this woman, virtually a stranger to her. 'How can she – so frail and beautiful? Why else would she say such terrible things? She doesn't mean it! Such things could never, never be true!'

'I know, Sylvie,' said the Countess simply. 'He was my brother.' She kissed the top of Sylvie's head and was suddenly gone.

Rosa seemed still oblivious of her departure and of Sylvie's woebegone presence. Then she suddenly waved her hand in the air. 'What does it matter?' she said wearily. 'I'm going to lie down in my room. Tell Kati to come to me.' And she brushed past her daughter without looking at her, and disappeared upstairs.

After calling to Kati to attend her mother, Sylvie went to her own room, and, taking Rudi's ring from her pencil box, she held it tight, trying to fathom the real cause of her mother's vicious attack. Most deeply, she felt that it had been the threat of losing her, Sylvie, that had thrown Rosa overboard. How her mother must love her! She blamed herself for her instant of longing for her aunt's protection. Guiltily, she felt her mother must have sensed her momentary disloyalty. That's what had upset her so and caused her to say those frightening things, things she never meant. Without quite understanding why, Sylvie felt that Rosa must have abandoned Rudi, jettisoned his memory in this callous way, for her own survival. For surely only grief could have prompted such an outburst against the man she'd loved? She had obviously not fully appreciated the depth of her mother's grief. From now on, she would – must – do all she could to help her mother in her task of forgetting, of burying the pain. For neither of them could survive another such scene. There could be no thought of ever following up her aunt's offer of friendship or protection. That was unthinkable. She would never allow herself even to think of Rudi's family again. Resolutely, she kissed Rudi's ring and placed it carefully back in its hiding place, as a symbolic renunciation of his family. And so Sylvie's generous heart, bruised and hurt as it was, went out to Rosa, adding a fierce protectiveness to the admiration she had always cherished.

At the end of the summer, six months after Rudi's death, Sylvie began to attend a local seminary for young ladies. It was housed in a low-built villa in one of the prosperous suburbs of Buda; the big schoolroom was dominated by a huge brown ceramic stove, and long French windows looked out onto a shady terrace, planted with lilac trees and geraniums in stone urns. Kati had found it, by asking amongst the other nurses and governesses, and had suggested it to Rosa as a way for Sylvie to make friends of her own age. There were only two dozen girls, taught by two elderly and indulgent sisters. Some of the pupils, at five or six, were only a year or two younger than Sylvie; the eldest were fourteen or fifteen. While Sylvie was delighted to make new friends, she was puzzled to find herself the focus of attention among the older pupils. As she played tag and hopscotch in the dust during breaktime, she noticed them glancing at her and whispering; far from laughing at her, they seemed almost in awe of her. When Sylvie told Kati about it later, the nurse clicked her tongue.

'They're just jealous. Your Mamma, she's so beautiful, and you, well you're different, too. Pay them no mind.' And she went on fussing with Sylvie's buttons.

'But I don't want to be different,' declared Sylvie, stamping.

'Stop wriggling!'

'But Kati,' begged Sylvie seriously, breaking free to look into her friendly face, 'I don't want them to look at me like that. They don't look at the other girls. I feel like a freak.'

Kati sighed. 'You're no freak, my little love. It's not my place to explain these things to you, but, well . . . ' She sat down heavily on the bed and folded her rough hands on her lap. 'Let me see how I can say this.'

'What, Kati?'

'You and your mother, well, what you want out of life is different to what other people want – or get, at any rate. And they're fascinated with it – fascinated with your Mamma's beauty and all the friends that come to the house, and that your poor dear Papa was a nobleman. You'll always be different, there's nothing to be done about it. But don't you ever let people tell you you're not as good as they are because of that, or old Kati'll have something to say about it!'

'I still don't understand. What were the other girls saying about me?'

'Now I've said enough. You'll understand when you're older. Let me finish unbuttoning you.'

Sylvie stood submissively while Kati slipped her nightdress over her head, but, as she sat before her dressing table to brush her hair, she asked earnestly: 'Kati, tomorrow, will you do my hair for me like Madeleine wears hers at school?'

'But she wears it like that because her hair's so wiry she can't do anything else with it!' snorted Kati contemptuously. 'It'd be a shame to braid your lovely hair like that!'

'Please, Kati?' At the sight of Sylvie's pleading eyes in the mirror, Kati nodded, but she sighed heavily to herself and shook her head as she plodded off downstairs after tucking Sylvie in.

Sylvie worked hard at being as much like the other girls at school as she could, and found that, by careful observation, she could pick up their slang and their mannerisms and reproduce them so naturally that she could never be accused of mimicry. As the months passed, she soon forgot about their earlier treatment of her. Indeed, flattered by her attempts to imitate them, the older girls made much of her, and she became quite popular. As February, and her eighth birthday, approached, she went to her mother to ask if she might have two or three school friends to tea on the day.

'Why, yes, Sylvie. I don't see why not. Kati will arrange it for you.' She barely looked up from her desk, where she sat writing one of the many notes required by her social life.

'Thank you, Mamma.' Sylvie was pleased, and she continued to stand beside her mother's chair, wanting to be close to her. Rosa went on writing, unperturbed, and eventually Sylvie trailed over to the window and stood breathing on the pane to melt the fine tracery of frost that coated the outer surface, and touching the cold glass experimentally with her finger. A further notion arose. 'Can I have a cake from Kugler's? Madeleine did on her birthday. Please?'

'Yes, yes, whatever you wish.'

'Oh thank you!' And the girl exhaled a noisy breath onto the glass in celebration, quickly sketching a smiling face with exuberant ringlets on the misted surface by way of sharing her pleasure with someone.

'Don't do that, Sylvie. Kati only has to clean the windows again.' Rosa had put down her pen and turned on her chair. Sylvie looked around guiltily, hands by her sides, but Rosa did not appear seriously annoyed.

'Perhaps I should write – to the girls' mothers,' said Rosa. 'It might be proper.'

'They usually just pass notes out at school.' This was said quietly. Sylvie disliked the tedium of proper decorum, and also something unacknowledged inside her wanted to keep her planned party small, within her own orbit. She wriggled with discomfort, refusing the impossible thought that she did not want her adored mother involved. 'You're so busy, Mamma, I don't want to bother you,' she murmured. Much as she longed for her mother's attention and praise, she unconsciously knew that, once Rosa got her hands on the birthday celebrations, her own delight in the proceedings would wane.

'No,' said Rosa, as much to herself, 'this way I can get to know some of the mothers. Then they'll call on me. No,' she said determinedly, 'I *will* write. We are almost out of mourning, and I don't see that they can fuss over a little celebration for your birthday.'

She looked over at Sylvie, standing silently by the window. 'Come here,' she smiled. Sylvie went willingly and was thrilled to be drawn to her mother in a light hug. Rosa kissed her cheek. 'A party for you is an excellent idea,' she said, already planning ahead how she could use the occasion to display her talent for entertaining.

'Oh, Mamma!' Tears came to Sylvie's eyes and she threw her arms around her mother's neck and kissed her passionately. Inside, in a struggle she would not acknowledge, exultation fought with resentment. She only wanted her three special friends to come to tea. Kati would have arranged it all, and they could have had high jinks alone in the nursery. Now it was to be Rosa's party. It wasn't fair! And yet, it was so wonderful to be noticed in this way that she hugged Rosa tightly, thanking her over and over.

When the day came, Sylvie basked in the attention Rosa gave her, stepping forward shyly to greet the mothers of the girls Rosa had invited. They sat down to tea at a table in the morning room, with paper lanterns and brightly coloured paper birds strung cunningly across the ceiling. The table was an absolute confection, with flowers and pink cotton napkins that Rosa had asked Kati to dye specially for the occasion, and a delightful cake in the form of a fairy castle, with turrets of icing sugar and a moat strewn with Parma violets. Mothers and children alike exclaimed over its beauty, but Sylvie felt curiously depleted of energy, and had hardly any appetite. She felt like a spectator at her own birthday. Kati noted the dark shadows under her eyes and, clucking to herself that the poor child must miss her father more than ever on such a day, made sure that she drank plenty of the foaming hot chocolate with whipped cream that she usually loved, to keep up her strength. When the visitors departed, Sylvie asked if she might go early to bed, and Rosa, still caught up in her own triumph, absentmindedly agreed and kissed her warmly: 'It was fun, wasn't it, Sylvie?'

'Yes, Mamma. Thank you for everything. It was lovely. So special,' said Sylvie, standing close to her, as if seeking shelter, and looking up into her face, searching for reassurance, but there was none. No one else had such a wonderful mother. Who else could have created such a magical party? What was wrong with her that she felt such a misfit? Suddenly all she wanted was the privacy of her bed, and the solace of Rudi's ring, and she ran to Kati, who waited at the door to take her upstairs.

CHAPTER FIVE

One day in September 1872, when Sylvie was eleven, a man knocked at Rosa's door. He was deeply tanned and carried himself with more assurance than was usual for a servant. He held a small, flat packet, no more than an inch deep, and informed Kati, who opened the door, that he was instructed to deliver it into the hands of Mrs Lapham herself. No one else. Rosa, who sat talking with Maria Zichy in the drawing room while Sylvie sat quietly sewing in a corner, was intrigued by Kati's account of the visitor, and instructed her to bring the caller up. The man entered quietly, made his bows all round and addressed Rosa seriously.

'Ma'am, I am sent by a gentleman who wishes, for the meantime, not to reveal his identity. He instructs me to present you with this gift as a token of his esteem.'

Glancing playfully at Maria, and suspecting that some young admirer was having a game with her, Rosa mimicked the man's strange formality of expression. 'If you're instructed to deliver this token directly into the hands of none other than Mrs Lapham, how can you be sure which of us is she?'

Maria entered willingly into this game, and both women smiled at him expectantly. But he remained serious and unsmiling and never took his eyes from Rosa's face. 'My master has previously identified you to me, ma'am, and so I know that you are the lady who is to receive his gift.' And he bowed to her once more.

'Your master is a most prudent man,' laughed Maria, thoroughly enjoying this unexpected intrigue.

Rosa, too, was charmed as the mystery deepened to include a secret admirer who watched her covertly. She gave a little laugh of excitement and decided to play along with him some more. She reached out her hands, and he solemnly placed the packet in them.

'There, I have the package and your duty is discharged.' Teasingly, she placed it unopened on the low table beside her. Sylvie got up from her chair, drawn towards the enigmatic little box.

But the man made no move to go. As if reciting from memory, he continued as though this eventuality had been foreseen and rehearsed.

'If you please, Mrs Lapham, I am instructed to stay until you have opened the package, to ensure that you are aware of its contents.'

'My, how the conditions mount! Are you also instructed to inform me how I'm to open it? Are you going to tell me how I'm to respond to whatever is inside it?' She and Maria giggled openly together, but the man remained impassive. Unwilling to be seduced so easily, and to tease him further, she impulsively handed the packet to Sylvie. 'Here. Open it!'

Sylvie took the box eagerly from her mother's hands and undid the bowed ribbon, glad to play her part in this unforeseen drama. The outer wrapping came off easily enough and inside was a flat padded case. She had some trouble finding the button that released the latch hidden in the bottom, and she looked for help at the man's tanned, circumspect face, but then the top suddenly sprang open and Sylvie gasped as the cold fire of massed diamonds caught the light from the window and seemed to dance in the sunlight. Silently, she handed the case back to Rosa, who was thrilled speechless, staring into the box, turning it this way and that, experimenting with its captivating glitter. Then she held it out to Maria, who took it silently, impressed now by the gravity of such a gift.

It was Maria who finally reached in and took up the necklace gingerly in her fingertips, feeling its weight. Both women stood up as she handed it back to Rosa and moved behind her to fasten it while Rosa looked at her reflection in the mirror above the fireplace.

'Oh, Mamma,' breathed Sylvie. 'Are they real, do you think?' Quickly, she blushed, thinking that the man who had brought them would consider her rude, but when she glanced at him, his face remained a blank.

Neither Rosa nor Maria, both lost in wonderment at the extraordinary whiteness and brilliance of the large single stones, replied.

'These have been cut and set according to the very latest fashion,' breathed Maria. 'A graded rivière, too, and stones of great purity. These are not the usual rose-cut Indian diamonds of family heirlooms, but specially commissioned. This is a gift of princely magnificence!' And she too turned to stare openly at the man who had brought the packet. He respectfully ignored her gaze: it was impossible to tell from his face whether or not he had prior knowledge of the package's contents.

For several moments, Rosa turned this way and that, overjoyed by the effect of the shining jewels, quite unaware of her audience, her mind already running over the mystery of who could have sent her such a fabulous gift. Over her shoulder, reflected in the mirror, stood the messenger, and Rosa finally turned to him, now without any of her previous archness, their seriousness matched. But once again he seemed to anticipate her. 'Ma'am, I may not disclose any further information about the gentleman who has sent you this gift. However, my master has asked if he may call on you today at three o'clock?'

'I cannot possibly accept such a valuable gift from a complete stranger,' Rosa protested uncertainly.

'My master understands that a lady may find these

arrangements unceremonious. That is why he would like to make himself known to you in person. Should you decline to accept the stones, you may return them to him this afternoon.' And by the time everyone had absorbed all that he had said, he had bowed politely, left the room and was gone.

'Well!' exclaimed Maria. She looked in speechless amazement from Rosa to Sylvie, then all three burst out giggling, slightly hysterical with the tension of such a denouement. Sylvie felt as though she were in a fairy tale; somehow it seemed to her entirely natural that such a magical, miraculous event should befall her mother.

'Who on earth can it be?' asked Maria. 'Rosa, you must know!'

'I don't. Really, I have absolutely no idea. The only man I know with wealth of that magnitude is well over seventy. He could never possess the imagination and panache for such a stroke!'

'Let me see the stones again,' demanded Maria. She and Rosa sat together on the sofa and examined the diamonds carefully.

'They really are superb,' said Maria, 'and perfectly matched.'

'I don't think I've ever seen such a clear blue-white colour before,' commented Rosa, who was a keen connoisseur of such things.

'Nor such cutting – you know that this modern brilliant-cutting is the most wasteful way to cut diamonds.'

'I wonder where on earth they're from.'

'Maybe the design of the setting will give us a clue as to the jeweller who made them. Only a top firm could possibly have been given so prestigious a task.'

But a careful examination of the setting and the box revealed nothing.

'Oh, it's so romantic!' breathed Maria. 'Aren't you

excited for your Mamma, Sylvie? Just imagine having a secret admirer so fabulously wealthy as to be able to present you with a necklace worth a considerable fortune before he has even so much as introduced himself! What a delicious mystery!'

'I must get dressed!' exclaimed Rosa, suddenly catching a glimpse of herself in the mirror, and running her hand through her hair. 'What shall I wear?'

'There are no hard and fast rules for such a predicament!' laughed Maria, looking at her watch. 'I must be going. I'd give anything to be here at three o'clock, though. Write me a note this evening, or I shan't sleep a wink. May I call tomorrow morning?'

'Oh, please!' begged Rosa. The two women embraced each other, and Maria whisked off down the stairs, eager to tell Sandor what had taken place, while Rosa threw herself and Kati into a whirl of contradictory activities as she selected a different gown each half hour and changed her mind back and forth about how she should dress her hair.

Rosa was delighted at this sudden return of portentous excitement. All her life she had made herself believe in the existence of a hidden dimension of romance and intrigue, in a world in which a single glance might signify secret admiration or a moment's hesitation an avowal of sensual possibility. Despite her enforced passivity since Rudi's death, the world remained for her a place of passionate gesture and unending drama concealed within the most subtle of innuendoes and the slightest of portents. It was this intense focus upon an emotional dimension, which survived in the face of the obstinate durability of ordinary life, that had always added an intoxicating allure to her beauty.

She had no idea who the author of this bold gesture could possibly be, but the sheer value of the gift thrilled her and stirred her sexually. A man of wealth, a man of power, a stranger who had chosen her from afar! But she was alerted from her speculations by the sound of a carriage rolling to a stop outside, and she got up and ran across the room to the window for a glimpse of the caller. But the gleaming landau in the narrow street below was empty; he must have jumped down without waiting for his footman to open the door for him. The bell rang. Sylvie, too, was ready at her familiar vantage point, out of sight behind the door that opened onto the upper stairs from the first-floor gallery. From there she would at least be able to see the arrival of the mysterious visitor before she was banished to the nursery. Rosa just had time to replace the stones in their case on a side table, regain her seat in the salon and suitably compose herself before Kati opened the door.

'A gentleman to see you, Madame,' she said.

'You may show him in, Kati.' Rosa was trembling with suppressed excitement.

He appeared at the threshold, smiling at her. Kati stood at the door gaping from her mistress to the new arrival, and Sylvie peered at the scene from her strategic position across the gallery. She was slightly disappointed by the outward appearance of the exciting visitor. He was dressed in dark colours, his coat impeccably cut, with a smooth, sleek look to his head. He reminded her of the kind of animal that one breeds for fur – quick and agile and luxurious. But he did not immediately strike her as someone who might do anything particularly thrilling, such as drive them off across the *pusta* to live in his castle, or sail them away across an ocean in his private yacht. For someone presumably so impetuous, and so fabulously wealthy, he did not really look so very different from Rosa's usual friends.

Nye stood in calm self-possession while Rosa struggled to recover herself. 'Thank you, Kati. You may go now,' she managed.

She and Nye were left alone together, separated by twelve feet of Persian rug and countless unspoken contradictions. It was nearly four and a half years since they had last looked into each other's eyes. His face and hands were brown, like his servant's, and a ruggedness about his figure had displaced the earlier slimness of youth, but he still had that taunting, daring smile that had come to haunt her dreams since that dreadful night at Count Karolyi's reception. Carefully, he strolled towards her but stopped the moment he saw the slightest movement of her hands. He spread his arms in a placatory gesture which Rosa did not know whether to take as sincere or ironic.

'It was unforgivable, I know,' he said.

Rosa wondered whether he was apologizing for killing her lover, or speaking mockingly of his ostentatious gift of the diamonds. She noticed that, mounted in a gold cravat pin, he wore a dazzlingly pure silver-white stone of at least twelve carats.

'You certainly have a way of gaining a lady's attention, Mr Nye.' Rosa skated across the ambiguity.

'Sometimes one must use extraordinary methods,' he agreed, smiling, as if dropping a mask. 'If one is to arouse a favourable interest, that is. Besides, the diamonds will look splendid upon you. They were made to be worn only by a woman of your beauty.' He gestured towards the case which sat on the table near them. 'Please. Honour me by wearing the stones.'

He was hypnotic. Rosa felt herself calmed by him. At the same time she felt uneasy at having her emotions controlled by this man, at his power over her. His dark eyes gazed at her as they had nearly four years before, and she felt the same sexual stirring, along with fear and an urge to escape.

'Only try it on. Let us see just for a moment the

splendour of the diamonds as they were made to be worn.'

She stood immobile as Nye crossed before her to the table. He glanced at her, a moment of anticipation, and opened the lid of the box. His eyes seemed to catch some of the fire of the diamonds as he, too, looked with awe and passion into great depths. For a moment, he seemed lost. Then he withdrew the necklace and held it towards her.

'May I?' he said.

It was like a sensual coronation. He advanced towards her, holding the fiery necklace as if it were a crown for his queen. Or a groom bringing the bridle. She glimpsed the sparkle and then felt the coolness of the setting, refreshing in the late summer heat, as he held it gently to her throat. She felt his face close to her, his eyes upon her, but she could not look at him, afraid that if she did he would gain possession of her, yet at the same time longing to give him responsibility for herself. He took the necklace away again, as if he had been merely trying it on her for size, and she almost cried out. Their eyes met in assent. He slipped away behind her, and she felt again the diamonds about her throat, warmer this time, a mark of ownership. Nye smelt the fragrance of roses in her hair, and as he drew closer, the aroma of her body. The necklace tightened about Rosa's throat as he fastened it, and then its weight was upon her.

With her love of the dramatic, she would later say that everything hung in the balance in that instant. For a few seconds, she retained the choice in her own mind of rejoining the pleasant, sophisticated, ordinary life she had led since Rudi's death, but she flung the option away with scarcely a second thought. Like many people who determine their future by one throw of the dice, Rosa was motivated by a curious mixture of the trivial and the profound. Among the trivial reasons for accepting Nye's claim upon her were simple boredom with the inaction of her days, hatred of her reduced circumstances and a longing for some future that would raise the tempo of her life. But, also, she imagined herself in a world of grand gestures so loaded with significance that they could never be repudiated, and so it seemed to her that, having felt the warmth of Nye's arms about her, and recognizing the look of desire in his dark eyes, it was then impossible for her to step back from that acknowledgement, that to do so would, in some obscure way, amount to a betrayal.

The spontaneous gesture once made, Rosa believed that she must remain loyal forever to that fleeting impulse, that she had made a commitment to whatever that moment was to signify in the larger sweep of things, and she must go forward to whatever destiny it cast for both her and her daughter.

But even this was a flimsy veil over the profound. In truth, her obscure loyalties hid a far deeper resolve than she recognized. Underlying all her actions was a selfish desire for passion and adventure which needed only a pretext to break its bounds and set her loose on a reckless road of wantonness and betrayal. And what better pretext for one so greedy for glamour and uniqueness than such a dazzling fortune of diamonds!

Their eyes met in the mirror over the fireplace. Nye coughed lightly. His quizzical smile and ironic manner were gone, and he stood before her in frank admiration.

'Glorious!' he said. And then he turned from her and strode out of the room, not seeing Sylvie as she whipped back behind the door, out of sight, and leaving Rosa at the peak of it all, with her emotions running wild.

CHAPTER SIX

Nye eased into their lives gradually, with so little said that he became part of the household before anyone was aware that he had installed himself, and he continued to maintain his own apartments in the centre of Budapest, which served as his financial headquarters, presided over by Racker, the servant who had delivered the necklace. Nye ran a plentiful household, and Rosa was soon back at the social centre where she liked to be, the social slights of previous years quickly forgotten. He subscribed to a host of newspapers and journals, in order to stay abreast of the financial news, and Rosa pored over the society pages from London, Boston and New York, delighted to have intelligence of the new plays and novels before any of her friends. During that winter, as in the old days before Rudi's death, she was once again busy on a round of visits, concerts and skating parties in which Sylvie was often included. She patronized the best dressmakers, and the following spring paraded at the racecourse with the most stylish ladies of the city. Sylvie loved to see her mother, once again dressed in beautiful clothes, driving off in Nye's smart carriage, her head erect and proud.

There were still some doors which remained closed to Rosa, and some which shut resolutely in her face when it became common knowledge that she now lived under the protection of Count Lazar's killer, but others opened to the pressure of Nye's financial power. The defection that hurt Rosa the most was Maria's: her friend had been thrilled to discover the identity of the donor of the princely diamonds, deeming it the most delicious scandal that had ever come her way, but she was genuinely shocked and horrified when she learned that Rosa had not only accepted the gift but had become Nye's lover.

'What about Sylvie?' she had pleaded with Rosa, during the last talk they had together. 'What about the day when someone tells her the truth?'

'No one will,' declared Rosa with defiant certainty. 'They're such cowards. Everyone will tut-tut about it, but no one will actually do anything.'

'How can you scoff at such a thing?' Maria was fascinated by Rosa's magnificent unconcern, and stared at her in disbelief as if she were a villain in a play.

'I'm not scoffing, Maria. But come, now. It's a time of *laissez faire*, of live and let live. Anyone would think that I had plotted Rudi's death. It was Rudi's own fault, not mine. Rudi shouldn't have publicly insulted me. Or he should have apologized, that's all. Nye only did what any gentleman would have done.'

Maria wanted violently to shake some sense of reality into her, but it was impossible to make any mark on the flawless surface of Rosa's immaculate self-deception. She didn't know whether to love her friend all the more for the grand scale of her faults, or to shudder and run away. It was the image of Sylvie that stuck in her mind and made her shiver for Rosa's wantonness; unable to have a child herself, Maria found it unforgivable that Rosa should expose the girl to the risk of such dreadful emotional injury.

'It's just so hard to believe that Sylvie doesn't know the truth,' said Maria sadly to Sandor when she had returned home. 'It's as though she must be some kind of evil changeling still to resemble an ordinary, happy little girl. I felt quite ill at ease with her. It's terrible to feel that way towards an innocent child. But what can one do?' Sandor watched with resignation as his wife wrung her hands, understanding the deeper cause of her distress. 'It seems just as terrible to tell her the truth, when Rosa won't abandon the man,' she continued, 'as to leave her in the dark. I don't know which way to turn.'

'Just leave them alone,' counselled her husband. 'There's nothing we can do. They'll have their day of reckoning.'

As the spring came to an end, Sylvie accepted Nye's continuing presence with surprising equanimity, partly because of the polite avuncular distance he had maintained with her throughout the winter months, never attempting to win her over, yet making sure that she was included in as many plans and outings as possible, and partly because Kati, who knew nothing of Nye's part in Rudi's death, agreed with Sylvie that he was somehow dependable. Kati was an important influence in forming Sylvie's opinions of people, and she approved of Nye wholeheartedly with the stubborn self-interest of an established servant who liked to see the family fall on better times. Only at school did Sylvie sometimes sense an undercurrent of scandal, a frisson of gossip, but no one said anything to her face and she put it down to jealousy at the new frocks and expensive French dolls that Nye's wealth now provided. Besides, she saw how her mother glowed with a new radiance in his company, observed the secret looks and disguised gestures that passed between them, and heard her mother laugh with a suppressed excitement that she had never heard before. The aura of Rosa's physical magic seemed to Sylvie more potent than ever, and she was utterly seduced by its appeal, content with her mother's obvious satisfaction.

But at home, Rosa became increasingly complaining of Sylvie's presence. She did her best never to consider the past, even in moments of private thought, pushing her memories of Rudi into the persona of a mere acquaintance and denying to herself the blood link with her daughter. The more Rosa buried Rudi's memory, the more she distanced herself from Sylvie, blaming the girl for her innocence. She vaguely felt it unfair that Sylvie's ignorance of what had taken place should tug at the place the killing occupied in her own mind, making it impossible for her to believe convincingly in her own forgetfulness. She would have abandoned Sylvie to Kati and the schoolroom if she could, and seen as little of the child as possible, but Nye, though he seemed to stand aloof from them, with a bantering irony to his tone, took an obvious pleasure in the public display of their increasingly comfortable establishment and liked to have Sylvie accompany them.

It was impossible that Sylvie should suspect the true reason why her mother became so uncomfortable in her presence. She suspected that, when Rosa had found happiness with another man, her own existence reminded Rosa of a sadder past. With an egotism rare in a child – an egotism obscurely bolstered by the secret she shared with her father, the discovery of his ring in her pencil box – she did not blame her mother for disowning her and did all she could to show her support for Rosa's relationship with Nye. Seeing her resilience, he quickly came to admire the shining surfacc with which Sylvie guarded herself, the consummate act she put on to hide her hurt. Most of all, he was struck by the child's pride.

During the summer, Nye took them away on trips: in June, to Rosa's almost speechless delight, they visited the Imperial Austrian resort of Bad Ischl, where Rosa promenaded with the best, and at the beginning of September Nye took a villa on the shore of Lake Balaton. On their return to Budapest, sometimes a month or more would go by when Nye would be absent on business in foreign parts, often suddenly and without warning. Occasionally, on his return, there would be gifts – a ship of spun glass for Sylvie or a musical box for Rosa. Once, the following summer, when his absence had been considerably longer than usual, he seemed somehow darker, and laughed at Sylvie's search for presents. 'Would you like an ostrich egg or a totem pole, then, my savage?' he asked, and neither Sylvie nor her mother could discover where he had been.

'One day I'll take you with me, shall I?' he asked Sylvie.

Sylvie looked at her mother wide-eyed, then back at him, thinking the suggestion was serious. 'Oh, yes please! Where to? Could we go on a ship, across the ocean?'

She was so excited she did not immediately see that the adults were laughing indulgently at her.

'I know! Could we go to America? To see where Mamma was born?'

Rosa's expression suddenly changed. 'Don't be such a silly goose, Sylvie,' she said crossly. 'Can't you see that Mr Nye is only teasing you?'

But Nye, with his customary sensitivity to such undercurrents of conversation, homed in on Rosa's evident desire to leave her past unexamined. 'But maybe Sylvie has a good suggestion. Wouldn't you like to go back one day and visit your family, my dear?'

'I'd have no pleasure at all in repeating that awful sea voyage, thank you!' she returned, instinctively sheltering any aspect of her life that could leave her vulnerable, for deep down she feared Nye finding any further advantage over her.

Sylvie looked from Nye, smiling broadly, to Rosa, who suddenly busied herself with picking up the paper and straw in which their gifts had been packed, and decided once more that it was no use trying to make any sense of what adults talked about: they seemed so confused sometimes. She took up the carved ivory figures that Nye had brought her.

'May I go and show these to Kati?' she asked. Rosa

dismissed her with relief and bustled out to order dinner.

Nye was easy in company and his invitations were seldom refused, but, as Sylvie noticed from her place at the edge of things, he, too, moved around the periphery; he seldom committed himself to the proceedings he had initiated; he was a good conversationalist, but no one could afterwards quote his opinion on anything but a general subject; he had a clear, precise understanding of the world of finance and manufacture, yet he never made it clear just what part he played in that world himself.

He preferred to surround himself with younger people; sons of Budapest's new bankers and industrialists rather than the Hussars and minor landowners whose gossip was full of the activities of the royal court. Nye openly despised the old aristocracy – the class from which Rudi had come – as weak-minded and gullible; nor was he a believer in democracy. 'You might as well give in to mob rule as be guided by the illiterate rumblings of public opinion,' was his view. He saw the future in the hands of men such as himself, able and well-informed, a new autocracy ready to take advantage of the discoveries of the age. 'The Renaissance princes who ran the city states in Italy,' he would say, 'didn't get where they were by lineage or by wooing the peasantry: they were merchants, astute businessmen and entrepreneurs. They saw what they wanted and had the foresight and determination to take it. That Darwin fellow is right: survival of the fittest is the only natural way, and those who can't compete, well, they'll die out and become extinct in time anyway.'

Indulgent to those who amused him, he behaved with a natural patronage that made him seem older than his years. Sometimes one of the senior men of Budapest's financial circle, or some visiting banker or entrepreneur from Vienna, would be entertained for dinner, yet it seemed as though it were Nye whom they looked up to, his word that counted. Even after the disastrous financial crash of 1873, when several leading financiers, utterly ruined, had ended their lives by a jump into the forgetful waters of the Danube, Nye had seemed as secure as ever, and the respect and even awe in which he was held increased.

'The power of veto is all the power that one needs,' Nye would say, as if pointing out the obvious, when asked for his advice about the new business opportunities that were opening up all over Europe. 'I once knew an American whose business was building rolling stock. He used vast quantities of wood and iron, and he owned vast tracts of forest and several smelting works. But he always bought his raw materials from other suppliers.'

Nye would pause, as if waiting for the company to supply an answer to this riddle. The young men around him looked at each other with anticipation, and at him with admiration.

'The American used to say: "Let the forests grow. Let others pay me for my steel. I don't mind having others share in my prosperity. But they know they can't get my back to the wall: if they raise their prices to levels I don't want to pay, why, I'm ready to cut down a few of my own trees until they see sense again." '

The young men laughed, and Nye would pass among them, refilling their glasses.

'If you ensure that you can always afford to say no, then the people with whom you do business will always find a way to say yes.'

Rosa understood little of such talk, but she felt the respect they paid him, a respect that she herself was always careful to show. When Stefan had come to break the news of Rudi's death, he had taken pains to tell her in detail about the duel, about Nye's indifference to the shattered corpse he had left beside the river.

While she had conveniently removed the identity of the victim, she seldom forgot that Nye was a killer, and if she did, a cold stare from her lover would soon remind her, with a thrill of pleasure at her own abandon. She refused to allow him to refer openly to the past, but she enjoyed the frisson of her association with the power of evil, and felt set apart, made special and unique, by her very licentiousness.

And she took quiet satisfaction in the unspoken certainty that Nye's ruthlessness was not without results. Although he had been her lover for nearly three years now, he still would tell her nothing of his business life, but she knew he was a wealthy man – all, she guessed, self-made – and a powerful one.

One evening, the son of an acquaintance provided her with an unlooked-for clue to Nye's background. The young man had studied engineering and, not wanting to work for his father, had struck upon the idea of trying his luck in the new diamond and gold fields recently discovered north and west of the Vaal river in southern Africa. Janos boldly asked his hero what he thought of the notion.

'There's no doubt,' answered Nye, 'that there are minerals worth a king's ransom in those God-forsaken, fly-ridden lands. But finding them is a lottery. Speculation is only worthwhile if you have room to manoeuvre, to manipulate conditions or facts to your advantage.'

The young man's face fell.

'But,' continued Nye, 'there is a madness that surrounds the scent of gold or precious stones, and that you can exploit!' He drew on his cigar as though a satisfying memory had come to mind. Then his eyes veiled over again and he spoke more curtly. 'My advice to you, Janos, is to leave the digging to the kaffirs and to barter in what drives them on – drink! If they find diamonds, they'll celebrate and drink more. If they hit bedrock, they'll drink to drown their sorrows. Either way, you take your profit. Or foodstuffs for the animals, or water, candles or shoes: any of the fundamentals of life that fools forget in the search for wealth, and then have to pay for twice over with their dreams.' Nye laughed unpleasantly.

'But I can earn a living as a trader here,' said Janos, unable to keep the disappointment from his voice, and stung that his image of romance and adventure could be turned to such tawdry account.

'Yes,' replied Nye, a touch of scorn in his voice, 'but you won't get paid in bags of diamonds or gold dust, will you? You saw what happened here and in Vienna two years ago, all because the Americans lacked the means to refund their bonds. Stick to gold and you'll be all right.'

With that he walked over to where Rosa sat at the piano and gestured to her to play, closing the conversation.

As they sat alone together by the fire after dinner, Rosa turned to Nye. 'I suspect,' she teased, 'that you dug those magnificent stones in my necklace out of the ground in Africa yourself. Did you?'

But he merely smiled and refused to answer.

Later, as she sat musing before her dressing table, she thought, 'He is not yet forty – only a few years older than me.' She fingered the jewels in the casket before her, remembering the afternoon when he had given her the diamond necklace. She met the reflection of her eyes in the mirror: 'What might he not become?' And she began to dream of travel, of gowns and parties, of princes bending to kiss her hand.

She was interrupted by Nye, who entered the bedroom and came to stand behind her. She picked up her brush and began to brush the blond hair about her shoulders. He stroked her throat softly, his beautifully manicured fingers fanned out in the shape of the diamond necklace on her breast. Their eyes met in the mirror just as he wrung a cry of pain from her as he suddenly forced his thumbs into her neck, pushing her head backwards. Another moment and he released his grip, and stood behind her smiling again. Gently, he took her in his arms and kissed her deeply. She trembled and clung to him. Without a word, he led her to the bed where he made love to her with a ferocity that thrilled her. The matter was never mentioned between them again.

A few days after this, Rosa heard that her old friend, the actress Sari Fodor, was returning to Budapest. Sari was one of the young hopefuls who had first befriended Rosa when she was new to the city, and had introduced her to many of the theatre folk of the place. But Sari's growing fame had taken her away, touring in Vienna, Bucharest, Moscow, Milan and Paris. Now she was returning, intending to play a few of her most famous roles before retiring from the stage for a few months' rest and recuperation in her home town.

Her arrival, by steamer from Vienna, halted traffic along the embankment, the Ferencz Jozsef rakpart, as the crowds turned out to cheer and throw rose petals at their national heroine. A magnificent party was thrown for her that night, and Sylvie could hardly wait until Rosa awoke the next day to hear some details of Sari's manner and dress. She begged, again and again, to be allowed to accompany them to the theatre, and at last Nye, laughing and expansive, turned to Rosa and said, 'Really, my dear, I don't see why not. How old are you now, Sylvie? Thirteen? Almost old enough for a first visit to the theatre, surely?'

Sylvie sat frozen with desire, praying that her mother would relent. 'To see the great Sari Fodor is part of her heritage, after all,' continued Nye, 'and she is a friend of yours.' In an unusual gesture, he ran his finger lightly along Rosa's bare arm, looking ironically into her eyes. She returned his look with pleasure and surprise.

'Well, of course, Jack, if you think so.' She turned to her daughter, a becoming flush on her cheeks. 'Very well, Sylvie, you may come with us, but remember, you're only a child, you must behave. Only a touch of enthusiasm, too much is embarrassing.'

'Oh yes, Mamma, I promise. Thank you. Thank you, too, Mr Nye.' She made her excuses and ran upstairs to commune with her breathless delight alone in her room.

For the next two days she went about in a dream, reading every snippet she could find in the newspapers and nagging her mother to tell her everything she could remember about Sari's younger days. At school, her friends clustered around her, envious of her luck but delighted at least that one of their number could be the eyes and ears for all of them.

That evening, when she went to her room to dress for an early dinner with her mother and Nye, she found a small packet on her dressing table. Unwrapping it, she found it contained an exquisite necklace of turquoises and moonstones, set in silver. She ran to show it to her mother, who was about to exclaim with delight when the thought possessed her that a similar packet might also be waiting on the dressing table in her room. Sylvie and Kati followed to see, and sure enough, a curiously carved bottle of exotic perfume was disclosed. The women rushed downstairs to where Nye was waiting for them in the salon below.

'Mere tokens to mark Sylvie's first visit to the theatre,' he declared, smiling at them. Rosa flew over to him, and Sylvie, standing in the doorway, was surprised to see her mother fling her arms around his neck and kiss him greedily on the mouth. Nye, seeing Sylvie watching over Rosa's shoulder, gently pushed her from him.

'You go and finish dressing, my dear, while I take Sylvie out for a stroll to stretch her legs before dinner. Kati,' he called, 'fetch Miss Sylvie her bonnet and gloves.'

Nye settled his hat and offered Sylvie his arm as they walked along the narrow street. She did not really like him touching her, but she felt very grown up holding a gentleman's arm. She had never sought affection from him – he seemed too immaculate, too polished, for the hugs and romps that she had enjoyed with Rudi. Besides, she was no longer a little girl, and was too old now for those sort of games. They went down into the main square, past the lines of waiting cabs. Sylvie always loved the quiet, steady sound of the horses munching softly in their nosebags. The late evening air was still and heavy with the scent of lilac, and the bell tolled for mass at the church of St Matthew.

'I hope you won't be disappointed by tomorrow evening's performance, Sylvie,' he remarked. 'Some people just don't take to the theatre, you know.'

'But I'm sure I shall,' breathed Sylvie. 'Thank you for persuading Mamma to let me go.'

He looked down curiously at her. 'I rather think you'd like to be an actress, wouldn't you?' he asked lightly.

Sylvie blushed to have her secret discovered, but was glad to have a chance to ask his opinion on a matter that had been bothering her. 'Mamma says I mustn't even consider such a future – it's not ladylike. Mr Nye, do I really have to be a lady when I grow up?' she burst out. 'I'm not beautiful like Mamma, and I shall never be clever and witty like her. I don't think I want to write notes and call on people like Mamma does.'

Somehow she trusted Mr Nye to enlighten her on her future: he seemed so much of the grown-up world, and at least he didn't fob one off with silly compliments. Sylvie knew all too well that she was not conventionally pretty, for Rosa often sighed over her pale skin and the dreadful russet hair which would never brush smooth, and wished that Sylvie had darker hair or her own rosy complexion to enhance her striking grey eyes – her father's eyes.

'What would you be if you weren't a lady?' Nye asked with a smile, looking down at her with interest.

Sylvie pulled a face. 'Don't know. Suppose I'll have to be one, won't I? What did you want to be when you were a boy?'

'Oh, I forget,' he laughed.

Although she was used to his customary silence on the subject of himself, Sylvie was disappointed. Rudi would have told her about his boyhood expeditions, would have made some adventure story about running away to sea or being a pirate. But Mr Nye never did, and she somehow didn't want to question him further. She couldn't really imagine him doing boyish things, anyway.

'Did you like the gift I left for you in your room?' he asked, changing the subject.

'Oh yes! But how could you bear to keep such a surprise? I should have had to tell someone if it was my secret!'

'It would be most improper of a girl your age to have secrets anyway,' he laughed.

She laughed with him. 'Thank you for the necklace,' she continued more seriously. 'I've never had a real present before – not a grown-up one like jewellery, I mean.'

'Did your father never give you jewellery?' enquired Nye, absently, as they paused to admire the view down over the river to the resplendent city below, where the lights of the cafés on the quayside shone in the evening sun.

Sylvie coloured slightly. Nye had never mentioned Count Lazar before. She wondered at the propriety of discussing her father with this man, and a deeper part of her winced: her mother never referred to Rudi, and he had become her sort of secret talisman. His ring was safely in her pocket, where it always lay, within touch, during the day.

'No.' Sylvie was an obedient child, but answered hesitantly. 'I don't think so.'

'In any case,' continued Nye, moving on and once more taking her arm, 'I thought perhaps emeralds were far too grand for a child.'

Sylvie was used to finding that adults often talked in a way she did not understand, so dismissed this odd reference to emeralds as something she would know about when she was older. 'May I wear the necklace tomorrow night, Mr Nye?'

'Of course, my dear. That's what it's for. Do you know how your father died, Sylvie?'

She was shocked, and merely stared up at him.

'I know that you're too intelligent to believe that he fell from a horse. He was too fine a rider for that. Why, Count Lazar was famed for his horsemanship.' He paused to smile down at Sylvie, while his sharp eyes scanned her face. 'He died in a duel. A matter of honour. You have heard of these things, I'm sure.'

Sylvie looked up into his face, dumb with pain at the memory of Rudi. Through her tears, she merely saw Nye smiling at her fondly, and felt that he was trying to be kind, to help her, by so suddenly choosing to reveal the truth. She felt grateful to him for respecting her feelings for her father and thus telling her that he had died protecting their honour. She felt prouder of her father than she had ever done, without realizing that, imperceptibly, her real memories of the man were fading beneath successive layers of idealizing fervour.

She wiped away her tears with her glove. 'May we go in, please? I think dinner will be ready now.'

'Certainly, Sylvie. You understand, of course, that you must not upset your Mamma by discussing what I have told you just now? Especially when she has just agreed to let you accompany us tomorrow?'

Sylvie nodded, and Nye squeezed her arm compassionately. Once inside, he allowed her to escape upstairs to her room, where she curled up, still in her outdoor clothes, on her bed, holding Rudi's emerald ring tightly in her hand, thinking about him. But somehow it was the memory of her mother kissing Mr Nye's mouth that remained obstinately in her mind as Rosa called her impatiently down again for dinner.

The next day seemed to drag interminably, but, at last, they were actually in the carriage on the way to the theatre, and Nye was ushering them through the throng of horses and footmen and elegantly dressed ladies and gentlemen up into a box overlooking the stage. Madame Fodor was to play her most famous role: Mary, Queen of Scots. Sylvie clapped madly when the curtains opened but was soon lost to everything around her as she watched the events unfold on the stage below. How beautiful Sari was! What a wonderful actress! How expressive, as she knelt by the empty throne of the murdered Darnley and rested her despairing brow upon its arm!

Nye smiled at Sylvie as she applauded at the end of the first act. 'Quite a performance! Don't you think so, Sylvie?'

She looked at him with shining eyes, unseeing, and stood with him as he rose to his feet. With an exquisite sense of timing, they stood at just that moment when the applause surged and fed upon itself, and, in one of those mass movements which feel perfectly spontaneous to its participants, their action brought all the men in the audience to their feet in unanimous ovation.

Sylvie leant forward, watching over the balustrade of their box as they called, 'Bravo! Bravo!'

Rosa at first tried to pull Sylvie back, but soon gave up. Finally, the curtain came down on the prostrate Queen, and Rosa could make herself heard.

'Really, Jack, you're so unpredictable. One moment you insist on us keeping to the strictest proprieties, and the next thing we know, you're cheering along with the crowd like a schoolboy.'

Nye smiled one of his smiles. 'We none of us grow any younger, my dear. We must seize whatever enthusiasms come our way. Maturity and wisdom can become a trifle too predictable. What do you think, Sylvie?'

Sylvie looked from Nye to her mother, not knowing how to reply.

'I'd just like to be like Madame Fodor!' she sighed. 'An actress is seemingly all things – as the play demands.'

'Seemingly all things?' echoed Nye, ironically. 'Only a child, and already duplicitous! How quickly you'll grow into a woman!' His eyes held hers, and, for a moment, she felt breathless.

'But surely acting and deception are not the same?' Sylvie spoke so earnestly that both Rosa and Nye paid unaccustomed attention to her, and Nye's gaze lingered on her after she had finished speaking.

Rosa laughed scornfully. 'The girl is altogether stage-struck! I knew we should never have brought her.'

She swept out of the box ahead of them, ready to greet her friends. Sylvie, used to her mother's irritation, followed behind. As they paused in the crush at the entrance to the foyer, Nye leant down and whispered in her ear, 'Don't worry, Sylvie. I've arranged for you to meet Madame Fodor at the end of the performance.'

Sylvie almost yelped with delight and looked at Nye as if he were a magician. He nodded confirmation of what she had heard.

'She is to receive us in her dressing room. I have a bouquet downstairs for you to present to her.'

Sylvie was too thrilled to speak during the interval, and during the remainder of the play she rehearsed the lines which she would deliver to the brave, poignant lady who went forward on stage to meet her death. She sat between her mother and Nye whispering her presentation speech over and over under her breath, experimenting with all the different permutations of inflexion before deciding to emphasize everything, but the play came to its heart-rending climax before Sylvie was quite ready for her own performance.

As she walked before Nye down the narrow corridor to the great actress's dressing room, she felt slightly queasy with anxiety and the smells of sweat and perfume and cigar smoke. It was cold down here, in the bowels of the place. Just as they turned a corner, Nye took the bouquet of roses from her for a moment to rearrange the blooms, and she noticed that he slipped a tiny envelope deep among the foliage. Their eyes met as he returned the bouquet and he winked at her in a complicity she did not understand. But she was too nervous to pay much attention and instead concentrated herself by staring deep into the flowers. She had her eyes fixed on them in this way when Nye knocked upon the dressing room door.

'Come in,' a lady called out musically from within.

At the moment when Sari Fodor's dresser opened the door to them, Sylvie became aware that she had been staring for some time, not into the bouquet, but at something in particular, and as the light from the open door fell upon her, she saw that what she had been looking at was a ring threaded upon the stem of one of the roses.

There was a flurry of introductions and bows as Rosa and Sari kissed and exclaimed and kissed again, and almost before she knew what was happening, Sylvie found herself delivering her lines.

'Madame Fodor, please accept these roses as a token of our heartfelt admiration for the sublimity of your performance tonight.'

The actress, still dressed in the plain black velvet dress in which she had mourned her fate on stage, swept up the bouquet with a practised flourish and, with eyes shrouded in ethereal languour, she inhaled the fragrance of the flowers. Slowly, her senses returned to earth, and with a shudder she seemed to regain possession of her body once more. As she gazed in apparent rapture into the dark blooms, there was scarcely a break in her performance as she noticed the ring. She turned the bouquet lovingly in the light to get a better look at it. It appeared to be a diamond of appreciable size.

Sari turned the full intensity of her attention upon Sylvie. 'Why, this can't be your daughter, Rosa? So poised, so beautiful, already! She was barely a baby when last I saw her!' And she placed a kiss of stirring voluptuousness upon Sylvie's cheek, which Nye found gratifying. Sylvie smelt the strong smell of powder and felt the wiry hair of the actress's wig.

'She is your most ardent admirer,' said Rosa, putting a protective hand upon her daughter's shoulder and gripping her tightly to control any outburst of enthusiasm.

'My most cherished ambition would be to follow in your footsteps, Madame. But I don't know where to start.'

The actress looked pityingly into Sylvie's eyes, and beyond. 'It is a matter of the soul, of expressiveness, of passion. The heart of an actress is like . . . a diamond! It does not have its own colour; instead, it takes up the light that is about it and intensifies it. Then, and only then, it shines forth, glittering and dazzling from within. As actresses, we must accept the passion about us, which suffuses us and glows within us. We must accept it, and return the passion of our audience. We must accept it, and all that it entails!'

Everyone in the room felt the truth of her words. She seemed to radiate passion, while they felt limp and emptied. Sylvie was cold and shivering with excitement. 'These are not things you can learn in the schoolroom,' she continued, holding Sylvie's chin rather sharply between her thumb and forefinger and looking woefully into the girl's eyes. She looked up and away, as if searching for inspiration, and her gaze brushed across Nye. She returned to her scrutiny of Sylvie's soul. She noticed the girl for the first time, and was surprised to see the beginnings of a finely expressive beauty emerging from the still-childish features.

'There is hope for you. I see potential within you,' she said, seriously. Suddenly she had the answer. 'It shall be done!' Before Nye could move to head her off, she had lurched into her plan. 'While I am here in Budapest I shall instruct you myself.'

Sylvie caught fire, and there was no stopping the two of them. 'You will come to my house at eleven o'clock on Saturday morning, and we shall make an actress of you.'

Rosa was taken aback by the precipitousness of it all, and turned to Nye for support, but his face was expressionless.

'Perhaps,' he offered, as though it were a matter of absolutely no concern to him, 'I might find some time to bring Sylvie myself.'

CHAPTER SEVEN

Rosa did not know what to make of the Saturday morning visits. They started innocently enough, at least on the surface. Sylvie would study a scene from one of the classics during the week, and would then perform it with Sari playing all the other parts, and usually taking over Sylvie's, too, before the hour was up. Once they even induced Nye to take a part in a piece from *Faust*. After the performance, Sylvie would be given some lemonade and left to look through all the actress's costumes and props or to read her annotated copies of Shakespeare and more recent successes, while the adults generally withdrew for their own conversation.

Out of the theatre, Sylvie found Sari to be softer and cleaner and far younger than she had first appeared in her costume as Mary, Queen of Scots; yet Sylvie still found it impossibly hard to hold onto her own emotions in the face of the actress's stirring and rather overwhelming spirituality. But she worked diligently and thoroughly enjoyed the engagement of both her heart and mind in what had begun as an ordinary adolescent passion. She was pleased, too, with Nye's uneffusive praise of her performances, in the carriage home, for, seeing how seldom he gave it, she coveted his respect. From Rosa she initially received a mixture of chagrin and indifference. In front of Nye, Rosa pretended unconcerned encouragement, not wishing to criticize the scheme he had put in motion but equally careful not to show a detailed interest that he might construe as jealous suspicion of his sudden intimacy with her old friend Sari. Privately, she casually questioned

Sylvie, but could detect no hint of insincerity or intrigue in her eager accounts of the morning lessons.

Over coffee and cake in Kugler's, Rosa thanked Sari for her interest in the girl.

'She so looks forward to the sessions, you know. And you're really helping her to grow up.'

Sari looked suitably gratified. 'But I enjoy it, too,' she protested. 'It's surprising what one learns oneself from teaching a novice. And, besides, I think that Sylvie has real talent.'

'She's certainly learning to imitate what she sees, which, when the original is so fine, can only be a good thing, but whether that amounts to a vocation I rather doubt.' Rosa laughed disparagingly, playing the modest Mamma.

'No, no, she has some skill. Leave her with me. You don't object?' added Sari, seeing a hesitant look on Rosa's face.

'Well, perhaps a few more weeks, and she will grow out of her craze. I don't want her to bore you.'

'It's Mr Nye who may get bored, I fear!' laughed the actress lightly, delicately wiping a crumb from her lips with the tiny white napkin that lay beside her plate. She did not meet Rosa's eyes.

'No man has ever been bored of Sari Fodor!' exclaimed Rosa, crashing her tiny cup into its little moon of a saucer. 'Why, your admirers would call such a creature to account for such blasphemy!'

'Ah, my public!' Sari raised her clasped hands in a consciously theatrical gesture, aware that half of Kugler's was covertly watching her, then laughed with Rosa. 'But seriously, I don't think Mr Nye is the kind of man to join the ranks of my public, do you? Where did you find him, my dear? Such a Mephistopheles!'

Rosa stared at her friend, completely at a loss to know whether the actress's eager expression was innocently ironic or cruelly mocking. Suddenly she was afraid. It was not necessary for Nye to deceive her; she had no hold nor claim upon him. If he was tired of her, he could simply leave her. Why should he choose to stay and betray her? To enjoy her humiliation and defeat? Then she was aware that Sari was looking at her strangely, waiting for her reply.

'Oh,' she recovered herself, 'such a romantic story! He sent his servant with a fortune's worth of diamonds as a gift before he ever called in person!'

'Imagine!' enthused Sari. Rosa watched as Sari absently twisted the large, glittering, blue diamond ring she wore on her long, pale hand.

The two women bade each other farewell in the square outside Kugler's, ostentatiously kissing each other in full view of the passers-by who gasped on recognizing the actress. Nye's landau was waiting to take Rosa home, across the Chain Bridge and up the hill to Buda. She sank back in its luxurious cushions, admiring as always its trim lines and gleaming bodywork. She had no wish to lose all this, especially not by some precipitant accusation. She knew that Nye had no time for tearful reproaches, still less for anyone who questioned his actions. Rosa was determined never to allow herself to be provoked into an open display of jealousy or petulance. For what if she were wrong? What if the lessons were entirely innocent? And if not, she still dared not risk any breach with Nye: she could bear neither the humiliation of the truth, nor the gnawing fear that Nye might leave her. She simply did not want to know. By the time that the landau had rattled up the last few yards of the hill, Rosa had decided that she would do everything in her means to facilitate Sylvie's lessons, but turn Sylvie, unsuspecting, into her eyes and ears.

Sari Fodor was a good teacher: she took her profession seriously and was hard on the girl, though generous in her example. She found that Sylvie had a natural ability and a clear, melodious delivery. 'No, no, no!' she would interrupt mercilessly as Sylvie read aloud. 'Hold your head up, up! Imagine you are in a theatre. They haven't paid to see the top of your head!' And she drew a wide, balletic semicircle with her arm to indicate an audience, then burst into a peal of laughter. 'Always look slightly above the other actor's head,' she explained, instantly serious again. 'From below it will seem that you are looking straight into their eyes. Now. Once more!'

Sylvie nodded, concentrating on everything that Madame Fodor said, then began again, lifting her chin high and watching her teacher out of the corner of her eye to ascertain her approval. Sari would mime the gestures with Sylvie, then, satisfied that she had learned her lesson, would nod and stand quietly back, watching. 'Good, good!' said Sari, and Sylvie's confidence rose. But, as Sylvie moved across the room, she erupted once more.

'No, no, no! You move like a brown garden snail, not even fit to eat!' And, as Sylvie giggled at her mock insult, Sari skimmed swiftly across the room with tiny steps that nevertheless contrived to look like giant strides. 'Like that! Try it!'

'Yes, Madame,' and Sylvie ran, trying to move with the same speed, then had to hold out her hands to stop herself colliding with the wall.

'No, no, no! This is a stage! Everything here is artifice. Don't think that, to look as if you are running, you simply run.' And she spent the next forty minutes holding Sylvie's arm and pulling her hither and thither across the room, demonstrating to her how to make expansive, rushing gestures within the confined space of a stage. That night, Kati exclaimed over her bruised arms, but Sylvie felt that no price was too high to pay for such experience.

Sylvie applied her newly learned techniques at home,

gliding down the staircase, head held high, or surprising Kati by projecting her voice calmly across the courtyard instead of running about the house with her earlier childish shouts and yells. Seeing how much Sylvie had learned, Rosa began to feel reassured, to believe that her old friend was indeed generously instructing her daugher in stagecraft and no more.

Part of Sylvie's adoration of Sari Fodor stemmed from her memory of the actress being as much her father's friend as Rosa's; while Rudi had teased the actress for her dramatic airs and graces, he had honoured and esteemed her for her patriotism. For, by her performances of Hungarian dramas, Sari Fodor had become a kind of national mascot, a rallying point for those who still resented Austria's bureaucratic hold over their country. For Sylvie, the chance to read the parts that Rudi had admired made her sure that her father would be proud of her, and she tried all the harder, never dismissing Sari's criticisms or resenting her high standards.

But, when she begged one morning to read one of the plays that had made Madame Fodor most famous in her homeland, rather than the modern dramas for which she had been acclaimed in Vienna and Paris, Sari looked sideways at Nye, sitting quietly, his legs elegantly crossed, at the side of the room where he could simultaneously watch them and their reflections in the vast mirrors.

'There is always time for these later, Sylvie,' she said, without looking at her. 'Perhaps today we should look at the classics, at some Greek drama.'

'Let her do the Hungarian plays if she wants to,' called Nye, smiling dangerously. 'There's nothing wrong in allowing a young girl a little romancing.'

'It's not romancing!' Sari stamped her foot and lifted her chin imperiously.

'The age of petty feudal states is over, my dear. You

must look at reality. You're not on stage now,' he said calmly.

Sari frowned. 'Don't mock what you don't understand!' she spat at him. Nye raised his eyebrows, but, instead of the anger both she and Sylvie expected, he smiled.

'The future lies with the railways, steel, shipping,' he said, as if discussing a merely academic point. 'The new princes will head financial empires: trade monopolies, not territorial boundaries. No, Sylvie,' he continued, turning his gaze on the young girl, 'you mustn't fill your head with dreams, unless, like Sari here, you merely wish to act your way through life.'

Sari did not argue further, but for the rest of that short hour, Sylvie watched her, spellbound by the fiery intensity with which she read the inert words from the tattered playbook. At the end of an act, however, she complained of a headache and said that Nye should take Sylvie home directly. At the door to the great rehearsal room, Nye turned, looking at her ironically.

'Shall I bring Sylvie next week, my dear, or is this drama over so soon?'

Sylvie watched as Sari bit her lip. She looked angrily at Nye but, meeting his gaze, faltered. 'Yes, yes. Next week, of course.' She managed a smile for Sylvie, and briefly caressed her cheek before she turned to go, immediately shutting the high door behind her.

But, as the weeks went by, Sari seemed less and less interested in developing Sylvie's budding abilities and, while she entertained Nye upstairs, Sylvie was left alone in the huge rehearsal room below. For Sylvie, what began as a thrilling opportunity to become an actress had turned into a lesson in the realities of the vocation she had chosen. As she was left alone for more and more of the morning, she wandered aimlessly in the echoing chamber, or in the dressing room that led off it, where she tried on Sari's costumes. She wandered disconsolately among the racks of clothes, her hand brushing against the sleeves, dreamily feeling the textures of the satin, velvet and net, a paste and paper crown upon her head, peopling the room with her imagination. A little glass of the orange liqueur to which the actress was partial began to appear on the tray with the lemonade. Sylvie sipped at it through the long, lonely hour, and wandered about the chamber, stamping her feet for effect, posturing at herself in the mirrors to liven her spirits, and giggling unhappily.

Dressed in some of the simpler tunics, she was pleased to see from her reflection that her body was beginning to take on some of the outline of adulthood, that the straight hips of her childhood were showing signs of a curve and that the bones about her neck and shoulders had lost their girlish plumpness so that her young breasts stood out more distinctly. She experimented with gestures and poses in imitation of Sari and her mother and other ladies whom she admired, pouting and tossing her head while peeping over a pretend fan. Studying herself with utter seriousness, turning this way and that, she could believe that this was not childish dressing up, but an apprenticeship for womanhood. Gradually, as she breathed in the air of professional theatricality, she found in its hopeful implausibility not only romance and glamour but also the thoroughly intoxicating belief that this was something at which she herself might excel.

But at the back of her mind was an uneasiness. While she was not entirely an innocent in matters of the adult world, the idealistic glow in which she saw Sari Fodor and the automatic respect in which she had learned to hold Nye prevented her from becoming conscious of the obvious. Yet she realized, from Sari's neglect of her acting lessons – the ostensible reason for their visits – and from the lavish and ingenious gifts that Nye regularly presented to the actress, who often allowed Sylvie to unwrap them and join in the exclamations of delight, that she was being caught up in some deceit. The apprehension grew within her that something bad was going on and that she was a part of it.

While Rosa continued to show a polite involvement before Nye, in private she began to question Sylvie more closely than ever about the Saturday mornings. 'Does Mr Nye always stay in the rehearsal room, watching your lesson?' she would ask, tugging at a recalcitrant thread in her embroidery.

'No, not always. That's a pretty colour you're doing those flowers,' answered Sylvie, hoping to distract her mother's attention.

'Well, what does he do, when he doesn't stay with you?'

'I suppose he just does errands and things in town, Mamma,' she said evasively. She had never confided in her mother and, comprehending that something was not as it should be, did not know how to reply.

For a moment, her mother went on sewing, and Sylvie breathed a sigh of relief. But then Rosa spoke again. 'Is he friendly with Madame Sari?'

'Yes, of course,' she answered, wondering whether she should say more. Or less.

'Does she like him?'

'I suppose so. I don't know. She was cross with him the other day because he mocked her for wanting to read the Hungarian plays.' Sylvie offered this nugget hoping that it would be enough to satisfy her mother. Again Rosa was silent for a while, sewing thoughtfully. The only sound in the room was that of her thread drawing through the canvas.

'Is Mr Nye ever alone with Madame Sari?' Rosa finally asked bluntly.

'No, I don't think so, Mamma,' lied Sylvie quietly, feeling dreadfully guilty.

For reasons she did not fully understand, Sylvie soon

found herself lying more and more often about how she spent her time at Madame Sari's, making real the scenes she had performed alone before the silent mirrors. And the more she lied, the more she had to invent to cover her previous duplicity. Later, Nye found an opportunity to discover what answers she had given her mother, and she found herself deeper and deeper in a conspiracy, the purpose of which she dared not guess at.

The deceit was wanton. Sylvie's presence was not necessary, yet compromising her seemed to be part of the affair itself. But Nye's desires were always complex. His tastes played on refinements of violence, on killing psychologically, without leaving a mark on the person's flesh. When he had returned to Budapest and sought out Rosa, he had been completely unaware of Sylvie's existence. But the discovery that his victim, Rudi, had a daughter added immeasurably to the possibilities for treachery inherent in the affair, especially when he realized that Rosa's own response to her daughter was far from simple. Now, the same perversity that had made him seek out the woman of the man he had killed, and to win the confidence of his child, impelled him to twist and turn, to spin lies, to predict and control the lives of the women and to entangle Sylvie in his affair, for Nye had an appetite for betrayal that reached a state of passion when it was infused with money or the erotic.

In a lesser man, this desire to entice and betray might have stemmed from spite. But Nye did not act from petty slights, although he had his secret vanities and took pleasure in revenge. Neither was he a vandal, filled with the brute desire to destroy. He was too complicated, too much the connoisseur for that. It was as if life itself were too straightforward for him and so needed to be decorated with concealments and duplicity in order to be pleasing. Above all, he liked to pass unnoticed. He enjoyed the subtle exercise of his influence, acting here to produce an effect elsewhere, without the two appearing related. For Nye, the trick lay in quietly knocking over the first domino, and in leaving the room before the chain reaction reached its end.

Things came to a head at the beginning of October. When Saturday morning came, Sylvie said she did not feel well, but Rosa, sitting reading the papers amid the elegant debris of her breakfast, was implacable.

'Nonsense. You cannot miss your acting lesson and upset other people's plans. Madame Fodor is expecting you, and Mr Nye is waiting to take you there.' As she spoke, she shook out the pages of the *Boston Globe*, one of several foreign newspapers Nye had sent to him. She turned the page and folded the newsprint down neatly, signalling to Sylvie that the matter was at an end. Sylvie stared at her. Rosa was becoming slightly long-sighted, although nothing would make her admit it, and she held the paper at arm's length in order to focus. Sylvie could read some of the headlines over her shoulder: 'Massacre at Gregory's Barn', 'Record Catch for Gloucester Fishing Fleet'. The paper was two weeks old and concerned a country Sylvie had never visited: why couldn't her Mamma pay attention to her, for once?

Suddenly, all the fear and unhappiness that Sylvie felt about the situation welled up. She felt ashamed of her evasions, and guilty that it was selfishness that had prompted her to lie, for perhaps if she had told Rosa that Mr Nye spent the morning alone with Madame Fodor, Rosa would have stopped the lessons. For Sylvie still passionately loved the atmosphere of the rehearsal room, the intimacy she felt she shared with her teacher, and did not really want to give up this intriguing contact with the theatrical world. But her customary protectiveness of Rosa surged up, and, in what she felt was a great sacrifice, she decided that the lessons must stop: there was something very wrong, and it concerned her mother. 'I won't go!' she declared stubbornly, watching Rosa's face for the first signs of expected wrath.

But Rosa did not look up immediately from the paper. Her eyes continued to scan the newsprint, but her face drained of colour and her mouth fell open, her bottom lip slack with shock.

'I won't!' protested the girl again, ready to flinch from her mother's opposition.

Rosa at last looked up, but she did not seem to see Sylvie's tensed figure standing beside her. 'What?' she asked irritably.

'I don't want to go to Madame Fodor's today!'

But Rosa's attention already seemed to have slipped sideways again. She was breathing quickly and looked distracted. 'Get ready, now!' she hissed, tucking the newspaper tightly under her arm, and suddenly pushing the girl before her out of the room. 'Kati!' she bawled up the stairs. The old woman appeared quickly. 'Kati, get Miss Sylvie's things. Now get out!' she said savagely, and ran upstairs.

Sylvie was both shocked and relieved. She had never openly defied her mother before, and had expected a terrible scene. And, in a way, it had been terrible, yet Rosa had not seemed angry, just . . . what? Sylvie considered her mother's strange behaviour as she climbed quietly into the landau beside Nye. Her mother had seemed terrified. But of what? It must just have been exasperation; and she tried to put the matter to the back of her mind to consider quietly when she got home again.

Whey they reached the actress's house and Sylvie seemed to hesitate before turning to go alone into the rehearsal room, Nye smiled at her as if, Sylvie felt, she were an adult, and when he patted her head, his hand lingered in her hair in a caress at the curve of her neck. Sylvie was confused and drew back. Sari laughed, and then she did something which seemed to Sylvie at once terrible and obvious: she wrapped her arms about Nye's neck and kissed him hungrily on the side of his mouth, pressing her body against his, just as Sylvie had seen her mother do. To the girl, the sudden, sensual disillusionment was obscene, and, coming so suddenly on top of her confrontation with her mother, was overwhelming. She was stricken at the thought that she had betrayed Rosa all the more by not being resolute ealier that morning.

Plaintively she appealed to Nye. 'What about Mamma?'

Sari and Nye, each with an arm about the other, laughed at the denouement, two adults chuckling at a child's concern.

'Come, Sylvie, you are not a little girl now. Your Mamma does not need to know all that you do. Why, you have been so sensible all these weeks in the matter of our . . . affections,' he said, turning his head so that his lips came close to the actress's ear.

He watched her as she broke into dry, angry sobs.

'Come now, Sylvie, there's nothing to cry about. With you as our chaperone, what can possibly be remiss? Your performances with your mother have been superb!'

Sylvie sat miserably throughout the morning, alone in the rehearsal room, trying to imagine Sari and Nye together. What was it that adults did together? Did she sit on his lap and kiss him, or was there more? Nye appeared alone at lunchtime, saying his farewells at Sari's doorway upstairs, though Sylvie heard the soft rustle of her skirts. He was cheerful and talkative on the way home, but Sylvie turned away from him, tears in her eyes, her face hot with shame.

As soon as she got home, she hid upstairs, listening

to every sound in the house and waiting until Nye went out again. Kati told her that her mother was resting in her room. At last she heard the door of Rosa's bedroom close and Nye's footsteps on the stairs. She waited until she heard him descend, then crept into her mother's room.

It was obvious that Rosa had been lying down, taking her afternoon rest, but as Sylvie quietly pushed the door open, she saw her take a newspaper out from under the cushions piled up at the head of the bed. She looked up in surprise at Sylvie's miserable face.

'Mamma, I have to talk to you.' Sylvie burst into tears and ran to the bed where she could bury her head in the quilt.

'Can't it wait, Sylvie?' asked Rosa sharply, sensing the confession to come.

'No, no,' wept Sylvie. 'Oh Mamma, I'm so sorry. I never knew. God help me, I didn't know.'

'Stop crying. What didn't you know?'

'It's Mr Nye. He's in love with Sari Fodor.'

'Well, half of Budapest is in love with Sari Fodor. Of course he admires her, child, that's not news.'

'But he kisses her, and holds her like . . . like gentlemen don't in public.'

This angered Rosa. 'Nonsense. You've imagined it. It's another of your dramas. You don't know the difference any more between play-acting and reality!' She breathed deeply, and carefully put down the newspaper. She had been afraid of such a confession; she was only surprised that Nye should have revealed the truth so openly. But she was not going to be betrayed into any act of rash accusation. Especially not today. Her nerves were shattered by what she had learnt that morning from the *Boston Globe*. She must enforce Sylvie's silence.

'Stop this crying at once, Sylvie,' she went on sharply. 'Sari Fodor is a dear friend of mine. She has been exceptionally kind in wasting her time on such a stage-struck little fool as you, and this is how you repay her! I'm ashamed of you, and I want to hear no more about it. Now leave me to rest.'

Sylvie, still racked by the long, shuddering sobs that came despite her efforts not to cry, continued to kneel on the floor beside the bed, her face hidden in the counterpane. Part of her felt the release of confession and the childish desire to believe her mother against all odds. Indeed, part of the bitterness she felt was that her idol, Sari Fodor, should turn out to have feet of clay.

With an effort, Rosa patted Sylvie's hair.

'Come, come, Sylvie. You're simply tired. Maybe Mr Nye was acting out a part from a play, and you didn't realize – you told me that he sometimes takes part in your little enactments. Raise your head. You see. I'm not in the least upset.' She held her daughter's chin in her hand. 'Nothing happened, do you hear?' she asked, firmly. 'Nothing.'

'Yes, Mamma,' answered Sylvie obediently, but her eyes escaped Rosa's gaze and rested on the paper on the bed. 'Why, Mamma,' she exclaimed, unconsciously eager to find a tunnel down which to escape all these overwhelming emotions. 'Here's your old name in the paper! And in Saratoga Springs, too,' she added, reading on down the column headed 'Massacre at Gregory's Barn'.

Rosa itched to snatch the paper away, but knew that that would incite Sylvie's curiosity all the more. 'Where?' she asked lightly.

'Here, look. This terrible story about a family murdered and left hanging in a row in their barn, even the baby. Didn't you read it? Listen:

' "The fiend who carried out this atrocity, Edmund Johns, had no known connection with the Gregory family, who were well respected in the local community," ' read Sylvie aloud. ' "Mr Silas Gregory was known and loved in Saratoga Springs for the flowers he supplied to all the hotels and for weddings and parties. The victim, whose wife and entire family of eight children were all horribly mutilated before being massacred by this insane monster, was a natural part of every civic celebration, bringing gaiety and colour to occasions great and small. His own flowers today poignantly graced the descending line of ten coffins laid out in Saratoga Springs's principal church. A posy of forget-me-not and heart's-ease adorned the smallest casket." What a perfectly dreadful story, Mamma! But didn't you tell me your name was Johns, before it was Lapham? Wasn't your brother Edmund? It can't be the same man, of couse, but what a strange coincidence.' Sylvie rattled on, hardly knowing what she was talking about, just wanting to get away from the cloying, impossible events of the morning.

'Edward Jones was my brother's name,' replied Rosa as calmly as she could, rescuing the paper out of Sylvie's hands, though her own shook imperceptibly. 'Not Edmund Johns. And after all the commotion you've caused today, I hardly think you should be reading such stories. You are quite overwrought enough with drama. You'll make yourself ill with your fervid imaginings.'

'I'm sorry, Mamma,' answered Sylvie. 'I'll go now. I'm sorry I disturbed you.'

'Go and rest. How silly of you, thinking my name was Johns. Edward Jones,' she repeated firmly. 'Not Edmund Johns.'

In her room, Sylvie took out Rudi's ring from where it was hidden in her drawer and lay down on the bed. Her mind was blank, her eyes hot and dry as she stared at the wall. She was no longer able to make any sense of all that had happened, of all the conflicting undercurrents and layers of truth and reality. But her Mamma had said she was not upset, that everything was all right, that nothing had happened. And Sylvie, confused and shamed, was only too glad to cling to the wreckage of her mother's lie. She lay like that for several hours, until Kati came to find her in the darkness to tell her that her supper was ready downstairs.

That night Sylvie awoke, sure that she had heard a cry. She lay quietly, listening, then heard the sound again. It was her mother! Sylvie crept from her bed, down the stairs, and listened, shivering, outside the bedroom door. She could hear her mother moaning clearly now. She wanted to run back to the safety of her room, but did not dare for fear of her mother's evident misery inside. She opened the door, choking back a sob that rose in her own throat. The bedroom was lit only by firelight: her mother was kneeling on the bed and Nye had mounted her from behind, savagely fondling her full white breasts as he thrust repeatedly into her. She could not see her mother's face, which was hidden by her thick blonde hair, but now she heard her groan aloud at each thrust of Nye's hips, calling out with undeniable pleasure.

Sylvie stood transfixed in the doorway, her hands over her ears. She thought that she was screaming, but no sound emerged. Then Nye raised his head, his dark eyes glazed with passion, and looked right into her face. It seemed to Sylvie that he did not really see her, but as she wrenched her gaze away, he too let out a cry and jerked his thighs in quick succession, as though electrocuted, squeezing Rosa's breasts so tightly that her flesh bulged between his fingers. He bit her shoulder so that her head shot up and her back arched in a spasm of pain before they both collapsed onto the sheet.

Leaving the door open, Sylvie ran for her life. In her room, she pulled the bedcovers up over her head and, taking Rudi's ring from its place beneath the mattress, held it tightly in her fist, weeping with fear and waiting for the door to open and Nye to come for her. She did not understand what she had seen, but she knew that she should not have witnessed such a moment. She must never question what adults did, and she must be silent as to what had taken place. Never again would she question what went on in the adult world. All night she lay there, listening to every noise in the house and in the street outside, but no one stirred from her mother's bedroom below. As dawn broke she fell asleep. Her dreams were filled with the image of ten bodies hanging in a line, reflected in the huge gilt mirrors of the rehearsal room, while her mother moaned with pleasure.

The following Saturday, events took place as though nothing had happened. During the week, Sylvie had avoided Nye's eye and was careful not to let him touch her. She stayed as close to Rosa as her mother would allow and was quieter than usual, but, at night, her sleep had been broken by nightmares. At first they were of soiling, of dirt which she could not get off her starched white night-dress; later the dirt turned unaccountably to blood.

As she sat alone, shivering miserably, in the rehearsal room, she no longer wanted to pretend or to let her imagination run before her, feeling her way into the parts she had read with Sari. She felt there was danger in allowing things to be other than how they seemed in the real, ordinary world. Finally she made up her mind to tell Nye that she wanted to stop the visits. She chose her moment when they were alone, in the carriage on the way to the acting lesson the following week. He continued to survey the passers-by from the landau, his mind taken up with some other matter. 'Soon, soon. All in good time, my dear,' was all he answered.

Sylvie spent the hour, as usual, alone in the rehearsal

room. It was cold, and, in order to keep warm, she tried on some of the fur-lined cloaks from the closet and practised pacing up and down an imaginary stage. She meant merely to rehearse the movements Sari had taught her, but lines from Shakespearian tragedies and other plays, things that she had overheard, snippets of songs she knew, all chased each other through her mind as in a dream. As she walked, swinging the swirling cloak around her as she made her turns, she was Portia, vehement and just, Desdemona, fated and betrayed, poor Cordelia, loved and lost. Her own personality seemed to dissolve and then reform itself anew, the thoughts and problems that had obsessed her during the past two weeks became printed lines in a torn playbook, the lines that charged through her brain became words that she had actually spoken at home. Was Rudi Lear, or Nye Othello? Was Rosa Hamlet's mother or her own? She no longer knew, and no longer cared. She was merely an audience of one, released and freed from misery and loneliness, watching her performance in the long mirrors that lined the wall.

It was the intense cold that slowly brought her back to herself. She was thirsty, and the usual lemonade and liqueur had not materialized. Silently, she crept to the door and opened it to look at the big ornate clock that stood in the hallway. Why, she had been in the rehearsal room for two and a half hours!

The huge house was silent. She closed the door and stood behind it, puzzled. Had they forgotten her? She thought she remembered hearing the front door bang shut, but she didn't know when, or if she'd imagined it anyway.

Sylvie did not want to think about what Nye and Sari might be doing upstairs for so long; she was cold and hungry and wanted to go home. She slipped out of the fur-lined cloak and hung it up carefully in the closet, then opened the door and crept up the stairs.

She listened at the doors that opened onto the first landing, but heard nothing, so tiptoed on up to the second floor. The door to one of the rooms that overlooked the street was ajar, so she went forward, shivering now with cold and fear, and peeped through the gap. The gas inside was lit and she could see the edge of a bed, a gilt chair and a pillow thrown carelessly on the floor, and she could feel the warmth of a fire. She knocked so lightly that no one would have heard her. She paused, looking back down the empty stairwell, then pushed the door forward a few inches so that she could see more of the bed.

The covers had slipped to the floor at one side, and, lying uncovered on the sheet, was Sari, asleep. Sylvie crept into the room and looked about. There was no sign of Nye. Sari's clothes were heaped on a chair beside the bed, and she was naked. Sylvie had never seen a naked woman before. Kati, who had slept in her room with her when she was little, had always undressed underneath her voluminous nightdress, and it was unthinkable that she should ever be present when her mother was bathing or undressing. Fascinated by the sight before her, she looked closely at the naked body of her heroine with a mixture of admiration and curiosity.

Her own body was changing in unaccountable ways, but, used only to the smooth marble of the sculpted figures she had seen in some people's houses, she was astonished by the mass of reddish hair between the actress's legs, so different from the light patch beneath her own smooth belly. The hair under Sari's arms was thick and soft-looking, running down towards the very dark nipples of her breasts, and her skin, Sylvie noticed with surprise, was covered with fine brown freckles. Her arms were thrown back on the pillows behind her head, and her legs were wide apart. The sheet was damp between her legs, as if she had wet herself.

Sylvie walked around the bed, meaning to cover Sari over gently with the fallen covers before waking her. Then she saw the leather strap around her ankle, tying her leg to the post at the end of the bed that supported a curtained canopy above. Sylvie looked quickly across and saw that the other ankle was similarly bound. Only then did the tautness of the pose strike her, and she took another step towards the bedhead before seeing that the actress's wrists were also caught fast with buckled leather straps.

Sylvie started to shiver again, despite the warmth of the room, and observed the red marks about Sari's thin wrists, as if she had struggled to free herself. Only then did she begin to realize that the normal gentle rise and fall of a person breathing in their sleep was absent. Unconsciously, Sylvie started to whimper and to look towards the open door, whether in fear or in hope of rescue she did not know. She thought of the cold, dim corridor outside and all those closed doors. Had she heard the street door close, or was Nye here, watching her?

Bravely, she climbed onto the bed, kneeling beside the woman, all but oblivious now of her nakedness. There was an unfamiliar smell about her body, a slightly sweet bodily odour that she now remembered noticing sometimes about her mother.

'Madame Sari,' she called quietly. She touched her cheek. It was warm.

'Madame Sari,' she said aloud. The actress's face was turned away from her, and she actually had to lean right across her breasts in order to look into it. The eyes were open, staring, fixed, dead.

Sylvie was never able to remember how she got out of the house, nor whether, as she imagined, she was in fact pursued as she darted between the smartly dressed people strolling beneath the gaily striped awnings of the elegant shops in Vaczi-utca. She recalled jumping on a horse tram, and the interminable ride across the river and up the steep slope to Buda. From the main square of Castle Hill where the tram stopped, she ran as fast as she could, knowing that people turned to stare at this dishevelled girl fleeing past, her face deathly pale and determined. The sound of her footsteps and her painful breaths filled her head.

Kati met her on the stairs.

'Where's Mamma?'

'In the drawing room. But Miss Sylvie, whatever is the matter?'

Ignoring the servant, Sylvie burst into the room, where Rosa was standing in the window feeding her pet canaries. She glanced around, but, dazzled by the light from the window, saw only Sylvie's outline.

'You're late, Sylvie. Did something detain you?'

Sylvie realized that she had to try to be calm. That the story she had to tell was unbelievable. She closed the door behind her, noticing Kati still standing on the gallery, wondering what was afoot, her face full of concern.

'Mamma,' she began, but stopped as she felt the hysteria rise within her. She tried again, fighting for control. 'Mamma, Sari Fodor is dead. I found her.'

Rosa had by now taken in the state of Sylvie's dress, her white face and the dark rings around her eyes. Now her eyes, too, grew round and frightened, and she grasped for a seat on the sofa beside her, fumbling for her handkerchief.

'What do you mean? An accident? Has she been in an accident? Where is Mr Nye?'

'I don't know. Oh, Mamma, I was so frightened. I thought he would kill me, too.'

At this, Rosa leapt up, rushed to the door and opened it.

'Kati,' she demanded, finding the woman still outside the door, 'what are you stopping there for? Go about your duties immediately.'

'Yes, Ma'am,' said Kati, curtseying, and even more agog to discover what had happened.

Rosa closed the door again carefully, and drew Sylvie down to sit beside her. She took Sylvie's shaking hands in hers. 'Now, tell me slowly what has happened. Are you absolutely sure that you're not making all this up?'

'No, Mamma. They left me alone for hours, so I went to find them to say that it was time to come home. Madame Sari was on the bed, she was tied to the bed, Mamma, with little belts of tough leather. She had no clothes on. I thought she was asleep, but she wasn't breathing at all and her eyes were wide open – like Clara's were when she died.' Clara was a servant who had died of a stroke when Sylvie was eight; Sylvie had been with Kati when they found her. 'I tried her smelling salts that I found on her dressing table, but her eyes never moved. And I couldn't close them, I couldn't close them.'

Sylvie began to sob loudly, but Rosa acted rapidly, hitting her hard on the face and shaking her by the shoulders.

'And what about Nye?' she hissed. 'Where was he?'

'I don't know.'

'Why did you think he was going to kill you?'

'He killed Madame Sari. And the other night, you and he . . . '

'What are you saying?' Rosa swept to her feet. Sylvie dared not look at her face. 'How can you even think of such terrible things?'

'Because he did, I know he did. They go there together every week. He goes to see her. She doesn't teach me any more. He did something terrible to her, I know he did.'

Rosa remained silent, watching her daughter's face closely, thinking. What if it were true? She knew only too well of Nye's sexual penchant for restraining his partner, for inflicting a little pain. Sylvie mentioned straps: Nye had never suggested using such a device with her, but how could Sylvie possibly have imagined such a thing? What if this time he had gone a little too far?

Sylvie could read in her mother's face that she did not entirely dismiss her story. 'What are we going to do, Mamma?' she asked plaintively. 'I'm frightened.'

'Nonsense,' said Rosa decisively, sitting down beside the girl again. 'You imagined the whole thing. She'd just fainted, or was asleep. That's if you went into her bedroom in the first place. You know how you imagine things. Kati told me that you've been crying out in your sleep recently. I don't know what we're going to do about you. It's all this theatre business, it's just gone to your head, unsettled you.'

She realized that her firmness frightened the girl more, so she softened her tone, putting her arm around Sylvie's shoulders.

'You need to spend more time with other girls. You're growing up now, and everyone feels strange things at your age; young girls do have unaccountable moods and fancies. Don't you cry. You needn't go to your lessons any more, I'm sure Madame Sari will understand . . . No,' Rosa held up her hand to silence Sylvie's exclamation. 'No, I'll hear no more of this ridiculous murder business. You imagined it all, overwrought with whatever play you've been acting. Now, my dear, go to your room, and Kati will bring you something to eat on a tray.'

She kissed Sylvie's head and tried to pull her gently to her feet, but the girl would not move. She sat like stone, her eyes never leaving Rosa's face.

'But Mamma, shouldn't you alert the authorities? What if he comes here?'

'Enough!' She rose angrily, standing in front of

Sylvie, who cowered down on the seat before her. 'You're hysterical. All this acting has been too much for you, and now you're imagining things – things that a girl of your age has no business knowing or thinking about. It's unnatural.' Rosa avoided Sylvie's eyes, looking over her head to the door where Nye now stood, silently watching the scene. His eyes glittered and he was breathing rapidly; Rosa sensed the air of suppressed excitement that hung about him. So it was true! She met his gaze and, controlling her voice, spoke to her daughter in a hard, unyielding tone. 'The only way to deal with these fantasies of yours is to empty the theatre. Go to your room.'

Rosa looked anxiously for Nye's sanction of the line she had taken, and he nodded imperceptibly to her. Sylvie rose submissively from the sofa, but when she caught sight of Nye in the doorway, she let out a little scream and clung once more to her mother.

'Sylvie, you are being ridiculous. Jack, dear, I hate to embroil you in our domestic difficulties, but Sylvie is behaving most oddly. Perhaps you should call a doctor to her?'

Nye adopted Rosa's tone, and went to call Kati. Sylvie still clung to her mother, but Rosa was able to guide her across the threshold and along the gallery outside to the stairs. She left her at the door to her room as Kati joined them.

Safe upstairs, as Kati unhooked Sylvie's dress and lifted the heavy skirts over her head, she looked curiously at her, concerned at the commotion and disturbed by the mechanical way in which the girl answered her enquiries and obediently got ready to get into bed. It seemed to her that Sylvie was oblivious to what went on; she reminded her of nothing so much as one of those automata she'd seen at last year's summer fair.

'Is there nothing I can do for you, Miss?' she asked solicitously.

'Poke the fire for me, please Kati. It doesn't seem to give out any heat. I'm so cold.'

'You're about to go down with something, mark my words,' said Kati, fetching a shawl and wrapping it about Sylvie's shoulders. She looked very tiny, pale and helpless. Her large grey eyes, lost in the haze of hair that had escaped its ribbon and now framed her delicate face, seemed to be gazing into a non-existent crystal ball, and her hands trembled as she pulled the shawl more tightly around herself. 'Get into bed, and I'll tell your mother that you'll not be down this afternoon.' She paused, hoping that Sylvie would speak and explain what had evidently taken place that morning to upset her so. But she remained silent.

Only as Kati tucked her into bed and quickly kissed her forehead did Sylvie seem to remember her presence, giving her a brief smile that almost broke Kati's heart: 'Thank you, Kati.'

'There's a dear. Don't you worry, old Kati will look after you,' she said, pausing in the doorway, but the girl hardly seemed to hear her.

Alone in the salon downstairs, Rosa put her knuckles to her mouth, biting them in fear. All the possibilities were equally fearsome. It was just possible, despite the strange expression of triumph she had seen on Nye's face, that Sylvie was mistaken, but what if Nye *had* accidentally killed Sari Fodor? Even though they might silence Sylvie, could he continue to evade detection? And what if – and she almost screamed aloud at the thought – what if Sari's death had not been accidental? But why should he do such a thing? And what were his intentions towards them? After all, he had killed before . . . With a small cry, she ran towards the door, thinking vainly of escape. She stopped, holding onto the handle. How dare Sylvie put her in this quandary?

As she paused, running all the eventualities in her head, the handle turned within her grasp, the door opened, and Nye walked in, perfectly composed. She backed away from the door, licking her lips and smiling nervously, not knowing how to proceed.

'No greeting, my dear?' He kissed her on the cheek. 'How is Sylvie? She took it into her head this morning to leave without informing me. I hope that she did not encounter any difficulty on her way home?' he enquired blandly.

'She is most out of sorts, Jack,' Rosa stumbled. 'I'm afraid that she has been sadly overwrought by these acting lessons. She came running in imagining I don't know what,' she ran on, unconsciously wringing her hands.

'I hope you told her that she is a silly fool?'

'Yes, Jack. Indeed I did,' she said eagerly. She took confidence, and continued. 'I hate to criticize you, but, in retrospect, these lessons have been too much for a girl of her age. I think it inadvisable to encourage such . . . such histrionics.'

She bit her lip, waiting for his reply. He was standing beside the canaries, looking into the cage, smiling. There was a satiated, almost sleepy, look about his eyes, like a cat that has eaten a bird. 'I think you're right, my dear,' he replied, replacing the water dispenser that Rosa had been in the act of filling when Sylvie burst in. His task finished, he turned, smiling at her. 'She's upset you, I can see. It is really most inconvenient.'

'I'm so sorry, Jack.'

'Most inconvenient. You see, some business affairs have been completed sooner than I thought, and I have to leave immediately. I had thought that, since I may be away for half a year or more this time, you and Sylvie might wish to accompany me.' He spoke nonchalantly, but Rosa watched him very carefully. Now, however, her own excitement and relief broke through.

'Where?' she gasped. 'Where do you have to go?'

He spread his hands and smiled at her, as if chiding her ignorance. 'Why, Africa, of course. We must leave tomorrow or the next day at the latest.'

CHAPTER EIGHT

'I'll go mad if I have to spend another summer here,' declared Rosa petulantly. 'I've had enough. Dust one day, mud the next. And the filthy stench and noise from that precious mine of theirs!' She swung herself off the cane-backed couch on which she lay in her shaded parlour in Kimberley and almost slammed shut the glazed doors that stood open onto the verandah, reducing the distant, confused hubbub from the Big Hole about a mile away to a low murmur. A small black girl sat in a corner of the room, unceasingly tugging a cord that kept a large, bladed fan revolving in the centre of the ceiling. 'Pull harder on that rope!' Rosa commanded irritably. She removed the beaded muslin cover that protected a jug of precious water from the flies, and poured herself a small tepid glass. 'I suppose the heat is no worse really than it was during the summer in Budapest,' she went on as she sipped languidly, dampening the corner of a handkerchief to cool her brow. 'It's just somehow harder to bear here, with no distractions.'

'Another concert hall has opened,' offered Lucy Tarrant, Rosa's only real friend in Kimberley. 'It's just off Warren Street, next to Johnson's Hotel. I saw the women arriving yesterday.' And she pursed her lips and shook her head in chagrin and disappointment. Lucy was a pretty little woman with red-blond hair and a noticeable cast in her left eye; she compensated for this slight disfigurement by the exaggerated, almost challenging, sophistication of her ways.

'Oh, the men have plenty to do!' snorted Rosa contemptuously. Lucy's mouth opened slightly in horror as she thought that Rosa was about to enlarge upon the nature of the male distractions in the diamond fields, but Rosa merely paced the stuffy room once more.

'Why do they have to keep us here?' she burst out, although both women knew their own private answers to that question: Lucy's husband, Edward Tarrant, simply could not afford to allow Lucy and Daisy, their daughter, to remain in a quiet villa in Cape Town. All his remaining capital had been spent on his claims, those tiny strips of mud and slime at the bottom of the vast man-made crater that contained the elusive stones that gave this amazing scene of hope and greed its purpose. There was simply no money for the niceties of life and Lucy had to make do with the little she had, except on the days when she took refuge in the relative luxury of Rosa's house.

Every day, Edward went to oversee work at the mine. Far below, amid the impossible network of terraced claims, each bordered by thin, crumbling walls, kaffirs shovelled the mud or dusty earth into leather buckets which were rapidly hauled up to the rim of the open mine by a system of wires attached to windlasses and pulleys. Thousands of wires were strung across the surface, like a monstrous cobweb, almost veiling the activity below. High above the toiling pit, the buckets were emptied and the precious soil carted off to be pounded and sifted. Close to, where Edward joined the swarms of men among the wheelbarrows, heaps of earth, sieves and sorting tables, the noise of clattering and creaking equipment, yelling and cursing men and lowing bullocks and mules was hellish.

Rosa had hated this crude frontier town from the start, but she could not leave. Nye had made it plain, by his manner and the odd casual comment, that, although Rosa and Sylvie were entirely free to move to more congenial surroundings, he would feel no obligation to support them or, indeed, ever to see them again. Rosa chafed at the uncertainty of her position. She felt trapped, owned, humiliated, although she did her best not to dwell on the true nature of her relationship. She knew that the presence of a beautiful and cultured woman to welcome Nye home and to play the piano – probably the only one outside a bar in Kimberley – before amusing him in bed, was an essential part of his well-being. If boredom got the better of her, she would undoubtedly somehow be replaced.

Meanwhile, she took comfort from the fact that she was the partner of one of the most ambitious and successful men in Kimberley. In contrast to most of the prospectors, Nye had not become involved in the Augean labour of the mine itself, but had set up as a dealer in diamonds, a 'kopje-walloper', initially riding among the open-cast mines in neighbouring Dutoitspan and Bulfontein, buying the stones direct from the claimholders. He was always accompanied by Racker, who carried the necessary cash in a strong-box attached to his saddle by thick chains. Nye had quickly diversified his interests. He now ran the fastest team of security despatch riders who took the precious leather pouches of stones south to the Cape. He also owned controlling interests in the Yellow Slipper, Kimberley's biggest gambling hall, as well as Jack's, the chandler's shop in the market square, where the huge waggons that had made the month-long trip northwards across the veld unloaded their supplies and re-stocked ready for the return journey.

Rosa had to console herself with Lucy's envy. Nye had furnished this house at vast expense, bringing every single chair, rug and crystal wine goblet across the karoo from the coast by ox cart. Everything was new, unworn, unfaded: but the plushness and sheen of all the objects Rosa handled had come to irritate her and she longed for the soft edges of age and use. Time lay heavy on her hands. Kimberley had absolutely none of the refinements of style or details of social finesse which, for her, had always spelt life and excitement. There was nothing to do but drift along with Lucy in their conversational games, reminiscing about their former lives in Budapest and in London and talking over past successes and projected future triumphs. Rosa dreamed constantly of the heady days when she and Nye would leave Africa, wealthy beyond imagination, to take their place in the most exalted society of Europe.

'If only I'd never married Edward,' sighed Lucy, who considered it her misfortune to have eloped with a man of great charm and sincerity, who had a romantic conception of money but no head for business. 'Such a ne'er-do-well! I'm sure those diggers who work for him are cheating him, pocketing half the stones they find. Well, this is his last attempt to make his way in the world. If he can't manage here, I'm taking Daisy and going back to England. I shall cast myself on the mercy of my brother!'

'Lord Falkirk?' murmured Rosa placatingly, for she knew that it comforted Lucy to talk of her aristocratic connections, and she was tired of Lucy whining.

'Of course Douglas never liked Edward,' Lucy continued. 'He had more or less banned him from coming to Castle Falkirk, which was what led me to so foolish a step as my elopement.' Lucy shook her head with the wisdom of hindsight. 'Douglas is not an easy man, but I should have listened to him. Or to my sister-in-law, Laura, for that matter. Her brother is Lord Glenmorach, you know. She's such a gentle creature.'

Rosa listened lazily, not really caring how Lucy went on, although some inner part of her mind automatically stored the information for future use. She had learnt the lesson well from Maria Zichy how a remembered connection or claimed acquaintance could further one's social ambitions in the most unexpected ways. She threw herself down once more on the couch, swinging up her legs and arranging her skirts prettily about her.

'Families are strange things,' she assented. 'Especially the most blue-blooded, such as yours,' she added, gracefully conceding Lucy's superiority. 'Count Lazar's sister – the Countess Karatsonyi – ignored me for years, you know. Then she had the absolute gall to come and beg my forgiveness after Rudi's death.' Having thus staked a claim for her own credentials, Rosa, who liked to get her own way without apparent force, sighed and stretched. 'Can't you pull a bit harder on that rope?' she cried petulantly to the little girl in the corner. 'It's stifling in here! What must Mrs Tarrant think! Oh, I wish it would thunder and be done with it!'

'Oh, I don't mind the weather as much as you do, Rosa,' said Lucy. 'It's the monotony that I can't bear. If we could even ride out! At least the men can go hunting, but the thought of passing those stinking kaffir compounds . . . If only Edward had the sense to put his money into some kind of supplies, as Nye has done, instead of dreaming always of sudden wealth,' declared Lucy with a burst of honesty.

'But it was prospecting that first made Nye rich,' confided Rosa. 'Back in 1871, before the rush here in Kimberley,' she explained. 'With his sharp eyes and the luck of the devil, he told me he collected dozens of diamonds in a matter of months in the gravel around the Vaal River.'

'You mean he worked his own river diggings? And found big stones?' Lucy saw little of Nye and, since he seldom responded to her conversation, did not particularly admire him, but she was nevertheless fascinated by the story of his success.

'Yes. I think most were pretty small. But some, which he sold back in Europe, were thirty carats or more.' Rosa held up her thumb and forefinger to show a gap the size of an impressive gem-stone.

Lucy digested this information silently. She was tempted not to believe it – the leaping hope that Edward might similarly strike it rich only made it harder to bear the impatience she felt, cooped up in this raw, embryonic town. Besides, she told herself, conditions in the diamond fields had altered drastically since Nye's first lucky prospecting trip five years before. Since those day, stones had been found in huge quantities in the yellow ground of the kopjes twenty miles south-east of the Vaal River, and Dutoitspan, Bulfontein and Kimberley had attracted men from all over the world: the days of the intrepid prospector alone in the veld were gone forever. There were just too many diggers living on their dreams now for them all to have them come true.

'It'll never happen to us,' she said at last in a depressed voice. 'Why do we suffer it, Rosa? What are we doing here, bringing up our children in this hell-hole? Fever and dysentery are rife in those camps. If I could only send Daisy safely back to school in England!'

But Rosa's eyes seemed fixed on something beyond the confines of the stuffy room with its ornate furnishings. 'I know, Lucy, I know it's awful. I hate it too. I could scream with boredom sometimes. But just think! There *are* riches here – no one can deny that – huge, vast, endless deposits of wealth stuck in all that mud. Someone is going to get it all. Let it be us! It must be worth a little endurance. Just wait and see.'

Following their arrival in Africa, Rosa had watched Nye covertly, intrigued by his evident familiarity with the terrain and its extreme conditions. Arriving in Kimberley, and dazed and horrified by the huge open crater of the Big Hole, swarming and foaming with activity like a terrible termite nest, Rosa could not help but recognize his dominance over the lower orders amid this venal, animal kingdom. She had no doubt but that he would triumph over this apparent chaos and emerge more powerful than ever. Although he had been more open with her about the sources of his wealth since they had left Budapest, he was still vague as to the full extent and scope of his interests and silent as to his ultimate ambitions. But, as he amassed his financial empire, he seemed to expand within himself, becoming a man of stature, more potent, more charismatic, more undeniable than ever before. Rosa felt in thrall to him, and submitted to his power, awaiting the day when she should share it.

'Oh, I do try to endure it, Rosa,' wailed Lucy. 'But Daisy is growing up without any conception of how real people go on in proper circles, and I can't bear just to wait out my days like this. Why, look at this dress! I've re-made it a dozen times! If only my brother would help us!'

Lucy's complaints were too much for Rosa, and she stood and beckoned to the little girl in the corner. 'Go and tell Cheong to serve luncheon now, and call to Miss Sylvie and Miss Daisy to come. Say to Cheong to put out some chilled hock with the lunch.' And turning to Lucy, indicating that Lucy should precede her through to the dining room, she said encouragingly: 'Tell me once more about the time you met the Princess Louise.'

Lucy roused herself, and, heartened by the promise of a cold glass of wine, let the day fall bearably back into its familiar routines.

Sylvie, as usual, had spent the morning with Daisy Tarrant, who, at fourteen, was a year her junior. Bored by the atmosphere of frivolous chat or clinging self-pity that united their mothers, the two girls had formed a firm friendship. Daisy, a plain, lonely child, alternately ignored or fretted over by her mother but much petted by her father, had seldom found real friends of her own due to the frequent moves demanded by her father's recurrent business failures. She entered eagerly into the intensely self-contained world of adolescent friendship. Sylvie, too, after the shattering experiences of Budapest, had been grateful and relieved to find a companion who made few demands upon her other than the exchange of ribbons and promises never to like anyone better. Rosa was only too glad not to have her troublesome daughter hanging around her, adding to her sense of frustration with the place, and hardly seemed to care what Sylvie got up to.

Sylvie's expectations of people had changed drastically since those terrible last days in Budapest. She was no longer certain what she knew or thought, and her predictions of how other people might behave shifted constantly like a kaleidoscope. On board ship, Rosa had once more assured Sylvie that her vision of Sari Fodor on the bed was nothing but a bad dream, a nightmare. Yet it was her dreams, dim and incoherent, that now occasionally reminded Sylvie that her happy, conscious memories of the Budapest of picnics, skating and gypsy music were somehow terrifyingly incomplete. Although she remained protective of Rosa, Sylvie, too, was relieved to be on her own, independent of her mother's ability to make her own perceptions seem so hollow and shadowy. If Rosa insisted, Sylvie felt, that black was white, Sylvie had little power to gainsay her. Instead, Sylvie welcomed Daisy's simplicity of spirit, her consistency and her loyalty. Not knowing quite how to reciprocate the sometimes overwhelming intensity of Daisy's comradeship, she even confided the secret of Rudi's ring, telling her with pride how her father had left it for her before going to his death in a duel, fought to protect their honour.

Daisy was content just to be in Sylvie's company. Sometimes the girls took themselves off to the stifling kitchen, where they were welcomed by Cheong, the

Malay-Chinese cook, who, in a good mood, fed them his delicious *Melktert*; sometimes they sat in the late afternoon in the nascent garden, Daisy swinging idly in a hammock slung from the spreading branches of a thorn tree while Sylvie read to her from *Redgauntlet* or *Jane Eyre*.

Today, accompanied by the Tarrant's houseboy as their guardian, they had ridden out in the cool of the morning a few miles away from the town. Sylvie loved to see the red earth and the faded colours of the trees, the marked plumage of a game bird as it scooted out from under a bush or the delicate lines of a springbok leaping away at their approach. Above it all stretched the vast, open blue sky. At that hour, the air had a bitter smell, mixed with the freshness of the dew. It was Nye who encouraged Sylvie to escape from the house. She thrived on the outdoor life and loved to listen to him and his friends boast of their hunting trips, and of the lands with exotic-sounding animals and fearsome peoples that lay further to the north. In the winter months, she had felt exhilarated by the sharp night frosts and revelled in the unfamiliar constellations of the Southern Hemisphere, bright in the velvet expanse of sky overhead. Now she welcomed her second spring, when the karoo would blossom and come to life again.

As they ambled on their ponies between the antheaps and wild olive trees, the two girls chatted amicably. Daisy, who always required Sylvie's opinion of any change in her dress or appearance, wanted to know whether the blue satin ribbon that Sylvie had procured for her from the Cape would be better used in her hair or as a belt for her best dress.

'The colour may be lost in your hair,' answered Sylvie judiciously. 'But it would set the pattern of your frock off well.'

'Oh, I wish I were pretty like you!' sighed Daisy, much to Sylvie's surprise.

'Me?' she asked, grabbing a tress of her thick auburn hair with one hand and pulling it around where she could inspect its colour. She shook her head in confirmation of her suspicions. 'I'm not pretty,' she declared. 'I'm far too pale and my hair's the wrong colour.' Sylvie's figure was lithe and thin like a colt, and her heavy mane of hair, still worn down her back tied with a simple bow, only accentuated the delicacy of her complexion. But her large grey eyes were lustrous and fascinating, and, given a year or two for her figure to finish rounding itself out, she would indeed be a beauty. 'Why, Mamma has completely lost interest in my appearance!' she laughed. It was not that Sylvie did not wish to be as lovely as her mother, but that, at fifteen, she was shy and self-conscious. The thought of men finding her attractive scared her just as much as it secretly thrilled her.

'But you are!' insisted Daisy. 'Well, maybe pretty isn't the right word. No, don't laugh at me. I do think you're . . . romantic!'

'Hardly,' smiled Sylvie. 'I don't look in the least like Mamma, and she is romantic. My Papa once said that I look like my grandmother,' she confided shyly. 'She was a Hungarian countess.'

Sylvie added this not to boast, but because, surrounded only by prospectors and labourers, both girls found the notion of gentlemen and princes, culled from the stories they read, entrancing. They were at an age when they longed to be admired, perhaps even kissed for the first time, and some far-away, idealistic prince was a far safer fantasy than any handsome digger in his hat and boots.

'I wish you could meet my cousin, Will,' said Daisy, bringing her pony closer beside Sylvie's, and glancing backwards to see that the houseboy did not follow too close behind. 'He's not really my cousin. He's my Aunt Laura's nephew, so is only related by marriage. He'll be Lord Glenmorach when he inherits the title. He's much older than me, but I think Mamma hopes that . . . ' She broke off, giggling. She dug her heels into her pony's sides and trotted off, calling back over her shoulder, 'You'd have to be a lot nicer to me if I were Lady Glenmorach!'

'But he's in London and you're in Africa!' Sylvie shouted gleefully after her. When she caught up with Daisy again, her friend looked serious.

'Mamma and Papa had another argument last night,' said Daisy sorrowfully. Both girls were aware of the tensions at home, of the unnaturalness of women like their mothers inhabiting such a place. Usually it remained a subject of unspoken sympathy between them, but Daisy had told Sylvie before of the ferocious rows between her parents.

'Was it about going back to London again?' asked Sylvie.

Daisy nodded. 'And about Papa's gambling debts.'

Money was not a subject about which Daisy had much understanding, but Sylvie had been coached over the last few months by Nye in the strange workings of economics and investment. She often sought sanctuary from her mother's irritability at Nye's office in town, where the cool logic of figures and finance seemed enticing after both the emotion-laden air of Rosa's parlour and Daisy's rather clinging admiration. He, in turn, seemed amused by her interest in the details of his business, and he instructed Racker to allow her to assist him in the office and even, occasionally, to ride with him to one or other of the mines. And she understood that here in the diamond fields, gambling debts were no light matter. But she remained silent.

'I hate it when Mamma shouts and shouts like that,' went on Daisy miserably. 'I don't really care about going back to London. We weren't happy there either. And I wouldn't want to marry Will MacKenzie anyway – he's far too clever for me. But from what they were yelling last night, it seems like we may *have* to leave here, if Papa gambles away his claims.'

'Mr Nye told me that people like your Papa will be all right if they hang on to their claims,' said Sylvie. She had accompanied Nye to inspect conditions at the Big Hole only the previous day. Accustomed now to the awesome place, she had surveyed the apocalyptic scene rationally, looking for signs of change. Bending down to shout into her ear to make himself heard above the din, Nye had pointed out to her several places where the reef had slipped, forming an avalanche at the side of the crater and burying several claims underneath the soft shale. He made her look, too, at the bottom of the pit, where many diggers were hard at work draining out the water that had collected and filled their little patches of ground. The task looked hopeless, yet it was as though this endless commotion could never cease, spurred on by laws of nature that were savage and unyielding.

Most of the narrow roadways that ran like bridgeheads between the claims, wide enough for an ox and cart, had been all but abandoned as unstable. 'See,' Nye had explained, 'the mass of individual tunnels are undermining each other; those walls between claims there are just paper thin; if there's a flash flood, it'll take days to drain the bottom-most diggings, even with these new steam pumps that they've hauled up from the coast at vast expense. You can see all that. Look! New cracks are appearing in the soft ground around the rim here every day. It's getting to be a waste of effort and money.' Riding back into town, there seemed to be already a feverish awareness that such a chaotic state of affairs could not last much longer before disaster – either natural or economic – struck, with calamitous results for those who had risked everything on the dusty soils of Africa.

'He says that things will change soon at the mine,' Sylvie explained to her friend. 'The Mining Board will have to pass new laws because, without people getting together, no one can afford to stop the Big Hole collapsing.'

'How can that help Papa?' asked Daisy irritably. It annoyed her when Sylvie showed off her cleverness. It reminded her that Sylvie could amuse herself apart from her friend. Poor lonely Daisy counted the hours each day until her mother released her back into Sylvie's company.

'At the moment, no one can own more than ten individual claims,' explained Sylvie patiently. 'That way it's more fair and people won't fight over the mine. But the mine has gotten so deep that the sides are forever caving in and the bottom is filling up with water. Three men were killed in a slippage the other day, you know. But no one makes enough money from only ten claims to pay to make the Hole safe. Mr Nye says it'll happen any moment, that the Mining Board will let people own as many claims as they like, otherwise the whole thing will go bankrupt. Then your Papa can sell at a good profit,' finished Sylvie, tugging her pony's head around to make for home.

'Then we'd go back to London,' said Daisy with excitement. 'And I'd never see you again,' she added miserably.

That afternoon, while her mother rested, Sylvie rode with Cheong into town. Before making his way to the crowded market, he left her at Nye's office, built, like most of Kimberley, of corrugated iron. In the sparsely furnished upstairs room, Nye sat silently in front of the window at a table spread with white paper, his scales before him. He always seemed comfortable despite the heat. He had abandoned his usual dark, close-fitting clothes for a loose white suit and, outdoors, his face was always shaded by the wide brim of a light canvas hat; his linen jacket hung neatly now on the back of his chair. Patiently wielding the tweezers with his manicured fingers, he was grading each small heap of dull, unpolished stones according to size and colour. Sylvie waited, silent and still, watching as he sat hunched over the table, examining these tiny trophies. At last he stood and stretched, stiff from sitting so long. He laughed when he noticed Sylvie observing him so seriously.

'What? You're still not bored with these playthings? Well, then, come and see what I've got today.' He handed her an eyeglass and made her sit at the table while he stood behind. 'I'm only interested in the close goods, mind. The pure, well-shaped stones that will go to the jewellery trade. You can leave the chips and boart to the bulk buyers.' As he spoke, he picked a stone from each pile, one by one, for her to examine.

'These stones from Bulfontein are white and pure – like the stones in your mother's necklace – but they're all small, you see?' He then directed her attention to the next pile. 'There are too many among these here that are yellow or brown: they won't go, won't sell. And here are some good white crystals from Kimberley itself. But, look, here are the finest stones, these truly blue-white Silver Capes from the small Dutoitspan mine. They'll lose half their weight in cutting, but these are the ones that'll be in demand in the jewellers' shops in Fifth Avenue, Bond Street – or Vaczi-utca!' he added, laughing again. He looked through the window, down at the noisy, bustling street below, a light of triumph in his eyes.

Sylvie could not help smiling at him as he turned back from the window and grinned at her. The scars of the Sari Fodor affair had left her with an animal aversion to Nye, but, strangely, her growing understanding of him amid this primeval struggle for gain had quenched her fear somewhat, and left her with an equal mixture of pity, faint disgust and admiration. She found she had intuitively understood the cocktail of raw emotions that held Kimberley together: hope, greed, disappointment, euphoria and, above all, the pervasive scent of fear. There was cruelty attached to the dreams of riches held by every man associated with this scene, a cruelty that Sylvie felt Nye savour like the aroma of food to a starving man. Seeing him here in these dusty streets, Sylvie felt that he was in his natural habitat, a hyena among a pack of dogs.

She knew that, unlike the other dealers, the *diamantkoopers* such as Alfred Beit, Barney Barnato or Anton Dunkelsbuhler, Nye sold the uncut gems direct to New York, side-stepping the merchants in Cape Town and the cutters in Amsterdam and London. He had recognized early that it was the rich Americans who wanted to enjoy their wealth who were going to become the largest consumers of diamonds. The cattle barons and the coal and steel magnates were unlikely to inherit jewels, yet their wives wanted to rival the European aristocracy in their grandeur. In New York Nye had friends, and some influence, and was a partner in a company that imported all the finest stones that he could buy, selling direct to the diamond brokers in Manhattan. Where the other dealers in South Africa received far below a quarter of the stones' ultimate market value, Nye earned nearly three-quarters, meeting the demand from a land with all the potential to be the world's richest industrial nation.

But this afternoon Sylvie wanted to ask him if he knew about Mr Tarrant's predicament, and how serious it might turn out to be for Daisy, so she put down the tweezers and asked him earnestly what he thought.

'Tarrant?' echoed Nye absently. 'He should be all

right. He was one of the first on the fields, and he's built up a nice little holding on Number Six Road. His trouble is lack of collateral – you know what that means?'

Sylvie nodded. Rigorously trained in the precise, careful habits of a diamond dealer, she moved away from the table with its precious cargo to a high stool at the back of the office. She sat fingering the large leather-bound ledgers that covered the counter, thinking. Nye glanced at her.

'What do you think he should do?' he asked.

'Diversify?' Sylvie ventured.

Nye bowed in her direction. 'There you have it. He should get into one of the businesses supplying the diggers, then he'd have a source of cash.'

'Can't you help him?' asked Sylvie eagerly. 'Couldn't he take over a little part of one of your interests?'

Nye laughed loudly, as if this were a great joke, but his eyes remained serious. 'Have you learned nothing?' he demanded. Sylvie blushed, feeling stupid. 'That's why it's a waste of time teaching women about business. Too sentimental! Racker,' he called out to his man in the office across the hallway. 'Did you hear Miss Sylvie's sweet suggestion, Racker?'

'Yes, sir,' answered the man impassively.

'The only help you can give people in business, Sylvie, is towards their downfall. Profit is your motive, always. And another man's ruin is generally cause for celebration, not commiseration. Always remember that.'

Sylvie nodded miserably, her face hot with shame and anger.

'All this hypocrisy about those men who were killed at the mine the other day,' he continued. 'No one really cares. It's the fact that no one can make a profit any more that really worries everyone.'

Sylvie slipped off her stool and stood ready to leave.

'Wait, Sylvie,' he said. 'You can learn from this. Listen! Your Mr Tarrant still holds a valuable bundle of claims. If he can hang on until the Mining Board lifts the Ten Claims restrictions and people can buy up as many claims as they can afford, they'll be queueing up to buy him out, and he can retire to a modest estate back in England, if that's what he wants. It depends how much of a fool he makes of himself until then.'

'Why can't he sell now?'

Nye shook his head. 'The economics of the diamond fields have got to change radically in the near future. Prospectors are under pressure from both ends to amalgamate and consolidate.'

'But how does that affect Daisy's father?'

'His claims are good ones; he produces a lot of stones. But look what it costs him to maintain his patch. Even the Mining Board is having difficulty financing the proper maintenance of the Hole. What chance does he have?'

'So why will it be better when people can own more than ten claims?' pressed Sylvie. 'Where will the extra money come from? The mine will still produce the same number of stones, surely?'

'What's been happening to the price of diamonds? It's all in those ledgers beside you,' he said, leaning across to indicate them by a slap of his palm.

'It's been dropping steadily for months,' answered Sylvie obediently. 'The market has responded to the glut.'

'And why is there a glut? Because, with so many hundreds of individual claim holders, there's no way to control production and stabilize the price. And few dealers can afford to hang onto large stocks of stones. That's why I've never wanted a stake in the mine itself. Until now.'

Sylvie nodded. 'But even if there are fewer owners, how can they afford to maintain the Hole?'

'If the mine's owned by a dozen or so syndicates, they can float joint stock companies, or raise capital in other ways, and modernize the operation. The railway will arrive in Hopetown soon, and then it'll be possible to import the engines and machinery of modern mining: new shafts can be sunk well outside the perimeter of the mine and, within the crater, drilling and blasting with this new dynamite will replace the pick and shovel. But much more importantly, production can be steadied. A cartel will control it. We'll be able to manipulate the price per carat gradually upwards once more. Hold out on the best stones, and make the cutters pay more for the run-of-the-mill stuff. You'll see: more and more diggers will sell out over the next few years as they lose the fight against the drainage and the slipping reef and are squeezed out financially by the muscle of the cartel. If your Mr Tarrant doesn't sell out at the right moment, it'll be too late. Only a handful of men can come out on top. I intend to be one of them.'

Sylvie was silent. She felt confused by the expression of savage joy on his face. To her, the finances of mining were a matter of fascinating mental agility and ingenuity, but Nye's unaccustomed openness this afternoon had made her realize that there was much, much more at stake. Power, success or ruin. She glanced across at the neat piles of crudely faceted pebbles on the white paper. Suddenly she hated them.

'In twenty years,' Nye went on, 'all this mineral wealth – not just diamonds, but gold, iron, manganese – will have created a new money supply that will be in the hands not of the landed gentry with their ploughs and prize cattle, but of entrepreneurs and financiers. Men with ambition and new ideas who can see the future clearly. Railways, steamships, factories: more wealth will be created in the next decade or so than in the whole of the past century! Wait, and you'll see!'

Even on his first trip with Racker, Nye had seen the

potential in Africa for a man with colonial aspirations, realized how easily a single man could amass a fortune, stake a claim, merely place a flag in the ground and name a town after himself – in the name, usually, of some queen or emperor, but that was merely to summon the threat of official support. Place enough flags in the ground, and he'd have himself a country, with no tom-foolery about democracy, either, such as confronted the settlers in America's virgin territories. Nye's fascination for politics was captured by such possibilities and for some time his imagination had dwelt happily on such a future. But first he was busy creating the power base to which he could attach the guy-ropes of such a flimsy but imperial edifice as he planned somehow to erect.

In the back office, Racker, too, was quietly listening, a look of pride on his face. Nye relished the unspoken praise. 'The safest way to become rich here on the diamond fields,' he continued, 'is to be like me, a broker or a supplier. But the chance to gain a real fortune, one that brings the power to control the flow of diamonds for sale, is to become a mine-owner. It's not money I want. I'm no naïve young prospector, out to escape the grinding existence of some poverty-stricken farm or industrial mill; money has none of the glittering attractions for me that it holds for those who mistakenly believe that it's an ultimate cure-all in life, some hidden elixir for happiness. Money's a tool like any other, a means of gaining power and influence. The moment is coming, Sylvie, when I shall buy into the mine in order to control its operation!'

But Sylvie felt no sympathy or admiration for his ambitions. She now began to see all too clearly how men such as Daisy's father could be crushed in the maw of profit-making. She already despised the indignities practised upon the black labourers by white overseers who treated them with less consideration than their mules. But she had somehow assumed that, among the prospectors, there was enough for everyone, that everyone stood an equal chance of striking it rich. She felt the disillusion keenly, amazed now at her own naïvety.

As she walked home that afternoon from Nye's offices, thinking long and hard about Daisy and her father, she felt the sharp, sore edge of the emotions that hung about the town like a malevolent swarm of bees or locusts. The destiny of so many hung in the balance. Ruin was imminent. Only a few of the thousands of prospectors who inhabited the corrugated iron shacks and rows of white tents that stretched across the plain would survive the coming change. She suddenly wondered feverishly what Rudi would have counselled her to do, had he been beside her, and longed for the familiar feel of his ring in her hand, her talisman.

Realizing that the sky was turning to the vivid colours of sunset, she hurried home, for Rosa had warned her that once the daylight went and work at the mine stopped, the bars quickly began to fill up with drunken, carousing diggers and Kimberley became no place for a young girl.

When Sylvie saw Daisy again the following day, however, her friend seemed happier.

'Mamma has got all Papa's gambling debts sorted out!' she announced as soon as she saw Sylvie. She took her arm and squeezed it against her thin ribcage. 'Your Mamma spoke to Mr Nye last night, and he has kindly taken up all Papa's markers, so that all the people he used to owe money to will leave him alone now. Mamma is so relieved!'

'What are markers?' asked Sylvie, a cold dread seizing her.

'Oh, I don't know. Bits of paper. It just means that he promises to pay Mr Nye back as soon as he is able – which, of course, he would anyway. And Mamma's headache is completely gone!' Daisy skipped delightedly beside her friend. Sylvie did not entirely understand the rules of gambling, but she now knew that to owe money to Nye was to be as free from anxiety as a rabbit caught by its leg in a trap. She remained sombre as Daisy danced along beside her, jerking her arm uncomfortably.

'Why, Sylvie, aren't you pleased for me?' Daisy looked hurt.

'Yes, yes, of course,' Sylvie rallied. 'But you will tell your Papa to be sure and pay Mr Nye back the money as soon as he is able?' she insisted earnestly.

Daisy instantly withdrew her arm and raised her little chin. 'My Papa is the most honourable man in the world. Your Mr Nye doesn't need the money anyway. Why, Mamma says it's pretty strange the way he always seems to make more money, even though she says the price of diamonds is falling,' declared Daisy stubbornly, dreadfully injured by Sylvie's misunderstood warning.

Sylvie forced a smile and tried to take her friend's arm once more, aware of the impossibility of explaining to her the terrible threat that Nye represented. But Daisy shook her off.

'I have to go home now,' she announced, her frail pride striking Sylvie to the heart. 'I promised Mamma I wouldn't be late for luncheon.'

'Shall I come over to your house this afternoon?' asked Sylvie humbly.

'I'll see. Maybe I'll be busy.' And Daisy flounced off, her sense of friendship deeply wounded by Sylvie's apparent disloyalty.

'Goodbye,' called Sylvie disconsolately after her.

She wandered sadly indoors, wondering how to spend the afternoon alone. To her surprise she came upon Racker standing in the centre of the parlour, dressed in his riding breeches and a sweat-stained shirt.

'Where's Mr Nye?' the man asked curtly, as she entered.

'I've no idea. Whatever's the matter?'

Racker picked up his wide hat from the table and pushed past Sylvie in the doorway. 'I must find him,' he said. 'This is important.'

'Tell me, then,' Sylvie demanded. 'I can give him the message.'

Racker paused, and seemed about to speak. Such was his respect for the girl's understanding of his master's affairs that he almost broke his lifelong habit of absolute secrecy where Nye's interests were concerned. But his customary deep reserve prevented him, and, shaking his head, he hurried out.

When Nye came in later than usual that evening, his eyes were glistening and there was a slight nervousness about him as he moved around the room and smoothed back his hair from his forehead. He looked youthful and excited, but ate his dinner thoughtfully in silence. As Rosa served him his coffee and brandy, he stretched out in his chair and looked at her and Sylvie victoriously. They returned his stare curiously.

'It has started, my dears. The next few days will seal the fate of Kimberley and everyone connected with it!'

'Is that what Racker wanted to tell you?' burst out Sylvie, despite Rosa's reproving gesture.

But Nye grinned and nodded. 'A few diggers at the bottom of the pit have found that the soft, yellow ground has suddenly given way to hard, dark earth.'

Rosa sighed, twitching her skirts impatiently as she sat down, exasperated with this endless obsession with dirt and earth. But Sylvie got up and went to stand beside Nye's chair. 'Is it the end of the mine?' she demanded. 'There must be a natural limit. I hadn't thought of that before.'

'Sylvie, don't be tiresome!' Rosa nagged. 'Come and help me tidy my sewing box.'

But Nye and Sylvie ignored her. 'That's what they fear,' he agreed, noting the intelligence in her cool, grey eyes. 'And they've hurriedly covered the barren earth over with yellow ground and gone into town, eager to sell their claims as quickly and quietly as they can before the news gets out and prices drop to zero.'

'There's going to be a panic!' In her mind's eye, Sylvie could imagine the fury, distress and fear that such news must cause, a tidal wave of desperation as everyone tried helplessly to save what they could from such a calamity. Speed would be the only way to salvage anything – sell first, before Kimberley became a ghost town.

'But Racker got word to me this morning,' continued Nye, almost purring with satisfaction; even Rosa looked up from her embroidery, startled by his rich tone. 'Together, we've been helping to spread some of the worst rumours, while I've quietly bought up thirty claims for about half their usual value. There'll be no way that the Mining Board can enforce the Ten Claims Clause after this.' His gaze returned from the far distance and focused on Sylvie, whose frowning face was searching his expression for a clue to his actions. 'It's merely speculation, of course,' he told her firmly. 'Pure speculation.' And he concentrated once more on his brandy glass.

Over the next few days, the diamond fields were rocked by rumour and speculation, and the bars and gambling halls were crowded with men desperate to drown their dashed hopes. Everyone was jumpy and nervous, wondering what would happen if this were indeed the end of the strike.

Sylvie never forgot the intense excitement of these days; the mass emotions that seemed to sway the very fabric of Kimberley were, to her, a natural phenomenon like a storm or a heatwave. Her enquiring mind closed around the economic realities of that time and place, and learnt, at a quite fundamental level, how cold, dry figures written across the pages of an accounting ledger were intimately connected with people's emotions, ambitions and fortunes. Luck itself was infused by these feelings; a hunch feeding on a rumour could drive people together in mass panic or mass euphoria just as effortlessly as an earthquake or the deliverance from some natural catastrophe. It was a lesson she never forgot, yet never consciously remembered learning: it was as though it were something she had always known and understood about the world.

For Rosa, such calamitous events had meaning only so far as they influenced her own life; that Lucy's supper party was cancelled or that the dusty streets were more crowded and impossible than usual. She railed at Sylvie's nervousness, at the girl's eagerness to question anyone who had the latest bulletin from the mine. Yet now even she and Lucy were affected by the town's sudden change in fortunes. Through the parlour door, Sylvie heard Lucy crying as Rosa tried to comfort her. 'Well, at least we'll get out of this God-forsaken place, Lucy, back where we belong. The town will be finished. We can go home.' But Lucy only wailed the louder.

'We shall have nothing. Edward's claims will be worthless. With everyone leaving, we can't even sell our furniture. Oh, the disgrace! I should never have married him, never!'

Quickly, before she should live to regret it, Sylvie ran upstairs to her room. She sat on the edge of her bed, breathing deeply. Resolutely, she took Rudi's ring from her pocket and tied it tightly in her handkerchief. She went into her mother's room, to her desk, to find an envelope. Taking up a pencil, she wrote hurriedly on a sheet of notepaper, agitated with conflicting emotions:

'Dearest Daisy. This is to help your father. He is to

sell it. Now I have your friendship, I can do without this. You need it more. Your devoted friend, Sylvie.'

Trembling and near to tears, she pulled open the little drawers of Rosa's desk, searching for an envelope. At the bottom of one of the drawers she found one. In it was a faded scrap of newsprint, something about Gregory's Barn. Impatiently, she stuffed the newspaper cutting back into the drawer and pushed the handkerchief containing the emerald ring into the envelope with the note she had written, and went downstairs. She could still hear Lucy murmuring and sniffling in the parlour, so she slipped down the passage to the kitchen.

'Cheong,' she asked, looking into his wide, smooth face and trying to smile. 'Would you take this immediately to Miss Daisy for me, please? I . . . I don't feel well enough to take it myself.'

The kindly man wiped his hands on his apron before accepting the package. Seeing her pale face and huge, pleading grey eyes, he smiled and nodded. 'I go right away, Miss Sylvie. Before I prepare dinner.'

Sylvie sighed with relief. Her heart ached to lose her father's gift to her, but, with all the fervour of a young girl's first real friendship, she was glad that she had done all she could to help Daisy. It was a placatory gesture, too, to mend the coolness that had persisted between them since Sylvie's earlier warning. And she felt not so much responsible for Nye's ruthlessness, as determined to thwart its effects if she could. She somehow imagined that this act could turn the tide of Daisy's family fortunes; that because the emerald held such awesome significance for her, its monetary value would be sufficient to work magic: after all, how could anything so intimately connected with her father be ineffectual?

The next morning, Daisy accompanied her mother on her usual call upon Rosa, and Sylvie was gratified and relieved when her friend hugged her warmly, their earlier coldness forgotten. 'I haven't had a chance to give it to Papa yet,' Daisy whispered in Sylvie's ear as Rosa took Lucy over to the piano to show her some new music that had arrived that morning. Daisy squeezed her arm gratefully. 'You are a darling,' she said.

But the next day, Lucy called alone. She looked strangely at Sylvie as she put down her parasol, as if she couldn't quite determine whether Sylvie were entirely serious and sincere in her usual polite greeting. She moved her head from side to side, in an irritated fashion, so that her errant eye could look also at the girl's face.

'Why don't you go and play with Daisy at my home today, Sylvie?' she said. 'She's waiting for you. And I have something particular to discuss with your mother,' she added pointedly, patting the small bag she wore on her wrist in a significant manner. 'You don't mind, do you, *chérie*?' she asked Rosa, who shook her head disinterestedly. 'Go on, then. After all, I think you know what I have to say to your Mamma.'

Sylvie went cold: it could only be the ring. Mr Tarrant must have asked his wife to return it! But to Rosa, who had never known she had it! Who would recognize it instantly! Sylvie ran, glad to escape to a friend to whom she could pour out her heart. But as she closed the front door behind her, she saw Nye dismounting from his horse at the gate. Desperate to get away, Sylvie waited reluctantly to greet him, looking at her feet while the houseboy came to lead Nye's mount away to the stables shared by the half dozen nearby houses.

'The news is out!' he called, waving his hat in the air. 'Someone's finally dug out a few tubs of the hard blue ground, pounded and sifted it and found that it contains even finer quality stones than the soft earth above it! What do you think of that?'

He stopped in front of her, still breathing fast from the exertion of riding. He smelled slightly of sweat and of his horse. Instinctively, she stepped back, away from his closeness. But, despite her misery, her imagination was caught by this new development.

'So it's not the end of the strike?' she asked.

'Far from it!' Nye threw back his head in exultation. Inexplicably, he reached out his hand and cupped the side of her head, reaching his fingers in amongst her thick hair. 'The mine is now worth incomparably more,' he continued, seeming not to notice as she wriggled free. 'My holdings have risen several hundred per cent overnight: now I've got a major stake in the mine itself.' And he walked straight past her into the house, leaving her to run next door and tell her friend that her father, too, was saved.

'You'll be rich now,' cried Rosa, hugging Lucy when Nye told them the news. But Lucy did not join in the celebration. She glared murderously at Nye and struggled free of Rosa's embrace. She was flushed and shivering with anger. As she walked towards the door, she attempted ineffectually to spit on Nye's dusty boots. Failing that, she choked on the angry sob that rose in her throat. She looked heavenwards, searching for some gesture that would relieve her. Looking downwards once more, she realized she still held Sylvie's ring grasped in her hand, where she had been in the midst of showing it to Rosa when Nye entered. She flung it in Nye's face, where it stung his cheek and fell to the floor. As she ran crying from the house, he stooped down and nonchalantly picked it up. A half smile played about his lips as he slipped it into his pocket and turned to Rosa.

'Why, Jack, whatever is the matter with Lucy?' she asked, astonished.

Nye laughed. 'I called in Edward Tarrant's gambling debts, just before the news broke that the blue ground is fertile. He had to sign over his claims to me. He's penniless, that's all. But it need not concern us. You and I, my dear, are wealthier than ever!'

Rosa's face changed and darkened. 'How dare you do this to me?' She spoke in a low, venomous tone. 'Ruin my only friendship, my only solace in this cess-pit of a place!'

'Come, come, my dear,' said Nye equably, though a dangerous glint shone in his eye. 'Anyone so weak as Edward Tarrant was to accept my offer in the first place was already a dying man. I thought you enjoyed the exercise of power,' he taunted.

Rosa was livid not only at Lucy's predicament and the fact that they would now have to stay here if the damned mine were still viable, but also at the shock, just a moment before, of discovering that all these years, Sylvie had secretly possessed Rudi's ring, with all that that might signify of what the girl knew of the truth. She felt called upon to feel shame at what Sylvie must have experienced all these years, at what she had all but succeeded in repressing, but instead was filled only with unutterable rage. And so, without pausing to think, anger clouding her better judgement, she now stormed over to Nye and raised her hand to slap his face. Swiftly he caught her wrist and pulled it high above her head, twisting it, his tight grasp making her flesh between his fingers white. He stood close to her, her breasts pressing against his chest, breathing into her face. He looked into her eyes, smiling dangerously.

'I am now a very powerful man in this place. Isn't that what you wanted?' he asked ironically.

Rosa saw that she had gone too far, that there was little hope of saving the situation. Sensing her own doom, rage, as much at herself as at him, welled up in her once more.

'I don't care how powerful you are!' she screamed into his face. He barely flinched. Sharply, he jerked her arm further upwards, pulling painfully at her shoulder socket. She yelped with pain, but continued to fight him. 'I hate this place. I hate you for bringing me here!'

Nye leaned his weight on her, standing on the hem of her gown, crushing her breasts and making her screw up her face with pain as the strain on her arm increased. Confused signals began rushing to her brain; was he aroused by the situation? Was she? So often they had fought together, naked, reaching for a sexual climax in the midst of pain. Or were her feelings for him over? She looked into his face, so striking, its slight foreignness accentuated by the cold irony that flickered always in his eyes.

Usually one look was enough to subdue her, to make her long for his touch, but suddenly she resented her powerlessness; hated him for making her into the cringing creature his violence evoked. She wanted to howl with helplessness and anger, not knowing whether to retreat or advance. Her clenched teeth were bared with the effort of struggling ineffectually against him, but the desire to fall on him, to bite him and to drive her tongue deep into his mouth, only an inch from hers, was uncontrollable, even while she wanted more than anything to be rid of him and this hateful place.

'Let me go!' she hissed viciously at last, as he gloried in her confusion. 'I don't want you any more!'

The door was flung open, and Sylvie rushed in, wide-eyed, gasping for breath. 'Mr Tarrant's shot himself!' she screamed at them. 'You ruined him,' she yelled, beating at Nye's back with her fists. 'You killed him, just so you could get his claims. Just for money, more money. You're a killer! You're a killer! You're a killer!' She continued to shout hysterically until her mother drew her away, out of the room.

Nye stood alone, smiling to himself.

CHAPTER NINE

Will MacKenzie looked up at the lights burning in the first-floor windows of the red-brick London house in front of him. The soft rain fell like a mist in the plane trees of the square, and he heard the melancholy sound of the departing hansom cab as, once more, he felt his emotions fall into their familiar pattern outside this door. A middle-aged maidservant greeted him with a delighted smile.

'Master Will – Sir William, I mean to say! I do forget how the years pass by!' She chattered on as she took his long dark coat and silk hat and laid them by his cane and gloves on the cluttered hall table. 'I'm well, sir, thank you,' she replied in answer to his genial enquiry. 'You'll never guess who's here! Arrived off the boat all the way from Africa! It's poor Mrs Tarrant and little Miss Daisy, come with another widow-lady and her daughter that they met out there. They look so cold, poor dears, that I've lit big fires in all their rooms – I just hope his Lordship doesn't catch me!'

Will went unannounced into the first-floor drawing room. It was freshly painted white and hung with a light green wallpaper decorated with pomegranates. Lady Falkirk had thrown soft Paisley shawls over the capacious padded armchairs and arranged a collection of blue and white vases on shelves around the mantelpiece, cleverly adding a touch of modernity to the comfortable solidity of the mid-century, without incurring any additional expenditure. She sat now at the back of the room beside the tea-tray, which was laid on a gilt and ebonized table already crowded with piles of books, photograph albums, newspapers and a

Chinese vase filled with huge stems of dried flowers, the colour of stones or driftwood. A fire burned in the hearth, and the old-fashioned red damask curtains, becoming threadbare, were tightly closed against the late November fogs. To either side of the fireplace hung life-size portrait sketches of Laura Falkirk, done in pastel on flesh-coloured paper and handsomely framed. Will glanced at them as he came in: he still thought them the best things he had ever done.

Douglas Falkirk, a rugged, stocky man with wily eyes, like a fox, beneath his thinning, sandy-coloured hair, stood before the fire, legs spread apart and hands clasped behind his back. He stared coldly at Will as he entered, then his gaze slipped away sideways: he had a look that could never quite be caught and pinned down. He left it to his wife to greet the young man.

'Will!' She ran with small steps across the room and kissed him. She wore a silk gown in shades of pale grey and fawn, with loosely draped scarves of old cream-coloured lace about her delicately wrought shoulders. Although her hair was now a colourless blond, turning here and there to grey, the overall effect she created was strikingly ethereal. Since boyhood, Will had unconsciously held his aunt – his father's sister and the woman who had all but brought him up – as an ideal of womanliness, and his eyes brushed hers lovingly as she looked up at him nervously. 'Your Aunt Lucy and Cousin Daisy are here!'

'I know.' He smiled down into her pale, bright face, holding onto her hands. 'Peggy just told me. How are they?'

Her large brown eyes, which seemed permanently brimming with tears, looked imploringly at him. She was about to answer, but her husband spoke first. 'Destitute, of course!' he sneered. 'Why Lucy expects me to pay for her mistakes, I'll never understand. Well,

I'm no fool like her late and unlamented husband – I won't house them long!'

'Douglas! She's your sister!' cried Laura.

'Then she should learn more respect for her brother,' he answered in a surly growl. 'I'm not her bank!'

'But she's never asked you for money before. Never!'

'And remember, sir, how recently she's widowed,' put in Will gently in support of his aunt. 'And a suicide, too. I'm sure she wouldn't have come to you unless she were absolutely desperate,' he added firmly, with deliberate irony, as if to remind Lord Falkirk that no one, especially his sister, could ignorantly presume upon his good nature.

'Don't lecture me, boy!' snapped Falkirk. 'I'll do as I please.'

Will gave him a long, hard stare of contempt, but kept silent: Laura's restraining hand upon his arm reminded him of what she had long ago told him, that any angry intervention on his part later provoked silent, secret abuse from Falkirk upon his wife.

As a youth, Will had longed to fight his uncle, to show to the world what a coward the bully really was, and he had learned discretion with difficulty. For Laura could not leave her husband: Falkirk had made it plain that he would never allow her to take their young daughters, Helen and Madeleine, with her, and the law of the land gave a wife no power whatever to protect her children from a violent or even murderous father.

Once more, Will cursed himself for his inability to prevent such cruelty, and all but cursed the world, too, for its complexity. Justice, he felt, should be a simpler affair. It irked and saddened him that life made this business of reward or punishment so indirect and indistinct. For all his quick intelligence and subtlety of mind, Will was slightly afraid of the whiplash tendency of life to spring back and hurt people, even when their paths seemed so straightforward. Despite his openness, he shied away from situations that were not clear-cut and kind.

Laura drew him now to sit beside her at the tea-tray. 'Lucy and Daisy and their friends will be down soon,' she said, steering the subject into less turbulent waters, as she had done so many times before. 'Let me make you some tea.'

Will gladly pulled up a chair. Although he still glanced over to where his uncle stood before the fire, his anger underlay a determination to bring his aunt some, albeit temporary, lightness and relief. Laura, long inured to Falkirk's cruelty, sensed how hurt Will was by such conflict. Will's mother had died when he was only nine years old, and since then Laura had always had him with her. He had spent all his holidays from Eton with her, until he went up to Oxford and began to spend his vacations travelling in Italy and Greece. Now he lived in Chelsea, he came to see her frequently, and often spent a few weeks in the summer with her in Scotland. Recognizing an essential goodness in the boy, she had always indulged him, and he had rewarded her with his easy-going charm and loyalty. She smiled at him now a little mischievously.

'There is one way in which you could be of help to your cousin Daisy,' she said quietly, passing him his cup.

'What's that?' he asked eagerly, although he guessed from her look that she was not entirely in earnest.

'As the future Lady MacKenzie, neither Daisy nor her mother would need to look to my husband for help.' She regarded him with a smile, but her eyes were serious. Laura knew that Will had had the usual boyish crushes, and that his relationships with some of his regular life models showed a thorough appreciation of their physical charms, but she was not aware that any part of him other than his eyes had ever been in love. Being handsome and gregarious, he was, she fancied, lazy about women, but sooner or later he would have to produce a suitable Lady MacKenzie, and he had always been particularly kind and charming to his cousin.

Will was horrified. 'Oh, no,' he began. 'Of course I'll help in any way, but not that! She's a sweet kid, but she'd expect me to give up the best painting hours of daylight and go calling on people. And even when she grows up, she'd never have anything in common with my friends. Aunt Laura, you don't really . . . '

She laughed and patted his hand. 'Don't worry. I just thought I'd ask. You see, I'm sure the idea must have occurred to Daisy's mother more than once, so it's best that you're aware of it. And now you know, you won't lead her on unintentionally.'

Will breathed a sigh of relief as the door opened and Madeleine and Helen, acting as family hostesses, showed the women into the room.

Will greeted Lucy Tarrant warmly; he had little in common with Lord Falkirk's sister, but he had always admired her pluck in defying her brother, even if it had led her into greater trouble. 'And Daisy,' he continued, kissing her cheek while she blushed. 'I was so very sorry to hear about your Papa. But you're such a young lady now that you can be of help to your Mamma.'

Daisy gave him a shy smile of gratitude for the small compliment, but her unnecessary glance towards Lord Falkirk told Will that she fully comprehended her uncle's attitude towards them. Here was Daisy, so guileless and vulnerable; could it really be impossible to act for her good? The curb on his generous impulses thwarted and hurt him. But Daisy was tugging lightly at his sleeve. 'And, Will, this is my friend, Sylvie Lapham,' she whispered proudly.

Will turned towards the two women who had accompanied Lucy and Daisy, while Laura performed the introductions. The mother, who surprised him by her American accent, was a beautiful creature, a slightly raffish version of a Botticelli cherub, an Alma-Tadema creation, thought Will to himself. Standing beside Laura, Rosa looked taut and sleek in her dark travelling dress. Her figure was plump, and there was a wonderful lustre about her skin, making the golden tints in the fluffy curls about her face seem like mere reflections of her glowing flesh, like sunlight dancing on water. She met his regard spiritedly and, though her sensuality was a little too obvious for his taste, he had to agree with the confident assertion in her gaze that she was in the full flush of mature womanhood.

Then he turned to greet Daisy's new friend. The girl was young, perhaps sixteen, slender and straight-backed, with a mane of untamed auburn hair tied with a wide, black velvet ribbon. She wore a simple close-fitted grey travelling dress edged with a deep scarlet that echoed the natural hues of her hair. Obviously tired from her journeying, the fine bones of her face seemed to him like ivory; the shadows under her eyes were a burnished gold. Her mouth was like one of those rare rose-coloured stones set into an inlaid Florentine table. And her eyes! He had never seen such eyes. Two huge silver-grey moons that burned with a painful intelligence and shone with all the hopefulness of her extreme youth. She was an angel!

Sylvie herself was curious to meet the cousin about whom Daisy had spoken so often in Kimberley. She looked at Will with pleasant interest, and saw a slim, long-legged young man in his mid-twenties, with thick, short, dark brown hair like an otter or some other aquatic mammal. He was elegantly dressed and not at all bohemian, for, having never met a painter before, she had half-expected him to wear a soft jacket and floppy necktie. But she saw the way his greenish-brown eyes looked at her with an artist's intensity, as if measuring the distance from her chin to her nose, or judging just how to mix the colour for her skin. She found she did not resent his examination of her in the least, and stood patiently while he accomplished it.

Returning with a jolt to his aunt's drawing room, and seeing that the girl did not take fright at his study of her face, Will smiled cheerfully at her. 'Delighted to meet you, Miss Lapham,' he said at last.

'How do you do?' answered Sylvie frankly, returning his friendliness.

Laura retreated with her daughters to the tea tray, and smiled vaguely at the visitors. Rosa, obviously intent on making an impression on Lord Falkirk, walked over to him and addressed him frankly.

'I'm sure that I'll soon be able to make proper arrangements for myself, and bother your hospitality no longer.' She spoke curtly, in a businesslike way, as if realizing that it would be useless to throw herself on the mercies of such a man, yet she smoothed the flat front of her gown provocatively with her hands.

Will saw the lazy flicker of erotic interest in Falkirk's eyes as he quite openly surveyed the woman from head to foot as she stood before him on his worn Persian rug. Despite his familiar manner, gained from a rough, outdoor life as a soldier controlling the interests of the British government in some of its more obscure outposts, Falkirk was accustomed to command. He had the practised look of a man used to dealing with local potentates, but used also to having the full weight of the British Empire behind him when he did so. Will knew that he would hardly stand on ceremony for a pack of women, but Rosa met his gaze with an insolence he knew his uncle would appreciate and understand, coming from such a source. Will saw with surprise that she most certainly wanted, and expected, Falkirk's help; what her raised chin and the smoothing gesture over her generous figure said quite clearly was that she was prepared to pay for it. He ironically wished her joy of her quest and washed his hands of responsibility for her.

'We go north to Scotland for Christmas in a few weeks, Mrs Lapham,' answered Falkirk casually. 'So you'll have to be out of here by then, come what may.' He laughed in an ugly way. But Rosa strutted nonchalantly past him to seat herself beside Lucy, to whom she chatted contentedly.

Will sat down beside Daisy and asked her questions about Africa. Sylvie was left quietly on her own, and Will glanced at her from time to time, struck by her self-possession. She was just beginning to grow out of the formlessness of childhood and showed the promise of great beauty. The girl had a presence in the room that even out-shone Laura's haunting, shadowy power. His eyes rested a moment on one of his studies of Laura; for the first time, its rare, languorous quality, its undeniable power to evoke a tangle of emotions, seemed lacklustre.

'So what do you mean to do with yourself here in London, Mrs Lapham?' demanded Falkirk, interrupting her conversation with Lucy. 'Have you the means to support yourself, or are you utterly impecunious, like my sister here?' His manner was familiar, almost jovial, but his eyes never laughed.

'Yes, I can support myself,' answered Rosa. 'Though eventually I shall have to find some way to amplify my income.' She looked demurely at her hands in her lap.

Falkirk guffawed. 'I daresay you'll do that the same way you did in Africa!'

A strangled exclamation of horror escaped Lucy's lips, and Laura looked angrily from her husband to her own daughters and then to Sylvie, but Rosa, though her colour heightened, did not look up. Will was about to intervene, when Rosa spoke calmly. 'I daresay I shall, sir.'

There was a moment's silence; sensing the tension, even Helen and Madeleine hushed their quiet chatter.

'Then I hope you'll allow me to furnish you with some introductions, since you're a stranger in town,' allowed Falkirk. 'You may use my name if you wish to open accounts and so forth.' Will could see that, inwardly, Falkirk was laughing to himself: still, there was no doubt that the American would do well among certain of Falkirk's friends, if that was the game she was after.

'I had hardly looked for such kindness, sir. Thank you,' answered Rosa, a touch of mockery in her voice. She turned to Lucy and patted her hand. 'You see, Lucy, I told you that your family would hardly abandon you.'

'As for you, Lucy,' continued Falkirk, the banter gone from his tone, 'you, too, will have to find some way of supporting yourself. I suppose you'll have to stay here temporarily, but you can make yourself useful to my wife, I'm sure.' Laura blushed and hung her head in shame to be associated with such high-handed meanness.

Lucy bit her lip in anger and disappointment and mumbled her thanks, pushing a reluctant Daisy forward to kiss her uncle. Will saw Sylvie reach out jerkily and grasp Daisy's hand as she passed, giving it a squeeze of support. Daisy smiled at her gratefully, and Will, too, inwardly honoured her loyalty. He rose and went to sit beside her.

'Are you familiar with London, Miss Lapham?' he asked politely.

'No, sir, not at all,' she answered demurely, though she looked directly at him with eager eyes. 'Daisy told me you're an artist,' she went on. 'What kind of things do you paint?'

'Oh, figures and portraits mainly. Are you interested in art, Miss Lapham? Do you draw?'

Some of the shine went out of her eyes. 'Not at all,' she answered rather curtly. 'Besides, I imagine that you would hardly like your work to be compared with the kind of drawing that young ladies are taught.' He felt rebuked and yet was amused. This girl obviously had little patience with the usual currency of the drawing room.

'You're quite right.' He smiled warmly at her, but, finding that his charm was not sufficient to melt the defensive look in her eyes, was puzzled as to how he should proceed. After a pause, he pointed to the pastel portraits of his aunt that hung beside the fireplace. 'Those are examples of my work. I think they're about the best things I've done.'

She looked over at the pictures and studied them quietly for a moment. 'They are very good,' she agreed seriously. 'You're obviously very fond of your aunt.'

At this quaint observation, Will laughed aloud, then glanced at his young companion, fearing that he may have upset her again by his lack of seriousness, but she laughed with him. Nevertheless, his practised eye registered that the eagerness with which she had first looked at him had not fully returned. He read in her expression that she was holding back just enough to protect herself from her own curiosity about life. As a portrait painter, it was a quality that he might have expected in a much older person, but not in one so inexperienced. Such reserve was, after all, a quality that he knew from his own face in the mirror, although he had learnt to disguise it beneath an air of stylishly ironic malaise.

As Will took his leave, he vowed to call upon the women the next day in Falkirk's absence, and see what his own personal wealth and contacts could do to smooth the way for Lucy and Daisy Tarrant. He also admitted to himself that he wanted very much to see what colours Sylvie Lapham's eyes might turn out to be in daylight.

The next day, when he called in at Cadogan Square, he found that Lucy and Rosa had taken advantage of the bright autumn morning to go shopping, leaving the girls in Laura Falkirk's care. They were in the morning room on the ground floor, where French windows looked out onto a terrace that bordered a garden shared by all the houses in the square. The last remaining leaves on the chestnut trees burnt orange and brown against the keen blue sky, and, seeing Sylvie's glowing outline against the low dazzling rays of the sun that streamed through the panes of leaded glass, he turned and whispered to Laura where she sat at her light rosewood writing desk before an elegant disarray of opened letters, invitation cards, pens and cut-glass bottles of purplish ink. She laughed lightly in return and urged him forward.

'Miss Lapham,' said Will, approaching her, 'I hope you don't mind my forwardness, but your colouring, your profile, your eyes are so striking, and you look so pensive by the window there . . . '

Sylvie, disturbed from the memories of Budapest that the chestnut trees had evoked, acknowledged his words shyly, while Laura laughed. 'He thinks you're a sublime creature. The colour of your hair is apparently all the rage now among these artists! You won't mind if he sketches you, will you?' She began to take the paper and chalks from the drawer where she kept them for him, for he often sketched her or one or other of her daughters when he came to visit.

'Will!' cried Daisy, anxious that Sylvie would be offended by such free talk, but Sylvie, too, laughed happily at his cajoling expression.

'Mamma says that I am far too pale, and that my hair is her despair,' she said, looking up into his pleasant face. More used to her mother's ripe looks, Sylvie had always considered her own colouring to be too strong, too definite, to be seen as pretty, but, recalling Sari Fodor's tutelage, she understood enough of the art of acting to know that versatility could outweigh mere beauty; now she welcomed this novel idea of her face being more interesting to draw than one of more fashionable loveliness.

And so she gladly allowed Will to pull up a chair for her facing the French windows, so that the light fell evenly upon her. He sat before her and studied her, leaning forward to take her wrist in order to position her arm slightly more to one side so that the slenderness of her shoulder, encased in its well-fitted bodice, was more evident. Unconsciously, he enjoyed that brief physical contact with her; her proximity gave him a feeling of happiness and excitement, adding to that almost physical intoxication that an artist experiences through his eyes alone.

For half an hour, Sylvie sat there in Laura's room while he sketched her profile. She concentrated hard, taking her task seriously and trying not to twitch a muscle and to move as he directed her. Daisy wandered from one side of the room to the other, alternately observing Will's work over his shoulder, and standing beside Sylvie where she could study his expression. Sylvie was just beginning to feel the strain of sitting so long, when he told her that she could move freely once more.

Laura came to join Daisy in looking over Will's shoulder and she exclaimed enthusiastically over the drawing. 'Worthy of Lord Leighton himself!' she declared, placing her hand affectionately on his shoulder as he looked up at her. She saw that his eyes had a bright, far-away look.

Sylvie came forward shyly and Will put the sketch pad into her hands.

'Oh, but I'm not so beautiful as that! This is like an angel!'

The others laughed. 'Not at all,' said Laura, taking it into her hands. 'It's a very good likeness indeed. Will is famed for his ability to catch a face.' Sylvie blushed, a delightful new world of possibilities flooding her imagination.

Laura handed the drawing back to Will, who continued to scrutinize his work, his head bobbing like a robin as his eyes darted from the paper on his knees to Sylvie's face and back again, as his long agile fingers added a slight thickening to a line here or rubbed at the chalk marks to lighten a shadow there. Now that the sitting was ostensibly over, Sylvie found the profound intensity of his stare disquieting. She didn't know whether to look away, or to meet his eyes. His face was handsome and joyful in animation, but this concentration made his features seem more determined, almost unyielding. But then she found that he did not see her at all. This burning gaze was seeking out the exact curve of her neck or the precise way in which her hands lay upon her lap, and then returning to his drawing, concentrating upon making subject and image one and the same. Laura and Daisy, too, grew still, watching as Will was absorbed once more back into his private vision.

'It's no good!' he declared suddenly, putting the pad from him and shaking his head. 'It looks like you, but it's not you at all. I must draw you again.' And he took the sheet on which he had drawn Sylvie's beautiful young head and, crumpling it in his strong fingers, threw it towards the fire.

'Oh!' Sylvie cried out as if she had been hurt. But Laura, with her quick, intuitive perception, rose and put her arm around the girl's shoulders, while Daisy darted forward and picked up the bruised sheet, trying to smooth it out.

'You don't belong to yourself, once you get into an artist's hands, Sylvie.' Laura spoke warmly to her. 'That's not you,' she said, indicating the drawing. 'I've sat many, many times for Will, ever since he was a boy, and more than half the studies he's done of me have ended up on the fire. What goes down on paper or canvas belongs to him. It's himself he's dissatisfied with, not you.'

Sylvie looked from the shelter of Laura's encircling arm at Will. He was looking at her once more with innocent detachment, a look of puzzled amusement on his brown otter's face. She felt mildly shaken, and suddenly remembered Sari Fodor's critical gaze multiplied in the mirrors of her gilt rehearsal room: this was like acting. Lady Falkirk was right – it had nothing to do with her.

'I don't mind,' she said shyly to him. 'Do you want me to sit still for you again now?'

'Would you?' exclaimed Will warmly. 'I don't mean right now. But I really would like to draw you often. If I could have you for a whole day!' The image of Rosa floated into his mind and he looked doubtful. 'Aunt Laura?' He turned to her.

'Yes, dear,' she answered vaguely, already busy with something else. She was used to Will with his bursts of enthusiasm and bouts of laziness, and paid him little heed, content, like a mother with her cubs, to have him there.

'Aunt Laura, you'll bring her, won't you?'

She looked up from the note she was writing. 'Well, not without Mrs Lapham's permission, Will.'

'But you'll ask her? Please, Aunt, you must!' With surprise, Laura recognized an urgency in his voice, quite different from the usual dilettante pose that he assumed, in common with most of his fashionable young friends. Sylvie looked from one to the other. She had already spotted Daisy carefully folding Will's drawing of her and hiding it under a cushion from where she could retrieve it later. Sylvie wanted to giggle. This sudden promising upturn of events did not dislodge the ball of misery caused by all the tragedy that had befallen her young life; it sat waiting inside her, she felt, until she should be old enough somehow to break it up and disperse it. But there was enough of the healthy young animal in her to welcome such flattery and fun.

'I will ask Mamma,' said Sylvie with quiet determination. 'I don't think she will object, if Lady Falkirk approves.'

The next few weeks, however, were taken up with their move into an elegant, white-painted house in Phillimore Terrace, a tree-lined street in Kensington. It had wide steps leading up to the front door, with a small garden at the back and an open square in front, fenced with iron railings, where nannies in grey uniforms marched sturdy children around in the drizzling rain. Rosa paid for the lease, with characteristic candour and lack of embarrassment, by the sale of the necklace Nye had given her. The stones, so perfectly matched and graded, were worth a small fortune, and she lost no time in disposing of them, with Douglas Falkirk's help, in Hatton Garden. It was not until the Falkirks returned from Scotland in the New Year that Will reminded Laura of her promise. Rosa, who seemed to Sylvie constantly to be discussing leases and money and other arrangements with Lord Falkirk, was glad to have Sylvie out from under her feet; not unmindful of Will's eligibility, she willingly gave her permission for Sylvie to sit for him as often as she liked.

Will MacKenzie's studio in Cheyne Walk, Chelsea, was in a wide, old-fashioned house set back behind railings and a narrow, shady garden of magnolia trees overlooking the River Thames and Battersea beyond. At the back of the house, French windows opened from the studio onto a large old-fashioned garden, where venerable mulberry trees stretched down to rest their heavy boughs on the grass. The walls of the studio were painted a dim red and were hung with an assortment of works by Will's friends, while his own paintings were stacked in racks along one wall, beside a small wooden quarter-plate camera on a tripod and an up-ended plinth. Two or three canvases in various stages of completion – oil paintings for exhibition or commissioned portraits, for Will was already beginning to make a successful name for himself – stood on easels of varying sizes.

The room was furnished almost like a drawing room, but the floor was of bare polished wood and the air in the huge, high room was filled with the pungent smells of oil paint, turps and size. Sylvie, hovering by the stove, was fascinated by the assortment of plaster casts, fossils, Isnik tiles, even a human skull, that lay neatly arranged on low shelves behind a huge wooden chest brightly painted with medieval knights and ladies. In an ante-room, hidden by a tapestry curtain of birds and flowers in shades of dull turquoise and blue, his studio assistant, Philip, a young lad of nineteen, reigned over a domestic domain of jars of bright pigments, evil-smelling pans of rabbit-skin size, rolls of canvas and wooden stretchers, and palettes, knives and brushes. Sylvie was forbidden to enter this ante-room, though she was fascinated by the almost harsh intensity of the exotic pigments.

Her first few visits were chaperoned by Lady Falkirk, but then, as Rosa did not seem inclined to bother herself about Sylvie's plans, she and Daisy went alone, until Daisy complained that there was nothing for her to do and she was bored, so she stopped coming. By then, no one seemed to mind that Sylvie went by herself. Rosa was glad to be free of the girl at last, for, since her discovery of Sylvie's unaccountable possession of

Rudi's ring, she had felt her relationship with Sylvie to be somewhat frail and tentative. Things were definitely better left unsaid, yet, without raising the subject, Rosa could not be sure what her daughter's state of understanding was about her father's death. Rosa found a welcome degree of certainty in recalling herself at Sylvie's age or thereabouts: she had been only a little older when she had run away with Onslow Lapham. Perhaps it was best just to let Sylvie fend for herself in London. She was such a close, secretive girl that who knew but that Sylvie might surprise them all one day.

Will worked Sylvie hard. For weeks, he was obsessed by his sketches of her. Dozens of studies of her neck, her profile, her hands, were tossed on the floor in despair. It was a new experience for him: he had always been passionate about painting, but now he really felt the limits of his power. Here was something that he absolutely had to capture, to make his own, and for the first time his skills seemed to fail him. The more dissatisfied he became with his work, the more he wanted to have her about him, so that he could just let his eyes dwell on her.

'Just shift around a little more to the right. Can you hold your hand up to your temple and pull your hair back? Try to look jubilant. The world is at your feet! Perfect.'

And Sylvie summoned up all the poise that Sari Fodor had taught her, and concentrated on ignoring her body's demand to flex itself, forcing herself to experience the emotion he wanted, so that the muscles of her face would respond perfectly. Will's brown head bobbed sharply like an automaton, his gaze piercing but unseeing of anything other than the line he was trying to capture on paper. Ten, twenty minutes would pass, disturbed only by the movement of the wintry clouds shadowed on the grass outside and the quiet, domestic sounds of Philip about his chores. Philip, too, would sometimes pull up a stool and, resting a board on his knees, sit a few feet behind Will, making his own likenesses.

'Perhaps you might like to read while I sketch you?' suggested Will one day. Philip handed her a novel that lay on the floor beside Will's armchair by the stove. Without thinking, Sylvie began to read aloud, her quiet tones filling the big, empty studio. Soon it became almost a habit, and, if Will was busy with something else when she arrived, she would go into his dim library upstairs, where she loved to pore over the thickly clad walls, lit only by the lovely lights of the morning sky, making out the twilight colours of a Whistler nocturne or admiring the etched features of a pencilled portrait by Will's poor, ruined friend Rossetti. She would pull a book from the shelves and stand for a moment by the window looking out across the brimming river, watching the seagulls fight in the wake of the barges, allowing the spirit of the volume she had chosen to enter her.

She read poetry, by Tennyson, by Christina Rossetti, by Matthew Arnold, or from the novels of Thackeray, Dickens and the Brontës, and many of Shakespeare's plays. She found that the physical effort of projecting her voice helped her to sustain the still position that Will required. He loved to hear her: she could make the words she read come alive, peopling the room with star-crossed lovers, the wry intelligence of Rosalind or Portia and the bare-faced cheek of Becky Sharpe.

Will found to his surprise that she was a natural mimic, and saw that, in play-acting, she lost her usual reserve and acquired an extraordinary emotional depth that was astonishing in its intensity. He found this sea change fascinating, and he encouraged her all the more to plunder his library for characters that he might draw.

'You've moved again. Tilt your head back to the left.

No, too far. That's it! No, you can't put your arm down yet! Just one more minute.'

His deft hand moved surely over the paper pinned to the small easel before him. One long leg, elegantly shod, stretched out to the side, the other was tucked under the stool on which he sat, straight and broad-shouldered. Finally his head tilted to one side, the sign Sylvie had learnt to recognize as the waning of the spell he seemed to be under whilst he drew her.

'You know Daisy's been sent away to school?' She had been waiting to tell him, and she knew that he often liked to chat when he got to this stage of his drawing.

'No, I didn't.' Will felt the sorrow in her voice. 'You'll miss her.'

'She hates it. She's miserable. And when she finishes, she'll have to go to strangers as a governess or an old lady's companion.'

'It's a damned shame,' said Will in a brotherly way. 'I'll talk to Aunt Laura and make sure she's sent some treat or other each week. But it's no good arguing with my uncle over it,' he added bitterly.

'He often calls on my mother.'

Will looked at her in surprise. He remembered Rosa's strange challenge to Falkirk to help her find her feet in London, but had heard no further comment to confirm that his uncle had remained closely involved in her affairs.

'Does he come often, then?' he asked, but the faint perturbation he felt barely disturbed his concentration upon his work.

'Yes. And in the evenings he sometimes brings his friends to meet Mamma, and they have parties,' continued Sylvie. 'In Budapest, Mamma's parties were famous!' she added with pride.

'That's where you grew up, isn't it? Daisy told me.'

'Yes. My father was Hungarian, Count Lazar.'

'Then your mother remarried?' asked Will gently. Sylvie looked confused. Rosa had impressed upon her that, at Lord Falkirk's suggestion, they invent a polite fiction about their past, which involved a Mr Lapham who died of a fever contracted on the boat to Africa, which he would publicly support and would order Lucy Tarrant to do likewise. Sylvie liked and trusted Will and hated to lie. But she saw it did not matter; Will was once more intent on his drawing and did not notice her hesitation.

'Mr Lapham was my mother's husband, yes,' Sylvie answered quietly at last.

'That reminds me,' cut in Will. 'Would you like to come to one of my parties? On Sunday afternoon? Most of the artists in Chelsea have open house on Sundays, when all the world and his wife can come and buy. Of course they don't! It's mainly my friends. And they don't buy anything. Just drink gallons of tea, then invite themselves to stay for dinner.'

'It must be nice to have lots of friends,' agreed Sylvie wistfully. Will, so full of generous impulses, suddenly realized how lonely Sylvie must be. He cursed himself for having failed to draw her out more.

'Tell me, did you hate Africa as much as Daisy did? She told me she loathed Kimberley.'

'It was terrible what happened there,' she agreed soberly. 'But I found the place exciting. Especially now, because I can see the effects here in London, where all that wealth ends up.'

'How do you mean?' asked Will idly, his flickering attention already drawn back to his portrait of her.

'It's just so strange that, because of some vast great hole in the ground in the middle of Africa, miles from anywhere, companies are founded, shares traded, railways and offices built, and people walk around with more money to spend than they'd ever dreamed of. Out there, it *was* just a dream – and endless digging and sifting and shoring up and dirt. You should see the mine itself at Kimberley!'

'But what do you mean? About railways and so on?' Will asked, as his eyes traced the line he had drawn: yes, he had the jaw right, but it still wasn't working. He despaired of ever capturing the thing! There was something about this girl, some quality of magic, of other-worldliness that was not in the least like his aunt's fragility, that he wanted to grasp and put down on paper. Sylvie's delicacy was at the same time robust, red-blooded, young. He wanted to paint a portrait that you desired to kiss, but dared not. A picture that captured the awesomeness of her young, fine beauty and the layers of feeling and experience that seemed to lie beneath it. But he could not get it!

'Well,' explained Sylvie, 'the proceeds from the sale of all the diamonds, and the commissions that people take each time the stones change hands, that money has to end up somewhere, doesn't it?'

She seemed indignant at his ignorance, as though he were teasing her. Used as she was to the company of adults, Will nevertheless made her feel young and awkward. She felt acutely aware of the nine or so years between them; he seemed so quick and ironical, to have so much promise to fulfill, while she had no idea where life would take her.

'Do you know,' he said, looking up, 'I'd honestly never thought about it. Yet I should, I suppose. My family's money comes from the coal they found in the land they'd farmed for centuries in Scotland.'

'Yes, but this is different. This isn't just coal. Imagine if they do find gold in Africa in the same quantities as diamonds. That could double world liquidity within a few years!'

Now he looked at her in amazement. 'Liquidity?' He chuckled to himself, but wondered who had taught her such concepts. Not her mother, despite her canny nose for an advantage.

As if she had read his thoughts, her chin instantly went up in defiance. 'Mamma says it's vulgar to talk like that, that it isn't ladylike. But why shouldn't I understand what goes on around me? I'm not an idiot just because I'm a girl!'

'You're certainly not!'

Sylvie continued stubbornly: 'If you'd been there, and seen men dig the stuff out of the ground with their bare hands . . . You *have* to understand why they do it, what it's all about! You can't ignore the brutality, the greed, the hopelessness of it all just because it's not good manners!' She spoke passionately, but her shoulders drooped and he saw her retreat into herself once more, become the obedient model, private as could be behind that stunning mask. He found himself deeply moved by her predicament. He put his pencil to one side and stood up from his stool.

'No, you're right,' he said gently. 'I'm the one who doesn't understand. Come this Sunday afternoon, will you?' he asked, walking over to her and putting a brotherly hand on her shoulder to confirm his offer of friendship. 'You may find some of my friends are more intelligent than me.'

Guardedly, she smiled her thanks.

Returning to his drawing, he sighed, shaking his head. 'Philip, come and take this. Put it in the chest with the others.' The lad came and took the paper from him. Will saw Sylvie give a little blushing smile and, with a delighted stab of curiosity, he glanced at Philip. He could not miss the adoring look in his eyes. So that was how it was! Will laughed to himself uncomfortably. The two dear children flirting with one another! From the maturity of his twenty-six years, he felt a voyeuristic pang at stumbling upon this nascent sexuality. As Philip came back to put away the easel, Will dismissed him. 'You can clear up later, Philip,' he said, and, assuming a preoccupied air that was half real, ambled away. Out of the corner of his eye he watched as Philip and Sylvie approached each other and stood close to one another in the failing light. For almost the first time, he felt some genuine interest in Sylvie as a person, and realized somewhat guiltily that the intimate knowledge he had of her physiognomy did not amount to much in the way of friendship.

'Let me tie your hair ribbon,' he heard Philip murmur.

'Oh, thank you!' answered Sylvie, standing patiently like a child as the boy slipped behind her, his hands disappearing into her mane of hair.

'Philip,' he called rather sharply, 'light the gas, will you? It's getting dark. Sylvie, why don't you come upstairs and have a glass of madeira by the fire? You look cold, sitting so long.' Suddenly he felt a little self-conscious, aware of her in a new relation to himself.

'Mamma does not allow me wine,' answered Sylvie simply, as Philip reluctantly went to light the lamps. Will instantly relaxed, laughing at himself. She was so young!

'Well,' he said, 'perhaps I'd better just see you home.'

After leaving Sylvie in Kensington, Will felt strangely restless and dissatisfied. Instead of heading south to Chelsea, he decided to take a walk in Kensington Gardens. As he struck out across the grass, leaving the noise of cabs and carriages behind him, he breathed more deeply and lengthened his stride, but still his feeling of restlessness did not leave him. He thought over his day's work, looking critically at his sketches in his mind's eye, as he often did, searching for the flawed line that had unbalanced the whole. But he could find nothing technically incorrect in those sweet faces he had done of Sylvie. Yet there was something lacking. His sense of puzzlement increased, and, finding himself near the Prince of Wales Gate in Hyde Park, he decided to walk down through Montpelier Square and see if his aunt were at home.

Laura welcomed him with her usual calm. She was alone and glad of his company.

'I haven't seen much of you recently. Work must be going well,' she greeted him.

'Not really,' he answered, reluctant now to discuss the very topic that had brought him there. 'How's Daisy? Sylvie told me she's miserable.'

'I think she'll settle in,' replied Laura. 'I persuaded Lucy that, since Douglas has given them such a niggardly allowance, it was better to choose a school that economized by limiting the accomplishments it taught, rather than by half starving its pupils. Poor Daisy won't have the best drawing masters, but I think it's a homely, friendly place. And I hope Daisy has the sense to see how irrelevant her mother's ambitions for her have now become.'

They sat in silence for a moment, both pondering the tyranny of the master of the house.

'And how is Sylvie Lapham?' Laura continued. 'Are you still painting her?'

'Trying to.' Will flung himself back on the divan on which he sat, swinging up his long legs, as he had done as a boy, and clasping his hands behind his head. Laura looked at him with amusement.

'But she has such lovely features,' she said. 'I would have thought she was a perfect subject.'

Will shook his head in reply. 'Tell me, Aunt Laura,' he began eagerly, sitting up with his feet on the floor once more, 'what do you know about her past? What did you make of the mother?'

'Not much happiness for little Sylvie, that's for certain.'

'I've found there's something I just can't get at in her,' he explained suddenly. 'That's why I can't draw her successfully. There's an absence in her, a quite striking reluctance to voice her own thoughts and beliefs and such an over-eagerness to agree with other people. Yet she's seldom shy, and when she does open up . . . This afternoon she started talking about Africa, about finance and liquidity. Now where does she get that from?'

'I don't know, dear.' Laura shook her head. 'I doubt that the few careful facts that Mrs Lapham let slip about her past are entirely true.'

'I should think Sylvie could tell quite a story about her past life with Rosa!' agreed Will indignantly.

'Mrs Lapham is certainly tough, and quite ruthless,' she agreed. 'But I don't see her now. There's no reason for me to call upon her, and as I can be of no use to her, she doesn't call on me!' Laura laughed. 'But do you think Sylvie takes after her mother at all?'

'No!' Will was shocked. 'Not in the least. Except that, just recently . . . Perhaps she has her mother's strength. I suggested she read while I work, and now she reads aloud. She has the most beautiful speaking voice, and, when she reads a part, she seems to take on a presence that's somehow reckless and free. It's as if she loses herself in other people's words, as if she can change the very tint and colour of her own persona. I've watched her face alter under my hand as I draw her.' Will paused, shaking his head in puzzlement. 'I've never known anyone like her.'

Laura looked at him wryly. She wondered how long it would be before he discovered he was in love. And she was not entirely sure that it would be an easy experience for him. Although Rosa had not remained long in her house, she had sensed with her customary perception that at a deeper level, under Rosa's ruthless veneer, lay the hysteria of a woman whose dreams had not come true yet still exerted a powerful hidden force upon her actions. She had seen, too, the tension in Sylvie, born of dealing with the edge of fantasy that crept into Rosa's thought processes, and suspected that, in the past, Rosa's precarious hold on reality may have plunged them both into some minor tragedy. Sylvie's guard had been carefully constructed, and would not be demolished just by Will's infectious enthusiasm. Laura suspected that Will would have to dig a little deeper into his own soul before he could win the girl's trust entirely. Laura adored Will, with his mixture of shyness and laziness, of courage and loyalty, but was glad that this girl might force her brother's child to embark on his own journey of self discovery.

'Perhaps you should take a break,' she suggested vaguely. 'Try a self-portrait or something.'

Will looked at her in astonishment, but Laura merely smiled at him mischievously.

Will's friends, all sons of gentlemen, were young men who had declared themselves free of the demands of money, land or property and had rejected careers in law or politics for art. Harry Lewis was the dramatic critic on *The Times*; Felix Partridge was a fellow painter who had turned his attention to pottery and frequently set on fire the kiln in the basement of his house in Gordon Square, but managed to bring from it, just the same, the most wonderful majolica and lustred pots; Fred Allingham was a friend from Will's Oxford days who now worked for the Foreign Office but spent as much time as he could lecturing on Ruskin in the working men's clubs of London's East End; and Charles Dunbar was an architect.

'So this is the face on all the studies you keep hiding from us, is it?' asked Fred, when Sylvie was introduced the following Sunday afternoon.

'You wait until I paint her in oils, then you'll see

what I'm after,' answered Will. 'Philip,' he called to the lad, who was carefully pulling a canvas out of its rack to show to the visitors. 'Make sure that Mr Allingham doesn't go snooping, will you!' Philip laughed at the joke.

'How's your own work coming along?' Felix asked, joining the young man. 'I hope he remembers he's supposed to be teaching you.'

'Oh yes, indeed. I've been doing a few sketches of my own of Miss Lapham.'

'Really? May I see them?'

Philip looked embarrassed. 'Sir William hasn't seen them yet.'

'What haven't I seen?' asked Will, coming up to them.

As Philip seemed to hesitate, Felix answered gently, 'I was asking him about his own work. He says he's done some studies of the girl.'

Will was torn between resentment at the light way Felix spoke of Sylvie as 'the girl', and a jealous curiosity to see his assistant's images of her.

'I can show them to you later, if you like,' offered Philip, sensing his master's disquiet.

'No, no,' said Will, as his natural generosity reasserted itself. 'I should have taken a proper look at your work before now.' Philip disappeared into the ante-room and came back with a portfolio case tied with soft tape. 'Bring it over here to the light,' called Will.

Philip spread open the wide portfolio and took out a smallish pencil study. It was unmistakably Sylvie, caught quickly as she turned in apparent surprise. It was a moment's observation, carefully captured and then worked on to show the lightness of her girlish figure, the strong, refined bones of her face and her long hands and wrists. It was a simple drawing, and had none of Will's style or technique, but Will saw with a sudden tearing in his guts that Philip had got that indefinable quality in Sylvie where he had failed.

'It's good, Philip,' said Felix, leaning over the group's huddled shoulders to see. 'Are there more?'

Philip showed them five or six further studies, all of Sylvie, and Will saw unbearably that, in each, Philip had captured not only Sylvie's grace, but a slight flirtatiousness, the self-consciously sensual drooping of her bottom lip, the slight caress of the hand that brushed the wisp of hair back from her cheek, the smile in the direct gaze of those wondrous eyes.

'Damn!' thought Will to himself. 'Damn, damn, damn!'

'Have you seen these, Sylvie?' Felix called over to where she sat leafing through a new book that Will had just bought about Japanese art.

'Yes,' she answered quietly, at first not looking at either Will or Philip. Philip's admiration of her beauty had been frank and undisguised, and his evident infatuation with her had given her the confidence to cherish her individuality and to carry her striking looks serenely and confidently. He was only a couple of years older than her, and they had giggled together secretly when Will was absorbed elsewhere. Once he had kissed her, and she had liked that, too.

'Well done, Philip,' said Charles. 'They're excellent, aren't they, Will?'

'Yes, they are.' He gave his assistant a warm smile, trying to hide his own chagrin. He liked Philip and did not begrudge him this highlighting of his own shortcomings. 'I see I must get on and start a proper painting of Sylvie myself!' he added ruefully. 'That's your job for tomorrow morning, Philip, to prepare me a big full-length canvas!'

Everyone laughed, and Philip hurriedly closed up his portfolio and returned it to the ante-room before going off to the kitchens to call for tea, but, at the back of Will's mind, the words of the stolen moment he had witnessed earlier in the week kept repeating themselves stubbornly: 'Let me tie your hair ribbon' . . . 'Oh, thank you!'

'There's an intimacy in the boy's work, don't you think?' Harry spoke privately to Will, looking at him with faint concern.

Will smiled mortifiedly at his friend. 'Yes, and you're quite right. I'm jealous! Though whether as a man or an artist, I'm not sure!' He glanced over to where Sylvie sat reading. With surprise, he discovered that she was watching him with a searching look in her eye, as if to observe his true reaction to Philip's drawings. He could not tell from her look whether she pitied him or whether she wanted him to be jealous. Aware of Harry's scrutiny, he coloured slightly. 'I don't know what my real feelings are, Harry,' he admitted. 'I know it's a cliché for an artist to become obsessed by a model, but I think about Sylvie more or less constantly.' He sighed angrily and looked away. 'Such a chit of a girl!' Will tried to laugh his feelings off. 'The sooner I capture her on canvas and work her up into some sublime representation, the better!'

The parlourmaid appeared and poured tea into creamy Worcester porcelain cups decorated with delicate golden Japanese birds and butterflies, and handed around silver dishes of hot, buttered currant buns.

'How are your working men, Fred?' asked Will, turning to another of his old friends. 'Is there to be a revolution in Deptford yet?'

Fred ignored his facetious tone, knowing that Will always responded readily to a request to lecture or to find some poor devil an opening that would enable him to escape the poverty and degradation that inhabited much of the East End. The two men discussed Fred's latest protégé with interest, while Charles drew Felix aside to ask him about the results of the latest firing of his kiln. Sylvie found herself alone with Harry Lewis, who looked at her with evident curiosity.

'Shall I tell you a secret, Miss Lapham?' he asked, his eyes twinkling.

'Oh, please!'

'I have arranged for a celebrity to come this afternoon. Will's hopeless, he doesn't even try to play the game.'

'What game?'

'Why, of becoming famous, of course!'

'But I thought he was,' cried Sylvie earnestly.

'Bless the child!' laughed Harry. 'We know he's a genius, and I daresay he does, too, but his pictures don't yet hang on the right walls. He's not talked about. He can't just wait until he inherits his title – Lord Glenmorach, the painter-peer! So I've made a start.' He paused dramatically.

'Oh, do tell me!' breathed Sylvie.

Harry looked from left to right as if afraid of being overheard. 'Miss Ellen Terry told me – promised me – that she would call this afternoon and see Will's work.'

'Oh!' Sylvie's eyes were shining with wonder. 'Of all the people I could most wish to meet – Ellen Terry, coming here?'

'And of course she knows a thing or two about painting, after being married to Watts more or less out of her cradle. And then she was Godwin's wife in all but name – the architect, you know. Did a house for Whistler up the road. Such taste! Says he decorated his house in colours derived from the pineapple! Imagine! Just Will's sort of thing, all those twilight greys and greens.' He had completely forgotten that, in English terms, this self-possessed young beauty should be still in the nursery with her governess. Like Will, he recognized in Sylvie a kindred independence of spirit and he welcomed her as one of their own.

'I should love to meet Miss Terry!' Sylvie could barely contain her excitement: she was to be in the same room with the most expressive, modern actress of the era. 'I went with Mamma to see her as Olivia at the Court Theatre. I've never seen such calm, such compression.'

Harry was almost taken aback at the sophistication of her observation, but before he could comment, there was a light commotion in the studio, and the actress had arrived. Sylvie peeped round Harry's shoulder and saw a mischievous, pretty, motherly woman, with a laughing, mobile face with straight brows and pointed nose, surrounded by a cloud of curly golden hair caught up by coral combs above a loosely draped dress of some wonderful oriental-looking stuff. Two slim white arms were held out in greeting to Will as Harry performed the introductions, and Sylvic saw the friendly gaze of the actress's dancing grey eyes.

Will's paintings were pulled out of the racks and exclaimed over, drawings scattered across the table. More people came and went: fashionably dressed couples and City businessmen who liked to include art in their busy lives. As the light in the north-facing studio began to fade and the lamps were lit, more tea was called for and, as Will predicted, only his old friends remained, together with Sylvie and Ellen Terry. Will forgot that Sylvie should have gone home long since; unable to tear herself away from the close proximity of her heroine, she had stayed in the background, all but forgotten by Will and his friends, chatting quietly to Philip, when he was not required to display his master's work. But now, as chairs were drawn up around the studio stove, Will called Sylvie to him.

'Miss Terry, may I introduce a young friend of mine, whose head you no doubt recognize from some of my work.'

Sylvie felt the cool, firm grasp of the actress's hands

and found herself drawn down into a seat beside her. Remembering how Sari Fodor had always loved praise, she said, simply and sincerely, 'I've seen you act, Miss Terry. I think you make the difficult look not only easy but effortless. Yet you never become familiar, you still manage to take the audience by surprise.'

'Why, thank you,' answered Ellen, wondering who this self-possessed young girl could be, here among these unfettered young men.

'I want to be an actress,' continued Sylvie directly, to Will's astonishment. 'I was taught by Madame Fodor in Budapest,' she added proudly.

'The great Sari Fodor!' exclaimed Ellen. 'Well, you were truly fortunate! Her death was a great loss to the theatre.' She began to question Sylvie closely about Sari Fodor's technique, and the two women were soon engrossed in an eager conversation about the art of acting. Will could hardly believe his ears. Here was little Sylvie, confidently explaining to the toast of London's West End how she studied people's gestures, how easy it had been for her to learn to imitate the different London accents she had heard since arriving in England, how she memorized parts and held lonely performances alone in the garden at home. And there was Ellen Terry treating her with a professional respect! Listening to the intelligent questions she was asking and the almost businesslike way in which she put them, Will's condescending attitude towards Sylvie was shaken to its foundation. Wanting suddenly to make amends for his stupidity, he interrupted their conversation.

'Here, why don't you read something for Miss Terry?' He thrust the nearest book into Sylvie's hands. It was *Jane Eyre*, and by chance it opened at the scene when Jane has run from Mr Rochester and is desolate on the cold moorside.

'Please, do.' The older woman encouraged Sylvie

with genuine curiosity, while Will's friends looked at each other quizzically in the lamplight. They all seemed to feel that something special was about to take place.

Sylvie ran over the first words silently, like practising a scale on the piano, then, more sure, she tried them aloud, feeling for the sense of them and recognizing the emotion they expressed. She had never read to an audience before, but she was so accustomed to the acoustics of the high studio that the sound of her own voice instantly reassured her. The familiar words seemed to fill her out gently like a breeze swelling a sail. The intent faces of the circle around the stove, illuminated only by the lamplight, were accompanied by the portraits hung on the dim red walls, all but lost in the gloom of twilight. The big room was hushed; only the rustle of the breeze in the trees outside and the low rushing of the fire within the stove challenged the clear tones of her voice.

Will listened silently to Sylvie's short performance, and saw the familiar sea change that came over her as a sudden new poignancy and vulnerability emerged from her young beauty. He saw that the clue to Sylvie's character was to do with layers, that she was many things where he had been trying to capture some single essential quality. Some people, like his Aunt Laura, like himself, were basically solid, whole, homogenous, based around a single theme; but Sylvie was different, and her being an actress seemed an apt metaphor for her duplicity, her many-sidedness.

Suddenly he felt triumphant: 'Now I can do it!' he said to himself. 'Now it's there, what I want to paint. It's surfaced at last!'

As she finished reading, Sylvie herself seemed confused, as if awakening from a trance, and Ellen, sensing this, left the girl to herself, turning to Will to say that she must return home to see her children before they went to bed. After a few more minutes, she rose and held out her hands to Sylvie.

'You must come and see us at Hampton Court one weekend. My little ones, Edy and Teddy, act as guides to the maze – when they are not being the severest dramatic critics the world ever held! And perhaps, if you should like to, you could come to the theatre and help my dresser, or attend a rehearsal with me.' She held Sylvie's hands tightly in her own, looking seriously at her now. 'That way you would see whether the stage seen from behind holds as much magic for you as it does from the stalls. Now I must go! Goodbye Harry. Thank you, Sir William, for asking Miss Lapham to read to us all. Farewell, Sylvie.'

For the first time since Rudi's death, Sylvie had fallen headlong in love. It was as if, crossing some threshold from girlhood into womanhood, Sylvie had suddenly sensed something of life which she could not have understood before; a self that had been coming into existence gradually, and without her awareness, cushioned by the confidence of Will and Philip's open admiration, by friendships independent of Rosa's pervasive influence, and now by Ellen Terry's praise.

She was young, with the resilience of youth, and she began to sense her own destiny, there, waiting to be grasped. In acting she could be safe from her mother, from the Nyes and Falkirks of the world. Sometimes, when reading a part alone at home, she had felt pain, fear, aversion, at experiencing such raw emotions through the words on the page. But now, before friends, these words had been true, these thoughts real, and she could think them without fear of contradiction. Like someone stranded in the centre of a great, frozen lake, bitterly cold, unable to move, Sylvie suddenly saw a series of tentative footsteps that might take her safely to the shore, back to human warmth and company. She could act! Ellen Terry's encouragement had been like the hand of a champion coming to rescue her. She could feel stirring emotions without incurring pain or punishment! She could dress herself in other people's words, other emotions, and hide and protect her own nakedness completely.

The experience did not lessen the burden of hopelessness and loneliness that she often privately felt, nor did it absolve the strange, guilty anger she felt towards her mother, but it condensed her experience in a way that enabled her to make it her own. Despite her difficulty in reacting with complete freedom or spontaneity, she could store her emotions and control their release before strangers into the irrelevant, free environment of the theatre. That knowledge led her onwards into the future, to a destiny that only at that moment became hers. Victoriously, as the door closed behind her heroine, Sylvie gave a great sigh and pirouetted around on the spot.

As Will came back towards where she stood by the stove, he caught her hands and looked wonderingly into her radiant face. 'You were magical. You held us spellbound.' He acknowledged her new-found power humbly.

But she broke away to stand by herself, not answering him, her chin defiantly in the air, smiling as if she were a queen, independent and aloof, and Will felt as though a door had been closed in his face.

CHAPTER TEN

'It's a quite remarkable work, what!'

'Certainly intriguing. And certainly the best thing young MacKenzie has done.'

'I wonder who the model was.'

'I can't believe she's real, can you?'

'Why on earth not? Such glowing hair! Such eyes! He's painted real flesh and blood, all right. The girl's fairly young, too, I'd lay odds.'

'But no young girl could have such a look of . . . well, such a knowing look. She's so stern, so . . . so divine. The avenging angel who knows perfectly well what sins you've got to account for. I shouldn't like to meet her on my way to Heaven.'

'Yet the fury is tempered by such a radiant innocence, the awesome innocence that only an angel could possess.'

'You're right. She does have a sort of blazing beauty that burns out the impurity. Yet, even if you call it divine wisdom, the impure thoughts are still there, just the same.'

'Maybe it's us who bring the improper thoughts, my dear! I think Saunders is right. She *is* an innocent. What's he asking for her?' enquired Lord Arlington, turning to face Michael Saunders, the manager of the prestigious Maybeck Gallery in Old Bond Street.

'Sir William hasn't put a figure on the work, my lord. We have the engraving rights and so forth, but the artist doesn't seem ready to part with the original yet.'

'I don't blame him,' murmured Lady Arlington.

'Shame, though,' added her husband, taking a last

look at the huge canvas that towered above them on the wall, framed in dull, reddish gold and lit by the long narrow skylights overhead. 'It would have gone well next to the Burne-Jones.'

'It would indeed, my lord,' agreed Saunders, who knew the Arlingtons' extensive collection of modern pictures well. 'Though I think you would have had competition to buy it, if it were for sale. The critics have hailed it as the painting of the decade, and, I must say, I think they're right.'

'Do you now?' mused Lord Arlington. He was shrewd enough to recognize the sincerity in the manager's voice.

'I agree.' Lady Arlington spoke up. 'I don't care what you say, the figure of the Angel is erotic, yet MacKenzie's managed to depict all the forces of divine morality. It's really a most surprisingly pious work.'

'We've had people agree wholeheartedly with the first part of your appraisal.' Saunders spoke quietly. 'Wickham-Smith in the *Athenaeum* said it's the work of the devil. That he would be ashamed to have his sister beside him as he looked at it. He was very angry when he came here and saw it. And he has his supporters.'

'What horrid nonsense!' exclaimed Lady Arlington. But Saunders's words made her uneasily aware of the polite jostling behind her as people crammed together to look at Will's portrait of Sylvie as *The Angel*. The gallery was uncommonly crowded, but few people were paying much attention to the rest of the show. True, the painting stood out, not only because of its size, and its position in the centre of the back wall, looking back down the two elegant exhibition areas to the wide street entrance beyond.

She looked at it again. The tall figure, garbed, it seemed, in light rather than in any material stuff, stood out against a dim woodland scene. It was clever of the artist, thought Lady Arlington, to place his angel in an earthly setting, among flowers and trees, birds and woodland animals – a Garden of Eden – which enhanced the connection with mortal sin and with Creation, all painted with gem-like intensity. The sun broke through the topmost branches, joining with the light that seemed to emanate from the angel's flaming hair. The wings, too, were intensely natural, like those of a bird of prey. But it was the face that haunted one. The pale, delicate skin, the innocent lips and those grey eyes that seemed like pools of holy water. She wondered again who the model had been, if, indeed, this angel was based on any living face.

'Come, my dear, we must give others their turn to see this extraordinary work.' Her husband's words interrupted Lady Arlington's reflections. 'But you'll let me know, won't you, if MacKenzie changes his mind about selling it?' he demanded of Saunders.

Saunders nodded sagely. 'He'll be in later, and I'll tell him of your interest. We have a rather good Millais over here,' he added. 'It would go well with the one you have.' And the manager led his best clients over to a painting that, despite its meticulous brushwork, seemed almost dull and lustreless by comparison with *The Angel*.

Rosa was among the well-dressed crowd who hovered around the painting of her daughter. The exhibition had only opened to the public on Thursday: now it was Tuesday and already the word had been passed around London Society circles that there was the makings of a *cause célèbre* on show at the Maybeck.

Rosa had of course seen the painting before in various stages of completion, slanting precariously forwards on its huge easel in Will's studio, but this was her first sight of it immaculately varnished and framed. Its power was undeniable, and Rosa was forced to admit to an uncomfortable truth that she had been trying for some months now to suppress; that Sylvie was not only a great beauty, but a character of some considerable force. Rosa consoled herself with the knowledge that Sylvie, who had just turned seventeen, had barely begun to recognize the extent of her own potential. She seemed to spend most of her free time either with Will and his friends in Chelsea, or backstage at the theatre, where Ellen Terry had taken her under her wing in the most remarkable way. But, looking at this icon before her, Rosa had now to admit that the interest Will MacKenzie or Miss Terry showed in Sylvie might not be so remarkable: the girl had a haunting power, an influence of which she was quite unconscious. And was it so very surprising, after all? Sylvie was her child! Had she herself not always been able to attract people to her, to charm them and inspire their loyalty?

'Mrs Lapham?' Her reverie was disturbed by Will speaking softly beside her. At once she was also aware of the rustle of interest among the throng surrounding them as people nudged one another and stared at Will.

'I think it's disgraceful!' A man of military bearing in a black morning coat and sharp wing collar stamped his foot and glowered aggressively at Will, who looked back in surprise. A murmur of approbation and dissent arose from the crowd. Aroused by the evident signs of trouble in the gallery, Rosa and Will were swiftly joined by Michael Saunders, who pushed his way expeditiously through the gathering mob.

'Come with me,' he said urgently, and shepherded them towards the wall beside *The Angel*. 'Shame!' hissed a voice in Will's ear as he passed by.

'Can't you see integrity when it stares you in the face, man?' countered another.

Rosa, not understanding where she was being taken, struggled against Saunders's outstretched arm, but then he opened a hidden door cut into the velvet-covered wall and ushered them through into a small, dark room crammed with books, catalogues, card indexes and folio-holders of mounted, unframed water-colours, prints and drawings. He shut the door behind them. This was obviously the inner sanctuary of the gallery. The only light came from a dirty window high up near the ceiling, which presumably looked out onto a back alley. An untidy desk and a well-worn armchair were somehow squeezed into the centre of the high, narrow room, with two rush-seated, ebonized chairs to either side, both piled high with books and papers, which Saunders now shifted to the floor so that Will and Rosa could sit down.

Will was familiar with the room; this was where negotiations took place and where money changed hands between artist and gallery, though not between gallery and customer. Saunders well understood the magic that the private, inner world of the gallery held for outsiders, and only serious collectors were ever granted the imaginary privilege of finding their way into this tiny, well-stocked reference library. Rosa looked about her with contempt. The rug was frayed and dusty and the desk looked shabby. But Will knew that, among the drawings and sketches, there were some real, enduring treasures.

Will introduced Rosa awkwardly: it had been agreed among them that no one outside Will's studio should ever know *The Angel*'s identity. It was Sylvie herself who had first tentatively asked that her contribution to the picture be kept a secret, nervous that Will might take her request as a sign that she did not like the work and did not wish to be associated with it. But such was Will's own passionate obsession about *The Angel* that he intuitively understood that it held deeper, darker feelings that could not yet – and perhaps should never – be explored between them. Will did not know whether the strong currents of emotion that had carried him on through this work were simply those of the true artist, or whether they were more intimately connected with Sylvie herself, but he had never before become so absorbed by a painting: he had dreamt of it at night, its shape and form had imposed itself like a shadow over everything he looked at; the studio seemed eerily bare without it.

Now that the painting hung, varnished and finished, in a gallery, he could see with a little more objectivity that the figure of the angel was precariously imbued with all the passionate ambivalence of his feelings towards art, love, Sylvie – towards his whole life – and he hesitated to unleash such intensity of passion on so young and trusting a girl, only to discover, as he simultaneously both hoped and feared, that his feelings might dissolve with time as the painting came to mean less to him.

So he introduced Rosa now to Saunders without mentioning her connection with the painting. In any case, Saunders quickly excused himself, and went back through the hidden door to quell the growing row outside. For a few moments, Rosa and Will listened silently to the swell of voices, only able to catch the odd accusation or statement of defence. Will smiled wryly at Rosa. 'She's making her mark, isn't she?' he remarked ambiguously of the image he had created.

'I would guess this is just the beginning. I hope you've a hard skin.' She looked at him closely, as if wondering for the first time what kind of mettle he was made of. She wondered briefly if he had made love to Sylvie, but rejected the idea – Sylvie herself was too diffident about such matters. But, had she been in Sylvie's shoes, she would not have let such an opportunity pass her by! He was a handsome young animal, strong and idealistic like Rudi had been when she first met him. However, she recognized that Will did not like her, and that thought made her contemptuous of him.

'Oh, sticks and stones, you know,' he answered her vaguely. 'But I'm glad that you and Sylvie won't be involved if there's a real stink about it.'

'What will Lord Glenmorach say?'

Will laughed. His father was a true aristocratic eccentric. An amateur archaeologist renowned throughout Europe, he spent most of the year in Greece or the Balkan states digging up ancient civilizations. On his infrequent returns to London, he devoted himself to the House of Lords, believing that the time spent indulging his private passion with trowel and sieve had to be paid for by the conscientious exercise of his constitutional duties. 'I hardly think he'll notice,' answered Will fondly. 'He seems to take it entirely for granted that my actions should always surprise him.'

'Will it make money, this picture?' she asked abruptly, settling herself in her chair as if a meeting had been called to order, and spreading the soft cashmere folds of her wine-coloured skirt about her, regardless of the piles of books and papers she disturbed at her feet.

'Yes,' replied Will, surprised by this sudden turn in the conversation. 'A great deal probably, for the outraged critics will only succeed in making it more and more famous.'

'What will you sell it for?'

'Well, I've told the gallery that I don't want to sell it yet. I don't need the money, you know.' He felt exceedingly strange, discussing such matters with this pert, complacent woman with her pampered looks.

'Perhaps not,' she said calmly, looking directly at him. 'But there are Sylvie's interests to consider.'

Will was puzzled. It had not occurred to him that Sylvie should have any financial stake in the fortunes of her likeness. But then, why not? He certainly did not care about the money other than as a sign of the painting's success. He paused, wanting time to consider what was happening here. Was this highway robbery? Rosa was courteous and respectful towards him, with the self-centred indifference that beautiful women often had. It was hard to decide whether or not the demand she seemed to be making was outrageous.

'The Maybeck Gallery has permission to have two or three copies made, which will go on tour,' explained Will, feeling that an honest examination of the facts could help him towards a decision. 'That can make quite a bit of money, for they'll charge the public admission. And either the original or a copy will go to Paris to be engraved – the sale of prints could also be considerable. And nowadays, of course, there are photographic reproductions – the ways in which the public can consume one painting have increased since old Gambart first marketed Frith's *Derby Day*!'

Rosa continued to stare at him. Will almost wanted to laugh, but he also remembered how cowed Sylvie had once seemed when her mother had accompanied her to his studio. Now he began to see the bullying streak in her. Yet, in a perverse way, he still found something to admire in the unabashed way she went for what she wanted.

'And obviously the Gallery will earn something from the commissions I am likely to receive as a result of my . . . my notoriety!' concluded Will, smiling.

But Rosa merely waved her hand. 'That's of no concern to us, naturally,' she said dismissively. 'But Sylvie should receive her due from the exhibition fees and from the prints and photographic reproductions. The original, since you do not seem disposed to sell it anyway, may remain your private concern.'

'Thank you!' Will laughed uncertainly. A deal appeared to have been struck! Here he was already thanking her for her generosity towards him. What cheek!

'What percentage does the Gallery take?' she asked,

taking a small notecase from the little bag that hung from her lace-trimmed wrist. Removing her pale lilac-coloured kid gloves, she extracted a tiny gold pencil. It hovered above the paper in her beautifully manicured fingers. Will watched these proceedings open-mouthed. 'Ten per cent?' she demanded. 'Or more?'

'Ten per cent,' Will found himself agreeing. 'After they've deducted their expenses for framing and so forth.'

'Then Sylvie should have fifteen. What do you think?'

Will had previously remarked on the strange passivity that sometimes fell on Sylvie like a physical malaise, a tropical lassitude, in her mother's company, and had wondered what it was that caused Sylvie to curb her own healthy and ebullient nature. Now he found himself putty in Rosa's hands. Brought up by his indulgent Aunt Laura, he had always learnt to be gentle and courteous with women. Unused to the exercise of female power, he had no weapons to use against such good-natured but implacable force of will. He felt a deep-seated anger at the assumption she made that she could control and order him in this way; a calm fury that, in Will, expressed itself in a rigorous politeness. Nevertheless, he felt no resentment at all at the notion of Sylvie gaining financially from her picture: he realized swiftly now that it *was* her picture, it was his homage to her, that the strivings of love and glory he had tried to put into colour and form were his true feelings for her, the flesh and blood girl, not his carefully constructed image of an angel.

'Make it twenty-five per cent,' he said decisively. 'I'll make arrangements with my banker, Sir Joseph Waldschein, to open an account in her name. The monies can be paid direct by the Gallery without anyone other than Sir Joseph needing to know her identity.' That way, thought Will to himself, bitter in his minor triumph, Rosa could have no direct access to Sylvie's money. For he felt sure that one day Sylvie would have need of some financial independence from this woman.

Sylvie was deeply shamed when she learnt what her mother had done. She was speechless with horror, embarrassment, chagrin, but powerless to lessen the certainty in Rosa's mind that she had brought off a great coup against a man who would otherwise, as she put it, 'have used you for nothing'.

'But I never went there for gain!' wept Sylvie. 'He'll think I . . . Oh, it's the worst thing you've ever done!'

Rosa drew herself up, tight-lipped. 'Nothing a mother does in good faith for the benefit of her child can be wrong.' She dabbed at her eyes with her lace handkerchief. Without recognizing its source, she was enjoying the triumph of her sadistic desire to destroy any pleasure or confidence that Sylvie might have derived from the success of *The Angel*. 'I cannot bear your ingratitude!' she whispered plaintively, and Sylvie, whose fierce protectiveness of her mother masked a far deeper, unacknowledged desire to placate the terrible capabilities for evil in Rosa, came obediently to console her, while her own grief and anger tore at themselves untended in her heart. Her hand opened and closed emptily, missing Rudi's ring, that tangible evidence of love and protection that her father had left for her.

'Besides,' continued Rosa, ruthlessly pressing home her advantage by increasing Sylvie's portion of guilt at her reaction, 'we need the money.'

In London, to Sylvie's surprise, Rosa had continued to spend money just as she had under Rudi and Nye's liberal regimes. An excellent cook had been engaged, together with a new maid; the house was always warm and luxuriously furnished; she pampered her body, lavishing it with expensive creams and perfumes, and the best hairdressers and manicurists she could find; and the tradesmen were never from the door, delivering baskets of hot-house fruits or cases of champagne for the dinners that were now a regular part of Rosa's life.

'You cannot expect Douglas Falkirk to pay your bills as well as mine, and now you are getting older . . . '

But Sylvie interrupted her. 'Lord Falkirk pays our bills?' she exclaimed.

Rosa realized that she had made a tactical error and swiftly retreated. 'He pays the cellarage, you know. It's only right – Lady Falkirk dislikes entertaining, so he makes himself free in our house to invite whom he chooses,' she answered airily, turning away to pat a curl into place before the mirror over the fireplace.

'Why? Why should he make himself free in our house?' Horrified by the advantage she felt her mother had taken of Will, Sylvie suddenly feared that she had taken Lord Falkirk's frequent presence in Kensington too much for granted.

'Would you begrudge me a little company? A little amusement?' Rosa whirled around to face Sylvie. 'How you question me! Oh, but I understand! You seek to judge me, your mother!' Rosa's voice rose in indignation, as she moved in with her familiar power to deny Sylvie's perception and silence her questioning. 'You always were a malicious child, with your melodramas and your truculence. You little angel!' she sneered. 'Stand in judgement on your own mother, then, you little angel!'

Sylvie retreated, vanquished and baffled as so often before. Her only safety lay in silence. She dared not voice her own confusion and suffering, even to herself, for fear of losing Rosa's continuing affection, but the torment of misery she expected to feel never came. Some essence of herself simply left her. She felt herself depart. Ever since the years that had followed Rudi's death, she had unconsciously learnt to empty herself, to deny the frightening contradictions of fact and emotion that Rosa thrust upon her, by side-stepping any recognition of the brutal collision of her senses and feelings. In emptiness lay safety, but she could never know the full price extracted by such a loss of selfhood.

Rosa's unerring instinct for nosing out an advantage, however, proved to be as astute as ever. *The Angel* made a great deal of money for everyone connected with it. The press could not leave it alone, and journalists came from all over Europe to see this icon. It was discussed in the smoking rooms of gentlemen's clubs and over tea in ladies' drawing rooms, and the public flocked to the Maybeck Gallery to see it. Its detractors purchased photographic reproductions to brandish as evidence of MacKenzie's shame, while its admirers paid their deposits for the half-size engravings to hang on their walls.

At the end of April, even though the Maybeck was still crammed to capacity during every hour of opening, the painting was sent to a sister gallery in Manchester to be exhibited, before also visiting Liverpool and going on to Scotland. The issue that the press seized upon, to encapsulate the excitement the painting caused, was whether or not *The Angel* could be real. The small but significant minority who thought the image depraved claimed it could only be a fantasy hatched in the artist's degenerate mind, that it was unthinkable for a woman even to comprehend the thoughts and desires displayed so brazenly on the hussy's face. The growing number who saw Will's portrait of Sylvie as a rallying point for modern ideas about relationships between men and women, as a clarion call to sweep away the hypocrisy and cant of the older reactionary generation, insisted that *The Angel* must be real, and called for her to reveal herself so that she could lead her eager armies into the battle to recapture women's minds and souls from the prisonhouse of the Victorian home. Sylvie was interested by the arguments of the latter camp, but felt frightened and threatened by the denunciation of her as something unclean. In the end, she gave up even looking at the newspapers and magazines.

Sylvie was also so ashamed of the financial deal struck by her mother that it was weeks before she could bear to have any contact with Will, who merely assumed that she was lying low so as not to be recognized. But when they met again, he quickly reassured Sylvie that his opinion of her was not altered in the least by her mother's interference in her affairs. With his usual charitable outlook on life, he had in fact quickly forgotten Rosa's outrageous behaviour and was even mildly grateful to her for a notion of which he wholeheartedly approved – supplying Sylvie with an income to which, he now felt, she was more than entitled and which she richly deserved.

Sylvie had called at Will's studio in answer to a note he had sent her, explaining that he had received word from his banker to say that the 'Angel Account' was growing fast and suggesting that a decision be taken soon as to the management of the funds that were now pouring in from the engraving rights.

'I'll happily take care of the proper investment of the account, if you wish,' he said, assuming automatically that she would accept his offer of help. He was astounded by her reply.

'Thank you, but no,' she said quietly but firmly. 'I would like to manage my own affairs. I don't mean to be ungrateful,' she added hurriedly, when she saw the amazement on his face. 'But . . . well, I have some ideas of my own about what I'd like to do with the money.'

'There's a lot of it,' he warned gently, surmising that she meant to spend an allowance on clothes and so forth.

'Good,' she answered, with a wry smile.

Will struggled with the unusual feeling of having been politely rejected. 'Well, you'll at least allow me to escort you to the bank in Threadneedle Street?' he asked somewhat tersely. 'Perhaps you'll let me know when is convenient, and I'll reply to Sir Joseph's note.'

'Thank you,' was her simple reply.

'Oh, come on,' said Will, unwilling to let this jarring note continue between them. 'Let's go into the garden; I'll call for some lemonade.'

Sylvie stood a moment at the garden door enjoying the fresh spring air after the familiar smell of turps and linseed oil. A parlourmaid appeared at the studio door in answer to her master's ring.

'Some of Mrs Brierley's best lemonade, please, Susan.' Will took Sylvie's arm and led her across the grass to an old bench in the shade of the mulberry tree.

'So what's it like to be such a mystery?' he asked jovially. 'A living, breathing enigma?'

'Thank God no one knows it's me! I couldn't have borne it.' The sincerity in her voice piqued him somewhat. Did she take no pride in his painting of her? He could not believe that she wasn't at least a little flattered by the legend of her that was growing up around the painting's fame.

'Don't you like to see yourself everywhere? Photographs of you are in every shop window in Regent Street!' he cajoled her, smiling.

But Sylvie shook her head firmly. 'They're not of me, they're of your painting!' she rebuked him sharply, then, as if thinking better of her tone, went on in a gentler manner. 'It's like there's a part of me that's become public property,' she explained. 'I feel as if I've lost some superficial delicacy that comes with privacy that I didn't realize I had until I'd lost it. I know it's not me they're all arguing about, only some creature of their own imaginations, but I feel sometimes as though I no longer belong entirely to myself. I don't know whether I am – or even should be – the Angel or not. You've made me lose sight of myself.'

'Do you mind it all so very much?'

'Yes. Yes, I do.' They sat together for a moment in silence, and the chimera of *The Angel* lay between them like a knife. She knew that Will's friendship remained sincere, but she felt she had only half understood Will's emotional confusion over the picture. There had been a point at which she thought he was in love with her, and she had waited, curious as to what her own reaction would be, for him to speak. But when *The Angel* had gone off to the framers, she had seen how drained he was by the emotional effort he had put into it. Then, although he still seemed to want to cling onto her familiar presence in the studio, she knew that he no longer wanted to draw her, he was not yet ready to invent another interpretation of her. She could not help feeling somehow used and finished with, bundled up like the canvas itself in old paint-smeared wraps and carried off into the Maybeck Gallery's horse-drawn van waiting outside on the roadway beside the river. It had been the painting, not her, that had temporarily beguiled him, and she resented her own image.

Suddenly she turned to him. 'Am I like that?' she demanded.

He was confused. 'Like what?'

'The Angel.'

Will could not answer her directly. It was the question that he had sought to answer in the painting itself. Almost unthinkingly, by way of reply, he leant forward and kissed her softly on the lips. At once, she leapt up, pushing away invisible demons with her fists and beginning to cry bitterly. She ended standing in a huddle before the trunk of the tree, her forehead resting against the old grey bark and her knuckles pressed into her cheeks while the tears poured over her hands. As

Will approached her softly, he caught snatches of speech between the sobs.

'It must be true. Mamma said it was so. You think so, too. Oh, how could you?'

'What has your mother said?' demanded Will. Surprise at Sylvie's sudden, unusual burst of emotion coupled with anger that Rosa could interfere from a distance with the expression of his feelings for Sylvie made him rough. It was as if it was only now that he recognized how strongly he felt for her. He pulled her round and hugged her to him, but she pushed him away.

'No, no,' she cried breathlessly. 'I didn't . . . Oh, it can't be true, what she said!' There was the slightest edge of hysteria in her voice. 'Why did you have to paint me like that! You just want me to be like the Angel, to fit into your canvas. Well, I'm not like that.'

Will stood there helplessly. 'What has your mother been saying to you?' he asked in as firm a voice as he could muster, hoping by some authority of tone to pull her together. He wondered if he should fetch Mrs Brierley, his housekeeper.

'Mamma said,' she began, taking gulps of breath, 'she said it was my fault. That he wouldn't have done it if I hadn't looked at him as if . . . as if . . . like the Angel looks!' she finished in a rush, looking at him challengingly. 'But you made the Angel – she's not me!'

'What did she mean?' probed Will, wondering what could lie behind this outburst, and already suspecting some vile jealousy of Rosa's at work. 'Something's happened. Tell me what it is,' he pleaded. 'What has your mother done to you?'

'Nothing. Mamma would never . . . '

'What did she say was your fault?'

Sylvie wandered a little vaguely about the lawn. She stopped before a small bed of ebullient yellow flag irises and stood, fingering one of the blooms. 'It was Lord Falkirk,' she began at last. 'He tried to . . . he tried to touch me, and Mamma says it was all my fault. She said he wouldn't have done it if I hadn't looked at him. She said I . . . enticed him.'

'My God, I'd like to put a stop to that man!' cried Will to himself through clenched teeth. 'But what did she mean, that you looked at him?' he asked gently. 'Here, take my handkerchief.'

Sylvie blew her nose gratefully and let out a deep shuddering breath. 'I didn't know what she meant. She just said I looked like the Angel . . . that the Angel looks as though . . . '

'As though she might want a man to touch her?' finished Will quietly. Sylvie nodded, not daring to look at him, her long fingers pulling at the damp fabric of the handkerchief.

'There's nothing wrong with wanting a man to touch you,' he began, but she started to cry once more.

'But I never looked at Lord Falkirk like that!' she pleaded. 'I didn't!'

'Of course you didn't. Your mother's talking nonsense. I know what Lord Falkirk is. He can't even hold a flower in his hand without crushing it. You're not to judge yourself for any outrage he commits. And you're to tell me if he ever lays a finger on you again, or insults you in any way. Promise me? I'd kill him!'

Sylvie nodded, and Will's contemptuous anger against his uncle died away for the present moment as he looked at Sylvie and tried to think what to do for the best.

'But why did you . . . ?' Sylvie's voice was a whisper and he had to step closer to hear her.

'Why did I kiss you just now?'

She nodded.

'Because you're lovely,' he said simply, taking hold of her hand and stroking her fingers gently. 'And the

Angel is beautiful, too. There's nothing wrong with either you or the painting. Believe me.'

She looked up at him; her eyes, still wet with tears, were like glittering mirrors. She pressed his hand and smiled a little. Then she whispered fiercely: 'I'm sorry, Will, but you should never have painted me like that. I hate the Angel! She's not me! She frightens me!'

Sylvie went alone to visit Sir Joseph Waldschein in Threadneedle Street. He was expecting Sir William MacKenzie, one of his wealthier clients and heir to several imposing titles, and was therefore astonished when, at three o'clock sharp, the door to his panelled office opened and a young lady, hardly out of the nursery, was shown in. In the dim light of the old City office, Sylvie's hair framed her delicate face like a halo, and her large grey eyes, though shy, met his with utter composure. She was very pale, but her face had a determined set to it.

'Thank you for seeing me, Sir Joseph. I know that you are doing so at Sir William's request, and I am grateful. I won't take up too much of your time.' And she seated herself on the edge of the chair, gracefully sweeping her skirts to one side, her back straight. She felt instinctively that she could trust this elderly man, small and rather ugly though he was, with bushy grey hair and craggy eyebrows.

'Please,' said Sir Joseph, gesturing for her to do what she had just accomplished. He actually rubbed his eyes as if he were dreaming, before composing himself and taking his seat behind the wide mahogany desk. 'How can I help you? It's not often we have the pleasure of serving an angel!' he added gallantly, but the young lady barely smiled.

'When my mother, Mrs Rosa Lapham, came to this city nearly two years ago, she was able to realize a large amount of capital – exactly how much, I don't know. My mother has always lived by her wits and has made no investment or provision for the future. But I must presume that, once her money is spent, we shall be destitute. However, as you know, my mother has arranged with Sir William for me to receive twenty-five per cent of the royalties accruing from the portrait of *The Angel*. If this money is to provide our sole means of support, I want to keep control of it in my own hands. And I want to invest my capital in a way that will quickly increase its value.'

Sir Joseph was inclined to laugh. But, at heart, he was too shocked. He remained silent for some moments, thinking. Sylvie sat as still as she could, her heart beating. She wanted to run, out of this imposing office, out into the street and away from Sir Joseph's stern face. What held her fast was, in her mind's eye, her own reflection in an imaginary tall, gilt mirror. She was acting, and she knew that her performance was flawless.

At last Sir Joseph, as if calmed by her iron control, spoke. 'To accumulate, one must speculate. There are no safe ways in which significantly to increase capital. In any case, I should consider it most improper – if not positively indecent – to advise one so young and innocent as you to engage in speculative financial affairs. I will happily advise you on a safe and steady placement for your funds, but for a young girl, for one so pure . . . I should be accused of corruption if I were to take any other course.'

'And what shall I be driven to if my mother ruins us?'

Sir Joseph's jaw dropped. He was appalled.

'I am sorry to speak so bluntly, Sir Joseph. I realize that it ill becomes my sex and years. But if I were a boy, would you not then praise my attempt to save my mother and myself?'

With the events of the past few months, which had

taught Sylvie the power that external events beyond one's own control could wield, she had felt the stirring of an instinctive sympathy for Rosa's predicament. She saw her mother unconsciously thrashing about in the web she had spun by her own illusions and vanities. She sensed the animal terror of the doomed creature, caught hopelessly in its own trails, and even pitied the woman for the iron clasps which bound her inexorably to the consequences of her own actions. Rosa spent money with a kind of desperation; the slightest setback or irritation was sufficient justification for a new purchase for herself, and the house was kept up to a standard, Sylvie knew, well beyond their means. Sometimes she suspected that Lord Falkirk picked up most of Rosa's bills, and it was precisely to deny him this power that Sylvie now clutched so desperately at this chance of financial independence.

'Have you no guardian?' pleaded Sir Joseph. 'No uncle or male friend? What about Sir William himself . . . ' But, instantly recalling both Sir William's youth and the present outcry over his latest painting, he saw the error of his own thoughts.

'Precisely!' said Sylvie drily. She rose to her feet. 'Please help me, Sir Joseph. You do see my dilemma. I can promise that I shall never blame you for any misfortune, and that I shall take full responsibility for any decisions on which you may advise me.'

Sir Joseph looked at her slim figure standing beside his desk. He thought of his own daughters at that age, and how he should have felt if they had been forced into such a situation.

'Please sit down, Miss Lapham. I will help you as you ask. But,' he held up his hand to prevent her thanks, 'I demand that one condition be strictly met. No one must ever know that I advise you. I shall place your portfolio under another name and will deal with all your affairs personally. I am making a very unwise decision. Should your investments fail, I shall be accused of leading you recklessly into the paths of ruination. I do not wish to be so accused. Do you understand?'

'Perfectly. I promise that no blame shall ever attach to you. Nor credit either, if you advise me well! In any case, I should have demanded the same condition from you. No one must ever learn from you that I am the subject of Sir William's painting. And you must promise never to discuss my affairs with anyone, not even my mother.' Sylvie held her breath, expecting him to remonstrate with this last request, but he nodded his head in agreement.

She rose once more from her seat, and held out her hand. He took it and held it limply, once more shocked, and shaken by his own decision.

'I will write to you tomorrow with some ideas I have about buying shares. Goodbye.'

'Goodbye, Miss Lapham.' As the door closed behind her, he sank into his chair, mopping the sweat from his brow. He hoped that, when tomorrow came, this interview would prove to have been a hideous dream.

Sylvie found her refuge in the theatre, glad to escape to the dim, high backstage wilderness where she felt so indescribably at peace. From her first afternoon with Ellen Terry, behind the scenes where the magic of the performance turned to the dross of flats and props baskets and even the odd forgotten sandwich, she had felt a calm descend on her, as if some ancient struggle that went on within her ceased as she breathed the cold, heavy air of the place. Sylvie valued her anonymity there: she was just Ellen Terry's girl. Ellen, who had seen Will's early sketches of Sylvie, had promised never to reveal her identity as *The Angel*. With her quiet ways and quick smiles, and her hair smoothed and coiled in thick braids unfashionably low on the nape of her neck, no one thought to connect Sylvie with the furore about the painting.

Sylvie had attended rehearsals, or waited in the wings during performances, holding Nell's kimono ready for when she came off stage. She had soon learned all Nell's roles by heart and begged to be allowed on stage. When Nell had joined Henry Irving's new company at the Lyceum Theatre, she promised to have a word with the actor-manager, and, soon afterwards Sylvie was employed as a member of the company at six pounds a week. At Nell's suggestion, she adopted a stage name, calling herself by her father's name, Sylvie Lazar. Rosa had at first been outraged and threatened to call on Miss Terry and accuse her of . . . But she did not know quite what social sin Nell had committed, and Sylvie was able to persuade her mother that a few months of hard work playing walk-on roles might be the best thing to bring her home to the leisure of the drawing room. Besides, on this one subject, Rosa sensed a stubbornness in Sylvie which recalled unpleasant memories of Rudi in his cups and made her loath to conjure up the ghost of Sylvie's father unnecessarily.

Sylvie had first gone on stage as a second gentlewoman in attendance on Nell. She was so flattered to be granted this honour, and so rapt at being able to observe her heroine at work at such close quarters, that she forgot all about her fear of stage fright as, straight and slender in a rather dusty old gown, she walked behind Nell out onto the centre of the stage. Then she had been too fascinated by the view out over the gaslights to the packed house, drinking in the sight of the absorbed, up-turned faces and studying their expressions and reactions, to remember to be nervous. She had soon risen to playing 'dumb' parts, and, quickly reassured by the genuineness of Nell's praise, was too busy ever to cultivate anything other than a professional confidence in her work.

The truth was that Sylvie was a natural actress, and she had had the good fortune to join the best English company of her day. The Lyceum provided not only a long and invaluable apprenticeship, but also Sylvie's first real taste of home. She was instantly taken to the bosom of the company, most of whom were of the old school, like Ellen Terry herself, from families who had been in the theatre for generations. They saw that Sylvie was far from stage-struck; she was merely a fish in water, in her natural element at last. There was no affectation among the cast, just an unquenchable love of method and technique. Sylvie loved to hear the tales the older actors told of the theatre of twenty or thirty years ago, or to listen to the stories they had heard in their youth of the great days of Astley's Amphitheatre and the swashbuckling melodramas enacted there amid the pervasive smell of horses.

As Christmas approached, Irving gave Sylvie her first speaking part in *The Bells*. She carried herself well, speaking her four lines in a cool, melodious voice that seemed to carry effortlessly to the top balconies of the theatre, her slim figure taut and confident. Will, who was in the audience, witnessing her slight but undeniable presence on stage, relaxed and wished her well.

Soon Sylvie was regularly given minor speaking parts in the Lyceum's different productions, and her life was gratefully submerged into the theatre. She remembered what old Kati had once told her – she was different: she was not to have a life like other women, and she didn't care. All she wanted was the exhilaration of acting. She played several different small parts each week – occasionally going on two or three times in one evening when Irving had his heart set on a series of spectacular crowd scenes – and, the following summer, from the windows of a second-class railway carriage, she saw the bread-and-butter side of the profession during their exhausting annual provincial tour. Once a new play flopped, and the entire company had to learn and rehearse a new crowd-puller overnight. But Sylvie thrived, and began to regain some of the animal confidence that had been dispersed when Rudi died. At first, she had been terrified that she would be recognized as the Angel, but when her worst fears went unrealized, and she completed her small parts on stage without exciting any undue attention, she relaxed and put it out of her mind. Although she still could not help noticing the endless reproductions of the painting in shop windows and magazines, she taught herself to disassociate herself from it completely.

Sylvie still went to some of Will's Sunday afternoon parties, and he occasionally joined one of the late suppers beloved by the Lyceum actors, but they were seldom alone together. Occasionally Will would send flowers and his card round to the stage door, always with a complimentary message written on the back. Indeed, he was sometimes lost in admiration of her brief performances and began to realize that she might become not just a professional actress but a great artist.

Off stage, he watched her growing confidence with pride, noting with satisfaction how happy she seemed. There was still the reserve, the sometimes urgent desire to avoid conflict of any personal kind, but, as a professional actress, even off the stage, she acquired a wit and buoyancy that, while it was a performance, also revealed something of the true depths of Sylvie's spirit.

He longed to paint her again, to have her near him with the familiar ease with which he had watched her and studied her movements and gestures, but he dared not ask her. He was aware, without being able to explain it, that his portrait of her had added greatly to her sense of vulnerability. Sometimes the tenuous fragility of her confidence was painfully obvious to him, and he was determined to protect her delicate and precarious sense of self from further shock. He longed to understand what made her so vulnerable – it could not just be Rosa's bullying insensitivity – but he was at a loss to speculate further.

Nell, too, kept a watchful eye on Sylvie, and Irving, knowing of his leading lady's interest in the young hopeful, made a point of giving her the choicest of the minor parts. As she waited in the wings, Sylvie listened carefully to the whispered comments of the other actors and actresses.

'Henry's good tonight, Bill.'

'Yes, he remembered to turn his head enough to catch the lights as he made the vengeance speech: saves no end of eye-rolling, that, and leaves him free to concentrate on the words.'

'I do love it when the audience is all worked up waiting for Nell's scream, and all she does is gently speak the words as though ordering more hot muffins.'

'Yes, it's a bit different from Mrs Winstead: she's so damned dramatic she could act the food right off your plate.'

Finding Sylvie so eagerly receptive, they watched her own small performances with care, advised her on her mistakes and suggested new ways of interpreting her roles.

Finally, the dream of every young actress came true. Arthur Hartwell, Irving's understudy who also played the younger romantic parts that Irving declined, was to play Hamlet for his benefit night, before leaving to join the Bancrofts at the Prince of Wales. Nell had happily agreed to be his Ophelia, but, on the day, sent word that she was unwell. Irving summoned Sylvie to the comfortable dressing room that also served as his office. His long thin face looked almost comically serious in this domestic setting.

'I take it you know the part?' he asked, handing her

Ellen's stage copy of the play, so that she could read the notes that the actress had made in the margins in her large pencil scrawl.

'Oh, yes, but . . . '

'But me no buts!' he commanded, looking down the length of his haughty nose at her. 'This is young Hartwell's benefit. You cannot let him down.'

Sylvie rushed, petrified and delighted, to find Arthur, who surprised her by showing almost no disappointment that he would be appearing opposite a young unknown instead of Ellen Terry.

'I wish you'd come to the Prince of Wales with me, too,' he said. 'You and I could challenge Squire and Mrs Bancroft themselves when it comes to all this modern drama! You know, I've always admired you, and you've outgrown the Lyceum and Henry's old-fangled ways as much as I have. You should be playing these new drawing room parts, don't you see? Miss Terry and Mr Irving are wonderful, of course, but they're too set in their ways. We're young, we understand these modern emotions and how to act 'em. If only you'd listen to me, you'd be such a success!'

Sylvie was surprised by Arthur's vehemence. She had known for a while that he always singled her out for a word of praise in the green room, or managed to sit next to her at supper, but this was no flirtation! Nevertheless, delighted as she was by his homage to her skills as an actress, she shook her head, laughing. 'Oh, I'm not ambitious like you. And you're older. I'm quite content to stay here, among friends. I'm learning all the time.' She shrugged, unable to explain that the Lyceum was her home, that she had no desire to venture out into a wider world that might engulf her.

'But you'd be perfect in these modern pieces,' he pleaded. 'And you wait, there'll be new dramatists writing for actors like us who can act naturally and move audiences to tears without all the melodrama that Irving loves so much!'

'I know you're right. Harry Lewis . . . ' she acknowledged her friendship with the critic shyly, ' . . . Harry Lewis says the same, about the way things are moving in the theatre nowadays. I know Henry's old-fashioned, but I like it here.' Sylvie felt a sadness swell briefly within her that she had to practise such caution, but she knew that she was not yet ready to give up the security she had been so lucky to find at the Lyceum.

'Things are changing,' he warned. 'Don't be left behind!'

'Small chance of that,' she laughed. 'I'm only eighteen! Besides, the Bancrofts haven't asked me to come to the Prince of Wales!' she added brightly. 'And I can see no reason why they should, either!'

'They might after tonight,' Arthur told her seriously.

They spent the rest of the afternoon rehearsing their scenes and working out her stage directions. The time seemed to alternately drag and rush by, until Sylvie found herself waiting in the wings, ready to go on. Her hands were frozen, but, as she stood watching the familiar early scenes of the play, she regained the calm that had always come to her in the theatre. She found that she was no more nervous than she ever was in her smaller parts.

Sometimes, on stage, she had found that she could call upon a reservoir of emotional experiences, as if she were reliving the most harrowing episodes of her life in clear detail, and she would use those remembered feelings to fire her performance. As soon as she left the stage, her mind clouded over again, pushing everything safely out of focus once more. All she felt after her performances was that she was strangely fatigued, as people feel after they have been crying for some time, and a greater vagueness than usual enveloped her. But she supposed that this was what all actors felt, and never questioned the leaden feeling that sometimes stayed with her for hours even after quite undemanding performances.

Now, during Ophelia's mad scene, Sylvie recalled, uninvited and unconsciously, the emotions – though not the circumstances – that had accompanied her lonely climb up the dim stairwell of Sari Fodor's house five years before. The truthfulness of the feelings that possessed her, as if from nowhere, gave her performance an authority and directness that was compelling. Arthur, responding to the purity of her acting, was equally fired to give the best performance he had ever given.

The calm misery of Sylvie's attitude and the haunted look upon her beautiful face held the audience spellbound and, when she took her curtsey at the end, the applause from the high, curving rows of balconies washed over her like a cool shower, refreshing and invigorating her. As she looked out into the blackness beyond the footlights, she could just make out the fleeting impressions of rows of smiling faces as she heard the applause feed upon itself.

Arthur, recognizing that the acclaim was not for him, handed Sylvie forwards, giving the audience what it wanted. She was amazed at the intensity of the audience's reaction and felt calmed and held by their admiration, for it was not just flattery for her technique, but an avowal, a ratification of her experience on stage. Not only could she voice her own emotions, but, far from being punished, she was extravagantly praised for her sincerity and depth of feeling! She thrived on the applause, that affirmation of her true self that satisfied her need for love and approval.

Someone was shouting out above the din of clapping, and Sylvie turned instinctively to smile and bow towards the voice. It shouted again and again, until the rhythm of the applause broke and created a pause for it to be heard.

'She's the Angel! She's the Angel!'

Sylvie's heart froze. The clapping stopped. For a nightmarish moment there was silence. Sylvie turned to Arthur, only to find that he and the rest of the cast were staring at her with open-mouthed curiosity.

'Bravo!'

Suddenly the shouting started again, different voices now joining the clamour. 'She is the Angel! Bravo! The beautiful Angel!' The audience were on their feet, clapping and shouting. At the front, a party of young men drummed their stamping feet on the floor. Sylvie stood, completely lost and bewildered, at the centre of the stage, desperately afraid of the noise. She felt naked, exposed, robbed of her own voice, her own insistence on who and what she was.

She had, almost unconsciously, come to see *The Angel* as a composite of all that was fearful and loathesome in herself, for all the parts of her damaged mind that Rosa had crushed and twisted and that she had denied and forgotten. She could not believe that this audience did not hate her.

Then Henry Irving was at her side, presenting her with a flourish to the audience while hissing in her ear to acknowledge the riotous applause. His overt theatricality brought her back to her familiar surroundings. Almost woodenly, she smiled and bowed her head, hanging on tight to Irving's bony hand. Her gesture brought another roar from the auditorium and a chant of 'The Angel! The Angel!' began.

After minutes that seemed to Sylvie like hours, Irving signalled to the stage hands waiting in the wings to raise the house lights. As the gas hissed in the glass shades and the audience were illuminated, Sylvie felt ready to flinch, expecting to see expressions of distaste and horror. Instead, she looked in amazement at row upon row of smiling, delighted faces, all focused on her, all encouraging her to accept their homage and pleasure.

'The Angel! The Angel!' The chant was softer now. Tears poured down her cheeks while Henry Irving stood back to leave her alone in the spotlight.

PART TWO

CHAPTER ELEVEN

As Sylvie entered the familiar panelled room in Threadneedle Street one hot afternoon in the summer of 1887, Sir Joseph Waldschein sensed an unusual excitement about her. He had watched her grow, over these past eight years, from that extraordinary young creature who had dared him to question her audacious claim to authority over her affairs, into this confident, pliant, intelligent young lady. She wore a slim, elegant afternoon dress of dark red material that fitted smoothly to her figure. The tiny waist was accentuated by the bustle that fell to a small pleated train at the back of the skirt. The high tailored collar, and neat cuffs just below her elbows, were embroidered with white and yellow daisies. She looked every inch the rational young woman. And there was no denying how much he looked forward to her visits.

'Come in, my dear,' he said, rising stiffly with his usual courtesy from his chair. 'You won't have heard the news already, surely?' As always, the two of them got straight down to business, a business they enjoyed and that placed them, the elderly man and the beautiful young woman, on an equal footing.

'What news?' Sylvie's eyes immediately shone with excitement, an excitement that she always made him share – he, a financier now for fifty years. Why, he shared a jubilee with the Queen herself!

'De Beers are buying again, just as you predicted!' answered Sir Joseph with satisfaction. 'Your Kimberley shares are rising even as we speak! Do you want to sell, or hold on a little longer?'

As soon as she had felt that she had gained Sir

Joseph's confidence, Sylvie had shyly explained her knowledge of the diamond fields, and had begged him to allow her to try some investments. Gradually, he had seen that she had a feel for finance, and, as she won his support and even respect for her dealings, she had begun to back her own hunches in the market.

Six years before, several of the new mining companies at Kimberley had failed and the banks had refused credit because the vast workings were threatening to collapse. Just as Nye had always predicted, the bottom of the vast hole had filled with water and the sides had constantly given way and slipped down into the workings below. To Sir Joseph's horror, as the depression bottomed out, the twenty-year-old Sylvie had insisted on buying a modest stake in one of the bigger conglomerates, but now, six years later, after a railway link had been completed, drastically reducing the price of raw materials and supplies, and as Cecil Rhodes began to mop up the smaller companies in his move towards Consolidated Mines' complete monopoly, share prices were beginning to rocket upwards again. The considerable earnings Sylvie had invested from the financial success of *The Angel* had multiplied several times.

'I want to buy some more!'

'Compete with Consolidated Mines! Why?'

'Because in the end De Beers will have to buy me out. The longer I wait, the more it will cost them.'

Sir Joseph shook his head admiringly. No longer did he toss and turn at night, anxiously wondering why he had ever agreed to allow a mere child to operate under his aegis on the Stock Exchange. For some time, he had been considering retirement, and now he felt reassured that, even without his advice, Sylvie's portfolio was in the very best of hands – her own.

'You'll have to realize some other assets, then. There's no floating capital in your account just now.'

He began to flick through the pages of the accounts book in which the details of her portfolio were recorded, a book that he personally locked away each night in his private safe. She interrupted him in his search for some stocks that could be sold to advantage.

'There's no need!' announced Sylvie proudly, and she held out to him what was obviously a legal document.

'What is this?' he asked, puzzled.

'Only the contract for my first American tour!' she laughed delightedly. She had looked forward to this moment, and felt that she was now, like a child, handing him her achievement. She had come to feel a great deal of affection for the old man over the years; he had always treated her with honesty and courtesy, taking the place of her grandfather she had never known. She waited for him to congratulate her.

The contract, from the great American impresario, Henry Abbey, stated that she was to play ten cities, from Boston to St Louis, Washington to Chicago, opening and closing in New York, and that she would receive $500 for each performance. Henry Abbey would pay all travelling expenses (so long, he had added, as Sylvie didn't insist, as Lillie Langtry had, on coupling her own kitchen and chef onto the end of the train) and – a gesture towards European customs – he would select the cast, call the rehearsals and arrange the lighting and scenery for her. It would be an exhausting itinerary, with little break between towns, but, wrote Abbey in his accompanying letter, Americans were always impressed by anyone who did things at breakneck speed. She was to receive an advance of $15,000 on signature of the contract. The tour, if successful, should make her at least $50,000, and Abbey had said that she could virtually double that if she wanted to, giving endorsements to manufacturers of beauty products and so forth.

But Sir Joseph said nothing. He sat quietly engrossed in the document, reading the minutiae of each clause with his customary thoroughness. They had seldom discussed her life beyond her financial affairs. In the early days at the Lyceum, she had sent him theatre tickets; he had politely acknowledged them, but never came to a single performance. She assumed that this was merely because of their mutual promise of absolute secrecy. Now, as he read through the contract, she suddenly saw, by the way he shifted himself in his chair, that he was far from happy with what he read.

She could bear the silence no longer. 'What's the matter? Is there something I've missed?'

'No, my dear. This is a perfectly fair and reasonable contract.' He paused, unable to meet her imploring eyes. He rose from his desk and walked stiffly to the window, looking down into the busy street below. He felt tired. Tired and old. Was this his doing? Was it because he had encouraged her in her legitimate desire to help her mother and herself that she now insisted on this unnatural course of action? Yes, he must take his share of the blame. How old was Sylvie now? Twenty-six? She should be married with her children about her knee, not proposing to go off alone in some rackety train across an alien continent in pursuit of what? Money! Something that no right-feeling woman should care about, beyond her immediate needs! It was intolerable, and it was his fault! He turned to face her, sighing. She sat, ashen-faced, scared.

'Tell me what you're thinking, Sir Joseph,' she asked gently.

He spread his hands, his bushy eyebrows raised in that timeless gesture of his race. 'Why?' was all he said.

Sylvie would have expected such a question from a stranger, but not from those very few people who were her friends. 'Don't you know?' she asked humbly.

'No!' he exploded. 'I don't know. You have money

enough for your means. You and your mother are perfectly secure, even if you placed all your capital into widow's bonds. You have no business to be competing with men! Go home!'

She rose, as if he had meant to dismiss her. But, as always when moved by her grace and apparent fragility, all his anger at her melted like mist. He went to her, putting his arm around her shoulder, pushing her back into her chair. He pulled up another chair beside her and sat, holding her cold hands in his.

'I don't understand you at all, Sylvie. I suppose I never have. But I know that, no matter how much I ought to disapprove of what you do, I don't, because if you choose to do it, then I know that it's right. There is not a vulgar, unfeminine bone in your body. But I wish you'd find the right man and marry him. I did think at one time that Sir William . . . but . . . '

Sylvie squeezed his hand, releasing hers to find a handkerchief to wipe away her tears but laughing somewhat now.

'Acting is me, Sir Joseph. It's not something I choose to do, it's something that I am, an actress. I love it. I should be a shell without it. And I love what we do here together, too. I like to be a part of the wider world, to understand some of what shapes our destinies. I can't explain myself any better than that, I'm afraid.'

'And you shouldn't have to, my dear. I'm a silly, foolish old man. You go to America. Take them by storm! I believe that's the expression, isn't it?'

Sylvie nodded and kissed him impetuously on the cheek.

He rose, delighted, and sat again behind his wide mahogany desk.

'So you've $15,000 to play with?'

'Yes!'

'I hope you're not still interested in this foolish gold-mining business?'

'Yes, I am.'

'Sylvie, I saw too many people get their fingers burnt when the De Kaap and Barberton share bubble burst last year,' he warned.

'I'm quite prepared to run the risk of this being another nine-day wonder, but my guess is that this Witwatersrand gold reef in the Transvaal is for real.'

'You know, these opportunities are often made to sound extraordinarily alluring. But always from a distance: it's the siren cry calling the unwary investor onto the rocks.'

'Yes, but on the other hand, there are so many strikes in South Africa that sooner or later one has to be the big one. It was the same with diamonds. And when it is, I want to be in on the ground floor.'

'So what have you been able to find out?' Sir Joseph sat back, resting his elbows on the arms of his chair, lightly holding the tips of his long, thin fingers together. His knuckles were red and gnarled with arthritis and, nowadays, it was an effort of sheer will to hold this habitual position. He looked as though he were composing himself for sleep, but Sylvie recognized this stance and smiled to herself. When he sat as he was sitting now, his astute mind was most active and most receptive. She knew that once he had been persuaded to listen seriously to her proposals, she had only to win the argument.

'Johannesburg, from all accounts,' she began, 'is still a collection of tents and corrugated-iron shacks, and the diggers are mainly accustomed to panning for alluvial gold, which this isn't. They're using kaffirs, native labour, to dig trenches to get at the outcrop reef – which seems to run quite deeply underground, though I haven't been able to get any more information on that aspect yet – and primitive engines to crush the rock. You see, there's no railway, so everything has to be hauled by ox-cart from the coast, which takes weeks and is very expensive, especially for heavy machinery. So they're desperate for capital.'

'And who is investing in this godforsaken place?' Sir Joseph spoke without opening his eyes.

'Well, that's what really caught my attention. All the big guns from the diamond fields were the first on the scene. Now that they've all become such gentlemen, they want to make their profits out of share dealing, not prospecting, but nevertheless, they're still close enough to the ground to get first-hand reports on what's happening at Johannesburg. If it's good enough for them . . . '

'And what assets can these mining companies boast?'

'The important thing is water. And grazing land for the mules and horses for the tramway system they've set up.' Sylvie was now leaning forward eagerly. One of the things she loved about her sessions with Sir Joseph was the chance their financial dealings gave her to use the experience she had gained with Nye and to discover more about the world of trade and commerce, a world generally closed to women.

Sir Joseph opened his eyes and sat up in his chair, clearing his throat as though awaking from a cat-nap. 'I'd give anything to know how you come by your information!' he snorted. 'I've not heard anything as thorough as that from our analysts.'

Sylvie laughed, pleased at the compliment. 'Men love to tell women things. All I have to do is express total ignorance and devoted curiosity and I can discover just what I need to know. Men are never guarded with me, because they don't think I'm capable of understanding, let alone remembering, a word they say.'

'Take a pair of sparkling eyes, eh?'

'Something like that,' she agreed, laughing.

'Very well.' Sir Joseph got to his feet with difficulty, wincing at the pain from his arthritis. 'I can see that you've set your heart on this, but I advise caution. Many of these companies are formed with the sole purpose of relieving the optimistic investor of his cash before the bubble bursts, as it inevitably does. So don't risk too much in any one company. Go for one that might be making a loss but is actually producing gold at the end of the day. In the early days of these strikes, you often find that the companies paying the dividends are the ones that don't even have a pick and shovel to their name, they're just fronts to collect the money and run. A company can't hope to pay a dividend if it's actually investing in plant and machinery.'

Sylvie nodded at the wisdom of his words; she recognized the voice of experience and always considered Sir Joseph's opinions seriously. Soon they were deep in an examination of the various companies quoted on the new Johannesburg Stock Exchange, comparing the advantages of water rights over the possession of working stamp engines and weighing up the relative experience of the mine managers and joint stock company directors for the task in hand. Their earlier quarrel was soon forgotten.

If Sylvie noticed Nye's name among the major stockholders of the Simmer & Jack Mine, she kept the information to herself.

Two months later, she stood once more in Will's studio, posing for her portrait. This was the first painting he had done of her since *The Angel*.

Despite its enormous public success, Will's painting had remained like a gulf between them. Sylvie would not talk of it, except to mock her own success as an actress, which she insisted was due to the curiosity value that being recognized as the Angel had lent her, but Will sensed that there was more to it than that. Any publicity given to the work always included a summary of the accusations that the figure was immoral, enticing, decadent. If such comments were made in Sylvie's presence, even if only in refutation, Will saw her shrink with what almost amounted to fear. Once or twice more, after she had told him of Lord Falkirk's drunken attempt to assault her, he had tried to talk to her, to explain his feelings for her, but each time she had managed to glide over his words as though some fellow actor had merely come in on the wrong cue. But neither had he been able to discover that she favoured any particular one among the throng of admirers who waited with flowers at the stage door, took her riding in the Park or for after-theatre suppers.

On stage, she was magnificent; as womanly, as passionate and as full of longing as those who did not know her believed her naturally to be. But privately, she retained such an almost child-like unconsciousness of her own sexuality that Will feared for the moment when she did discover it. Despite her thrilling self-confidence, she was ravishingly innocent, and he himself would do nothing to challenge that state of affairs, for he sensed how necessary it was to her emotional survival.

Seeing how the painting upset her, Will had sold *The Angel*, to a new collector and for a fabulous sum, but he often saw reproductions of it. He still believed it to be his greatest work, and a true homage to Sylvie's elusive power, but he felt guilty that the image he had created seemed to haunt her so unpleasantly. He remained convinced that it was Rosa's jealousy of her daughter's beauty and acclaim that had whispered the malicious innuendoes that Sylvie was so afraid were true. And, if the rumours he had heard over the past couple of years about Rosa's parties with his uncle's 'friends' were accurate, they perhaps went some way towards explaining Sylvie's own deliberate maintenance of her innocence.

Now, however, Will had used the news that Sylvie

was to tour America as an excuse to ask her to pose for him again. He had asked once or twice before, but had been pleasantly rebuffed with excuses of having no time and being too tired. He had been delighted when, this time, she had readily agreed. It was sheer pleasure to have her there, alone in his studio where he could look at her to his heart's content, and the sittings were progressing well.

'Come along, back into place,' he said to her, taking her by the arm to position her once more beside the delicate gilt and ebony sideboard set on a dais against a background of the dim pattern of a William Morris tapestry. As his eyes flickered about her, and his hands gently manoeuvred her limbs and head into place, one white arm resting negligently on the black and gold sideboard, the toe of one black and gold slipper peeping from under the hem of her gown, he felt with a surge of pleasure how comfortable and at ease she was with him.

Sylvie was dressed in her favourite plain black evening gown, its close-fitting bodice cut low, with wide straps worn off the shoulder. The skirt fell in heavy, elegant folds, accentuating the magnificent curve that ran from hip to breast, and the pearls that Henry Abbey had made her buy, unwound into a long single string, drew attention to the more subtle grace of her throat. Pinned to one shoulder, she wore a huge and unusual French brooch: five black enamel and gold wasps with diamond-set wings buzzed ferociously about a carved opal flower, its sinuous stem and leaves also of enamelled gold in various shades of green and lavender. In her hair was a similarly wrought gold, enamel and opal flower, but one as yet untouched by wasps, its pinky-violet tones blending with the russet shades of her hair.

'Throw back your head as if in the first gesture of laughter,' Will instructed her. 'As if your eyes are still on the person who's made you laugh.' The pose highlighted the white arch of her neck and caught the daring that she had so recently made her own inimitable style, for there was a strength in her beauty, no doubt, thought Will, derived from her Magyar ancestry. Her stance took full advantage of the unmistakable signs of a new and commanding presence in her manner. The background he had arranged would become, in the painting, a shadowy, bejewelled mystery for this triumphant *belle dame sans merci*.

'Wonderful! You know you're the best model I've ever had?'

Sylvie laughed, falling precisely into the pose he wanted. Glancing up at her, Will caught a glint of irony in her eyes. 'That wasn't a trick to get you to laugh,' he chided her. 'I wouldn't presume to try such amateurish methods on the great Sylvie Lazar!'

'Oh, acting is full of tricks,' she murmured dismissively. 'Besides, when Sylvie Lazar meets the immortal William MacKenzie, one of them must give way,' she teased.

'Ah, but I owe my success to you!' he answered gallantly.

'And I, mine, to you,' she added roguishly. She laughed, but a perceptible touch of bitterness underlay her lightness of tone. Will stared at her, but she had retreated into her pose. He sighed inwardly: their relationship seemed as volatile as ever. It was not that she did not trust or confide in him, but that there was always this edge of challenge, of niggling resentment, in her attitude towards him that he could not get past. Yet he felt that it was something that she did in spite of herself, as an unconscious defence against their comradeship.

But gradually his frustration at the friction that always seemed present between them melted away as he abandoned himself once more to his work. As he looked at her, his eyes seemed to swallow her whole. He absorbed her into his mind and reduced her, by the soft touch of his sable brushes, to the perfect colour and line on his canvas. It was a form of possession that drew them together; she, content to give herself up to this transformation; he, lost in his regard of her.

The clock ticked. The shadows on the grass outside lengthened imperceptibly. At last Will came back to himself, surfacing upwards out of the deep waters of his concentration. He surveyed his handiwork. It was not just the beauty of her flawless skin and Titian hair that had kept audiences leaping to their feet to applaud her, he thought, striving once more to see if he had captured her elusive appeal. There was still something mysterious about her, something impossible to pin down, that had not merely been the formlessness of youth. Nor was it eroticism: it was glamour – there was just something freakish about her that made it impossible to take your eyes off her. He handed his brushes and heavy palette to his assistant – not Philip, who now had his own small studio, painting Society portraits, thanks to the attention his sketches of Sylvie had brought him – and stretched out his arms.

'You can take a rest now, if you like.'

Sylvie rather gingerly removed her arm from the sideboard. It was red where the flesh had lain so long on the hard edge and her fingers were stiff and cold. Her neck, too, felt as though it would creak if she moved.

'I'm expecting a visitor at four o'clock,' said Will as he climbed down the ornate library steps on which he stood in order to reach the top of the high canvas. 'I don't know whether you'll want to meet him or not.'

'Who is he?'

'The collector who bought *The Angel*.'

She laughed nervously. 'I hope he doesn't buy this one as well,' she said. 'I'd feel like part of a harem!'

'Don't worry. This portrait goes to the Royal Academy before anyone gets their hands on it.'

'Will you need another sitting for it?' she asked.

'I wouldn't mind one more. When do you leave?'

'I sail next Friday.'

'Are you nervous?'

'Of the voyage, yes,' answered Sylvie. 'I have bad memories of sea voyages. They make me feel like I'm a fugitive.'

Will laughed. 'You're hardly a fugitive now. With British audiences at your feet, you're off to conquer new frontiers!'

But Sylvie shook her head and smiled ruefully.

'Come now! This American impresario you've signed up with isn't whisking you off on the biggest American tour since Sarah Bernhardt just because of some picture I painted of you when you were a kid. The only reason you're not as famous here as Lillie Langtry is because you refuse every chance to be as big a star! I know – Harry Lewis told me of the offers you've turned down!'

'I'd say Lillie Langtry is infamous rather than famous,' she answered quietly. Nevertheless, she took satisfaction in provoking Will to her defence. She liked to hear him eager on her behalf: it gave her a glow of pleasure that she hardly dared acknowledge. 'If she hadn't been a royal mistress I doubt even her beauty would have brought her quite so much acclaim.'

'Fair enough. But you can act her right off the stage any time you want, and you know that. You know how good an actress you are!' Will was impatient with Sylvie's lack of courage to claim what she had earned. In public, she was the actress – thrillingly confident: only he and a few other close friends saw this genuine and deep-seated diffidence and reserve. He sighed, and tried another tack: 'It would be facetious of me to pretend that I'm not a good painter, wouldn't it?' he asked.

'I know. I know I can act. But, somehow, I still feel a fraud. I don't know who I am, and I'm afraid that, one day, the audience will discover that . . . that there's no one inside . . . ' Her voice trailed off.

Will was quiet, hoping for more: it was not often that she spoke about her inner life. She was silent, thinking for a moment. Then she said, 'I dream sometimes, you know, that I had a twin, a sister, who knew all the important things about me, but that she went away, and took that knowledge with her . . . that Mamma sent her away . . . ' Sylvie gave a little yelping laugh and Will saw a glimpse of fear in her dark grey eyes. 'How silly!' she said, forcing the gaiety back into her voice. 'I wonder what made me say that!'

'I'll show you who you are,' said Will quietly. He went and took hold of her hand, and drew her to stand before his canvas. 'Look.'

Sylvie stood and studied the half-finished but already magnificent portrait in silence, a slight smile playing about her lips. She pressed his hand warmly.

'This is how I see you,' he said softly.

'Sylvie Lazar,' agreed Sylvie. Somehow she dared not accept this image as herself. *The Angel* had betrayed her: she would not be so trusting again. She paused, then began, 'Often, discussing work with other actors, someone'll describe how they'd lost themselves in a part, became the character they played, like a mask temporarily possessed them body and soul. I don't. Before that silent, intense concentration of an audience, I feel more purely myself than I can ever manage alone! As an actress, I can be anyone, I can be myself!'

It was true: for her, the acting was the chance to be complete, to reveal feelings and emotions that, off stage, were suddenly shadowy and hard to grasp. The fight to reconcile conflicting truths ended, and she could be first one thing and then its opposite with nothing but a professional glide across the intervening void. The lightness she felt on stage gave a zest and gaiety to her acting that was magical to watch, and she had merely accustomed herself to the unaccountable depressions that sometimes followed her successes.

'That's Sylvie Lazar,' she went on. 'She'll stand in for me. It doesn't matter about the rest.'

'It matters to me,' answered Will. He was suddenly aware of his assistant busy in the ante-room. 'Let's go out in the garden.'

Without a further word, they stepped out into the lovely old garden. 'I've got some new plants to show you,' continued Will, returning to old ground. 'I met someone who'd been out in China for years and brought back some wonderful things. He gave me one or two plants. Some are still in the hothouse, but just come and see this creamy-yellow tree peony. It doesn't look much . . . '

'But at least it's actually flowered!' she finished for him, joining excitedly with his passion for flowers. 'Henry Abbey says he'll send me to California next year, so I can bring you some desert blooms,' she went on. 'I saw a big collection in a hothouse in Edinburgh, would you believe. They were wonderful – strange and unreal.'

'Wouldn't it be fun to build a garden together!' They smiled conspiratorially at each other, relishing the moment that could draw them together on such simple terms.

As they walked around the garden, companionably absorbed in their familiar inspection of the flowers, neither saw the parlourmaid show Nye into the studio. She was about to accompany him to the garden door and announce him, but he waved her away and walked around the big polished mahogany easel to stand and examine Sylvie's portrait. On the table beside the library steps were scattered a dozen sepia-coloured photographs of Sylvie in various casual poses, with the chosen one pinned up on a small stand and almost obliterated by the pencilled grid on its glossy surface. He looked sharply from the photographs out to the woman in the garden and, smiling to himself, sauntered over to join them.

'Sir William!' he called. 'How kind of you to receive me when you're working.'

'My Nye.' The painter nodded politely, and walked over the grass to greet his visitor. 'Sylvie, may I introduce Mr Jack Nye. Mr Nye, Sylvie Lazar.'

Sylvie started in involuntary fear, too shocked to extend her hand as he walked across the grass towards her. She recognized the half-smile that habitually hovered about his finely chiselled lips, and noticed that his clean-shaven face was less mobile than it had been and a touch of grey streaked his hair. But time had been kind to him, and there was little doubt of his worldly success, for the nimbus of power that played about his stance and expressions was more marked than ever. His physique had broadened and strengthened and his figure, sheathed in conventional plain, dark clothes, obviously cut by the best tailors on Savile Row, commanded authority and respect. The only slight show of personal vanity was the massive ice-blue diamond, set in a simple gold shank, that he wore on the little finger of his left hand.

As he came up to her, he extended his hand, and, with astonishment and relief, Sylvie realized that the frank admiration in his eyes was no more personal than that of any of her other new and unknown admirers. Nye did not appear to recognize her as the child he had known! She forced herself to overcome her agitation, and gave him her hand, meeting his cool, quizzical gaze with equal calmness.

'Delighted to make your acquaintance, Miss Lazar.' Nye bowed before her. 'I was one of the lucky few to see your farewell performance. You were superb.' He had, against all the odds, it seemed to Sylvie, retained a veneer of delicacy, a lightness of touch, that would continue to win people to him.

'You're very kind,' she answered demurely. She focused all her attention on the recent months in which she had been watching his financial movements so closely. The advantage of her knowledge of him gave her confidence, and also made her feel that he was, in some clean and isolated way, her foe. Almost unconsciously, she now began to play with him, taunting him and flirting with him.

'I was surprised that you chose a comedy, though I thought it very entertaining,' continued Nye smoothly. 'I hadn't realized you were known for comedy.'

'No, but I enjoy it, and this one is so trenchant, and very up to date, you know. My manager thought that if I closed with something witty and out of character it would catch the critics' attention and prevent them from writing my professional obituary.'

'It's certainly a roguish part, and you played it flawlessly.'

'Well, I do a lot of flouting!' agreed Sylvie. 'In New York I shall return to tragedy.'

Will looked on in amusement as Sylvie took this man's admiration and laid it so coolly at her feet. Sleek and dark, Nye was impressive in his way, and Saunders had told Will of the extent of his wealth, much of it apparently gained from diamond mines, and the quality of his collection. What artist, even one as financially independent as Will, could turn a blind eye to such romance!

'I'm working on a new, full-length portrait of Miss Lazar,' said Will. 'Sylvie, would you mind if I let Mr Nye see the work in progress? He is quite a connoisseur.'

'Not at all. Why don't you show him some of your early sketches?' She turned to Nye, giving him a straight look, but trembling inside, knowing that, once the past was revealed, the moment could never be undone. 'Sir William has used me as a model since I was a girl, Mr Nye. I'm sure that you would find his early portraits especially fascinating.'

Will led the way indoors. Sylvie remained behind.

'I shall walk in the garden where it's cool, if you'll excuse me.' The two men bowed and entered the studio together. Will first took Nye to stand before the tall canvas. 'When this is finished,' he said proudly, 'Sylvie will begin to realize just how famous she is.'

'She has a rare beauty,' agreed Nye.

'Here is the portfolio of the early sketches I made of Miss Lazar – I had them out as an *aide-mémoire* for my new portrait,' explained Will as he drew Nye over to the library table at the side of the room, where he laid out the smaller paper sketches where Nye could study them. 'You'll recognize these studies for the portrait you already own.'

Nye picked up first one, and then another, looking at them with interest. 'I can see why you were so struck by her features,' he agreed. 'Fame has merely given her the absolute right to be herself.'

'Here it is!' cried Will, handing Nye a rough, crumpled sketch of the fifteen-year-old Sylvie in Cadogan Square. 'This is the first study I ever made of her!'

Nye took it and looked at it appraisingly, then started suddenly, looking quickly from the paper in his hand out through the window to the woman strolling in the garden outside. 'But it can't be!' The words broke from him. Will watched him curiously, puzzled by the evident emotion on this man's otherwise impassive face. A long sigh escaped Nye's lips, and he stood a moment in silence, gazing into nothingness. He was amazed that he had never made the connection before – *The Angel*, for which he had paid such a price, was none other than little Sylvie Lapham!

In truth, after the first flash of recognition and inexplicable emotion, he had to strain to remember clearly exactly where Sylvie fitted into his past. So many faces crowded his memory, so much had happened in the intervening years. And lately his passion had been for his growing wealth and power rather than for women. His instant association with the girlish face had been of some unfinished business, and, as he laboured to pin it down, odd incidents from that period of his life ten years or more ago came to mind – Rosa's full, white body amidst the primitive dark red hangings and oak furnishings of her bedroom in Budapest; Sylvie strutting around in Sari Fodor's spangled costumes in the gilt and mirrored rehearsal room; Sylvie's intelligent face watching his as he explained the vagaries of the Kimberley workings in that first office he had there. Then his attention was caught once more by the drawing that he still held in his hand: 'I must have this!' he exclaimed vehemently.

Will was struck by the urgency in his voice, but, used to the odd vagaries and sudden, intense passions of art collectors, he shrugged. 'I'm sorry, Mr Nye, but that sketch is not for sale. Sylvie and I are old friends, and I should be sorry to lose so personal a memento of a great lady. However, I would be happy to look through these other studies and select a few from which you may choose.'

Nye recovered himself, burying the sudden incoherent rush of memory. 'Of course,' he said, putting down the sketch, and turning with real interest to the others now spread out on the enormous table, watching as Sylvie grew to womanhood; her stem-like neck appearing when she first put up her hair; the true outlines of her face emerging as she lost the last vestiges of girlhood; her striking dark grey eyes growing larger and more lustrous as her hair darkened and thickened. As he stared long and hard at these pencilled and painted snapshots, he was aware of Will's steady observation. Now he met his gaze, smiling coolly. 'It seems that I may be an older acquaintance of Miss Lazar's than even you, Sir William, though I fear the lady has forgotten our old friendship.'

'Indeed!' Will was astonished, but too well-bred to show his avid curiosity.

'I was a friend of the family's at one time.' Relying on Will's politeness, Nye was deliberately vague. He knew that the painter would not question him, and, until he learnt from Sylvie what past Rosa might have created for herself, he would not for the world betray a confidence unless he meant to for a purpose.

Will could wait no longer. 'Don't you want to reveal your identity to the lady?'

'And shame her into pretending to remember me?' laughed Nye.

'But I do remember you, Mr Nye.' Sylvie's voice carried as clear as a bell across the room from the doorway where she stood behind them.

A cloud passed at that moment over the sun and, as Nye turned, he saw the unmistakable challenge in her eyes, the taunt of one who has the advantage. He experienced a strong sexual thrill. She was a queen! She had been a lovely little thing as a girl, though Nye's tastes had never veered towards the immature, and now she was magnificent! If she had only half the sexual robustness of her mother . . . But then, she was the Angel, the subject of that painting that he had paid such a price for precisely because of its erotic power. He looked at her with new eyes, and smiled, openly allowing his gaze to sweep the full length of her figure. His look made Sylvie shudder inwardly.

And now, finally, the full flood of recollection washed over him. The way he had entangled the girl in his affair with Sari Fodor; the childish hurt in her eyes when she had discovered it. Of course, Sari's death had been quite unintentional; Sari had enjoyed their sexual games, and had herself produced the straps and other restraints that she encouraged him to use. Having made herself so willingly helpless, it had been exquisitely tempting to smother her with her pillow, then he simply let himself out of the house, and alerted Racker to remove all traces of his presence once Sylvie, too, had left. And Rosa had done the rest, without so much as a hint from him. She was magnificently voracious, that woman, and hated her daughter. She had been quite happy to deny Sylvie's terror in order to preserve her own frail, vain world.

But, he now recalled with slight elation, there was not only the affair with the actress; there was the father! Nye could not remember what Rudi Lazar looked like and could now only dimly recall the body flung awkwardly on its back beside the swollen Danube by the force of his bullet. But the familiar frisson of betrayal came like an actual taste in his mouth. He licked his lips and smiled at the beautiful figure, merely outlined now against the bright sunlight from the garden beyond her. Here was a fruitful situation he had not looked for!

She walked calmly towards him, holding out her hand. 'I do remember you. And I'm sure that Daisy Tarrant does too.'

Still dazzled by the light, Nye took her hand and, brushing it quickly with his lips, let it go again, while his eyes met and locked with hers. The name Daisy Tarrant meant nothing to him, and he did not entirely understand her look of challenge, but he was quite content to pick up the glove thrown so boldly at his feet.

Will stood looking from one to the other. He saw the sexual interest in Nye's eyes, and watched aghast as Sylvie calmly appeared to acknowledge it. The stab of jealousy made him nauseous. He was suddenly enraged that this man should possess *The Angel*. He should not possess the original, by God!

'How is your mother?' continued Nye urbanely.

'Well, thank you.' Sylvie dreaded the idea of Rosa renewing her relationship with Nye.

'I must call on her to pay my respects. Miss Lazar, I am delighted to have met with you again. Sir William . . . ' He turned to Will, who looked at him coldly. 'I would very much like to add the pair to *The Angel* to my collection, especially now that I realize I have such a personal connection. Maybe I might call on you another time?'

'I leave such matters entirely to the Maybeck Gallery, sir,' answered Will curtly. He felt the force of the man. As a boy he had had to witness his uncle's bullying without being able to do anything to protect his adored aunt other than being there to console her. In Nye he recognized a similar cruelty, although of a different, higher, magnitude. At that instant he determined inwardly that Nye should never get the better of him.

Nye took his leave adroitly.

'A strange coincidence,' said Will, as soon as the door had closed behind him, hoping to probe his way into this strange situation. 'When did you recognize him? Surely not when I introduced you?'

'As soon as I saw him,' Sylvie answered suavely. She felt that she had triumphed, though over what or whom she could not say. Not over Nye; he was not discomfited in the least. Not even over the situation, although she was glad that it had passed off so easily. No, she felt obscurely that it was herself that she had triumphed over, some unacknowledged boundary that she had crossed, some unknown travail she had survived. She laughed aloud and shook herself.

'What are you laughing at?' enquired Will, watching her in utter bemusement.

'I wonder whether you shouldn't paint me as St George instead! I feel like I've just killed a dragon!' she answered lightly. Her habitual guard over the secrets of her past made it impossible to confide in him, and she raised her instinctive shield of confidence over her fears and doubts, all too perfectly concealing her longing to hand this burden over to someone else.

'Well, it was a novel death then,' answered Will with some relief. 'Not many dragons just roll over at St George's feet and present their hearts to the blade. Tell me, what did that reference to Daisy mean?'

'It was Nye who ruined Daisy's father,' answered Sylvie seriously. 'It was because of Nye that he shot himself.'

'Ah, of course,' said Will. 'You met him in Africa. I knew his money came from diamonds, I just never made the connection. He always struck me as being somewhat sinister, despite his impeccable taste.'

'I suppose you're right. He is a menacing man, despite his rather ostentatious veneer of civilized behaviour. But, looking back, I guess Daisy's father would have ruined himself anyway. Hundreds of men were ruined in Kimberley. The shares I've bought and sold may well have been some poor soul's last hope of salvation.' She paused, looking puzzled, like a little girl again, her brow puckered by a frown. Why was it that her own memory kept tugging at her, begging her to listen to some song that always seemed snatched away, as if by a wind, every time she thought she heard its plaintive, familiar strains?

Far from feeling revived at having survived this meeting, a familiar torpor fell on her. Her mind felt heavy, as if she had awoken from some vivid dream that, strive as she might, she could not remember. What was it about Nye that challenged her so? She tried to remember the things her mother had said to her in Kimberley the day that Daisy's father killed himself, the day Rosa discovered Rudi's ring, but the words were blurred, the images out of focus: she knew only that Nye had ruined Edward Tarrant, an improvident gambler who no doubt would have ruined himself by some other means if left to his own devices, poor man.

Puzzled, she sighed. Why did she feel frightened? Even though Nye could not know of her financial dealings, thanks to the holding company that Sir Joseph had always used to protect her identity from prying eyes, now, seeing Nye in the flesh, she worried about being so close to him. His predatory movements on the Rand were not without some purpose, some grand design. His presence brought back to her the memory of him when she first saw the Big Hole at Kimberley, how she had felt the animal emotion of the man aroused by the splendour of the economic potential of the apocalyptic scene below. She had not been on the Rand, but she could imagine the same cocktail of greed and fantasy. She felt afraid, as if she had taunted a bull in a field, and only now discovered that there was no fence between them.

'And to think that I should have sold my Angel to him, of all people,' declaimed Will bitterly.

'I'm afraid that painting never brought me any luck, Will,' she said sadly. She felt their moment of harmony together in the garden recede and slip once more behind an impenetrable wall of emotional complexity.

CHAPTER TWELVE

The Maybeck Gallery had been delighted to act on the suggestion of Sylvie's new American manager, Henry Abbey, that they should throw a farewell party for their Angel. A small supper upstairs in Old Bond Street was to be followed later in the evening by a more general gathering in the gallery below.

Abbey himself had already returned to New York, to prepare for Sylvie's arrival, but before he left he had accompanied her to several dressmakers to arrange not only her stage clothes – some of which had already been ordered from Worth in Paris – but also, to Sylvie's astonishment, a new winter wardrobe.

'You're gonna be a star,' he'd told her forthrightly. 'You gotta act like a star, dress like a star and think like a star. I've never been so certain of anything in my life as I am of your magic on stage. You're quite a girl! But you've got to live up to it off stage, too, or the Americans won't understand what you're up to. Now what about that silver frock over there, the one with all the lace?'

Sylvie liked this handsome, easy-going New Yorker, with his cool confidence, and found his matter-of-factness and lack of obvious flattery intoxicating; she felt, obscurely, that this was the greatest praise he could give. She was aware, too, of his tireless work promoting Henry Irving and Ellen Terry's American tours, and knew that he could be trusted.

'Remember,' Abbey had continued, 'I'm not having you billed as an English actress, but as the daughter of an American coming home at last. This is what makes it so right!' he exclaimed. 'We Americans have no female star to rival Modjeska or Bernhardt or Terry, and we'd just love a darling of our own. You put your heart and soul into it and you'll see – there won't be a more loyal audience in the world.'

Abbey was fond of discovering reasons and explanations to back his totally intuitive hunches about people. He had known that Sylvie was star material within minutes of seeing her act, yet nevertheless laboured to argue the case to himself and to everyone about him.

'You and I know, in our heart of hearts, that the "grand manner" of the old-style performers like Irving is coming to an end,' he had confided to her. 'It's all the new realism nowadays. And I know just how to sell it! Glamour! It's not a word that people use much, but they will! And you've got it in bucketfuls! You've just gotta stand on stage or walk into a room of waiting journalists and they're gonna be taking it down in shorthand. Glamour! You are what you play on stage – not just some girl playing history. And you've gotta live up to it – and dress up to it.'

So Sylvie arrived at the Maybeck Gallery garbed for the first time in one of the gowns that Abbey had chosen for her. She felt good in it, and was thankful to him for having given her the confidence to wear it well.

The dress was daringly simple, of white tulle shot through with silver thread, the over-skirt looped lightly across her flattened hips by clusters of violets and gathered up into a confection of a bustle at the back. Her long white kid gloves were edged with a purple so dark it was almost black; the narrow sleeves, worn just off her shoulders, were fastened with more bunches of violets; and her creamy pearls, wound into a triple row, hung round her neck. Crowning it all was the nimbus of her russet hair, in which she'd fastened baroque pearls tied with fresh woodland violets.

Will, immaculate in his evening clothes, his brown

hair well-brushed and shining with health, was waiting for her with Mr Saunders at the door of the Maybeck as she and Rosa alighted from their four-wheeler. Saunders stepped forward to take her cloak while Will beamed and spread his arms admiringly.

'Splendid! Doesn't she look magnificent, Mrs Lapham?' As he asked the question, Will knew that he had said the wrong thing, and he quickly covered his traces. As he slipped behind Rosa to take her cloak from her shoulders, he murmured into her ear, just loud enough to be deliberately heard by the others: 'It's not every daughter who has the advantage of inheriting beauty! Or who has a mother to teach her how to carry her beauty as you do.' And he bowed gallantly before passing her cloak to the waiting footman. He was rewarded by a quick smile of gratitude from Sylvie as she took his arm and followed Rosa and Mr Saunders down the length of the gallery, past an impressive array of paintings, to the grand staircase that rose from the centre of the chamber.

'Saunders has, naturally, invited some of his best customers, and I'm afraid your mother took it upon herself to have my uncle invited,' whispered Will as they mounted the stairs.

'Oh, but how lovely to see your Aunt Laura again! Mamma said she was back from Scotland.'

Will squeezed her arm appreciatively. But he looked at her solicitously as he added: 'And Saunders could hardly neglect to ask Mr Nye. Especially since he insisted on transporting *The Angel* here from his own fireside for the occasion, and at his own expense. It's hanging in its old place downstairs.' He felt Sylvie's body jerk involuntarily, and experienced a slight spark from the long-neglected embers of resentment at Sylvie's enduring recoil from the image he had created of her.

He had stood for a long time alone downstairs before

the guests arrived, taking stock once more of his work, for he had not seen it in its original form for some years. Now, of course, its qualities were widely imitated and the picture looked almost unsophisticated. His own style had become simpler, more refined, in its appeal to the emotions, though he had to admit that *The Angel* still had an undeniable power and directness. But he failed to see anything in it to account for Sylvie's aversion – no, it was more – abhorrence. For her sake, he now swallowed the accusation of injustice that arose in his mind. 'I'm sorry,' he said simply. 'I'd have much preferred them all to see my new portrait of you, but it'll be months before it's properly dry and can go to be framed.'

She looked at him in surprise, as though her thoughts had dwelt on something else entirely, then her countenance cleared and she smiled at him and tapped him playfully on the arm with her fan. 'For shame! Do you think I would bear a grudge against an old friend! I'll greet *The Angel* again with pleasure!'

But she immediately lapsed back into thoughtfulness, and seemed to hesitate. She looked at him, searching his face, before making her decision to speak. 'I did not tell Mamma yet that Mr Nye was in town,' she began, so softly that he had to bend his head down close to her face, catching the scent of some light perfume in her hair. But then they had reached the top of the stairs, and were immediately greeted by cheers from the assembled guests. Will had to let her go as she went to hug Ellen and shake Henry Irving warmly by the hand. Saunders presented Lord and Lady Arlington and Joseph Hargreaves, a northern industrialist, immensely rich, and another great collector of Will's work, whose taste Will esteemed greatly. Then Philip slipped forward and Will saw Sylvie blush prettily as he raised her hand to his lips. With a pang, Will forgot the young man who stood before him, now a successful illustrator and portraitist, and only recalled Sylvie and Philip standing intimately together in the failing light in his studio nearly ten years before: 'Let me tie your hair ribbon . . . Oh, thank you!' Why could Will himself not treat her with such simple ease? Since having her back in his studio over the last couple of months, he had recognized without a doubt that she was the only woman for him, yet he could not seem to speak, or touch her. Now Philip had made her laugh and he saw that the younger man had no difficulty in letting Sylvie see his open admiration – or she in accepting it.

But he had no time to pursue his thoughts, for Rosa stood suddenly beside him. 'Sir William! Who is that man?' she asked breathlessly.

He looked at her face, where a hectic flush had spread across her lightly powdered fair skin, then followed the direction of her shining eyes. They led to Nye, now being formally presented to Sylvie by Mr Saunders.

'Do you not know him?' he asked, unwilling to be made a pawn in any game of hers.

'Why . . . ' she laughed feebly. 'Why, I may . . . I had an old acquaintance . . . ' Her words trailed off, after the slightest pause before her choice of the word 'acquaintance'.

'Then let me present you,' said Will firmly, taking hold of her arm and leading her over to Nye. He was determined to take charge of the situation.

Rosa had initially been speechless when she first caught sight of Nye; emotion after emotion had hit her, hard. First was the shock of seeing a man whom, in her imagination, she had long since buried in some faraway and obscure grave; this was swiftly followed by anger at Nye's treatment of her in Kimberley; and then by confusion and fear that he might, by some unguarded question, disclose her present fictions of widowhood. She must, she decided, be very, very careful.

Will and Rosa arrived beside Sylvie and stood facing Nye. 'Ah, Mrs Lapham!' said Nye at once. 'I was just telling Miss Lazar that I had not yet found time to call upon you and leave my card. Most remiss, having rediscovered the whereabouts of an old friend, not to seek her out immediately.' And he bowed over her trembling hand.

Rosa glanced sharply at Sylvie. 'I don't understand,' she said. 'You knew that I was in London?'

'Only for a day or so. Be assured that I should not let so great a time elapse before paying my compliments. Which day was it, Miss Lazar?' he asked, turning politely to Sylvie, 'that I had the pleasure of meeting you?'

Will saw the murderous look that Rosa gave her daughter, and saw, too, the bitter resignation on Sylvie's features.

But once again they were disturbed, as Mr Saunders interrupted them.

'Miss Lazar, would you be so kind as to allow Lord Arlington to take you into dinner? And Mrs Lapham,' he added, gallantly offering his own arm and falling into line behind Sylvie and her companion. The guests formed a procession, the men smooth and elegant in their black swallow-tail coats and high white collars beside the full, frothy skirts of the ladies, and walked through the wide mahogany doors into the room where a large table was laid for dinner. The panelled walls were hung with English watercolours, including, Sylvie noticed, several glowing Turners, and the long table, covered in stiff, white, linen damask, was set for more than twelve with, in the middle, a huge gilt candelabra thickly covered with gardenias, whose heady scent hung in the air.

As Rosa found her place card and seated herself, slowing drawing off her gloves, she had the leisure to watch for Nye as the other guests entered the dining room. He, however, merely bowed and turned his attention to the soup that had been placed before him. A woman who relied so much on her physical, animal instincts as did Rosa could not bear to be thwarted in anything that promised physical satisfaction. Her initial terror at the consequences of seeing her former lover had swiftly dissolved – as all unwelcome perceptions, for Rosa, simply faded into nothingness – and all her thoughts were now of Nye himself. The intensity of her erotic memories of him left her breathless and unable to concentrate on anything. She wanted to run her hands over her full body, to feel her breasts, to touch the still-silky hair between her thighs, to cry out with longing at the memories the mere sight of Nye evoked. The hysterical flames of a sexual fire that had never been extinguished leapt into life once more as she remembered his overpowering sexual presence, the way in which he had held her in thrall, controlling her, bending her to his will, until, finally ready himself, he would allow her to join him in a shattering, searing climax.

For all her circumspection surrounding Nye during their years together, she knew that she had satisfied him, that he took real pleasure in her sensuality and boldness. Now, as she waited for the party to gather itself around the table, the years fell away, and, in her fantasy, she believed that she had only to let him know of her continuing desire for him and they would resume their mutual passion.

'I shall return to a lonely house tonight, Miss Lazar.' Nye was the first to speak across the table to Sylvie.

'How so?'

'My Angel is downstairs!'

Sylvie was discomfited by such unabashed gallantry. From another man, she could have tossed the compliment aside, but she felt that this was the opening salvo in a campaign that Nye meant to pursue to the end.

'You're a lucky man. I wanted that picture of young MacKenzie's.' Lord Arlington's interruption saved her from a reply, but, turning her head away gratefully, she ran into Rosa's gaze along the table, full of barely disguised, naked jealousy. She turned back quickly, only to find Nye's ironic eyes still upon her. She felt cornered and panicky, and instantly rebuked herself for her childishness. She looked down the long table, the silver and cut glass glinting deliciously in the candle-light, to where Will sat beside Ellen Terry. He smiled encouragingly at her, and she felt calmed. Then her attention was claimed by Joseph Hargreaves, who sat next to her.

'Tell me, Miss Lazar, what sort of themes do you think modern drama ought to treat?' he asked, introducing, with old-fashioned courtesy, a topic that they, as strangers, might profitably discuss. 'It seems to me it dwells too much on our sins, on betrayal and depravity. But then I suppose I'm of another generation.'

'I dislike the obsession some dramatists have with evil,' she agreed politely. 'Especially since evil people, in reality, so often appear to be banal, even good-natured – a difficult contradiction to portray convincingly.'

'But should a play not be uplifting?' pursued Hargreaves.

'Drama certainly has to stir our dreams,' answered Sylvie.

'And what are people's dreams made of, nowadays?' asked Lady Arlington, who had been listening to their conversation.

'It seems to me,' said Sylvie, 'that it's money that is the romance, the poetry of our age.'

'Of course!' agreed Ellen, clapping her hands. 'Everyone dreams of wealth.'

'You'd stage a play in the Stock Exchange, would you?' questioned Hargreaves humorously.

'I'm no playwright!' laughed Sylvie. 'But finance is a new science,' she continued seriously. 'It attracts the popular imagination, yet repels comprehension. And there is about financiers an aura of magic, of alchemy, a Hey Presto! change of base metals into gold, of bits of paper into millions, turning pedlars into kings overnight. I'd like a play about a financier.'

'I think Miss Lazar is absolutely right,' enthused Lady Arlington. 'Financiers do secretly like to be thought of as magicians!'

'I agree,' said Irving. 'I've found that men who find themselves without this financial legerdemain have an aura of something unexpressed, unattained about them, as if they were out of step with their age.'

'But there are no grand opportunities for magic now, my dear. The decade of speculation is over,' declared Lord Arlington.

'What about Africa? The gold and diamonds in the south make it a difficult continent to ignore.' Gold was an exciting topic. Sylvie had everyone's attention. She avoided Nye's eye, but she felt compelled to make him speak, to hear what he had to say on the subject. He shifted slightly in his chair before inevitably beginning.

'But the diamond fields are already too well organized, and the gold must be got profitably out of the ground,' he countered with quiet authority.

'The Rand gold-field isn't alluvial like California; it needs heavy capital outlay, but who wants to speculate in such savage territory?' added Falkirk, glad to display a little of his own first-hand experience, and to belittle Sylvie in public. 'It's bad enough keeping the Zulus in check,' he went on, 'as we British have discovered to our cost. We've let the Transvaal slip through our hands twice now.'

'And then to have to deal with a scurrilous, arrogant peasant like Kruger,' said Nye.

'Oh, but tell us more,' put in Rosa in an inappropriately flirtatious tone, hoping to pull Nye's attention to her. 'We ladies know nothing of such affairs.'

'President Kruger in the Transvaal is just using the goldstrike to raise money to finance the Boers' antiquated farms,' explained Nye curtly. 'He won't even allow an electric tramway through the gold-field because the farmers make money supplying fodder for the pack animals.'

As the servants came and went with fresh dishes of food and filled their glasses with a ripe burgundy, the guests were content to let Nye monopolize the conversation. Rosa, who had leant forward into the pool of candlelight to smile invitingly across at him, irritably retreated into the relative gloom as a gold-rimmed plate of roast partridge was put before her. 'Kruger's policies are pushing prices for dynamite and so forth sky-high,' he continued. 'As the Rand is organized at present, the gold is better off left where it is. In the ground.'

'You paint a paradoxical picture, Mr Nye.' Will's tone was faintly questioning, as if challenging Nye's good faith in making out such a poor case for the new goldstrike. Will knew almost nothing of the subject, but he instinctively sensed Nye's insincerity. Nye looked at him as if surprised at his impertinence, but Will smiled at him charmingly. 'I imagine there must be safer ways to earn money?' he added.

'Like art,' put in Saunders, raising a laugh and easing the way for a change of subject.

But Sylvie would not be silenced. 'You're wrong.' A quiet fell upon the table: the other guests felt uncomfortable that she should challenge a man on such a subject in this way. Finance and politics were a strictly male preserve. But she seemed oblivious. 'The stakes involved are vast.'

'I certainly didn't enjoy our defeat in the Transvaal being rammed down our throats at the London Convention, nor the sight of Kruger being banqueted by Bismarck and the Kaiser afterwards,' commented Lord Arlington patriotically. 'As you say, Miss Lazar, after this latest goldstrike, the stakes are far too high. If someone doesn't take a firm hand soon, this goldstrike could lead to war!'

'What about you Americans?' asked Will lightly of Nye, still probing gently. 'Have you no interest in spreading democracy into Africa?' The mocking irony in his voice was virtually undetectable.

'Oh, the Americans have no imperial ambitions,' said Nye, ready to lecture indulgently as if at his own dinner table. 'They already have everything they need – land, timber, coal, ore, manpower. They might invest abroad, but they don't seek control. Unlike the Europeans, they have no interest in telling the rest of the world how to govern itself!'

'What? You think that Carnegie with his steel trusts or Rockefeller with his oil is not in a position to control a mere President?' laughed Will, to Nye's discomfiture.

'I'd like to know who will gain control of the Rand,' resumed Sylvie, seriously. 'It would be fairly easy for someone to buy up a controlling interest in the gold mines, just as Cecil Rhodes has done with the diamond fields, and then dispose of Kruger.' She looked challengingly at Nye.

'But there are somewhat more serious implications,' added Lord Arlington gravely. 'At the end of the day, diamonds are mere trinkets. But gold is where the political power lies.'

'With sufficient gold, a man could control governments and nations,' agreed Hargreaves, turning politely to Rosa as if to continue the explanation she had requested earlier. 'No nation has ever been held to ransom for a shortage of diamonds, but gold is quite a different matter.'

'They've still got to get the gold in Africa out of the ground at a profit,' insisted Nye stubbornly.

Sylvie's clear grey eyes glinted delicately in the candle-light like mother-of-pearl as she gazed apprais-ingly at him. 'The Witwatersrand gold reef runs under-ground at a gentle slope for a good thirty or forty miles to the south of the outcrop reef,' she answered coolly, ignoring Will's stare of surprise and continuing to look at Nye. 'It's true that the nature of the gold-bearing rock changes at about two hundred feet down, and, as yet, there's no effective way of releasing enough of the gold from this rock. But it can only be a matter of time before someone comes up with a process or formula that will.' She ignored the looks of amazement around the table and pressed on. 'Then whoever owns that land to the south will have the power to bring every economy in the world to its knees.'

'Just like magic,' added Nye drily, raising his head to stare challengingly at her.

'But what drama!' exclaimed Irving. 'You're right, my dear. Absolutely right! It would make a magnificent subject for a play.'

'Pandora's Box, perhaps,' murmured Sylvie, not taking her eyes from Nye, who now stared back with a mixture of admiration and conjecture on his smooth features. After a slight hesitation she went on determin-edly: 'And I know from my own childhood, in Kimber-ley, that the type of financial adventurer who finds his way to southern Africa in search of hasty wealth is not always the sort to demonstrate the highest side of European civilization.'

Saunders shuffled uncomfortably on his chair, assuming that Sylvie must be ignorant of the source of Nye's wealth, while Rosa fanned herself vigorously.

Will sat back, as if understanding for the first time where Sylvie's unlikely show of expertise was leading.

'Look at the poverty and destitution that flourishes here in London, or in Manchester or Birmingham or Glasgow!' Laura Falkirk spoke softly for the first time. 'See the conditions to which financiers and industrialists are prepared to reduce their own people in this country, let alone so far away.'

Will, too, gladly gave his support to this argument, remembering the boastful stories of whippings and beatings his Uncle Falkirk had told him with such pride of his days in colonial Africa. 'What might some all-powerful financier do if he got control of the goldfields?' he asked. 'There would be few men to stay his hand, and plenty willing to out-do him in savagery.'

'The pity is that it's so childishly simple for one man to gain dominion,' ended Sylvie.

'I had no idea that you had time to take such an interest in politics,' said Nye dangerously. 'Let alone in such fine detail.'

'I take an interest in drama, sir,' answered Sylvie spiritedly, suddenly aware that she had gone too far. For the first time, she had broken her promise to Sir Joseph never to reveal her knowledge of the financial markets. As always, she acted her way out of trouble: she laughed deliberately and leant across the table to reach for a stick of celery. 'An actress can hardly avoid being fascinated by such a situation,' she declared airily. 'The sweep is grand, the themes are universal, the characters are larger than life, everything is writ large. Who can fail to be interested in that?'

'You live life so romantically, Miss Lazar,' said Lady Arlington admiringly.

'Had I known that you were so well-informed, I'd have considered my comments more closely,' said Nye, with an ironic bow of mock submission. Sylvie in turn inclined her head and twirled the stick of celery absent-mindedly. 'There, Miss Lazar, I have brought a smile to your lips.'

'But you're mistaken, sir. I'm not smiling,' she said, turning upon him the full force of her stage technique, lips parted and teeth sparkling, but her eyes hard and penetrating with a suppressed anger that she herself barely acknowledged or understood. The stick of celery, like a riding crop between her fingers, slowly arched as she applied tension. 'I am showing you my teeth.'

Nye was both charmed by the zest of the fight she seemed to offer him, and nonplussed. Did she expect him to return this insolence? All the while, Sylvie had him transfixed in the beam of her ambiguous smile, and the rest of the company looked on in amazement. Rosa was furious: at that moment she hated Sylvie with a white-hot resentment and jealousy that she had to struggle hard to conceal. Interpreting Sylvie's actions in the light of her obsessions, she was convinced that Sylvie meant to seduce Nye, to take her lover from her under her very nose! Will, too, was astonished at Sylvie's performance – for surely that was what her challenge to Nye was? A theatrical gesture only? He wondered what struggle from the past she could possibly have with him to betray such fine scorn, such an instant of concentrated fury? He felt somehow afraid for her.

The celery snapped and Sylvie broke into a peal of mischievous laughter. 'Don't be alarmed, Mr Nye. I've already had my dinner – and an excellent one too. I don't think I could manage another morsel.'

Amid general nervous, excited laughter and a swish and flourish of dresses, all were relieved to leave the table and join the new influx of guests downstairs.

Will made his way to Sylvie's side as soon as he could, where he found his uncle already in possession of her arm, an ugly smile on his lips, his face close to hers, as she struggled to free herself. Will, however, was glad to see contempt rather than fear on her face.

'What a spectacle you made of yourself,' Will heard Falkirk hiss in Sylvie's ear. 'Be careful! Even fame such as yours doesn't always last, and then you'll be glad of your friends, remember!' Falkirk deliberately leant his full weight against her, pushing the back of his hand, where it held her arm, across her breasts. The muscles of Sylvie's face tightened as she tried to force him away without attracting unwelcome attention from the people about them, and she reddened as Will arrived beside them. Seeing him, Falkirk merely laughed loudly and slowly released her. 'I'll go and find your mother,' he sneered at her. 'There's more satisfaction to be had there.'

Sylvie hung her head in shame before Will, who stood in front of her, sheltering her and giving her time for the angry flush on her cheeks to subside. 'It's a pity in some ways that your mother couldn't go with you to America,' he said at last, wondering how far Sylvie would allow him to invade her privacy, not daring, by too overt a comment on Rosa's conduct, to risk Sylvie raising her defences against him. 'Sooner or later my uncle's behaviour is going to attract some very unpleasant gossip.'

Sylvie's eyes now sought Will's anxiously, and she put her hand on his arm. 'Mamma will be all alone while I am away. She's never been alone before. I worry that . . . ' Her eyes slipped over his shoulder, and Will turned his head to follow her gaze to where Rosa stood talking animatedly to Nye. 'Will you look after her for me while I'm away?' she asked, continuing to regard her mother. 'I know . . . I know you don't like her very much, but her life has not been easy, and her heart tends to rule her head sometimes. That's all. She doesn't mean . . . ' She transferred her gaze back to Will now, and he looked down into her clear grey eyes and smiled.

'I'll do anything you want me to, you should know that.'

She let out a deep sigh. 'Thank you. That makes me feel much easier. I was very concerned about leaving her.'

'I would have thought she would have welcomed the opportunity to return to America,' Will went on. 'Has she no family there?'

Sylvie smiled naughtily, retreating from their moment of intimacy. 'It's a family secret! Mamma ran away when she was seventeen! She thinks they would never acknowledge her if she suddenly turned up on their doorstep after all these years. She seems quite scared of them – if Mamma was ever scared of anything! But I plan to go there, to Saratoga Springs, and find out what family I have left. I don't know if my grandparents would still be alive, but Mamma had a brother. Maybe I have cousins!'

Will had no chance to reply, for they were interrupted once more by Saunders, who wanted to introduce the artist and his famous model to a wealthy Viennese collector who was visiting London. Will was forced by politeness to give way. He felt angry with himself that she was to leave so soon, for she was catching the boat train to Liverpool the following day, without his having found a way of penetrating that magnificent reserve. But the rest of the evening was taken up by friends, acquaintances and strangers, and he could do no more than share glances with her across the crowded gallery. He stared at her as she stood beside *The Angel*, lost in the tumult of his own feelings for her. Laura Falkirk, coming to stand beside him, laid her hand upon his arm and smiled sympathetically at him.

'She's very lovely tonight,' she said simply.

Will sighed. 'At least I have my new portrait of her to work on. I shall enjoy putting the finishing touches to it, so it's ready for her return.'

It had been arranged that Sylvie would leave early, to prepare for her departure. Her trunks, long since packed and bound with leather straps, had been collected by the carrier that morning and would be waiting for her on board ship. A little after half-past ten, Sylvie slipped upstairs to put on her cloak. As she climbed the stairs, the noise of the throng below gradually lessened and she could hear the rustle of her own skirts. She smiled to herself. The dress had been a success: it augured well for Henry Abbey's future management of her. She let out a sigh as she reached the top of the stairs: tomorrow she would be alone. She would have eleven or twelve days' journey in which to let London slide away into the past, giving her time to renew herself for her assault on America. She looked forward to it. She had always enjoyed new audiences and the chance they gave her to woo them and win them to her.

'Whore!'

Rosa came forward out of the shadows at the top of the stairs. She was shaking visibly. Sylvie stopped, appalled, on the top step. 'But then you always were a selfish child, thinking only of yourself and your own pleasure, never of me!'

'Mamma!' Sylvie cried out in fright. 'Whatever is the matter?'

'You've tried to take him from me, but you shan't! You hypocrite! Complaining to me about Lord Falkirk, then going behind my back to take Jack Nye away from me!'

'Hush, Mamma. Let me come past. You're wrong!' Sylvie, standing precariously at the top of the staircase, tried vainly to squeeze past Rosa.

'You with all those silly stories, your play-acting! You were always so jealous of me. You drove him away! He never did anything wrong! But he saw how things were, and wouldn't come between a mother and her child; he, also, was too sensitive for that. I never let you see how heartbroken I was. I never blamed you.' Rosa paused now, triumphant in her madness. 'In Budapest, too, you tried, with your crazy stories about Sari Fodor. As if he would ever have been unfaithful to me! You see how you lie! He would never look at you!'

'Let me come past!'

But all Rosa could hold in her mind was the fresh red cloud of her desire for renewed contact with Nye, to feel his masterly hand on her trembling flesh once more, and she was insanely jealous of Sylvie, of her youth, her success, and the attention Nye had paid to her this evening. It was intolerable to Rosa that Sylvie of all people should seem to threaten the slim promise of renewed sexual excitement that Nye's reappearance heralded. Once again, as she had done so often when Sylvie was a child, Rosa now set out in all the ignorance of her brute desires to challenge her daughter and overcome any opposition to the fulfilment of Rosa's physical needs. If Sylvie had to be crushed, so be it.

'You, who have so much! Now that you hold the purse strings, you deny me all the things that would give me pleasure.'

'That's not true!' began Sylvie, but Rosa was lost now inside her own head.

'In your cruel selfishness, you'd even take the love of my life from me!' And she started to mumble almost incoherently. Sylvie could just make out that it was a train of reminiscences of times in Budapest with Nye – outings to the racecourse, holidays at Bad Ischl, shopping trips to Vienna – proofs of his loyalty to her.

Sylvie looked up at Rosa standing above her, and for the first time saw that what her mother said about her was absolutely, undeniably wrong. She had expected the usual crushing weight of defeat, as Rosa forced her to overturn her own perceptions and substitute whatever truth her mother wanted her to have. Now, for the first time, she saw that Rosa simply could not succeed in persuading her to accept her lies, nor even in making her doubt her own mind. Sylvie simply turned and, stepping back down the stairs, walked away, leaving Rosa alone in the shadows.

When Will got home, Mrs Brierley was waiting up for him. 'There's a gentleman in the library to see you, sir,' she said in a worried tone. 'He insisted on waiting, though I told him you wouldn't be back till very late. He said as how it didn't matter. A foreign gentleman. Very ill, he looks, too. I've made him as comfortable as I can. He looked so wretched, I didn't like to send him away.'

'Thank you, Mrs Brierley. I'm sure you've done the right thing,' he answered, handing her his overcoat, hat and gloves.

In the dim room upstairs, Will could barely make out the thin figure huddled in a chair beside the comfortable fire. A glass of port, barely touched, stood beside him on a table. The face was sunken, the skin like parchment and the teeth already protruded unnaturally, but the dark hair that hung lankly on his brow was barely touched with grey. As the man rose to greet his host, Will could see that he had once been tall and even broad shouldered.

'I'm Sir William MacKenzie,' Will introduced himself gently. 'Please sit down again.'

'My name is Stefan Kadar,' replied the man, sinking gratefully back into his chair. The effort of it seemed to sap his strength temporarily.

'I'm sorry you've had such a long wait for me,' Will added, as he walked over to where Mrs Brierley had laid out the decanters and glasses. He poured himself a small glass of port and came to sit in the armchair on the other side of the fireplace. He smiled and raised his glass in a companionable gesture. 'How can I be of help to you?' he asked. He could not for the life of him guess at what this strange, ill creature could want with him so late at night.

Stefan Kadar shifted in his chair to take hold of his drink. He did not return Will's gesture, however, but sat looking down at the glass as he turned it slightly between his hands. 'I was a good friend of Count Rudi Lazar,' he began at last, looking up as Will, startled, leant forward in his chair towards him. Kadar nodded imperceptibly, as if to acknowledge that he had brought his story to the right house. 'I came to London for medical treatment, but the doctors here have told me that my case is hopeless. Tomorrow I must return to Budapest.' He paused. As Will waited for him to go on, he had the oddest feeling that, in the morning, this stranger's visit should prove to have been a dream.

'Before I die,' Kadar began, glancing challengingly across at Will, as though the idea of his own death were still something alien and ungraspable to him. 'Before I die,' he went on once more, 'I have something on my conscience that I must put right. It's a lie I told many years ago, to a little girl, about her father and how he died. It was my friend's daughter, Sylvie. She is your Angel, I think?'

Will, with a feeling of mounting dread, nodded silently.

'Then I can tell you, and you will know how or when to tell her the truth. I know of no one else who is close to her. I cannot tell her myself. I don't want to frighten her. And it is a pitiful tale. For it was not just I who lied. It concerns her mother, also.' He shook his head sadly and sighed heavily, staring into the fire before beginning to tell Will his story.

CHAPTER THIRTEEN

Henry Abbey was right: Sylvie had to work for her success. She arrived in New York to find the Hudson frozen and the city virtually cut off by snow. Ellen Terry had described to her the racket and bustle of the harbour and the wharfs, and the onslaught of the press who boarded the boat before it docked, but she arrived in a magically quiet metropolis, the ferryboats frosted, Brooklyn Bridge like a spangled spider's web from an old pantomime and, driving up Fifth Avenue along the Park, the newly built birthday-cake chateaux seemed covered in white icing. Abbey had filled her luxurious hotel room with flowers, but she barely had time to look at them before he whisked her downstairs to a hideous Moorish parlour where a pack of reporters was gathered.

They fired questions at her – tell us about working with the great Henry Irving, what did she think of New York, was it what she expected, was it good to be home, would she look for an American husband while she was here, did she plan to stay, was she used to such cold? She hardly knew what she answered, but Abbey seemed pleased and the reporters quite amiable.

'Are they always like that?' she asked Abbey, as they dined that evening across the Square at Delmonico's.

He grinned broadly at her. 'That was quite a restrained performance! They were there because they know I never cheat them on a story, and I told them they'd kick themselves later if they missed your arrival.' He chewed meditatively on his cigar and looked at her appraisingly, a shrewd look of humour in his eyes. 'Nobody's really heard of you now,' he went on. 'That whole thing about the painting doesn't mean so much over here. I guess it's old news. But by the time your tour finishes and you get back here, your publicity will be a whirlwind. You'll see.'

'And for now?' asked Sylvie.

'The secret for now is to undersell. Promote the play not the star. I'm going to let you prove for yourself that you're the star! I'm not saying it's gonna be easy. You gotta remember that you're dealing with an audience whose favourite play is *Uncle Tom's Cabin*, and you're gonna open with something completely new.'

Over dinner, Abbey had assembled the cast with whom she was to work. They arrived now, stamping their feet with the cold, and emerging from thick coats and scarves. They greeted her politely but without effusion, then set themselves to attend to the serious business of eating, drinking and talking amongst themselves. She studied them closely; although the unfamiliar accents were sometimes hard to follow, their gossip and tales did not seem so very different from the Lyceum company after all. They seemed curious to learn from her about the London stage, but not about her personally, and she sorely missed the friendliness of London.

As they settled to their coffees, and the noise in the crowded restaurant died down a little, they, too, were eager for news of the play that Abbey had commissioned specially for Sylvie's opening. The one clause in her contract that Abbey had reserved for himself was complete control over the plays and parts that she would perform, but Sylvie knew of his expertise and experience in publicity and promotion, and felt assured that, if she placed herself in his hands artistically, he would never betray her.

'You're all gonna have to work hard to get this new psychological drama across,' insisted Abbey seriously. 'Everyone's discussing it right now, but none of the critics and columnists have quite made up their minds which way they're gonna jump. My hunch is that this new stuff by that Norwegian fellow – what's his name? Ibsen? – that they're calling perverse and degenerate now has gotta take the theatre by storm. It's just a matter of timing. I've had my ear to the ground for long enough and I'm pretty confident. I've got you some good naturalistic dialogue, a good modern theme, and I'm just gonna leave the rest to Sylvie's magnetism.'

The other actors all looked at her directly as if assessing the odds on Abbey's speculation. She looked back steadfastly, determined to base her confidence on Abbey's estimation of her alone and not to allow herself to get rattled by the responsibility he seemed now to be placing squarely on her shoulders. Besides, she knew that she was a thorough, tenacious professional – all she could do was try her best.

Abbey understood that there was indeed an element of risk in allowing her to open with such a radically new drama, but then he had too long a string of successes behind him seriously to consider failure. And the rewards of success, as he knew well, were generous. 'No, sir!' he summed up, waving his hand for the check, 'I just can't wait for the fun to start!'

Over the next few weeks, the company worked tirelessly together at rehearsals and Sylvie gradually got used to the American actors' wise-cracking and their businesslike attitude to their work. It was Henry Abbey himself on whom Sylvie came to rely most: he was unfailingly courteous and affable, though he pushed her, and the rest of the cast, hard. He always found time to chat with her alone at the end of rehearsals, just to make sure she was content with the way things were progressing. No problem was too small; he seemed positively to enjoy any challenge. She accepted the security he offered and never sought to confide in him.

Soothed by the hard work, she found herself too busy to dwell on thoughts of London, especially on the situation she had left between Rosa and Nye, and she cherished this solitary period. Sylvie relaxed and simply got on with the job, confident that Abbey seemed happy with their progress and with the way the tickets were selling for the opening night.

And then the blizzard began. All thoughts of nervousness about performing before a strange, alien audience were lost in the tumult that reigned outside. The snow whipped along the long, straight streets faster than a racehorse and blew into gigantic, constantly shifting drifts. Sylvie had to leave for the theatre in the afternoon while there was still light to see and before the vicious wind froze her eyelashes together, then sit in her eerily quiet dressing room until it was time for the performance to begin. Her dresser, Louisa, who had accompanied her from London, stayed with her, slowly and rhythmically brushing her hair with long strokes while Sylvie mentally rehearsed her lines.

Of course, the theatre was almost empty and the lights burned blue and dim in the cold. The overture started late and some of the orchestra had not made it to the theatre. Sylvie had never worked to an empty house before, and her voice trembled, her gestures faltered and by the last act the company were more or less walking their parts. There were no bouquets, no curtain calls, no champagne and early notices to read excitedly late at night. Instead, both the audience and the cast were intent on reaching their homes safely before the city came to a total standstill. She was left alone in her dressing room with Louisa.

'I feel like running home myself,' she sobbed to her dresser. All the excitement that Will, Nell, Irving and the others had felt for her now seemed to have been tempting fate. Sir Joseph's cry of 'Go home!' echoed in her ears. 'I should never have aimed so high. Never!'

'That man is your destiny,' Nell had said of Abbey: now Sylvie could hardly face him. But when he appeared, as punctually as ever, at her dressing room door, he appeared to be perfectly sanguine.

'By the time you get back to New York the reporters will be telling this story as a far-fetched yarn,' he reassured her, dismissing her fears and smiling as charmingly as ever. 'It'll all add to the Sylvie Lazar legend another day, you wait and see.'

She dried her eyes, looking at him in disbelief.

'You know what happened at the start of Mrs Langtry's first tour, six years back?' he asked cheerfully as he bundled her into her wrap. 'The theatre burnt down on her opening night! They accused me of arson as a publicity stunt!' He grinned broadly. 'Trust me,' he added more seriously, taking her hand in his. 'The only thing I worry about is bad notices, not people staying at home because it's cold. Come on, let me get you safely back to your hotel before the weather gets even worse.'

He made sure that Sylvie and Louisa were tucked warmly into the cab and, chatting all the way, never gave Sylvie a chance to dwell on the night's failure. He saw them safely back into the torrid splendour of the hotel lobby before bidding them goodnight and making his own precarious way home.

As the blizzards roared up and died down again, people drifted into the theatre and the seats filled up once more, but to Sylvie things didn't seem to improve. She was a flop. There was no apparatus within her to live a half-life; either she was going to succeed, to follow in the footsteps of Rachel, Ristori, Modjeska and Madame Sarah, or she might as well return to the pleasant existence of the Lyceum company, where no one was expected seriously to rival the theatre's founders.

Her performances on stage were so instinctive, so

unconscious, despite her long and arduous apprenticeship, that she could only take this apparent failure as confirmation of what had always been her deepest unspoken fear: it was not she, Sylvie Lazar, whom the British audiences had flocked so eagerly to see over the past few years, but the Angel, that figure of scandal, intrigue and innuendo.

As she sat before the mirror in her dressing room after a performance, Rosa's frequent sarcastic comments flooded her mind – that she was mad to have believed that she had any theatrical talent, she was merely an exhibit, a fairground freak. Despairingly, Sylvie realized how deluded she had been to think that the theatre was her rightful home. Of course Rosa was right; without the interest generated by *The Angel*'s publicity, she would still be playing second lead at the Lyceum. Now she feared that the cold expressions on the up-turned faces of the audience that evening meant nothing but personal dislike at this imposter gesturing emptily before them. She felt an unbearable sadness and loneliness well up inside her, and she longed for some intimacy and affection. If only Will were here! The thought surprised her. She had never consciously missed him before. But the flash of memory of his pride in her success, of his constant support and encouragement, seemed to rise up and strike down the childish nightmare of Rosa's destructive jealousy. She recalled her first meeting with Ellen Terry in Will's studio: the magic hush, the quiet splendour that she knew had filled the big room as she had sat reading aloud beside the stove. That had been real! Nell hadn't picked her up and helped her because of *The Angel*. Suddenly, to Louisa's perturbation, Sylvie began to cry. Great hot tears of relief and gratitude ran down her cheeks, streaking her thick make-up.

'Mind your stage clothes,' murmured Louisa, gently

placing a wrapper around her shoulders, and giving her a slight hug.

Sylvie began to laugh, and caught at the woman's hand. 'I'm all right,' she said, sniffing and wiping her face. She gave a shuddering sigh. Rosa was not to be believed! She didn't want to think too deeply about her mother's motives, but she knew, as the little crack of light found its way into her life and illuminated some dark corners for the very first time, she knew that Rosa had been malicious. She decided to concentrate instead on the image of Will's new portrait of her. She would look into that mirror instead, and reject her mother's attempts to undermine her! Her new-found acceptance of her own opinion in the face of Rosa's haunting, bullying whispers to the contrary felt very shaky and raw, but she clung to the knowledge that she *did* belong on stage, that only in the theatre could she find acknowledgement and understanding, as well as the approval she so desperately craved. She determined at that moment to make herself as radiant and invulnerable as Will's most recent painted image of her claimed she was, and to drown out her mother's sly, threatening innuendoes with the noise of real applause.

Abbey saw what was happening to Sylvie, and, still full of confidence in his decision to make a star out of her, he closed the New York run and let her open earlier than planned in Brooklyn in order to give her a fresh start. 'My stock's not gonna fail me now, is it?' he demanded, chewing on his cigar and giving her a big, friendly wink as she looked at him in surprise.

'No,' she assured him, smiling at his kindly use of the language he knew they both understood. 'Your investment's as sound as ever it was.'

She began to rebuild her confidence, but the magic had gone, and now, crossing the bridge whose tinselled beauty had thrilled her as her boat drew into the harbour, she saw only the tramcars, carts, carriages and endless hurrying people, bent over against the weather. Coming home late at night, she slept in the carriage, wrapped in her sealskin cloak. All her energies were directed at her audiences, whom she wooed now as never before, desperate for their approval and praise.

Sylvie's only expedition outside the theatre, other than the early suppers with Abbey, was to Wall Street. Sir Joseph Waldschein had given her the name of a New York financier, Elliot Statten, who would, in the strictest confidence, enable her to keep her share deals up to date. He often handled the American end of Sir Joseph's own affairs and could, the old man assured her, be trusted implicitly. The situation on the Rand was changing constantly as existing companies amalgamated or expanded and new mining companies were floated on the stock exchanges of Johannesburg, London and New York, and Sylvie could not afford to remain out of touch for weeks at a time while she was on tour.

'He's a true Yankee gentleman,' Sir Joseph had said of Statten. 'His grandfather founded what is now Van Schuyler & Statten, one of the oldest and most respected banking firms on Wall Street. I knew his father, a cautious, courtly man who lived by quaint, outmoded codes of conduct that were a model of almost eighteenth-century propriety and restraint. You'll find Elliot, too, has an old-fashioned courtesy, though I think underneath he's made of rougher, more grasping stuff. See what you make of him, anyhow, my dear.'

Sylvie took a cab from Washington Square to Van Schuyler & Statten's offices. She sent up her card, then waited in the marble-floored banking hall, watching the soberly dressed men in their dark chesterfields talking together in low, solemn voices or sitting at the various tables attending to sheaves of paper. At the far end of the hall, half a dozen wide steps led up to half-glazed double doors. These now opened, and a large, athletic-looking man, only a few years older than herself, came down the stairs and, catching sight of her, immediately smiled widely and walked briskly towards her, holding out his hand.

'Miss Lazar! How d'you do? I'm Elliot Statten. Sorry to keep you waiting here. Won't you please come up to my office?'

He was self-confident and at perfect ease in his surroundings. As Sylvie walked beside him, she had time to take him in, and saw a tall, loose-limbed young man with the classic good looks of the Eastern Establishment. But, although he had the advantage of a natural charm and an admirable physique, he had a hard, dark face and a controlled, obstinate set to his mouth. As he turned to look down at her, however, there was a twinkle in his eye, and he addressed her with a warmth of tone which passed for cordiality, but hinted at familiarity.

'It's a great pleasure to see you again,' he said, pausing playfully.

She opened her eyes wide in surprise. 'I wasn't aware that we had met before,' she answered with some acerbity.

But there was no hint of discomfiture in his reply. 'No, we never met,' he said. 'But I see you today under better circumstances, just the same. The weather certainly has improved.' He laughed as he held the door open for her to pass through before him, then strode ahead of her to lead the way down a corridor lined with polished mahogany doors. 'I was lucky enough to see your opening performance in New York – one of the select few, I guess you'd say,' he laughed again over his shoulder at her.

Sylvie was both pleased and irritated; the actress was flattered to encounter a loyal theatre-goer who had been willing to see her performance in spite of the blizzard raging outside, yet she was annoyed that he should make a game at the expense of her unfortunate American début.

Statten paused now at one of the rich mahogany doors, his hand upon the wide brass handle. He seemed to smile in wry sympathy with her: 'We'll have the sun shine for you when you return to New York, I promise.'

'How reassuring, Mr Statten,' she countered ironically, rather resenting his patronizing arrogance. 'Perhaps while you're about it, you would be so kind as to arrange a few curtain calls, a standing ovation or two, and – oh, yes – perhaps a dozen dazzling reviews?'

'From what I saw last night in Brooklyn, your own performance will assure you of those,' he answered with obvious sincerity. 'I'll stick to making sure the sun shines!'

Sylvie and Statten stood smiling at each other on the threshold of his office, unclear whether they were allies or sparring gently with one another. Statten was surprised at the tough edge he had so suddenly encountered in her, and wondered what vulnerability made her so quick to mobilize at the slightest questioning of her self-sufficiency. Sylvie could not help being flattered at his constancy in twice attending her performances. He bowed and ushered her before him into the room, watching her figure appreciatively as she rustled across his carpet.

She sat in an elegant Duncan Phyfe armchair before his wide partner's desk. As she pulled off her gloves, she looked out at the bare trees in the churchyard opposite, outlined against the bleached grey sky. She was reminded of her first visit to Sir Joseph's in Threadneedle Street and felt a frisson of excitement uncurl inside her at the thought of sitting here, in Wall Street, ready to discuss her portfolio of stocks. Unthinkingly, recalling her familiar comradeship with Sir Joseph, she gave Statten a dazzling smile as he settled himself opposite.

'Sir Joseph has written to me, explaining your situation,' he explained in a serious tone, settling down to business. 'How can I be of help?'

'I've brought the details of the stocks I'm interested in. I need you to buy and sell for me while I'm on tour, though of course I'll send whatever instructions I can.' She handed him a neat bundle of papers covered in her distinctive handwriting. 'I'm gradually releasing my African diamond shares, which of course De Beers are snapping up at once, and I want you to make sure that the revenue is invested immediately in the Rand gold shares I've indicated.'

Sylvie sat quietly as the young man scanned the papers, his dark brows knit together in concentration. At length he pursed his lips and nodded his head appreciatively. 'I must congratulate you on a most shrewd campaign,' he said. He scrutinized her closely now, willing to allow her a measure of masculine respect. 'Sir Joseph wrote that I should take care not to underestimate you. Now I see that I should have heeded his warning more carefully.'

Sylvie did not know what to make of this rather grudging compliment, but Statten returned his attention to her papers. 'You are very wise to stake a claim in the deep-level mines, even though they can only be a speculative investment at the moment.' He paused fractionally before continuing. 'You may even find that your patience is rewarded more swiftly than you expect,' he added, with conscious mystery.

Sylvie was instantly on the alert. She had grown used to encouraging elder statesmen and foolish young men to divulge information that she had often turned to profitable use in Threadneedle Street. 'Why should you say that?' she asked casually, smoothing her gloves upon her knee.

Statten could not resist the urge to claim this bewitching woman's complete attention – and admiration. He had always loved the theatre, from the minstrel shows of his youth to the often bawdy vaudeville that he had visited in his college days. He enjoyed the robustness of it all, the camaraderie that had to exist between audience and players to bring off the charade successfully. And, accustomed as he was to the seamless image of womanhood supplied him by his mother and her class, there was something about actresses that had always secretly aroused him.

Intrigued by Sir Joseph's brief account of Sylvie Lazar, he had braved the blizzard to watch her performance on stage, and had indeed been struck by her beauty and the steadfast poignancy of her bravery in the midst of disaster. He had been drawn to ride out to Brooklyn to see her once more, and could not help but admire the subtlety of emotion she conveyed. Now he wanted her to notice him; he wanted to impress his personality on her, just as forcibly as her performance on stage had struck him.

'Oh,' he answered in an almost cavalier manner, watching carefully for her reaction, 'I've just bought a controlling interest in the patent on a process that may extract gold more profitably than the present way of treating the tailings with mercury,' he announced. 'I say "may" advisedly,' he went on, holding up his hand as if to prevent an outburst, although Sylvie had not moved a muscle. 'I'm waiting for some ore samples to arrive from the Rand so that we can try it out for real. It's worked in laboratory conditions, but it may not adapt commercially in the field.'

Realizing that he had said far too much to a woman he had only just met, Statten shrugged his shoulders and laughed uncomfortably. 'Still,' he added, hiding his embarrassment, 'I can tell you more about all that when you return to New York. Meanwhile, I'll take good care of all this for you. And I gave Sir Joseph my word that I would betray no inkling of your affairs to any third party. I'll attend to everything myself.'

'I'm sure I can trust to your discretion,' answered Sylvie, suppressing all hint of sarcasm. She had decided she liked Elliot Statten after all. Despite his slightly overbearing attitude, she had warmed to the impetuosity in his nature that had led him to give away the secret information he should have kept to himself. She was charmed by such an almost boyish failing in a man of such impeccable self-confidence. As he bid her goodbye amid the noise and bustle of Wall Street, she was delighted to spy a look of confusion soften his otherwise determined expression.

After two weeks in Brooklyn, Abbey introduced Sylvie to the railway car that was to be her home while she was on the road. It had a large brass bedstead, a comfortable armchair, a pretty dressing table and a smaller compartment with a desk that swivelled around and became a dining table, while a low chest contained the requisites of a small kitchen. There was also a larger drawing room that Sylvie would share with Clyde, her leading man, and any other members of the cast whom they cared to invite of an evening. Also on this miniature city were the rest of the company, Louisa, and the stagehands who would pack and unpack the scenery in each city, for Abbey had insisted on their taking their own cloths, flats, wings and props.

She said goodbye reluctantly to Abbey, promising to telegraph him in the event of any problems. Although she had settled down well with the members of the company, they knew that, in a few months, she'd be gone, so, despite their friendliness, there was no one person on whom she could rely.

'You've served your apprenticeship here,' said Abbey, his cheery manner positively exuding confidence. 'I don't want anything less than all you've got from now on.' He gave her an unexpected hug and climbed down the steep steps to the platform. 'Come back a star, mind!' he shouted to her, and waited to wave as the train finally drew out of the crowded station.

CHAPTER FOURTEEN

Rosa's natural and impulsive reaction was, of course, to shriek that it was an infamous lie, to insist that Stefan was a malicious old gossip who knew nothing of what he was talking about. But something in Will's grim expression warned her that she must be more careful than that. She looked at him imploringly, but he sat before her impassive, unmoved.

Rosa had been totally unprepared both for what Will came to tell her and for the murderous glint in his eyes as he had brushed aside her offer of tea, and, ignoring her customary bright chatter, briefly recounted Stefan Kadar's sad and shocking story.

'Herr Kadar told me that the fiction of the riding accident was your suggestion,' he stated plainly, staring coldly at her. Remembering the remorse with which the sick man had told his simple tale, Will did not attempt to hide his distaste for this spoilt, pampered woman. 'He described to me how you begged him not to complicate little Sylvie's life by telling her the truth, that her father had died in a duel. You can perhaps imagine the horror, repugnance and guilt he experienced when he finally learnt that you were living under the protection of Count Lazar's killer. The man to whom you let me introduce you at Sylvie's party at the Maybeck Gallery the other evening.' Will ended with a quiet, ironic laugh. He did not bother to ask Rosa whether or not it was all true, just waited to see what her response would be.

No one since Maria Zichy had ever directly raised the subject with Rosa of Nye's hand in Rudi's death, and she had long ceased to consider the consequences should the truth come out. Now she felt clammy and faint and found it hard to catch her breath. She put one hand to her heart and with the other took out a lace-edged handkerchief to wipe away the beads of sweat from her brow. The cosy room, the fire bright in the grate and the curtains already closed against the darkening winter afternoon, seemed to her suddenly claustrophobic, but Will's stony glare defied her to find a means of escape in any display of hysteria. Struggling to compose herself, she willed him to ask her questions, to give her some lead as to how she could proceed, some clue as to what he wanted to hear from her. But he remained silent and unyielding, just watching her. His very handsomeness made her feel old and tired: her normal reaction would have been to flirt, charm, seduce, but this was her daughter's champion, and she felt, with a grievous blow, that life had put her to one side. The world seemed suddenly a frailer place than she was used to.

She licked her lips nervously. She wondered whether, if she threw herself on his mercy, confessed and wept and begged for his forgiveness, he would protect her from the unpleasant train of events that must surely follow the disclosure that she had knowingly taken the killer of her daughter's father as her lover. But she sensed the force of his will oppose her. The thought crossed her mind that she could say that she had never known the identity of Rudi's assailant, that, on that point at least, Stefan must have misunderstood. But, greedy as ever, she realized that she would then have convincingly to repudiate Nye now, in the present, and to pretend to be sickened at his evil duplicity. But Nye had already called on her twice since Sylvie's departure, and Rosa, like the monkey who would remain trapped by the paw between narrow bars rather than drop the ripe fruit that prevents his fist from escaping, could not bring herself to deny the possibility of pursuing an erotic future with him.

Will sat immobile, watching her, wondering with distaste what devious web she was weaving. He knew that his silence was unbearable to her, and was determined not to ease her way.

Then, suddenly, it came to her, and without further reflection she lurched into the explanation that would exonerate them all. 'Can I trust you, I wonder?' she asked, looking at Will now appraisingly, turning the tables presumptuously.

Will's reply was an indignant laugh. 'If you know the meaning of the word!'

'Yes,' said Rosa, as if to herself, ignoring his rebuke, 'I'm sure I can. After all, I know you have Sylvie's best interests at heart – as, God knows, I do myself.' She paused significantly. 'No one understands the loneliness I have suffered. No one knows the countless times I have wanted to tell Sylvie the truth, to unburden myself. But the moment never came. And how can you abuse a small child in such a way?' Rosa gave a heavy sigh.

Will stirred in his seat with disgust. 'Surely you're not going to elicit my sympathy for having made love to the killer of Sylvie's father?'

Rosa shook her head in sorrow before going on. 'Children are so quick to seize on an idea, and so romantic, so unable to believe that their heroes may have feet of clay. You see, Sylvie got it into her head that Rudi was this marvellous, noble character, her champion, her prince. And it seemed far too cruel to force her out of such a belief so soon after his death.' She sighed once more. 'Of course, I know it's entirely my fault for ever letting her believe that Rudi was her father.' Rosa paused sublimely for effect, glancing up out of the corner of her eye to see the young man's reaction as she sat in a chastened pose.

Will gasped and shot to his feet. 'What! Then who . . . ? Tell me, damn you! What are you talking about?'

'Rudi Lazar was not Sylvie's father,' stated Rosa with magnificent simplicity.

'Then who . . . ?'

'Why, Jack Nye, of course!' Rosa's eyes were large and innocent, as if she were astonished that the truth was not self-evident. Then she shuddered and sank back into her comfortable chair, clasping her arms about herself. 'Oh, you are not the first to believe unutterable evil about me! I knew, of course, what my former friends were saying about me in Budapest. Friends!' She snorted in contempt at the word. 'But the only alternative was to shatter little Sylvie's dream. I felt I had to protect my baby. I was wrong, I realize that now. But Jack and I decided that we'd forgo the company of people who could conceive of such wickedness, and leave our little daughter's illusions intact. You see, she loved Rudi. God knows why, the man was little better than a drunken brawler, despite his high and mighty title. And then, when we left for Africa, we believed we could leave our past and our confusions behind us. All that mattered was that we were together. A family at last!' Rosa almost crowed with delight, the story was going far, far better than she could have hoped!

Will was stunned and utterly confused. Somewhere at the back of his mind was the memory of the overtly sexual looks that Nye had given Sylvie that day in his studio. Surely no father . . . ? But then, perhaps the truth accounted for the vast price Nye had paid for *The Angel*, and his constant pestering about wanting to buy Will's latest portrait of Sylvie? The unacknowledged father, wanting a portrait of his daughter: what in the world could be more natural?

Although Will felt instinctively that Rosa was lying

through her teeth, it all seemed so incredible that he was just tempted to believe that it was the truth. Rosa could not seriously expect to get away with such a blatant fabrication? More to the point, surely not even she could stoop to such a conscious, wily, duplicitous manipulation of her own daughter's well-being . . . surely no mother could risk her child's very sanity in such a way? For what? Will was frightened for Sylvie, yet felt temporarily compelled to accept Rosa's fantastic assertion as the truth, for the simple reason that the alternative – that she was so brazen a liar – was even harder to swallow. In his momentary confusion, he had a flash of insight into Sylvie's reluctance to voice her own thoughts – a reluctance that had hitherto seemed so strange and almost wilful. Now his heart flew out to her: whatever the truth, how she must have suffered at this woman's hands!

He struggled to put things straight in his mind, clear, as always, that the best way to the truth lay in a direct examination of the facts. If Sylvie's future was at stake, he would leave no stone unturned, no matter what ugly creatures he might uncover. He cursed himself for not having forced his way past Sylvie's reserve before now, for not having perceived more of her mother's reign of terror, even though he recognized that Sylvie would never have come to trust anyone who had tried such an assault upon her private self. And Sylvie did trust him, he was sure of that.

'If Mr Nye is Sylvie's father, where did Rudi fit in?' he asked at last.

'Simple. Jack went away before he was aware that I had conceived a child. I didn't know where he was. But I needed protection for my unborn baby. Rudi Lazar offered his services. But I paid the price!' she ended somberly.

Will nodded. 'And the duel?'

'When Nye returned from America, now a wealthy

man, we met once more, and I told him that Sylvie was his. Naturally he went to Rudi and said that I and the child belonged with him. Rudi threatened him, and apparently abused me – dear Jack would never tell me what Rudi said – and they fought a duel. Rudi was always a coward, and was probably drunk, too, and missed his shot. Nye stayed away until he felt that he could safely return, and the rest you know.' Rosa was exultant. She had succeeded! She'd brought it off! It was perfect – just perfect!

Will nodded once more, as if in understanding, and sat silently in thought. Then he frowned to himself. 'Where did you meet Nye?' he questioned.

'Oh, he brought me to Budapest from America. We're both Americans, you know.' Rosa was so confident that she had totally convinced Will of her story that she no longer had any anxiety over lying about details that he was unlikely to be able to check. She didn't want to complicate matters now by being too scrupulous about such inconvenient details as her early, impetuous marriage.

'And why didn't he accompany you to London?'

'Ah, Will,' Rosa sighed, and shook her head. 'You're young. You don't yet know of the terrible misunderstandings that can arise even between people who have shared a love as great as Jack and mine for one another. We had such an argument, and I left. I was headstrong, and very hurt by something that someone told me. It was only after I had settled in London that I learnt that my so-called friend had lied, was jealous of me and had lied. I wrote to Jack, imploring him to forgive me, but the letters never reached him. You can imagine my joy at seeing him here again in London!'

'And – excuse me, but I must fully understand all this – why did he never marry you?'

'Alas, he was married already.' Rosa shrugged. 'A

youthful indiscretion. They parted after only a month, and there were no children. But no divorce, either.'

Will didn't like the way in which Rosa was answering his questions so casually, all trace of her vaunted anxiety and concern for Sylvie gone. She had not lied to protect Sylvie: she was lying now to protect herself! Of that he was now completely convinced. But how could he ever prove it? Stefan Kadar, a dying man, had already sailed for Europe. And he knew just how susceptible Sylvie was to Rosa's insistent and forceful bullying. If it came to it, a stand-up row between himself and Rosa over such terrible allegations could only cause Sylvie irreparable harm if she were to witness it. And if, as he supposed she must, she sided with her mother, he would lose all opportunity of helping her.

'Yes,' went on Rosa, almost oblivious of him now, lost in reverie in the scenario she had so skilfully conjured up. 'You can imagine my joy at being reunited with Sylvie's true father. With the only man who ever meant anything to me.'

Will looked at the flush that had risen on her cheeks and at her unnaturally bright eyes, and was sickened by the sight of her. After hearing Stefan's tale, he had waited a week or so, thinking it all over, considering what he should do, before he decided to call on her. He had almost persuaded himself that Stefan's story, somehow, God knows how, must have been wrong. He had almost concluded that even Rosa's selfish lust and greed could not have driven her to such depraved actions. He had prayed, for Sylvie's sake, that Rosa would straighten the story out and make it possible for him to forget the Hungarian's visit entirely. But these audacious lies were evidence of an even more degenerate corruption that terrified him. Who could believe that this elegant, hospitable woman, reclining like a Turkish concubine among the soft pillows of her chair, could have visited such miserable confusion and turmoil upon her defenceless child? And was prepared to do worse violence – for what? The promise of a reunion with Nye? Will wanted to wring her neck.

But he forced himself to calmness. All that mattered now was Sylvie. 'Will you tell Sylvie the truth?' he asked, wanting to test out Rosa's future intentions. The excited attention she had paid Nye at Sylvie's farewell dinner prompted Will to fear that she planned to use this new deceit in some way to further her obvious desire for him.

But Rosa sighed heavily once more and shook her head. 'Sylvie can be very obstinate when she chooses. You must know that. As I explained before, she has this childish notion that Rudi was some kind of sainted hero. And, try as we did to dislodge it without cruelly shattering her pathetic illusions, Jack and I could never bring ourselves to make her replace him in her affections, with the result that, tragically, she never loved her real father as she should. She is such an unstable girl. I don't have to tell you that. She simply hasn't the wisdom or understanding to accept the truth,' ended Rosa, feigning a poignant disappointment.

Will wanted to take hold of this whore and shake her until she was limp and dead between his hands! His face was white and grim, but Rosa was too lost in her own extraordinary fantasy-world to notice. Will restrained himself with the thought that at least he had the answer he wanted: Sylvie was to be left alone. And he very much doubted that Rosa would be able to entangle Nye any further in her lies: Nye had already made it plain, both to Will and to Saunders at the Maybeck Gallery, that it was Sylvie – or certainly Will's painted images of her – that obsessed him now, not some ageing lover from his past. In any case, as Will also knew from Saunders, Nye planned to leave England at the end of the week, putting him temporarily at least beyond Rosa's grasp. Will blessed the fact that Sylvie's absence gave him respite to work out the best way of dealing with the situation. He needed time to decide how and when to tell Sylvie the truth about her father's death, about Nye. Sylvie must judge her mother's actions for herself, but, knowing of Nye's interest in his portrait of Sylvie, Will felt determined to protect her from her father's murderer.

Will stood to take his leave. 'Thank you for telling me your story,' he said in as dull and non-committal a tone as he could muster, looking at the carpet at Rosa's feet, unable to trust the expression she might find in his eyes. He judged it safest to leave her with a sense of victory. That way, she was unlikely to take any further action that would upset the fragile balance she now believed she had achieved. Then, at least, he knew where he stood and could choose his moment to reveal the truth to Sylvie.

'Oh,' breathed Rosa, rising also and clasping her hands before her. 'You cannot imagine the relief at sharing this burden with someone after all these years! Thank *you*!'

She held out her hands to him, but Will ignored the gesture. He felt the bile rise in his throat, and swallowing hastily, he collected his hat and gloves from the hall and escaped from Rosa's warm, comfortable house into the cold foggy air outside as swiftly as he could.

CHAPTER FIFTEEN

Sylvie soon came to love the thin, empty beauty of the American landscape, and the Americans came to love her – she won them to her, begged them and implored them in a variety of guises from the stages of Philadelphia, Baltimore, Washington, Cincinnati and St Louis to make sense of her life, to give meaning to this endless succession of less than clean dressing rooms, hot hotel rooms and the odd, rackety gypsy caravan of a railway car that was her home for nearly three months.

She would remember all her life the anticipation of drawing into a new town or city and peering out of the carriage windows to gain some impression of the character of each new place. In Minneapolis they arrived in the streaming rain. As the stage hands laboured to load the flats and props baskets onto the back of a waiting waggon, Sylvie was greeted on the station platform by a deputation of local ladies, the feathers in their hats sadly wilted by the dampness, who begged to take her, not to her hotel, but to one of their homes. Sylvie loved their infectious enthusiasm, and generally gladly accepted such invitations, although she learnt that she often had to endure speeches and even poems written in her honour. These same ladies would reappear later at the door of her dressing room, their husbands in tow and their eyes shining with excitement after the intoxicating glory of her performance. The menfolk were introduced with an almost proprietary air: 'This is Miss Lazar, who came to our house for tea this very afternoon, Clarence dear. Wasn't she just divine? Why, I declare she spoke each line as if she'd just invented it!'

Their humble awe and homage gave Sylvie unfathomable faith in herself: if these women had heard of *The Angel* at all, it was only as a snippet in a newspaper article. She knew that they were responding initially to the wave of interest that swept before her as local journals reported on her remarkable stage performances, but that their reaction to her presence, to her alone, was entirely genuine. They loved Sylvie Lazar! And she loved them in return. It gave her great joy to visit their houses, to sip tea out of their best china, to taste the special delicacies they had prepared for her. She felt, obscurely, as though she were coming to meet herself, allowing her spirit to rejoin the animal vitality and health she had experienced as a child.

And now, on stage, her magic was complete: not only could she become more fully herself, drawing on experiences and emotions that she hid from her daily self, but she was more intimately involved with her audience than ever before. She looked to them not just for flattery, applause and confirmation that she had done well, but for love, companionship, humour and emotional reassurance. Whether or not a deputation of ladies met her at the station, the audiences became her friends, sitting there expectantly, night after night, waiting for her. And they, sensing that she needed them and honoured them, gave in full measure. The Sylvie Lazar legend was born from a railway car.

The private car was in fact Sylvie's saving, although by the end of the trip she was glad to escape its caging influence. From it, too, she had seen America, and had been surprised to feel a spirit rise inside herself that she had not before been able to name. For the first time in her life she became intensely curious about her family. She lingered over the word. She realized that, in this strangely uncomplex land, she had family – she knew she had an uncle, possibly grandparents, and maybe also cousins and second-cousins – people whom she might resemble in looks or temperament, people who could explain her mother to her. Sylvie had little idea how such relatives would view a sudden meeting with Rosa's child – if, indeed, her mother was still remembered in Saratoga Springs – but she began seriously to entertain the notion of visiting her mother's people. Meanwhile, the very fact that she might claim kinship with someone somewhere in this vast land made her all the more determined to make America accept her. Henry Abbey was right, she was an American, and they should know of her existence.

As she sat in the darkness on the platform of her railway car en route to New York, she pulled her sealskin cloak closer round her. The air was cool but a feeling of spring was in the night air. This last winter had been hard but, if her performances in New York were received with the same rapturous applause as had so recently rewarded her in Boston, her life would be changed for ever. She thought of the terrifying blizzards and awesome miles of clear, bright snow, hardly broken even by animal tracks, let alone any sign of man, that she had seen from the train. So much beauty, when there was no one with whom to share it, made her intensely lonely: it made her long for the familiar rattle and congestion of the London fog. She thought of Will, and what he might be doing, of her friends at the Lyceum, and, with apprehension, of Rosa.

She consoled herself with the thought that she would soon be seeing Henry Abbey again. She was thrilled at the idea of her triumphant return to New York – and whatever lay beyond. She was intensely grateful to Abbey for his virtually flawless arrangements, his honesty and, above all, that he had, by backing his hunch about her ability, allowed her to discover her true self. She had repaid his faith, and she knew, too, that when they met again, he would see a difference in her. She was grown up at last; she had found a core of identity hiding within the self that embraced the theatre like the child who creeps into the warmth of its mother's cast-off cloak. She still felt at home, at peace, in the theatre – any theatre – but now she also felt a real sense of her own tremendous power. And that discovery excited her.

Sure enough, Abbey met her at the station to take her to the hotel, where a private dining room was laid for breakfast, the table surrounded by flowers and, in one corner, a basket full of letters and small packages. 'They're all from your admirers,' explained Abbey, his dark eyes smiling as he fingered his moustache elegantly. 'You're famous! Just as I said you'd be!' He held Sylvie's chair and handed her a table-napkin, but remained standing himself, too full of his success to sit down.

'Let me read you some of the reviews,' he exclaimed. 'Listen! "Miss Lazar was delightful . . . Her natural vivacity and eloquence won the sympathies of the audience at the very outset; she makes us thrill to the contemporary pulse" – that was the *Philadelphia Inquirer*.' He cast the newspaper cutting onto the table before her. ' " . . . poetic, delicate and true . . . Her performance was a revelation; Sylvie Lazar has shown us our souls for the very first time" – the *Chicago Record*.' Another cutting fluttered down onto the table like huge confetti. ' "Sylvie Lazar stole the hearts out of our breasts. A more joyous, graceful and wholly charming figure has not in a long time entered upon our boards . . . " – the *Baltimore Evening Call*. "Her beauty was more than a refreshment, it was a luxury . . . " – the London *Times* no less. I'm hoping that some of the Parisian newspapers will send their stringers to see you here in New York. You're an international phenomenon! And that torchlit procession through Harvard Yard the other night – wonderful copy!' Abbey finally sat down, breathing heavily and leaning back in his chair from where he regarded her with enormous satisfaction.

Sylvie smiled with delight. She felt too overcome to eat, but to hide her embarrassment at his effusive praise, she took an orange from the silver basket in the centre of the table and began to peel it into segments.

'Tonight's house is sold out,' Abbey went on, 'and we've auctioned the tickets for ten – twenty – times the usual prices. I heard the way people were talking at the box office. Sure there were comparisons with other actresses, but there was something different too. I heard 'em talking about "our Sylvie", "our angel". They've most of 'em never seen that picture, but the story seems to have touched a chord just the same. Their angel.' He paused thoughtfully, then began again on a slightly different track. 'They've been impressed by the European imports, maybe a little intimidated, but now they want one of their own. After tonight, you may just wake up to find yourself the American actress they're waiting for. Didn't I tell you I'd make you wealthy? Believe me, Sylvie, you could do a minstrel act and still get rave reviews.'

As she looked up, Sylvie could barely make out Abbey's dark features against the morning sunlight streaming in through the window behind him. She was too choked by pride and gratitude to speak. But he did not appear to be looking for any reply from her, as he continued enthusiastically.

'The photographers are falling over themselves for the honour of taking your likeness – so they can sell it, postcard size, all over the country! I've also got a few products lined up for you to sponsor. It's entirely up to you, of course, but a shampoo company, a shoe manufacturer and, of all the darndest things, a piano store, are all queueing up to pay handsomely for your endorsement. Do you play the piano, by the way?' he asked innocently. As he leant forward to help himself to coffee, he smiled at her and gave her a broad and friendly wink.

'And I've got a little reception ready for you that'll make the stunt those Ivy League men pulled in Harvard look like chickenfeed! Don't worry,' he continued, 'I'll keep the press away from you for today, but tomorrow you must be ready to be magnificent!'

Sylvie laughed, but Abbey seemed serious enough. 'Well, if you keep refusin' to sweep extravagantly into hotels with a retinue of servants and admirers, or to publicly spend a fortune on furs and jewels, what else am I to do?' he asked in mock exasperation.

'I've better things to do with my money!' laughed Sylvie. Abbey looked at her in surprise, and she met his gaze coolly. 'In fact I've rather lost touch with things on tour, and I'd like to catch up on the stock market,' she explained, as though it were the most natural thing in the world. 'If you've really no other plans for me this afternoon, I may just take a stroll down to Wall Street.'

Abbey agreed heartily with Clyde, who remarked, after Sylvie had taken her leave, that she was, indeed, quite a card.

As Sylvie awaited Elliot Statten once more, in the marble hall of Van Schuyler & Statten, she felt an unfamiliar lightness and zest. It was as though success had at last enabled her to lift her eyes from the stage and look around her; triumphant after Boston and confident of her return to New York, she was ready for something more. She felt ready to burst through into some fresh phase of her life, to grasp hold of some new thread that would lead her on into – she had no idea quite what, but that was what made it so exciting! She remembered how Elliot Statten had flirted with her before, how he had – in, she instinctively felt, a quite uncharacteristic way – recklessly made a bid for her attention by telling her about the formula for extracting gold, and she speculated idly on whether he would flirt with her again today. She was also impatient to find out whether the experiments with the southern African ore had in fact proved a success. As she stood waiting, facing the double doors at the top of the low flight of steps, a smile upon her face, she unconsciously tapped her foot and swayed slightly to an imaginary melody. He came upon her unexpectedly from another direction, with a broad grin of welcome as he witnessed her gaiety and answered it with his own.

'Why, hello again!'

'Oh,' she said, surprised into a slight blush. 'Hello!'

Immediately, he leant in towards her, as if to whisper in her ear. 'I hope you've noticed,' he said, conspiratorially.

'What?' she asked, startled.

'The sun is shining!'

She laughed. 'You're too ridiculous!'

'But the rest will be true,' he answered seriously. 'The reviews, the ovations, the curtain calls. I read all about the ecstatic reception they gave you in Boston – and the Boston Brahmin are not easily moved, you know. We New Yorkers simply can't wait to take you to our hearts.'

She blushed again, and instantly felt half annoyed at herself for her susceptibility to his flattery, but also so brimming with her new-found confidence that she entertained a wicked urge to encourage him further. Normally, Sylvie accepted the compliments and often audacious flattery that inevitably came her way with courtesy, but conveyed the firm intention not to encourage it. She tended to be embarrassed, not by the admiration expressed, but by not knowing what to do with such unwanted gifts. She didn't really know where flirtation was supposed to lead, and had seldom wished to find out. On the few occasions when she had experienced a flicker of erotic interest, she'd been nervous and fearful; she didn't know how to be playful, but sensed that a serious manner was out of place. Now she felt that she didn't care. She deserved a reward for all her hard work, and here was this self-assured, serious young man obviously determined to flirt with her.

'Then you'd better take me to your office, hadn't you, Mr Statten!' she replied spiritedly, raising her chin and looking him straight in the eye. He was immediately discomfited, not knowing in the least whether to take her invitation seriously. After all, actresses had the worst reputations in the world. Yet he could not for an instant believe that Miss Lazar could mean *that*! And if she did . . . Statten swallowed hard and decided that it was *definitely* out of the question to take her seriously. With her perfect sense of timing, Sylvie waited just long enough to acknowledge his speechlessness before releasing him from her ambiguous gaze.

Silently he led the way across the banking hall, acutely aware of the dozens of pairs of eyes upon them, up the steps and along the corridor to his office. Once inside, the sight of his father's old Federal-style desk and the pale walls hung with marine paintings by American artists of twenty or thirty years ago, returned him to his senses. He seated himself in the worn leather chair that had also been his father's and immediately immersed himself in a sheaf of papers, already prepared, on the desk in front of him.

'Now, Miss Lazar,' he began, clearing his throat. 'We've followed your instructions and I have here the present state of your accounts.'

He handed her the topmost sheet of paper, but was disconcerted by the impudent smile with which she met his gaze, before she laid the paper before her on her side of the desk in order to take a neat Morocco-bound notebook out of her bag. One by one, as he handed them to her, she scanned the reports, press clippings and prospectuses that he had mustered, sent by the various mining companies on the Rand who were hoping to attract new shareholders by their gaudily printed advertisements. He tried to hide his astonishment at the knowledgeable way in which she flicked through the pages, comparing figures and occasionally writing in her notebook. When she had read through the entire pile, she began again, tapping her pencil on the desk thoughtfully as she read.

Statten took the opportunity to survey her openly, since her attention was now completely claimed by her financial affairs. She wore a loose coat of deep turquoise-blue velvet that fell in hundreds of miraculous soft pleats at her feet. Her beautiful hair was swept up and secured by large combs of what looked to be carved horn, tinted green and set with moonstones and enamel the colour of blue wisteria. Her white neck, curved into an arch that he desired to kiss as she bent her head to read, was partly hidden by a transparent, silvery scarf. She had a calm that was both inspiring and vulnerable, and he longed to be able to keep her by him, always.

It was months since Statten had embarked on a flirtation, and he felt the need of a little pleasure. And Sylvie Lazar was, by anyone's standards, a bewitching subject for a romance. Adored by his mother and younger sister, he had grown up enjoying the company of women and, since his interest in the girls of his acquaintance was nearly always met with blushing delight, he had found no reason to be anything other than at his most charming in their company. He liked the little attentions that gentlemen are supposed to show to women, and took an easy interest in the unimportant details of their lives – the colour of their gloves, the design of their embroidery or the latest novel to be devoured. He felt kind and good and strong when he was among them, and understood why it was that they, in turn, liked him. So far, Elliot Statten had never been in love.

Only a few days before, he had accompanied his mother and the friends with whom she was staying to one of Sylvie's performances in Boston. As the lights had begun to dim and a rustling sigh went up from the audience, Elliot had sat back in the gloom of their box and prepared to open his senses. He adored the magnetism that Sylvie radiated on stage, but now she was real to him, was made of flesh and blood, not the paint and plasterboard of the theatre, and he could almost smell the lingering scent of violets that had clung to her at their first meeting.

He had been transfixed by the candour of Sylvie's performance. Here was no mercenary, brazen girl, but a vibrant, sensitive woman, alive to a man's real needs and emotions. Elliot had felt as though her words on stage had stripped him bare, felt that here was a woman before whom he could stand naked and not be ashamed.

As the play had reached its climax and come to an end, the curtain had swooped down upon Sylvie standing alone on stage, and as quickly risen again with a plashing rush. Suddenly the grave heroine stood before them as a laughing, beautiful woman, her eyes shining at the tumultuous applause that rose against her like a physical force. Her fellow actors had handed her forward, given her to the crowd who demanded her, and she kissed her hands, looking upwards, as roses showered onto the stage around her. Each time the curtain fell, the audience had shouted for her, only to redouble their clamour when Sylvie's still figure appeared once more. The house lights came on, and the heat in the crowded theatre had been almost unbearable, but still the audience had made no move to go, clapping and shouting as though unable to stop. Elliot had stood at the back of the box, clapping his hands together slowly, as if in a dream, and watching as Sylvie acknowledged the passion of the audience and accepted their praise. Her expression was gentle and loving as she stood like a child before these noisy strangers. Understanding their arousal, he felt jealous and helpless. He realized that it was her right and her destiny to belong to these people, but he wanted her to belong to him, and he had longed, foolishly, for her to look up to where he stood and to smile, privately, to him alone.

Sylvie looked up at him now from her papers in a frank manner that he found ravishing. He was not used to such directness, and he was enjoying the novel feelings she evoked in him. He felt suddenly as if they were somehow communing under water, as though real life and its niceties, his father's familiar room and his responsibilities to the family bank, were just rippling, distorted images far above them, and that they swam together in the grip of some deep, exciting current far below.

But Sylvie's frankness was reserved for the state of her investments. 'This Paardekraal syndicate,' she began directly, 'is the stock closely held?'

'It doesn't seem so, no,' Statten answered stumblingly, somewhat taken aback to be dispelled so abruptly from his reverie. 'There are five mining companies which own mineral and other rights to land lying a few miles to the west of the central Johannesburg reef on a farm called Paardekraal, which covers nearly three miles along the main reef series – that's about ten per cent of the total width of the present outcrop reef.'

'That's a fair slice,' agreed Sylvie. 'But what about the land lying to the south? Does anyone own a controlling interest in that?'

'Impossible to say. I have a hunch someone is operating a system of holding companies when it comes to buying shares in companies such as Aurora Deep, South National and Angle Tharsis – you'll see their positions on the map you have there: it's a little crude, but you can see that those companies own rights to land well to the south of the outcrop reef.'

'And they've just offered a new share issue?'

'Last week,' agreed Statten. 'Knowing that you already held shares in Main Reef before it joined this new syndicate, I guessed you'd be interested in the others. But the stock is moving pretty fast, despite the fact that investors are unlikely to see a return on their money for quite some while.'

'Yes, I suppose the majority of the capital raised by the share issue will go on equipment and development costs. Sinking shafts, stamp mills, winding and pumping engines, boilers, mercury amalgamation plants and labour costs will soon take care of a few hundred thousand dollars.'

'Exactly,' commented Statten drily, unused to hearing such nuts and bolts detail from a woman, especially from one who delivered it in such an expressive, musical voice. If he had not been warned in advance by Sir Joseph Waldschein what to expect, he would have felt inclined to pinch himself awake from this bizarre dream.

Sylvie, however, ignored him, as she rifled through the sheaf of papers she held, scanning the pages once more. She was not only checking on her own investments, and looking to spot some likely new ones, but also tracking Nye's financial movements, for his name appeared on the directors' lists of several companies, and it was obvious that his holdings on the Rand were now considerable: Nye was what the London stock market was learning to call a Randlord.

Sylvie didn't know why she now chose to stalk Nye in this way since he had re-entered her life. She had told herself that she had bought her first small stake in the Simmer & Jack Mine, on which his name appeared as a director, merely because it looked a sound investment – which indeed it was. But now, after seeing him again in London and learning that he already possessed *The Angel*, and as she saw his interests spreading across the Rand like a stain, it became a kind of challenge to her to match him, like a game of chess. Whatever he bought, she intended to buy too.

Now, however, she discerned the pattern to Nye's share-dealings that she had feared to find. He was buying just enough of each of the major Rand mine-fields either to hold an outright majority share of the stock or to have a controlling interest as the owner of the largest single block of shares. Could he be trying to corner these gold-fields, just as Cecil Rhodes now held a monopoly on the diamond fields? The reason why was obvious. The true extent of this strike had yet to be established, but Sylvie saw that there was every reason to suppose that the Rand could eventually seriously challenge every other world supplier of gold. At the moment, confidence in Rand shares was wavering as it became clear that the gold-bearing ore was uneconomic to mine, and that the deep-level mines depended on the lucky break of hitting upon the right formula for extracting the gold from the pyritic rock. If Nye could establish a monopoly before too many others saw the vast potential of the Rand, and then wait patiently for the right formula . . . his wealth and power would be infinite.

Realizing this, Sylvie's attitude to her own investments subtly altered. It was no longer a matter of skill, like mastering a spirited horse, but a battle in deadly earnest. Financially, of course, she could only muster a pawn to his queen and could not hope to rival him, but it gave her a feeling of satisfaction to shadow him in this way, using her own money, impersonally and unseen, a means of staking her own claim, of asserting her identity and independence next to his. It was no use trying to understand her own motives too closely. Every actress knows that there are some aspects of human behaviour that can never be explained and are best not examined lest the spark of life flies out of them. But, stubbornly, she explained to herself that the Rand was a new field, and she had as much right to be there as he did: she refused to be pushed out of the way by his power.

Alone in her railway carriage over the past couple of months, Sylvie had questioned her passion for the stock market. She had realized that there was more to the secrecy of her dealings than Sir Joseph's gallant intention to spare her modesty: it was the very anonymity of financial power that had attracted her, for money was a faceless weapon, apparently without malice or jealousy. It was only now that she had achieved power of another sort, to win and hold an audience, that she recognized the urgency of her need for autonomy. For too long she had pushed and squeezed herself into other people's images of her, so that she could be bullied or directed or framed and hung on a wall for them to control, or even buy and sell.

She had been astounded when she first recognized her desire for power for what it was; being defenceless, she had never thought that she sought to control events around her. But she recognized the same sense of flying freedom when absorbed in figures and the names of companies and endless pieces of paper, as she did on stage. And now, in Statten's elegant Wall Street office, far from Nye or her mother, she was enjoying a heady sense of autonomy that she regretfully acknowledged had earlier been impossible elsewhere: the emotional risks had simply been too great.

'Tell me more about your hunch,' she asked at last. 'Why do you think someone's operating under the cover of a holding company?'

'Not one, but several holding companies,' Elliot stated firmly. 'And the reason is obvious. Whoever it is doesn't want everyone following him into the market. Investors are like sheep. If they get the idea that someone else has found some lush grass on one side of the meadow, they all follow him. And if this someone is big and important – as he must be to have the kind of capital he's been outlaying – the sheep would follow him off the side of a cliff!'

'And you think he's buying into this Paardekraal syndicate?'

'Trying to,' answered Statten a trifle smugly. 'But I think we beat him to it this time!'

Sylvie looked at him enquiringly; a look of interest and curiosity that he enjoyed being able to satisfy.

'Van Schuyler & Statten took a short option on most of this new issue for the deep-level companies. You can have as much of it as you want.' He shrugged casually as if to dismiss his own cleverness, but was delighted when she looked at him gravely with those large, clear grey eyes of hers.

'Thank you!' she said gratefully. 'I was well advised to come here!'

As she smiled at him, he felt an impulsive wave rise inside him, just as it had done that last time she had sat opposite him in this office. Throwing caution to the winds, he didn't even try to fight it. 'There's more!' he announced with pride.

Sylvie sat silently, her hands folded expectantly in her lap, waiting to be told. Statten rose and came around his desk to where she sat. She felt a tingle of awareness of how close he stood to her as he bent over and pointed to the map that still lay on top of her pile of papers. She looked up into his face: the short hair that fell forward over his forehead was very dark, but his skin was smooth and close-shaven and she caught a faint, attractive scent of soap or pomade.

'Look here!' he said, pointing at the map on her lap. His hand was strong and sprinkled with vigorous dark hairs. 'Right in the middle of the deep-level companies here, but not belonging to the Paardekraal syndicate, is this one, Edinburgh. I've looked into it, and the majority of its shares were held in reserve at the time of issue last autumn and the company has remained inactive since. I've traced the owner. Seems he won it as a gambling debt and had no idea what to do with it. But he's prepared to sell – for the right price.'

Sylvie shivered with excitement. Thanks to Abbey's astute handling of her affairs, she would soon have much more money to invest. And he had already offered her another, even more lucrative contract, for a short European tour and a second exhaustive American trip next year. If she could gain a controlling interest in this Paardekraal syndicate, just to the west of the main Johannesburg reef . . . Well, it would not exactly put a stop to Nye's ambitions – for she had no doubt that he was the 'someone big' behind Statten's hunch – but it would be a definite thorn in his side.

Elliot Statten, still standing close beside her, felt the slight tremble of excitement and anticipation that went through her. He felt himself go hard, and moved slightly to hide himself behind her chair. He fought the uncontrollable urge to bury his face in her silky hair, to grasp her in his arms and kiss the breath out of her.

Sylvie remembered his reckless indiscretion of her last visit: the disclosure of the patent that might unlock the gold from the pyritic rock in the deep level mines. Whoever owned the rights to that formula could hold the entire Rand to ransom – Nye or no Nye. Excitedly, she swivelled around on her chair to look up into Statten's face, her lips open as she began to ask him about the patent, but he silenced her by crushing his mouth on hers.

CHAPTER SIXTEEN

Out of season, the main street in Saratoga Springs presented a similar face to Sylvie to the other Eastern seaboard villages that she had passed by on the train. But the porches and facades of the white-painted hotels set back across wide grass verges planted with budding elm and maple trees were larger and more imposing, and the windows of the houses seemed used to looking outward rather than in, ready to be amused by the spectacle of the summer tourists promenading past.

Abbey had booked Sylvie, accompanied by her dresser, Louisa, into the Grand Union Hotel, and the hotel fly had picked them up from the Hudson steamer the previous evening. The black driver had pointed out the sights as he was always accustomed to do: 'That there's the road out to the lake, goes right past the racecourse and the parks where you'n taste the waters. 'Celsior, that's the best'n, though Geyser's kinda pretty, too. But you won't like the waters, no ma'am, not at first.' He paused to give a high-pitched laugh. 'You'll come over all giddy as they fizzes up insida you, yes you will! But then, after a while, you'll feel real calm and ready fo' your dinner!' And he laughed good-naturedly once more.

Sylvie had told no one other than Abbey where she was going, nor why, and Louisa merely thought that they had come to this out-of-season resort for reasons of privacy, for a short break before taking the boat home to England. With Elliot in particular, who was so firmly rooted in his own background and who seemed to derive such a powerful and enabling sense of identity and place from being the principal representative of the Fifth Avenue Stattens, Sylvie had felt strangely reticent on the subject. It seemed disreputable, shameful even, not to know anything about your family further back than your parents, and she had already detected a hint of tension lurking in the background of her new relationship between Elliot and his mother. Abbey had told her, with an amused twinkle in his eye, that Mrs Dorothea Statten was regarded by many as *the* social arbiter of 'old' New York, and Sylvie suspected that she most certainly did not approve of her son being seen at dinner at Sherry's or walking in the Park with someone so socially disreputable as an actress. It had been simply impossible to explain to Elliot her predicament – or even her parentage – despite his urgent pleas to accompany her wherever she was going, and his ill-concealed jealousy when she refused to tell him.

Nor did Sylvie really know how she was going to set about discovering Rosa's family. The usual ways, such as asking at the local newspaper office, were too public – Abbey had warned her that anything that Sylvie Lazar did would be instant news – and she could not bear to descend upon her family with a train of reporters in her wake.

Her success in New York had been, as Abbey had always predicted, legendary. Broadway had been thronged with carriages, and the crowds who waited for a glimpse of her as she arrived or left the theatre had spilled off the sidewalks. Her rooms at the theatre and the hotel had been filled to capacity with flowers, and, despite Mrs Statten's opposition, she had received invitations from several of New York's younger and more fashionable hostesses to house parties in Newport and Southampton. As Abbey remarked drily: 'There's enough folks claiming to have braved the blizzard for your opening night to have filled half a dozen theatres!'

The manager of the Grand Union Hotel greeted her

personally on her arrival and showed her up to the best suite on the first floor overlooking the front, and she realized that if any family reunion were to take place, it would be held under a hateful glare of publicity if she involved anyone who knew who she was. She wanted to keep her secret to herself until she discovered whether she did in fact have family in Saratoga, and, more importantly, whether they would acknowledge her kinship.

In the morning, Sylvie was glad to let Louisa go off to try the efficacy of the fabled spa waters, while she walked slowly by herself up Broadway. She had dressed in her least striking outfit, a plain grey skirt and coat, and had tucked most of her abundant hair under a small but fetching hat. She did not expect to be recognized, but she hoped to be able to get the feel of the place without attracting attention of any kind. Abbey had suggested, in a practical if disillusioning way, that she should begin by looking in the burial ground. That way, at least, she might discover if her grandparents still lived.

She was on her way there now, but she did not even know their Christian names, and could only guess at their ages. She was sure that Rosa had a brother, Edmund, and it was on finding him that Sylvie pinned her real hopes: maybe he had children – her cousins! She had never mentioned to Rosa her plan to visit Saratoga, and her mother had always spoken so sparingly of her past life, before she came to Budapest, that Sylvie, as a child, had pieced together her slight knowledge of her mother's family only by odd comments of Rosa's and by nagging Rudi to tell her the little that he had been able to discover of Rosa's childhood.

As she walked, she looked with longing at the painted picket fences, enclosing neat paths leading to front doors beside cosy curtained windows, at the distant red barns and the white steeple of the church at the end of the thoroughfare. As she looked at each house she passed, she wondered whether this one was where her grandparents had lived – might be living still? As one or two people passed her on the street, the men raising their hats politely but unemphatically and the women smiling vaguely more as if to themselves than directly at her, she felt a lurch of hope. Might this be her uncle? How could she find out?

All the winter snow had melted now, and the grass and spring trees looked lush and full of promise. The sun shone, the sky was a cloudless blue and the distant woods had that mysterious haze of rising sap. Inside, she felt a glittering hub of excitement. Never had she felt so optimistic or so full of affection for her surroundings.

The small cemetery proved fascinating in its own right: between the pillar-like trunks of ancient oak trees, the headstones inside the lych gate were carved with a simple, flowing eighteenth-century script, recording the names and dates of those buried below. Many bore military titles; many of the women and children had died young, bravely and poignantly before their time. Sylvie was becoming absorbed in the mute eloquence of these old-fashioned names inscribed in the rain-washed stone when she started: Johns – she saw the family name at last! Ambrose and Sarah Johns. A sob almost rose in her throat: so they were dead after all! But then she looked again more closely at the dates: Ambrose and Sarah belonged to her great-grandparents' generation! She looked about her, unconsciously stroking the rough headstone. There were other names, other dates – great-aunts and uncles, perhaps. Who knew? But she felt that those simple folk who now lay beneath the thick, green grass were aware of her presence, that they thanked her silently for having come amongst them, her family, to pay her respects.

A tear ran slowly down Sylvie's cheek. She thought of Budapest, of skating with her father on the Varosligeti To, the smell of roasting chestnuts mingling with the tang of sulphur from the spa. She felt her blood pull at her. Two heritages, two families, two traditions, each with their own honours and codes, had met in her. She felt she must, at all costs, bring them together in harmony within herself, acknowledge and love them both. Smiling with a strange joy, she once again ran her hand along the rough, arched surface of the headstone that marked the grave of Ambrose and Sarah Johns and looked over towards the white wooden church. She saw a man standing there, watching her, but he gave no sign and made no move to come in her direction.

She sighed, and, smiling at herself, slowly made her way out of the burial ground. Abbey was a wise man, she thought. He was right to have her start with her ancestors before facing up to the living. Now, even if the Johns family should repudiate her, because of the way in which her mother had absconded, she had had her moment alone with her kin; she had felt the tug of America at her feet and had rooted a small but special part of herself there. She felt she belonged, regardless of the immediate future.

The man had disappeared when she reached the church, but the door was open and she went inside. It was large, presumably to accommodate the transient tourist population in the summer, but plain, with whitewashed walls and honey-coloured oak pews, very different from the ornate Eastern European churches of her childhood. A woman who was busy arranging flowers at the side of the nave looked up briefly and nodded to her. Sylvie looked about her aimlessly, then decided she might as well approach this woman for help.

'Excuse me,' she said, her light tone ringing in the

empty building. The woman straightened herself up from where the greenery lay on a sheet of newspaper on the wooden floor. She looked at Sylvie enquiringly, but did not speak. 'I'm sorry to bother you,' continued Sylvie, 'but my family came from these parts – a long time ago,' she added quickly, suddenly afraid to approach the subject too directly. 'The name was Johns.'

'What!' exclaimed the woman, staring at her. Then she bent her head and leant over to pick up another stem. She said something that Sylvie could not quite catch.

'I beg your pardon,' said Sylvie, taking a step closer. 'I didn't . . . '

But the woman interrupted her. 'I said there's no one called Johns in Saratoga Springs,' she declared challengingly. She looked angry.

'But . . . '

'There's no one of that name in the town,' she repeated firmly, and deliberately lifted the half-filled bowl from its stand and marched away from where Sylvie stood, leaving the flowers where they lay on the floor.

Sylvie shrugged, unable to figure out what the woman's strange attitude could mean.

As she walked back towards the hotel, she racked her brains, trying to think of how else she could approach the task of discovering her family. Perhaps, the thought now struck her, the hotel would have a business directory that might provide some help: she was certain that Rosa's people had run some kind of business, although she did not know what. She could surely ask to look at a directory without anyone suspecting her real motive. And she quickened her pace.

The manager brought up the directory himself, and paused to ask if he could be of any assistance in obtaining any service Miss Lazar required. Sylvie was about to dismiss him, then paused. She laughed and, as usual when nervous or in difficulty, instinctively began to act. 'Oh, it is nothing, really. But a friend of mine in London supposes herself to be related to a family here in Saratoga. I had meant to look the name up in this book you've so kindly fetched for me, since she has really given me absolutely nothing to go on. I didn't want to begin bothering innocent people with my enquiries!' She laughed gaily.

'Saratoga is a small town, Miss Lazar,' answered the manager readily. 'I'm sure I would know the name – if you would care to trust me with it.'

Sylvie bit her lip, hoping that if this enquiry were productive, her story would prove sufficient to disguise the outcome from curious eyes. 'Johns,' she said. 'The name was Johns.'

The smile on the manager's face faded instantly and he looked at her guardedly, but Sylvie's expression betrayed none of her real concern, feigning only the polite interest in executing a friend's casual request. The man studied her closely for a few seconds, then appeared relieved to find that she seemed genuinely disinterested in the subject.

'No,' he replied slowly, as if considering the matter anew. 'No, I don't recall anyone of the name of Johns here in Saratoga.'

'Well, never mind,' answered Sylvie lightly. 'My friend was far from certain herself. But at least I can tell her that I consulted the very best authority!'

The manager bowed gallantly at her compliment and, after renewed assurances that he and his hotel were completely at her service, seemed glad to let himself out.

Sylvie had just closed the directory, which indeed contained no mention of the name Johns, when Louisa, with her usual discreet knock at the door, entered the room.

'I hope you didn't need me?' she asked, a little breathlessly. 'But the park was lovely, and I got talking to a lady.'

'No, not at all, Louisa,' smiled Sylvie. 'Anyway, you deserve a break after all your hard work. Don't worry about me.'

'I thought you might like to hear the story she told me, anyway,' said Louisa, pulling off her gloves and automatically tidying up the room as she spoke. 'It's the kind of thing Mr Abbey would make a play out of!'

'Tell me,' invited Sylvie, putting her feet up and willing to be distracted from the puzzling mystery of Rosa's family. She sat with one eye on her companion and one eye idly on the street below the window as Louisa told her tale.

'Up on the hill, above the park where I went to try the waters, there's a ruined barn. It stands out clearly against the sky. The lady saw me gazing at it as I sipped my glass of water – which is, by the way, quite horrible – and announced in a voice of dread and gloom that quite intrigued me: "That's Gregory's barn!" '

Sylvie's attention wavered for a moment as a familiar-looking figure stopped opposite the hotel and stood for a moment looking up at it, before he crossed the road and disappeared beneath the wide verandah under Sylvie's window. It was the man who had stood watching her from the church while she was in the burial ground.

'Apparently there was a perfectly dreadful killing there, years ago,' continued Louisa, as she bustled about the room, plumping up cushions and straightening the books on a table. 'A whole family was killed and found hanging in the barn, even the baby. Imagine! Apparently no one likes to talk about it, and, at the time, the place was besieged by writers and reporters wanting all the gruesome details!'

'Edward Jones, not Edmund Johns,' murmured Sylvie to herself, almost unconscious of what she said.

Louisa paused in her story, confused: 'What did you say, Sylvie? Have you heard about it, then?'

But Sylvie was on her feet, her face white. 'Edward Jones, not Edmund Johns. That's what Mamma said to me when it was in the papers. "Massacre at Gregory's Barn". But I always remembered it as Johns. I forgot she ever said it wasn't. Oh poor, poor Mamma!' She buried her face in her hands, struggling to recall that morning in Budapest. Why hadn't she paid more attention? Why hadn't it registered? Then she remembered: Nye. Nye and Sari Fodor. She hadn't wanted to go to her acting lesson with Nye because . . . because he was using the lessons to conduct his affair with Sari Fodor. Sylvie groaned, and Louisa was beside her at once, her arm around her.

'Sylvie, whatever is it?'

'Poor Mamma,' said Sylvie again, looking up wonderingly into Louisa's face. She half expected to see old Kati's roughened features. 'No wonder people won't mention the Johns family. It was my uncle who was the murderer. The uncle I hoped to find,' she added unhappily.

Louisa could not make any sense of what Sylvie was saying, but instinctively she went to fetch the heavy silver brush from the dressing table and, like a child, made Sylvie turn around on her chair so that she could stand behind her. One by one she took out the tortoiseshell hairpins, allowing Sylvie's hair to cascade down her back. Slowly and rhythmically, she began to brush it with long steady strokes, just as she did in the dressing room when Sylvie went over her lines before a performance. The familiar action calmed Sylvie, who gave a long shuddering sigh, shook her head and stretched her neck and shoulders, allowing her hair to fall freely down her back as she gave herself up to the relaxing attention.

But almost at once the two women were disturbed by a debonair knock at the door. Louisa went and opened it a crack.

'Yes, what is it?' she asked sharply. An elderly man stood outside in the hallway, his hat in his hands. He looked over Louisa's shoulder to where Sylvie sat.

'I've come to talk to Miss Lapham,' he said.

'There's no Miss Lapham here,' retorted Louisa, and began to close the door on him, but he put out his hand to stay it, as Sylvie swung around to face him, her eyes wide and afraid.

'Miss Lazar, then,' he conceded, his eyes fixed on Sylvie.

'Let him come in, Louisa,' said Sylvie quietly.

Surprised, Louisa let go of the door, and the man pushed it open and walked through. Louisa shut it behind him, and looked from one to the other in silent amazement.

'Stay here, please, Louisa,' commanded Sylvie, as she rose and gathered her hair to twist it into a thick plait. Louisa rushed to fetch her a ribbon from the bedroom, then all three sat down, waiting to see who would be the first to speak.

The man – whom Sylvie had seen earlier that day outside the church – smiled oddly but seemed content just to look at Sylvie. At last, she spoke. 'Why did you call me Miss Lapham?'

'Because you're Rosa Lapham's daughter. And Count Lazar's bastard.'

'How dare you speak to Miss Lazar like that, you . . . ' burst out Louisa, rising from her chair, but Sylvie hushed her with a wave of her hand. 'It's all right, Louisa,' she said resignedly. 'He only speaks the truth. It suddenly seems to be a day for truths,' she sighed.

The three of them sat once more in silence, regarding one another. Again it was Sylvie who spoke first. 'Who are you?'

'Can't you guess?'

'No.' She shook her head.

'I'm Onslow Lapham.' He introduced himself with an odd mixture of pride and chagrin.

'So it was true,' said Sylvie wonderingly to herself, looking at him with interest. Suddenly she laughed, despite herself. 'I always thought you were one of my mother's fictions!'

But her laughter made him colour angrily. 'I daresay that's all I was to her,' he agreed bitterly. 'But I've nothing to reproach myself with. I was true to her. I'd have given her anything she wanted.' He paused expectantly, staring at Sylvie and rocking slightly in his chair. The knuckles of his hands were white where he gripped the arm-rests. 'You don't look much like her,' he added, almost with reproach.

Sylvie was amazed. She had come to find Rosa's past, and had somehow magicked her mother's husband out of thin air. She looked at him now with interest. He was quite tall, and had probably once been handsome in a conventional sort of way. Now he seemed faded and spiritless, as though his life had been used up on some pointless obsession. Which, she instantly realized sadly, of course it had: Rosa.

'Tell me what happened,' she asked him gently.

He let out a long sigh. Sylvie sensed that this was a story that he never ceased telling himself, but that it was a luxury to tell it aloud, to have it heard and witnessed by someone so intimately connected with its events.

'I came up from New York for a fortnight in the summer, a year or two before the Civil War. I had my own business, importing ribbons, braids, trimmings, that sort of thing – fancy goods for the dress trade –

but it did well, and I fancied a vacation. I was sick of travelling, didn't want to go far, so jumped on the river-boat and came here. Then I met Rosa Johns. Boy, was she beautiful; most beautiful thing I'd ever seen. And didn't she know it! Used to walk past on the arm of that brother of hers and look all the men right in the eye, like she was daring them to . . . Well, when she heard that I was due to go to Paris, France, at the end of the month, she wouldn't leave me alone. Pestered me all the time for what gowns they wore there, whether ladies ate out in restaurants, what kind of jewellery shops there were – I don't know what all!

'But it wasn't like it sounds. It wasn't just that she wanted gowns and knick-knacks. She wanted a man, too. She was hot. Just seventeen years old, and hot! I wanted to ask her old man's permission about marrying her, do it all right and proper. I really loved her! Clarence Johns, her father, owned one of the little resort hotels down by the lake, a temperance hotel, it was. They were quite well off, but he had funny ideas about religion. Kept seeing the devil in everything. When it came to his children, he was just about right, too. But Rosa wouldn't listen. She said he'd never countenance her being engaged to a man she'd just got talking to in the park. I was afraid of losing her, so I gave in, and we got a special licence in New York, with her brother saying he was her guardian. I just couldn't believe my luck.

'I took her to Paris with me and bought her everything I could afford – which was something: I wasn't Croesus, but I was doing well enough. Then she just went. Not even a note. I soon enough discovered that she'd gone off with that Hungarian aristocrat she'd been making eyes at. I even considered going after them to get her back. But what was the point? I reckoned she'd only run off again. Besides, she was still my wife – I've always known that some day I can pull on that string and get her back. When it suits me.'

Onslow Lapham paused for breath at last. Sylvie was surprised at how much of the story tallied with what she'd gleaned from Rudi and Rosa, for she had always supposed, if only because of the frivolous way Rosa had occasionally spoken of her early marriage, that there was every chance that it was pure invention.

'What did you do then?' asked Sylvie.

Lapham's face twisted with misery and bitterness. 'Oh, I followed them to start with. I hung about Budapest whenever I could and watched 'em. That's how I knew you were born. I followed you once when you went out with your nurse, when you were just a scrap of a thing, and I heard her croon your name. So when I saw all this publicity for your tour, for Sylvie Lazar, I knew it had to be Rosa's child. I've been waiting years for something about one or other of you to surface.' He paused triumphantly. 'I always thought she'd try and marry him – your father. I rather hoped she would, so I could get a hold on her . . . Did she ever try it?'

Sylvie shook her head.

Lapham remained silent for a while. Sylvie looked across at Louisa, who sat dumbfounded by all she had heard, then back at Lapham. She felt sorry for him. He wasn't her father, but he was her mother's husband, and she felt she ought to make it all up to him, somehow.

'Then the war started,' he began again. 'I fought for the Yankees, but by the time it was all over, my business was ruined. So I came here. I told old man Johns who I was, and what his daughter had done to me. He and his wife were decent people, and he took me on as manager in the hotel. I built it up a bit, and he began to talk of making me a partner. But Rosa's brother Edmund didn't like that one bit. He hated me. He didn't want to do any work, but he expected to get it all just the same. Then came the massacre. Who knows why he did it. But I can't say I was surprised. He was getting more and more unstable. I caught him once, out in the stable, cutting up a rat that had died of the poison we'd put down. I had the strangest feeling he was planning to eat it.' Mr Lapham shook his head in disbelief at the memory. 'There was a pretty odd look on his face, anyway,' he continued.

'You don't know what he did to those people, do you?' he asked darkly. Sylvie, afraid, shook her head. 'I won't tell you. No need for you to know. But there was no way his parents could stay put in this town after what he did to those little children. I got them settled out in Kansas City. Said I'd run the hotel, and they'd always have half the profits. But after two years they just died, of shame and grief I guess. I stayed. I could stand a little scandal. And the folk here in Saratoga were pretty eager to hush it all up, anyhow. Wasn't so good for the tourist trade. And besides,' he added, drawing himself up a little as he sat, 'I wanted to be here in case she ever came back.'

'She knew what Edmund did,' said Sylvie quietly. 'She saw it in a Boston paper.'

Lapham nodded. 'I guess it would've shook her up. They were pretty close, those two. And both had that same streak of wildness.'

There seemed nothing more to say, and Sylvie and Lapham sat regarding one another. Abruptly he spoke again. 'You're not like her, though. I thought you would be, but you're not. You're OK.'

Sylvie smiled weakly. She stood up. 'So I have no family at all here in Saratoga?' she asked.

'No. Just me,' he answered.

'Thank you, Mr Lapham,' she smiled, holding out her hands to him as he rose also. 'That's kind of you to say that.'

But he looked most taken aback. 'Oh no,' he said. 'You don't understand. I am your family. I'm owed. I've been waiting for this day and now it's dawned. Old man Johns, he always said, "Justice will come to those who wait". That's why I've stayed here. Waiting. Don't you see?'

Sylvie looked puzzled. Louisa came over to stand beside her, ready to repel any threat. But Onslow Lapham did not seem a threatening man. He seemed sad and lonely and betrayed.

'What do you want?' asked Sylvie, unable to guess what he had in mind.

'I'm your family,' he said, gabbling slightly now in his eagerness to be heard, to be acknowledged. 'That's why you came here, wasn't it? Looking for your family? Well, I'm your mother's husband. Or are you going to explain to the world that the great Sylvie Lazar is a bastard?' He spoke in a desperate manner. Sylvie could not believe that this was a serious blackmail attempt, yet he seemed so intense, so obsessed with what he said. He put out his hand and touched her arm, and she shrank back.

'I don't want to hurt you,' he pleaded. 'You've worked hard for what you've got. I admire that. I said, didn't I? You're OK. I won't go telling the world that I'm your father, because they'd soon sniff out the old scandal, and you don't want to be known as the niece of a notorious mass-murderer, a suicide, do you? No, you don't have to acknowledge me publicly. But I want to come along with you. I want to share in your success. I want to sit at your table. I want Rosa to be my wife again.'

Sylvie felt the hurt that lay behind his words, but also sensed the desperate obsession that fuelled his gamble. And she felt sorry for him. She would make amends if she could, but she knew that his instability was dangerous for her and her career. She must get back to New York and find Henry Abbey. He would know what to do.

She smiled agreeably at Onslow Lapham and patted him on the arm. 'You've given me a great deal to think about, you know,' she said gently. 'Let me sleep on it, and come and see me tomorrow.'

The look of relief on his face was palpable, and he willingly allowed Louisa to hand him his hat and to close the door behind him. Before Louisa could say a word, Sylvie had begun to gather up all her belongings in the room.

'Quick,' she said, 'we're going back to New York right now, even if we have to walk!' She realized that it was futile to think she could escape him, that he would find her easily enough in New York, but she wanted Abbey to deal with him. She didn't feel able to help him to confront Rosa. She and Onslow Lapham had both been damaged by Rosa's selfish mania for self-exultation, but she did not yet feel ready to deal with her mother's legacy. Her hopes of finding a sheltering family had been utterly dashed, and nothing remained for her here. She just wanted to get back to her own world, to New York. She might not like what she had found, but her visit to Saratoga had certainly served its purpose in scratching up the past.

CHAPTER SEVENTEEN

Pier 33 was crammed with people as Sylvie's carriage made its way slowly through the mass of humanity to where the first-class gangway led upwards to the gleaming, dark blue side of the Cunard liner *Etruria*, its magnificent funnels rising against the paler blue of the sky. On either side, the ships of the rival lines lay at berth like chariots in a race, the tugs on the river noisy in their support of their particular champions. Further down the pier, the steerage passengers waited patiently, holding their bundles and baskets, and having to endure the black dust that blew up from where the coal was being shovelled into the ship's hold. Sylvie smiled to herself, remembering her lonely leave-taking in Liverpool last winter: how different things were today.

'You'll have a private suite for this journey – and better weather, too!' said Henry Abbey at her side, as if reading her thoughts. 'Now, where's that damned florist? I told him what time we'd be here.'

As Sylvie started towards the gangway, a shout went up of, 'There she is!' and Abbey's carefully planned pandemonium broke loose as three florist's boys rushed at her with huge bouquets. However, several young women, recognizing the immortal Sylvie Lazar, also fainted obligingly into their companions' arms, causing yet more heads to turn. Abbey's hand on her arm, apparently guiding her safely up the gangway, was in fact holding her back, giving the milling crowd below time to pause, look up and see her triumphant exit, centre-stage of this gigantic arena. With consummate timing, Abbey led her to the railings, and bit back his whispered instruction to her to wave: Sylvie needed no guidance in how to bring her audience to its feet, and was kissing her hand and waving as if throwing butterflies to the assembled crowd. The reporters who always hung about the piers, waiting to see who might turn up, shouted up questions to her. Even the porters fell silent as Sylvie's musical voice rang out clearly in answer: yes, she would miss America; yes, she would return; her final words? 'Thank you to every American who has taken me to their heart.'

His face trembling from the effort to hide a huge smile, Abbey led her away from the railings and the staring faces below and, summoning an awe-struck steward, went in search of her suite.

Among the cheering crowd, frozen immobile as he bade his mother farewell, stood Elliot. As Sylvie's neat figure finally turned from view, he shivered with excitement. His mother looked down at him fiercely from her carriage and hatred welled up in her when she saw the glazed look of passion in his eyes.

'Elliot!' She sharply regained his attention. 'If you are seasick – and even the strongest men are – tell the steward to bring you a dish of plain cooked arrowroot, nothing else!'

'Mother, it was kind of you to see me off, but I beg you not to wait in this crowd. Thomas,' he addressed the coachman, 'make sure you take my mother straight home. Don't loiter here.'

Dorothea Statten bowed to her son's male command of the situation – it was unthinkable to argue the point before a servant – and sank back into the depths of the carriage as it rolled slowly away through the crowd.

Abbey lost no time in finding Sylvie's staterooms, which opened directly out onto an upper deck, and discreetly slipped the steward a couple of greenbacks to ensure her well-being on the ten-day voyage. He then despatched Louisa to apply to the head steward for her place at table, and insisted on accompanying Sylvie on a stroll around the ship. They looked into the great saloon, with its heavily buttoned and tasselled velvet sofas and vast expanse of carpet, already filling up with brightly dressed women and sober-suited businessmen.

The doors to the cabins that opened off the vast room banged open and shut, as noisy families explored their new quarters, while a young woman sat at the piano, playing some simple, soothing songs to herself. After a peep into the panelled library, with its stained-glass skylights, Abbey proposed a turn on deck, where they spent some time watching the crowds that still choked the docks, the waiting horses restive with all the commotion around them, and the drivers and porters shouting at one another as they manhandled heavy trunks from waggons or the roofs of cabs.

As some order seemed to emerge from the chaos below, Abbey broke their companionable silence at last. 'Well, my dear,' he said. 'I guess I must take my leave of you.'

Sylvie did not trust herself to speak. She stood, holding both his hands in hers, her grey eyes shining with gratitude.

Abbey nodded and smiled, squeezing her fingers. 'Now, you got those letters of introduction that I gave you safe?' he demanded in a businesslike way, still grasping her hands. She only nodded in answer. 'Good. And you remember what I told you about greeting Irving and the others? You're a big star now, Sylvie, don't forget. Bigger even than them. You're your own publicity and you gotta strike the correct note right from the start. I'll be joining you in a coupla weeks when I've finished my business here, but I don't wanna find my stock's fallen just because my back's turned!'

Sylvie leant forward to kiss him warmly on the cheek.

'You're an absolute darling!' she laughed at him. 'I'll miss you!'

'And don't you worry about that Mr Lapham. He'll soon get sick of running around after you.'

'Have you seen him?' she asked anxiously. 'Is he on board?'

Abbey nodded, his face serious. 'But I've told Louisa how she's to deal with him. Nice and polite, but don't let him near you.'

Sylvie sighed. 'He doesn't really mean any harm.'

'None at all, to you,' answered Abbey cheerfully. 'If he did, I'd have found a way of easing him off this boat by now. Anyway, if there is any trouble, at least he can't say you've been anything but ladylike to him. But I guess there's no one but your Mamma can give him what he wants. Let her deal with him. By the sounds of it, it's something she should'a done a while back.'

Sylvie was silent a moment, and Abbey looked at her still profile, at her pale forehead and her wide grey eyes, with a trace of concern. 'You mustn't let him get to you this way,' he murmured. 'His business is with your mother, not you. I had a long, long talk with him. He means you no harm. He's just gotten hold of an advantage for the first time in his life, and he don't mean to let it go until he gets what he wants. Deliver him to your Mamma, and the job's done.'

But Sylvie shivered as she turned her head to give him a wan smile. 'I know,' she admitted. 'But he's the spectre at the feast, isn't he? The albatross. I feel like he's a punishment for my moment of elation. I went to Saratoga so full of expectation . . . and he's crushed it out of me, somehow. Ridiculous, isn't it?' she ended lamely.

'Well, I've never yet met an actress who wasn't superstitious,' countered Abbey, as if that summed the matter up to his satisfaction. 'And you're right. He is an albatross. Just dead weight. Forget all about him. Louisa will see to him. They're gonna take away the gangway. I have to go. Besides,' he called back with a mischievous grin as he shouldered his way through the cluster of people who blocked the way to the exit, 'I'm sure young Statten will take good care of you! There's many a Society gel down Fifth Avenue stomping her foot in rage, seeing you walk off so coolly with the season's most eligible beau!'

Sylvie watched Abbey go, thinking of all the times his nonsense had soothed and cheered her, and waved as he reached the dock and turned to kiss his hand to her. Then his debonair figure plunged into the crowd and was lost.

She made her way back to her own staterooms, where she found Louisa busy unpacking her travelling trunk. She lingered outside on the deck, leaning over the rail. Once all the ramps that led from the decks to the dock had been removed, and the huge ropes that bound the ship to American soil had been cast loose, she felt a surge of excitement as the band of dark water widened, the noise of the wharves was drowned by the sound of the ship's engines and the cry of the seagulls, and the black smoke from the funnels obscured the backward view. Gradually she became completely engrossed in watching the tugs manoeuvre the great steamship down river and out towards the ocean and in observing the other steamers that passed by on their way into New York. The sense of voyaging out into the great ocean replicated her inner feelings. She, too, had ten or eleven days in which to complete a journey of her own.

Her most immediate anxiety was the sad and obsessed Mr Lapham. She knew that her fear of him was unfounded, and recognized a deeper fear that she shared with him – their ultimate dependence on Rosa's goodwill. And Sylvie could not delude herself that Rosa would harbour any benevolent feelings towards either of them. She sensed that a day of reckoning between herself and her mother loomed; there was no way of averting it. Her star had risen just as inexorably as Rosa's was waning, and Rosa would not forgive her for that. Sylvie quailed at the thought of introducing the hapless Onslow Lapham to Rosa's Kensington drawing room.

And she admitted to herself that, childish though it might be, she held Lapham accountable for spoiling her dream of finding some anchorage, some sense of identity, hidden behind one of those low, white-painted picket fences in Saratoga Springs. He remained obstinately in her mind as the symbol of her lost hopes. Just when she had felt on the verge of finding somewhere to belong, her dream had been torn from her grasp by Lapham's revelations. America had failed to provide her with a home. Yet her experiences had made her recognize her need of one. She couldn't go on relying on anonymous audiences, on the homage and love of strangers, on the magic of her intense onstage presence, to provide her with the illusions of security and love. She had to belong somewhere when she wasn't acting, too. And she knew now that Rosa's house was emphatically not her home.

She looked out at the wide expanse of ocean curving towards the distant horizon. She was far from despair. She had never felt so confident and alive. But she had to take control of her own destiny, arrange her own future, decide who she wanted to be and how she wanted to live. Disturbingly, she recalled how Abbey had told her a few days before that someone had offered, anonymously through the lawyers, to purchase his contract with her: a considerable sum of money had been named, which Abbey had automatically refused, but the occurrence had kept Sylvie awake at night. First *The Angel*, and now the contract for her stage performances: was she a commodity to be bought and sold in this way? A gardenia in some capricious businessman's buttonhole?

Sylvie recognized that her restlessness and tension were the stirrings of a struggle to oppose other people's desires for her to be what they wanted. For so long, she had striven to fit herself into other people's images of her. Now she had to be herself.

Where is home? she wondered, leaning out over the rail and staring down into the deep, dark waters below, feeling the strengthening breeze tug at her hair. Would Elliot Statten provide it? Over the past few weeks, Sylvie had almost persuaded herself that she was in love with him. It had been thrilling to work so closely with him, riding the wave of the stock market. Her success on stage, before her visit to Saratoga, had given her a deep feeling of security, of inviolability almost, and she had enjoyed the novelty of her reckless desire for experience. Sylvie had for so long buried her sexual nature, as she had buried so many other aspects of her personality, partly from inexperience, and partly, in recent years, in fear of her mother's increasing jealousy and competitiveness and the sense of unpleasantness that Rosa's sexuality imparted. But Elliot had aroused her passion and she had enjoyed his physical desire for her. In her hotel room, in his carriage, hidden behind the palms in a conservatory, he had covered her face, neck and hair with kisses, and run his hands over the smooth, corseted outline of her breasts and hips, and they had kissed endlessly, breathlessly, their lips red and swollen with passion. The directness of his need to touch her reminded her of Philip, Will's studio assistant, but Philip had been too young and too respectful to succeed in arousing much response in her. Now she felt her body was ready for physical satisfaction, she found Elliot's urgent embraces exciting, and she guessed with a little thrill of anticipation that he would want to make love to her during this voyage.

Sylvie was so lost in her thoughts that she hardly noticed the dark figure who came, silently and calmly, to lean beside her on the rail. Aware only of his eyes upon her, she turned her head, smiling vaguely, waiting for Elliot's kiss. Startled, she jerked back, catching her breath with surprise and sudden fear.

Nye's gaze shifted about her. He thought she looked frail and tired after her tour; a few strands of hair blew about her face, and he was eager to pick the silky threads from where they adhered to her fine nose and her full, half-parted lips. Seeing his look of admiration, she drew herself up and gave a smile full of grandeur and pride. Sunlight fell on Sylvie's face, and Nye looked at her, thinking that he had never seen a countenance so lovely, or so full of hidden pain and confusion. It had been a long time since he had experienced such a stab of physical desire.

'How fortuitous a meeting, Miss Lazar,' he said with a slight ironic bow. 'I had resigned myself to a dull crossing.'

'Mr Nye,' she replied, offering him her hand with deliberately calm courtesy. He bowed over it, giving her a long, appraising stare. Used now to exciting passion in men, she understood his ardour, but, almost out of habit, discounted it.

He stared at her a moment longer, then laughed and spread his hands in a deprecatory gesture. 'You must be bored of compliments on your success. What can I add to what the world has already said?'

'It would be pleasanter to talk of something else,' she acknowledged with an answering smile. 'What took you to New York?' she asked.

'Oh, meat and potatoes business affairs. Nothing that would interest a young lady. But I forget, don't I?' he paused, giving her a shrewd glance. 'I seem to recall that you do take a rather informed interest in such matters.'

'I keep my ears open. And being an actress,' she added carelessly, 'I learn my lines! I merely have a facility for remembering what I'm told, Mr Nye. No more than that.' Sylvie suddenly felt it was important not to betray her intimate knowledge and thorough understanding of his financial affairs. Knowing the very real power that he could one day represent – no less than a stranglehold on the world's bullion supply – she felt in awe and dread of him.

Nye leant over towards her, speaking in her ear as if the wind might snatch his words away. 'But you forget who taught you the basics of economics, my dear.' He sought her gaze, and crowed inwardly with delight to see the look of puzzled hurt in her eyes. 'I am an old friend, remember?'

Sylvie caught the almost imperceptible glint of insanity that flashed in his glance, only to disappear as rapidly under his seamless veneer of civilized charm. For a moment, she doubted what she had seen, but her slight panic, lending a becoming flush to her complexion, merely heightened the effect she made on him. His victorious smile made her shiver.

'Then you must excuse me if I treat you as such and go in now,' she answered. 'I am feeling rather cold.' And she rustled over to her cabin, the ribbons on her dress flying behind her in the breeze. He watched her go, content to bide his time.

Sylvie had intended to take supper alone in her cabin that night, but a steward arrived with a note from Elliot who was expecting her to dine with him. He waited at one of the entrances to the great saloon, immaculate in his black suit and pristine white waistcoat and tie, his grandfather's sapphire studs sparkling on his shirtfront. He watched with pride as Sylvie calmly entered the crowded room. A woman sitting with a group at one side of the door recognized her, and called out excitedly, 'Miss Lazar. It's Sylvie Lazar. Bravo, bravo!' The people with her began to clap, the men rising to their feet, and soon all heads were turned in her direction, lorgnettes were raised and all those who recognized her joined in the applause.

Elliot was surprised to find that he relished the attention he received as he now led Sylvie across the crowded room. Their progress was soon interrupted, however, by Nye standing in their path.

'Good evening, Sylvie,' he said. 'And Mr Statten.' Nye moved smoothly to shake Elliot's hand, as consummate an actor as Sylvie herself. 'The son of Charles Statten, if I'm not mistaken?' he enquired disinterestedly, as Sylvie had no choice but to introduce them.

Elliot was amazed at this fellow's cool familiarity with Sylvie, but was stung into curt, old-fashioned politeness by the reference to his father. He drew himself up, meeting Nye's ironical eyes. He recognized Nye's name as one of the most powerful financiers of the decade, but inwardly refused to pay him the respect that he would have done in other circumstances. Elliot was a good few inches taller than Nye, though the elder man, his dark, heavy frame compact and neat, was every bit as rugged and strong in physique. Both stood, elegantly clothed in black, both dark and hard; instant, unprovoked antagonists.

Nye was the first to smile and ease the moment. 'I've taken the liberty of asking the head steward to seat us together, Sylvie,' he went on, taking command of the situation. 'But I'm sure that I can arrange for Mr Statten to join us.' Without waiting for a reply, or to witness Elliot's angry expression, Nye flicked his fingers and at once a waiter appeared at his side. Sylvie shrugged helplessly at Elliot while Nye gave his orders, but she saw all too plainly his smouldering jealousy.

'Sylvie and I are old friends,' Nye explained, turning to the younger man, while taking Sylvie's gloved hand, drawing it through his arm and patting it in a proprietary way. Elliot stared at him aggressively, but Nye met his look with a quizzical raising of an eyebrow. Sylvie moved to disengage herself, only to find her arm locked in Nye's. She looked in angry astonishment at him, but he merely smiled, then, after a brief instant more, released her.

'Shall we go in?' he asked pleasantly.

The table seemed to run almost the entire length of the ship, with rows of revolving chairs on either side, so that the passengers could seat themselves without clambering over one another. The room, at this hour, was lit by scores of electric lamps suspended from the ceiling. The vibration of the ship's screw seemed less here in the centre of the ship, and Sylvie, entering the narrow, noisy room, felt the highly charged atmosphere of infinite isolation as this crowd of people settled down together to pass the leisured days of their voyage.

'You'll be glad to rest in London again after all your travelling?' Nye opened the conversation politely, once they were all three seated.

'Oh, this is only a brief respite,' said Sylvie brightly, determined not to be disconcerted by his persistent attention. 'I'm soon off again, across Europe.'

'How far do you travel?' he asked blandly.

'Budapest is my furthest point,' answered Sylvie curtly, loath to be reminded of their mutual past. 'I'm not like Bernhardt who dares to play in Cairo or Alexandria.'

'Ah, Budapest!' sighed Nye. Elliot looked at him sharply, but Nye, deliberately allowing his gaze to rest lightly on him, merely smiled again. 'Have you visited the city since you and your mother left it?'

'No.'

'It must evoke many memories for you.'

Sylvie's head jerked back suddenly, but her voice was unchanged. 'Perhaps one chooses one's memories more than one realizes, Mr Nye. My thoughts of Budapest dwell mainly on the times when I was a little girl. When my father lived,' she added, defensively.

'Mr Lapham, of course,' continued Nye urbanely. She looked at him sharply, wondering how far he meant to taunt her, but he bent his head over his plate. Catching sight of Onslow Lapham's pale, lined face, much further up the table, watching her submissively, Sylvie began to sense danger. She perceived, as the hunted do, that Nye had her within his sights, and she felt his physical nearness like static electricity, like a thunderstorm hovering over the horizon, lowering and threatening, although, on the face of it, harmless.

'Were you a friend of Miss Lazar's father, then, Mr Nye?' demanded Elliot almost rudely, determined not to be excluded any longer.

Nye put his head back and laughed, drawing attention from the other diners seated around them. 'Not of her father, no,' he answered, as though it had been a droll question.

Stung by the other man's barely veiled insolence, Elliot was about to reply, when he paused, reddened, and looked interrogatively at Sylvie. Sylvie recalled the look on his face the first time he had visited her backstage, when he had been shocked by the caricaturish appearance of her stage make-up, and how he had continued to show distaste at the curious mixture of the tawdry and the depraved that the far side of the footlights presented, although she had laughed and assured him that it was all as circumspect and correct as his own banking chambers. She had always known that Elliot's social attitude towards her was disquietingly ambiguous, that while he took pride in having the toast of New York on his arm, in reading in the Society pages the lavish accounts of how she had danced with him the night before, he had also unquestioningly accepted his mother's dictate that his young sister should not be asked to meet an actress. Suddenly she felt inexpressibly weary. She hated to be at the centre of the two men's silent struggle, the passive rabbit caught in the trap while they fought for possession. She saw now where Nye was leading, and submitted to the inevitable, meeting Elliot's glance with frank, silent dignity.

But, having hit his mark, Nye, to Sylvie's surprise, immediately changed the subject and began to ask Elliot in flattering terms about Wall Street. Gradually the younger man's antagonism ebbed as Nye put himself out to be undeniably charming; recounting his well-told tales with the unmistakable authority of personal experience, he succeeded in winning Elliot's grudging respect. Sylvie sat miserably, barely attempting to join in their conversation. She could sense the coldness growing in Elliot as he unconsciously began to distance himself from her, holding himself more rigidly in the seat beside her. With a sigh, she was forced to recognize that arrogant obtuseness in him that, until now, she had told herself was faintly endearing.

Elliot had in abundance the qualities she felt she lacked. She admired his directness, his energy, his determination, and she found it refreshing to be with someone who so consistently acted from the impulse that whatever he did was right. But now she realized the impossibility of any real closeness between them. She saw that she had been tempted to give herself up to him so easily precisely because she did not really care about him, and she felt disappointed, cheated of the trick that would have allowed her to lose herself, for once, in some spontaneous, sensual gesture.

As they moved through to the saloon for their coffee, Nye casually detached himself from them. 'Excuse me if I go and smoke a cigar in the library.' He bowed politely to each of them, and was gone.

'How do you come to know him so well?' Elliot asked

with exaggerated casualness the moment Nye was out of hearing.

'He was a friend of my mother's in Budapest.' She answered defiantly, and watched as Elliot accepted her statement and began the inevitable internal adjustment.

'And what was all that about your father being Mr Lapham, when your name's Lazar?'

'My father's name was Lazar,' she explained, flushing with indignation at being so crudely required to confirm the suspicions that Nye had planted in his head. 'My mother was and is Mrs Onslow Lapham.'

Elliot nodded, his face red with embarrassment.

She looked at him calmly. 'Does it really make such a great difference to you?' she asked.

Elliot was at heart an honourable man, and he was stung by the dilemma now created by the clash between his passionate feelings for Sylvie and the equally strong codes of propriety according to which he had been raised. He struggled to remain her champion. 'What a cad to raise the subject like that!' he exclaimed, finding it easiest to blame Nye for his own distress. 'I'm surprised you allow him to address you at all!'

'I don't have much choice. If it's the truth, after all . . . ' She shrugged.

Elliot looked at her in amazement. In 'old' New York, it was often considered less indelicate to lie than to face such unpalatable truths so brazenly. But one glimpse of the brave and vulnerable expression in Sylvie's beautiful grey eyes, and all the rules of his inherited code seemed far too simple to deal with the real complexities of life. He passed his hand over his eyes, suddenly weary and unsure. For the first time in his life, Elliot Statten was plagued by self-doubt, and it rocked the very foundations of his personality. He felt a flash of resentment that Sylvie could make him question his own values, could make him feel tinged with such dishonour.

Sylvie saw the struggle that went on inside him, and knew with the finality of an inner logic that this was the end of their brief affair. But, with her instinctive candour, she recognized that there was nothing personal in this rejection of her, that she was merely a sacrifice on the altar of his inner necessity. There could be no protest; they were both in thrall to their own private destinies.

Another moment, and he, too, saw the inevitability of their renouncing their claim to love one another. He read in her eyes the clearness of her understanding and acceptance, and he honoured her for it. He felt the greatness of her spirit in contrast to the narrow rooms his own had been brought up to inhabit. 'I won't leave you at the mercies of that man,' he vowed. It was all he had to offer her.

Sylvie smiled weakly. 'I shall need more than your protection,' she said. And she began to explain to him how she had been tracking Nye through the Stock Exchange, that he was the hidden identity behind the holding companies that Elliot himself had detected operating on the Rand. She knew that, whatever their personal relationship, his compulsion to wield the upper hand on the stock market – especially when pitted against such an adversary as Nye – would bind his remaining loyalty to her. As Elliot heard her out, his gravity disguised his astonishment at her stock market manoeuvres; even while acting as her banker he had never suspected that she had been waging so coherent a campaign against a financial baron as powerful as Jack Nye. His respect for her filled the empty places where his love had been.

'The patent you mentioned to me,' she went on. 'You said the trials have been successful. If so, then no one can mine below the outcrop reef at a profit without it.

That patent lies between Nye and what I'm certain is his ambition – to corner the market in Rand mining shares and so control the supply of gold.'

Elliot nodded. 'I told you, that's the reason I'm going to London now. All the major mining engineers are based there, and I'm going to negotiate with them to see who can put the process into production. The basic formula is fairly simple – using cyanide instead of mercury to treat the tailings – but cyanide has obvious handling problems which have to be ironed out.'

'But the patent is still secret, so far?' she persisted.

'Of course. The minute the technological problems are settled and news of the process becomes public, shares in all the deep-level mining companies will go through the roof. Van Schuyler & Statten want to make sure that their clients can take full advantage of the disclosure – which includes you, of course.'

'I don't believe Nye has any inkling yet that anyone is so close to solving the geological problems on the Rand. But if he gets a scent of this, I think he'll stop at nothing to wrest control of your formula into his own hands. It's the key to everything he wants.'

'Well, he's not going to get it, is he?' said Elliot, his earlier jealousy of Nye re-awakened by the faint accusation of inferiority that Sylvie's concern evoked. 'It won't be the first time that some financial mogul has come so close to a monopoly and failed at the last fence,' he declared with irritable arrogance. 'If, as you say, he's the identity behind these scattered holding companies, he's still have plenty to console himself with. He's a fabulously wealthy man. If he owns as much of the Rand as you say, he'll make J P Morgan look poor!' Elliot laughed, his excitement at the coup he was about to bring off on his own account rising inexorably. 'But, in the long term, he may not end up as wealthy as the partners in Van Schuyler & Statten!'

he added, his eyes shining, almost shivering with the thrill of it all.

Sylvie laid her hand on his arm. 'Be careful,' she pleaded. 'I'm not so sure he will be content with mere wealth. He wants more.'

But Elliot was impatient of her warning. 'He'd never get it anyway,' he answered dismissively. 'Politically, you don't imagine the great powers would ever allow a single individual to control the supply of bullion?'

'There's very little to stop him ousting Kruger and proclaiming himself president of the Transvaal. There's already bad feeling between the Uitlanders – the men who work the mines – and the Boer farmers who support Kruger. I'm not so sure the Uitlanders wouldn't rather have one of their own in charge than either a Boer or some pen-pusher held in place by an occupying army. The Transvaal's a long way from either Queen or Kaiser.'

Elliot merely shrugged. Sylvie did not know how to warn him more effectively. What could she say? That, when she was a child, she had witnessed a man's suicide, after Nye had knowingly ruined him? That she had seen the expression on Nye's face as he had looked down into the Big Hole at Kimberley? Somewhere at the back of her mind another memory tugged at her conscience, something that would persuade Elliot to take her fear of Nye seriously. But, like a word she knew but could not utter, she couldn't pin it down.

Elliot looked at her exhausted face. 'Don't worry about the fellow. I'll take care that he doesn't get near you on this voyage,' he said kindly. All she could do was smile her thanks, and they parted that night, at the door of Sylvie's stateroom, as friends.

Over the next few days, Elliot was true to his word, and he kept close to Sylvie; between them, he and Louisa never allowed anyone an opportunity to find her alone. After the daily rituals of baths, hairdressers and meals, they played deck-quoits, placed bets, along with most of the first-class passengers, on the distance the ship would cover that day, or sat, wrapped in rugs, content to stare silently out to sea. Besides, their fellow travellers created a social scene that enveloped and carried everyone along, so that there was no area of the ship that escaped this mass movement of sociability.

One evening, however, towards the end of the voyage, Sylvie found herself unable to sleep, and, wrapping herself in her thick cloak, went to walk on deck outside her stateroom under the stars. She had had nightmares the past few nights. There was something about this forced enclosure and inactivity that was affecting her badly. Something, like a door at the bottom of a corridor, glimpsed only out of the corner of her eye, behind which some terror lurked. Just lately, in her dreams, the content of which she could not remember in the morning, though the lingering scent of fear was unmistakable, she felt that she already knew what lay behind that door, but had forgotten. Something was pushing at her conscious mind all the time, beating on the doors of memory and insisting that, sooner or later, it would come in. She didn't know what it was, or even what form this unknown terror would take, but she instinctively felt that she had to keep it out at all costs. The more she tossed and turned at night, the more she craved the familiar safety of the theatre. As she paced the silent deck, listening to the sounds of the sea and the wind out in the darkness, she willed the great vessel to steam faster, to reach its destination quicker.

Almost unseeen, a dark shadow detached itself from the shadows and came towards her.

'You must know that you cannot escape me forever, my love.' Nye announced himself abruptly. Sylvie whirled around to face him, drawing her cloak more tightly about her.

'Why should I wish to escape you?' she replied firmly, although inwardly she felt frightened, and wondered if she should call out and waken Louisa. 'I have no business with you.'

Nye laughed. She went to pass him, to gain the door to her stateroom, but he grasped her arm and held her.

'That fellow Lapham,' he said softly. 'He could be a nuisance to you in London. Do you want me to get rid of him for you?'

She tried to shake herself free of him. 'Whatever do you mean?'

'A simple accident, a man overboard, perhaps. You see, I'm not afraid to act in your interests. Just speak the word and you'll be safe.' A gleam of light from one of the lanterns that lit the decks illuminated his dark eyes.

'You're mad! Mr Lapham can't hurt me!'

'Ah, but he already has, hasn't he? Young Statten didn't much like the mention of him, did he? You see, my dear, I don't want anything to threaten your happiness. Don't you see what kind of man I am? Don't you see how I could shelter you? I can give you anything you want.'

'You don't have anything I want!' she spat at him. 'Let go of me!' Sylvie looked down and with her other hand tried to prise Nye's fingers from her arm. But what she saw made her suddenly weaken and moan aloud: instead of the massive diamond he usually wore, his little finger bore an old-fashioned emerald ring, her father's ring that Nye had picked up that day in Kimberley, the day that Daisy's father shot himself.

'You must let me go!' she whimpered. Echoes of her mother's voice began to play in her head, familiar snatches of sentences that made no sense. But as she hung helplessly on Nye's arm, staring at Rudi's ring, the words began to arrange themselves into order, and she heard her mother tell her, that long-ago day, that

Nye was a murderer. Not only was he indirectly responsible for Edward Tarrant's death, but he had killed Sari Fodor: did Sylvie not remember coming home and telling her mother how she had discovered the actress's body, buckled naked to the bed?

There was more, but once again the words faded and those Sylvie heard were random and made no sense. But she was afraid, far more afraid of that tug of incoherent memory than of Nye's bulky figure beside her. She began to sob. 'Let me go! Please!' she begged him. She felt as helpless as she had as a child under her mother's venomous gaze.

'Very well,' he hissed triumphantly in her ear. 'But one day – sooner than you think – you'll beg to come into my arms. I'll wait for you! I shall make you a queen!'

He let her go, and she stumbled to her cabin, where she stood inside, trembling, behind the bolted door, listening to his departing footsteps. At last she roused herself and knocked on her dresser's door.

'Louisa, Louisa! Wake up, please!'

The woman emerged, her eyes still small with sleep, her hair tied in curling rags.

'Come and talk to me, Louisa. I can't be on my own tonight.'

Louisa nodded. Henry Abbey had told her all of Mr Lapham's story, and she had witnessed enough of the change that had so recently come over Elliot Statten's attitude towards Sylvie, to guess at the troubles she had on her mind. Louisa picked up Sylvie's silver-backed hair brush and began to stroke her long, thick hair.

After an interval during which neither woman spoke, Sylvie sighed deeply. 'Tell me about your mother, Louisa,' she asked.

Unperturbed, Louisa spoke quietly and soothingly, as though she were telling a bedtime story. 'There were ten of us, and I was the ninth, so my mother was a fairly remote person to me. It was my sisters who dressed me and took care of me, and told me off! My mother died when I was fourteen, but I remember her with respect. She was always fair. She'd never let us tease each other, or gang up against another child. But she was always, always tired – hardly surprising, really.'

'I thought my mother was – I don't know – some kind of fairy being. She was remote, too, but so beautiful. But, oh, Louisa, how cruel she's been!' Sylvie bowed her head into her hands and began to sob.

Louisa laid down the brush and sat down on the bed behind Sylvie, hugging her shoulders. 'It's all right,' she murmured. 'Everything will be all right.'

Sylvie turned and, laying her head on the woman's breast, sobbed like a child, as Louisa hushed and rocked her gently.

'How can it hurt so much?' Sylvie cried out. 'How can it be so painful just to remember what really happened to me?'

She began, incoherently at first, to tell Louisa how, on that other long voyage from Budapest to the Cape so many years ago, Rosa, by the force of her implacable will, had forced her to deny her own perceptions, had made her believe that her discovery of Sari Fodor's body had been only a nightmare and that her fear of Nye was just an ugly symptom of her adolescent jealousy of her mother's lover. Louisa could not make much sense of Sylvie's story, but she didn't interrupt, realizing that this outpouring would help to assuage the pain.

'I'm not even certain what I really know, and what I was told, those last days we spent in Budapest!' Sylvie struggled in Louisa's arms as though the effort to remember were almost physical. 'It's impossible,' she almost screamed. 'Mamma has crushed so much out of me!' She sat up, breathing deeply, before going on.

'On that other ship, in a cabin like this, bound for an unknown destination, I was alone, enclosed for weeks on board ship with the two adults on whom I felt my life depended. I was so isolated. It was impossible to hold out against Mamma. If I questioned her in any way, she accused me of being unnatural, hysterical and malicious. I wasn't old enough to oppose her, to believe that I wasn't as ugly as she said. I just wanted so desperately to be loved, to feel safe; so I capitulated. How willingly I gave up that vital portion of myself into Mamma's unkind keeping!' And Sylvie realized that she could never be sure just how much of her Rosa still retained.

'I'll never find the power to defy her, to confront her with the truth about the past,' she moaned.

Louisa finally calmed her enough to persuade her to go to bed, while she sat dozing in a chair close beside her in the narrow stateroom. But Sylvie's memories were like the thrusts of a sword, and, tossing on her pillow, she sweated with the anguish of the feelings of hurt and anger that threatened to engulf her. In an effort to lessen the unbearable pain, she scanned her mind for something, anything, that would enable her to believe in Rosa after all and to resume part of her old habit of obedience. She longed for the possibility of reconciliation, for a resolution that would heal the dreadful hurt caused by what she now knew beyond the shadow of a doubt to be the truth of their relationship.

As the dawn broke, she was forced to recognize that, while she could distance herself from Rosa, could try to avoid her company, she was still unequal to the task of confronting her. Feeling hopeless at her own craven betrayal of herself, Sylvie resigned herself to having to go on enduring her mother's crazy vision of life, however much she might now know it for what it was, and she ruthlessly and unconsciously suppressed the boiling anger that she really felt. Determined to pity Rosa – it was the safest way of continuing a relationship she did not know how to end – she at last fell into an exhausted sleep.

When, in the full light of morning, Louisa excitedly reported that there were gulls circling above the ship and that she could see land, Sylvie pulled the covers from over her head and roused herself. The events of the previous night seemed like another bad dream – until she remembered the obscenity of seeing her father's treasured ring on Nye's elegant, manicured hand. By lunch time, when she ventured on deck, heavily veiled and closely accompanied by Louisa, she could see, on one side, the dim, soft outline of the Irish coast and, on the other, the bolder lines of Wales. She almost cried with relief. Finally, the steward knocked at Sylvie's door to say that the ship had entered the Mersey and they would soon be docking at Liverpool; she must be ready for the custom-house officer's inspection. New York seemed an age away, yet, far from the intervening days having given her time to prepare herself for her return to London, everything had yet to be resolved. The voyage of self-discovery she had hoped to make had brought only more terror and uncertainty.

CHAPTER EIGHTEEN

Will approached Rosa's house with a feeling of disgust. The evening was already dark and the pale pink cherry blossom seemed effervescent in the gloom of the square. Normally he would have looked at the phosphorescence created by the moonlight among the branches with pleasure, but, associated with Rosa, the white trees made him think of dead flesh. He did not know why she had so suddenly summoned him at this hour. He had called on her several times over the past months, keeping his word to Sylvie that he would do so, but neither of them had wanted to prolong his visits past the usual polite ten minutes, and he had generally chosen a time when there were likely to be other people there. But tonight, as he ate a companionable dinner with Harry Lewis, who, as *The Times*'s theatre critic, had given him the welcome news that Sylvie's ship was due to dock in Liverpool any day, a messenger had arrived from Rosa, begging Will to come without delay. A cab had been summoned, and Harry had dropped him off at the bottom of Phillimore Terrace on his way to the Garrick Club.

The door opened before he had even rung the bell, and Rosa, dressed in a loose velvet robe, her hair around her shoulders, drew him into the dark hallway.

'I've sent the servants to bed,' she whispered. 'Try not to let them hear you.' She pulled him into the drawing room, and closed the door before turning up the gas. She stood before him, wringing her hands, a mixture of craftiness and terror on her face.

'Whatever is it?' Will asked irritably. He had little

desire to be drawn into some sordid scrape of Rosa's, yet he remembered his promise to Sylvie.

'It's your uncle,' answered Rosa. 'I thought, for your Aunt Laura's sake, that I should call you. I don't know what to do for the best.'

'What's happened? Where is he?'

'He's upstairs. He's had a heart attack. He's dead.'

'Why on earth haven't you called a doctor?' demanded Will, moving towards the door. 'Are you sure he's dead?'

But Rosa laid a hand on Will's arm. 'Oh, quite sure. I called you because he's too heavy for me to move, and I didn't think your aunt would thank me for calling a doctor in his present state.'

Will paused as he realized what she was saying. 'You said he's upstairs?' Rosa nodded slowly in confirmation of the real question in his harsh expression. 'You'd better take me up, then,' he added resignedly.

Falkirk's body lay spread-eagled on Rosa's sumptuous bed. He was naked, except for the red satin ties that bound him to the bedposts. Will spoke only to issue instructions, as he ordered Rosa to undo the satin ribbons and pass him Falkirk's clothes, while he knelt with distaste on the sheets and pushed and pulled at his uncle's heavy, inert body, forcing the lifeless arms into the sleeves of his cast-off dress shirt. 'Here,' he said curtly. 'You can put in his studs and cufflinks while I get his trousers on. Do it properly. But you can leave his tie – we can say we took that off when he was taken ill, to give him more air.' By the time that Will bent to knot the laces in Falkirk's shoes, he ordered Rosa out of the room. 'Go and lay three places at table downstairs. Turn on all the lights. Make it look as though we were halfway through dinner. I'll carry him down in a moment. Then you can get yourself dressed while I send for a doctor.'

Within an hour, the house was in uproar. Rosa sat

shaken and shocked in a corner of the settee, as silent as Will had commanded her to be, while her housekeeper stood beside her, shaking her head in sorrow. Will explained to the doctor that his uncle had been taken ill with violent chest pains, and had died within minutes. The body must be removed from the house, and he would go and break the news to his aunt. As soon as the doctor and the undertaker's van had gone and he had dismissed the housekeeper for the night, Will came to stand before Rosa.

'To spare my Aunt Laura embarrassment among her friends, I shall stick publicly to the story I just told. But I shall tell her the truth.' The furious glare in his eyes silenced Rosa's astonished protest. 'It will come as no surprise to her, and I see no reason to lie. But my collaboration in this charade has a price.'

Rosa snorted. 'There is always a price!' she said contemptuously. 'What passes for honour is merely that some men have no commercial value, which is their saving.'

'I can do without your cynicism. My price is Sylvie. She is not to return to this house.'

Rosa started angrily. She had been planning to induce Sylvie to agree to a move, to use her daughter's newly-earned wealth to set them up in a nice little house in Park Street or South Audley Street – after all, it would be better for the parties that Sylvie really ought to give now she was apparently so famous – but another cold glare from Will's hard greeny-brown eyes convinced her that she would gain nothing from an argument.

'Very well,' she assented wearily. 'I see you're determined to set her against me.'

'I want your promise that you won't try to force her to come back here.'

'How can I do that?' said Rosa in a mock-poignant

tone, turning her head away from him. 'After all, I'm only her mother!'

Will saw no point in extracting further empty vows from this woman. He stood helplessly before her a moment more. 'It's late. I must go and see my aunt,' he said at last. Rosa did not look round, but merely waved her hand for him to leave.

Sylvie was puzzled at Rosa's sudden decision to have the house-painters in the very week of her return to England, but she accepted with pleasure Laura Falkirk's invitation to stay. The Cadogan Square household was in deep mourning, but Laura, although more serious than usual, did not have the hypocrisy, at least among friends, to hide her relief at her deliverance from her husband's bullying oppression. And Sylvie was glad of the isolation that Falkirk's death imposed on them all. Carriages were constantly rumbling to a halt outside in the square, as grave footmen presented cards and letters of condolence, but few people came in person.

To Elliot, too, when he came to call on Sylvie a day or so after establishing himself at Brown's Hotel, it was a relief to find that the constraints of a recent death provided a fitting framework for their altered relationship. He was able to suggest that they meet with Sir Joseph Waldschein as soon as possible, and entrust him with the secret of the patent, without the embarrassment of making it explicit that the dinners and other meetings they had enjoyed together in New York were at an end: the black dress that Sylvie wore out of respect to Laura and Will made any such assignations impossible.

Nevertheless, Will burned with an agony of jealous curiosity while Elliot paid his brief visits. Will could not help but see that the American was everything he should be – handsome, wealthy, well-connected – and

Harry Lewis, who took the New York papers in order to keep up to date with Broadway productions, had also read him the snippets in the Society column that told Will how much time Sylvie had spent exclusively in this elegant Yankee's company. And now he had followed her to London! It was unbearable, but it could only mean one thing: Will had lost her!

Will came every day to help Laura with the arrangements for the funeral, the reading of the will, paying of debts and other practical necessities. But it hurt him now to see Sylvie and to feel the insurmountable barrier that the other man had raised between them. Especially when she looked so tired and even a little anxious. Will could not understand how she could be in love, and not be blooming with health and happiness, but he no longer dared to take his old place as her closest friend. Nor did he yet feel able to carry out his plan of gently breaking the news to her of Stefan Kadar's visit. He had seen Nye's card on the hall table, but, with the house in mourning, it had been easy to refuse him entry. Will did not believe that Sylvie was in any immediate danger from that quarter, and decided to await events. Perhaps if she announced her engagement to this Statten fellow, then Will could tell her the facts of her father's death, and she would have Statten – damn him! – to comfort her.

Laura noticed Will's acute discomfort. It was not her way to cajole a confidence out of him, but she guessed at the source of his pain, and did not press him to prolong his visits to Cadogan Square. But she also strongly suspected that her beloved nephew had completely misunderstood the situation, as men were so prone to do. As Sylvie helped her one morning to sort through the drawers in Douglas Falkirk's desk, throwing away what was now irrelevant and putting aside the many overdue bills to be paid, she decided to throw a little light on Sylvie's state of mind: women were far more able to see the truth of their own hearts, given a little help.

'I'm so glad you're here,' Laura said to her simply. 'You and I have always been friends, haven't we?'

Sylvie smiled in gratitude as she sat beside Laura on the floor. Since the circumstances of Elliot's withdrawal of love, she had realized that she could never afford to forget how dependent she would always be on the benevolence of other people's attitudes towards her. After all, a woman so publicly known as herself was never, somehow, quite proper, even if her parentage were spotless.

'You must come and stay with us in Scotland when you get back from this tour. Castle Falkirk is my sanctuary,' said Laura. She paused, as if she were about to continue, but seemed to shake herself and smile instead. Yet her private thoughts about her marriage were partly expressed in her next words. 'You're so lucky, you know, having the means to support yourself.'

'Most women would be shocked,' answered Sylvie quietly.

'It saves them being envious of your privacy.'

'My privacy! I earn my money by being looked at!'

'Yes, but when you are at leisure, you're not at the beck and call of the demands that propriety says I must make on my daughters – the endless notes to write and flowers to arrange. You can think of larger concerns than servants and children's illnesses and other people's betrothals.'

'When I'm stuck with train timetables and costume fittings,' laughed Sylvie, 'I often think how very pleasant it would be to think about flowers or children.' She blushed despite the lightness of her tone.

'You're not at all what I expected,' declared Laura. 'I thought you'd have become hard and brittle with your success, that your emotions would have grown artificial, but they're not. Why, I think you're quite romantic!'

Sylvie was slightly embarrassed at such artless candour, but delighted nonetheless. 'I could never live without romance. Why, you might as well replace the sky with a ceiling!' she laughed. 'That's a line from a play I do, but I rather agree with it!'

'Yes, it's good,' answered Laura. Sylvie knew of old that Laura Falkirk's vagueness of manner concealed a sharp, though intuitive, intelligence, and she was warmly flattered by her evident intention to remain firm friends. But Laura's next speech astonished her.

'Your friend, Mr Statten, seems to be of a more literal temperament. I'm sure he thinks he can be romantic, but he actually views romance as an easily disposable addition to life, not an essential. You must feel that yourself.'

Sylvie was speechless.

'Excuse me,' said Laura, blushing. 'I speak as I think. But I'm always interested in the relations between men and women. Take Will, now . . . he is far too romantic, and can hardly equate it with real life at all. Except in his painting. Then he wears his heart on his sleeve for all to see. That of course was the great secret of that lovely painting he did of you, *The Angel*.' She fell silent, allowing her words to sink in.

Sylvie's eyes dropped back to the pile of papers in her lap, but she shuffled them aimlessly for a few moments before speaking. 'Did you really like *The Angel*?' she asked shyly and hesitantly.

'It was the greatest love-letter that any artist could hope to write. I think his new portrait of you is a much better likeness, but that other one – well, it just showed all the confusion of a man in love who didn't know it yet. It's as much a portrait of himself as of you. Now, of course, he does. And that's why his latest picture is so much more realistic. You haven't seen it yet, now it's framed, have you? It's more beautiful than *The Angel*, but not as powerful. I loved *The Angel*!' Laura laughed. 'But then I love Will!'

Laura stood up and took another drawer out of the desk and put it down on the floor. She glanced at Sylvie. The girl was breathing deeply through her open mouth. The transformation was almost visible, like snow melting and slipping off the branches of a tree, making the possibility of spring vivid and alive.

'Do you mind carrying on with this?' asked Laura softly. 'I think I'll just go and ask about some tea. I'm sure you'd like some?'

Sylvie nodded, smiling seraphically.

Sylvie could not believe her own happiness. Nothing had really changed over the past few days, but the fears and nightmares of the sea voyage had turned out to be nothing but chimeras. Amid the familiar panelling of Threadneedle Street, Sir Joseph had managed to assuage her dread of Nye. She trusted Sir Joseph's judgement so implicity that if he pursed his lips and shrugged his shoulders when she explained her theory of Nye's political ambitions, then, with a shuddering sigh of relief, she was prepared to treat her fears as all part of her ship-board nightmares. She was even prepared to believe that Nye's lunatic offer to dispose of Mr Lapham for her must have been somehow unreal; she did not confide that bizarre episode to either Elliot or her old friend – it was too impossible. Besides, Nye had not been heard of now for several weeks: he had not called again in Cadogan Square, nor in Kensington, nor even at the Maybeck Gallery.

Sir Joseph had also persuaded Sylvie, for the first time, to cede control of her financial affairs. Elliot, moved by the chivalrous feelings Sylvie now evoked in him, had willingly agreed to form a syndicate with Sir Joseph's firm, which would include Sylvie's own holdings on the Rand. By amalgamating their joint shareholdings, the new syndicate would enable both the Threadneedle Street bank and Van Schuyler & Statten to cushion the expense of trials of the cyanide process should it not adapt itself economically to local conditions, or to take the fullest advantage of its success – in which case, the syndicate would also constitute a more than convincing challenge to Nye's financial muscle on the Rand.

'This will be my last great campaign,' Sir Joseph had said. 'After this I retire. I give you notice, now, Sylvie. My old bones can hardly keep up with you any more!'

Henry Abbey had recently arrived, and had clacked his tongue and pretended to fuss that she had not been out on a round of balls, parties and luncheons, making the most of the acclaim of her American tour, although secretly he was relieved to see her look so rested, and eager for her departure to Europe. Sylvie, delighted to see her manager again, had teased him in return. 'I declare that if I was to cut your heart through the middle, I'd find it made of solid gold – I mean the kind you can buy theatres with, not the kind that children's stories are made of!'

'Well,' he'd replied, his dark eyes dancing with pleasure, 'I can't make you the toast of Europe if you won't go where the champagne flows!'

But the most improbable surprise was a visit Sylvie paid to Rosa, where she found Mr Lapham ensconced in a corner of her drawing room, quietly sipping tea with a satisfied air. He smiled bountifully at her, an entirely changed man.

'All he wants is to be near me,' Rosa had explained in exasperation to Sylvie out in the hallway. 'He comes here every morning and stays an hour. He doesn't even want to talk! He just sits and smiles and drives me mad!' But Sylvie detected the slightest note of pride in her mother's vindication of her unaccustomed spirit of tolerance: such evident devotion as Mr Lapham's could not be entirely disregarded, after all. Sylvie secretly hoped that Onslow Lapham's constancy might go some way to compensate Rosa for the loss of other passions in her life, that Rosa might even find it possible to grow old gracefully after all.

Sylvie had been astonished, on her return to London, to find that Rosa seemed almost uninterested in her and her plans and had since tamely acquiesced to all Sylvie's suggestions regarding both meetings and domestic arrangements. Will and Laura had agreed not to tell Sylvie the circumstances of Douglas Falkirk's death, and Rosa had no reason to tell Sylvie the truth. She had merely apologized for not being able to have Sylvie stay with her, and had never since even demanded that she visit her. Feeling guilty at her unlooked-for release, Sylvie had trebled the allowance she paid her mother, and joyfully accepted her freedom.

As she drove back to Cadogan Square after witnessing the spectacle of Mr and Mrs Lapham's unexpected harmony, Sylvie thought how lovely London looked, how much she preferred it to New York. She found herself thinking longingly of Budapest. It lay at the end of her tour, beckoning, enticing her with thoughts of both happiness and dread. 'If only Papa had lived,' she thought with a pang of deep regret. Her experience in Saratoga had persuaded her that it was useless to think of any contact with Rudi's family in Budapest, but she missed her father now with all the force of the little child she was gradually learning to rediscover inside her. It seemed to her sometimes that all she needed to be complete was to have someone with whom she could evoke the happy memories of her early childhood with him.

Looking forward to beginning her European tour, now that Abbey had arrived, she decided that afternoon to begin her packing. She was on her knees before a large open trunk when there was a knock at her door and Will entered. Delighted, she jumped up to welcome him, laughing shyly and looking somewhat embarrassed at the strange assortment of paraphernalia that was neatly stacked in various sized piles around her. Most of it would have looked extraordinary even in a Wardour Street curio shop.

'It's my props trunk,' she explained, giving him her hand in greeting. 'I thought I'd sort through it in case there's anything I can use on tour.'

She did not question why he had come upstairs to find her, instead of paying his visit in the drawing room as usual. She felt light-headed this afternoon: she was happy that he was there, and that seemed to her sufficient explanation of his presence.

Will kissed her on the cheek, catching the lovely scent of her skin, and longed to pull her to him in an embrace. She was dressed simply in a loose, clinging tea-gown of a pale pink that accentuated her russet hair, caught at the waist with a silver-buckled belt. Her embroidered slippers had been kicked off to the side of the room, revealing her cotton stockings, of a slightly darker shade of pink than the silk of her dress. She looked so young, reminding him of when he had first sketched her, downstairs in his aunt's morning room.

'I expected you'd be at the costumiers again this afternoon,' he said, still holding onto her hand.

'Yes, I was supposed to be. But . . . I wanted some time to myself,' she said lamely. Will was surprised: Sylvie seldom let people down and, since his arrival, Henry Abbey had kept her to a very tight schedule. But he cherished her old familiar frankness.

'I feel I have to prepare myself here, too,' she explained awkwardly, clasping her hands to her heart, but smiling happily at him. 'It's no good having the right wig or costume if *I'm* not ready.' She shook her head, as if dismissing her own fancifulness, and knelt down again beside her trunk. She had obviously been arranging her odd collection of trophies for quite some time, and Will noticed that apparently natural cheerfulness about her which re-surfaced whenever her energies were directed back into theatrical channels.

Will knelt down beside her on the floor, wondering how he was to break the news to her. As they leant together over the motley collection of old playbills, albums of costume designs, fashion plates, paste jewels, hats, buckles, shoes, fans, handkerchiefs and tattered acting copies of old tragedies, he felt that she derived some comfort that she obviously needed from her evident affection for these mementoes, and he gladly joined her in her task. For some minutes they laughed together over Sylvie's props as she recounted the stories and memories that the quaint, faded stuffs evoked. Their fingers touched as she passed him things, and their eyes met as they spoke. Sylvie felt her joyousness increase with his nearness. Since Elliot Statten had awoken her sensuality, she had begun to acknowledge to herself how attractive she had always found Will to be, how right and comfortable she had always felt in his physical presence. Looking at Will, with his sleek, brown head and his sharp, candid eyes, she felt how very dear he was to her. She was suddenly glad that she had never slept with Elliot.

'Anything remotely connected with a performance that went well must never be discarded,' she told him playfully, 'whether it's an old power puff or an entire coat of arms.' At this point, a faded bouquet came to light, which she hastily placed on a pile behind her: Will suspected with pleasure that it was one he had once sent her.

'It's also very unlucky to throw away anything with your name on it,' she continued, 'so every playbill, programme and fly poster that lands in your lap must be religiously kept, no matter how small the print in which your name appears.'

'What's this?' he asked, taking up an old calf-bound volume from a pile on the carpet. Opening it, he flicked through a few pages. ' "Rodolpho! Rodolpho!" ' he read, holding out his arm in a stagey gesture. ' "Come to my aid else I perish!" ' She tried to take the book from him, but, teasing her, he picked up some of the others. '*The Haunted Tower*, *The Lying Lover*, *Clandestine Marriage, or, Aldobrand's Revenge*. You didn't really appear in any of these, did you?'

'Indeed I did! Complete with tinselled costumes!' declared Sylvie, giggling as he let her take the books from him and replace them on the stack. She caught her breath, wanting this moment to go on for ever. 'They used to go down a treat in the provinces, especially at matinées. Though sometimes we had to play them for laughs.'

'I should hope so!' He pulled a face, but now his eyes remained serious.

'What is it, Will?' she asked, looking steadily at him. 'Is something the matter?'

Will sighed and nodded. He stood up, then gave her his hand to pull her to her feet. How lovely she was! How rare! How beautiful she smelled and how candidly she looked into his eyes! He rubbed his other hand over his face.

'It's Elliot Statten,' he said. At once her eyes widened with fright. 'Sir Joseph Waldschein sent me a note an hour ago, and I came over here right away.'

Sylvie's face was white. 'What's happened to him?' she whispered.

Will looked down at his feet. He knew that Sylvie had hardly seen anything of the American over the past few weeks, but he still did not know how far her emotions had been committed. 'There was a fire in one of the courts near Shepherd's Market a few days ago,' he began.

Sylvie nodded. 'I heard about it. In one of the buildings the prostitutes use, wasn't it?'

Will nodded uncomfortably. 'They found a man's body in the room where the fire started. They've only just managed to identify it.' He took a deep breath. 'It was Statten.'

'I warned him,' cried Sylvie. Her hands flew to her mouth and she unconsciously began to bite her knuckles. 'I told Sir Joseph, too, but they wouldn't listen. They wouldn't take me seriously. He must have found out what Elliot was up to. I knew he'd stop at nothing!' She began to rock on her stockinged feet until Will took her in his arms and steadied her.

'Who found out?' he asked, murmuring the words into her hair, completely at a loss to understand her meaning. 'What did you tell Sir Joseph?'

'Years ago, in Budapest, he killed someone. I know. I found her body. Then, on the boat, he said he'd kill Mr Lapham for me, if I wanted him to. I warned Elliot he was dangerous! I told him he'd have to get his hands on the patent!' Her voice began to rise hysterically. She looked at Will with wild eyes. 'He killed Elliot, I know he did, I know he did.' She began to repeat herself, becoming more breathless until her voice rose almost in a shriek.

Will shook her by the shoulders. 'Who did? Who are you talking about?' he asked, although a cold hand clutched at his heart as Stefan Kadar's warning voice whispered the name in his ear.

Sylvie looked at him in disbelief. 'Nye. Jack Nye, of course.' She began to sob. Will bent and scooped her up in his arms. He carried her over to the bed, where he sat, cradling her against him, stroking her hair, kissing her face and hands and murmuring that everything would be all right. But the questions went round and round in his head. Will could not guess why Nye had killed Elliot Statten, he knew nothing of Sylvie's investments or the new syndicate that Sir Joseph had formed, yet he had no doubt that Sylvie's instinct was right. But how could they do anything? And how could he begin to tell her that it had been Nye who killed her father? As she clung to him, still sobbing gently, he dared not risk inflicting such a further, grievous blow. Will hugged her tighter, whispering words of love into her hair.

CHAPTER NINETEEN

Only in the theatre could Sylvie feel fully in control again. On her opening night in Paris, Abbey sat in his box with his guests and watched in open-mouthed admiration as Sylvie carried off the most impeccable and moving performance of her career. She received rapturous applause and ecstatic reviews. The next day, all Paris, normally so hostile to foreign influences, was talking about the new star, and they welcomed her as one of their own. For the next ten days, Sylvie was safely cocooned by her success. Invitation followed invitation. At every luncheon, soirée and ball, she was applauded, admired and complimented. The easier it was for her to hide from herself, the more robust and confident she once more became. The exhaustion of each day finally gave her the luxury of deep, dreamless sleep. Only on stage, where she had always held secret communion with her inner self, did that richness of experience, that special luminosity born of pain, shine through every line of the parts she played.

Abbey had been horrified when he had seen how wan and tired Sylvie looked on the day they set out for Paris, but had assumed that she was grieving for her American lover. As he watched her closely from the pit during rehearsals in Paris he had immediately sensed the change in her, noticed a new fragility and vulnerability in her performance. It made him tingle with excitement so long as she was on stage; off stage, it made him more fiercely protective of her than ever. Yet, off stage, she seemed to have acquired a new hardness, a new brilliance. Sylvie's new-found confidence in her public self surprised Abbey, and, for the first time, he felt somewhat in awe of his protégée. He only hoped that she wouldn't wind herself up to such a pitch that she would shatter like glass – or shatter the nerves of everyone around her with her fine, pure intensity.

Sylvie seldom sought or relished the attention that her fame invariably bestowed on her in public, but at times in Paris she seemed to be afire, like a crystal reflecting the low-angled sun, burning with some inner need for power and forcefulness, and the people around her in restaurants or at parties glanced constantly in her direction, attracted by the strange, provocative nimbus that hung about her. Abbey shook his head. There had to be a trace of instability in every genius, after all, and he had often felt that there had been something repressed and over-controlled about Sylvie's earlier docility and ease.

In truth, Sylvie was experiencing pure, unconditional anger for the first time in her life. Like a dynamo, the feeling was gathering speed and momentum the more she fed it. She felt like a comet, full of blazing energy, whizzing around the firmament, her tail spread in beauty behind her. She knew that no one could withstand her cauterizing heat as she set out, at last, to take her fate into her own hands and to put a stop once and for all to the man who had taken her young life and wrung it out of shape for his own mad and miserable ends, and who still dogged her footsteps.

After the news of Elliot's death, she and Will had immediately sought out Sir Joseph. He had listened in grave astonishment and sorrow to her tale. He blamed himself for never having found out more about her background, about Rosa, when Sylvie had first come to him: how he could have helped her if he had only known! But he had been forced to agree with Will that it would be pointless to go to the authorities about Elliot's death. Who would believe them that such an influential, distinguished man as Nye was a common murderer? They had nothing concrete to connect him with a prostitute's flat in Shepherd's Market and were unlikely to be believed. 'They'll say we've cooked up some fantastic theory of conspiracy to protect Statten's reputation,' he had counselled wisely. 'After all, it was an unseemly place to die, as I'm sure Mr Nye took into full account.' Privately, he also thought that, in her present condition, it would be unwise to present Sylvie as their principal witness against Nye, and her accusations could lead to some most unpleasant and persistent publicity.

'But,' he went on, sitting bowed with care in his chair, looking older than Sylvie had ever known him, 'what concerns me most is what he'll do next.'

'You mean about the patent?' Sylvie had asked.

'No, my dear. More serious than that.' Will and Sylvie had looked at him in confusion. 'I mean what he'll do about you, my dear,' he had said. 'You must be his next target. I discount myself.' He waved his gnarled hand in the air. 'He can wait for me to die of natural causes before he has to turn his attention to me. But you are the remaining member of the syndicate that now owns the patent. If he knew about Elliot, he must know about you. He will want you out of the way next.'

But Sylvie had disconcerted them both by laughing. 'Oh no. He has other plans for me! After all, if he marries me, what's mine becomes his automatically. He said he wanted to make me his queen!' She laughed again, but tears trembled on her lashes.

'Then marry me now!' declared Will, rising impetuously from his chair. 'That would put paid to his sick fantasies.' Sylvie had thanked him silently with the full power of her glistening grey eyes. She held out her hand to him, and he came to stand beside her chair, holding her hand tightly between both of his.

'No!' Sir Joseph almost shouted. 'No,' he repeated, more calmly, though with equal vehemence as they looked at him with shock. 'There's nothing I should like to see happen more,' he explained, 'but don't you see? If he can't marry you, he'll have to kill you,' he said simply.

The clock ticked loudly in the old panelled room, as each wrestled with their own thoughts. The only other sounds, besides the rattle of traffic in the narrow street below, were Sir Joseph's slightly rasping breath and the occasional rustle of Sylvie's full skirts.

'Can't Sylvie just renounce her part in all this?' Will had broken the silence. 'I feel so helpless. Can't she just give her share away? I've enough wealth, God knows, for us both.'

'And leave others to face the risk?' asked Sylvie. 'We can't let him win. And besides,' she added, hanging her head in shame, 'he won't give up. He wants me anyway. It's not just because of the Rand. He told me he wanted me before he ever knew of my part in all this. He already has *The Angel*.'

Will's face, too, had burned with colour. He still had not told Sylvie that Nye had killed Count Lazar. Realizing how dangerous Nye was, and learning of the vast stakes involved in Nye's infatuation with Sylvie, he had been afraid of unleashing a passion for vengeance in Sylvie that he could not control. What if she were to confront Nye and be crushed? He dared not take the risk. Although sometimes, as at this moment, he felt that neither dare he any longer accept the responsibility of hiding the truth from her. But once more, discretion and his innate desire to protect her made him bite back the terrible words he knew he had at some time to say.

Sir Joseph had sighed, interrupting Will's desperate thoughts, and shifted awkwardly in his chair. He was studying the lovely woman who sat before him, considering her last words. He could not deny the likelihood of what she said. Sylvie was a prize for any man. 'We have no alternative,' he had said at last. 'We must be cleverer than Mr Nye.' He tapped both hands on the desk before him in a gesture of finality. 'We must set a trap.'

On the train south to Italy at the end of the Paris run, Abbey surveyed Sylvie as she sat in their private railway carriage looking serenely out of the window at the parched rocks and sheer mountainsides of Provence. He was relieved to see how she thrived on her work. The pressures of such a tour as this would have sent a lesser woman into a fit of the vapours long before, but she positively enjoyed every aspect of it all – the journeys, inspecting the theatres, the socializing, not to mention all the different plays she carried in her head. Always a ready traveller, she had watched the miles of vineyards and romantic castles of Burgundy give way to the more rugged landscapes of the south. She was enchanted by her first glimpses of a more ancient past as they steamed past the ruins of a Roman viaduct or the fragments of an overgrown wall or arch, until, at last, they had their first sight of the Mediterranean, quickened by a fleet of frigates at anchor in the bay, motionless on the sapphire waters.

In Rome, Sylvie's magic had flown before them, and they were awaited at their hotel overlooking the Piazza di Spagna by a pile of invitations and *permessi* to visit the best private art collections and gardens of the magnificent Roman villas. In Vienna, too, she was fêted as she entered the hot, crowded rooms of the old palaces or the elegant restaurants of the Prater, still with the spell of the applause upon her. Every evening, at the end of the performance, Louisa had waited in the wings with her cloak. 'Now get your breath. You were magnificent,' she breathed, sending Sylvie forth to receive the ever more rapturous homage to her powers.

When Sylvie and Abbey left for Budapest, driving around the Ringstrasse from their hotel early in the morning to catch the little boat from the Prater-Quai which joined the Danube steamer, a slight mist had hung about the young trees between the newly-erected edifices of Imperial might and Sylvie had felt the clear, sweet tang of autumn in the air. Vienna had grown considerably since her last, brief visits as a child, and, as the steamboat plied its way downstream, she looked with sadness at the dirty barges and crowded tenements that had sprouted beside the Danube Canal. It seemed to her a miracle of political skill as great as any feat of engineering to keep so many people uncomplaining in the face of such squalor and unnecessary degradation.

She didn't know what she would do with her own steadily accumulating wealth – perhaps create a garden like the one Laura Falkirk spoke of in Scotland. It made no sense at all to Sylvie, nurtured as she had been by Will and his friends, men who had deliberately turned their backs on accounting ledgers and legal briefs, not to use her money in a way that created beauty for all. That the promise of the nineteenth century should come to this! This clatter and smoke and endless harrassed throng, oppressed by the philosophies of progress and profit! Surely the gold that lay beneath the southern African veld could be put to better account than such tyranny!

Once out of the city, however, as the sun banished the morning mists, Sylvie's spirits rose. She walked up to the boat's highest deck and looked eagerly at the steeply-rising green terraces of the vineyard villages and the never-ending, silent blue miles of forest that stretched way to the east, to Russia and beyond. The familiar onion-domes, the monasteries and palaces that they passed, all sang to her of home. In her mind whispered a beckoning voice, like an echo of haunting gypsy music. Wrapped in her furs, she stood for hours at the rail, staring at the choppy waters, and would not come inside until the boat had passed Pressburg and the scenery finally gave way to flat and uninspiring grasslands.

At last, towards dusk, the river became busy with mills, rafts, barges and the local screw-steamers. They passed under the Margaret Bridge, only completed since she had left Budapest, and then Sylvie was able to point out excitedly to Abbey their first sight of the long city of Pest on the left, with its new palatial buildings fronting the river. Handsome new apartment buildings, smart shops and offices had also been erected in the districts around the new Government and Stock Exchange buildings. She looked longingly up to the right, to the hills of Buda, and felt her heart beat more swiftly. She fought the tears and clung to Abbey's hand. It was dark by the time they went under the suspension bridge and stopped at one of the piers of Pest, where they disembarked.

At Sylvie's request, they took a one-horse cab like quite ordinary tourists. She looked out at the town with excitement as they drove to the Grand Hotel Hungaria on the Ferencz Joszef rakpart. How Budapest had grown during the years since she had lived there! Trams clanked and clanged, their noise penetrating every street, and the city bustled fit to burst. Count Rudi Lazar's Budapest had gone, forced to give way, she thought bitterly, to the Nyes of this world.

The following afternoon, freed by Abbey until she was due back at the theatre, Sylvie put on her plainest dress, wrapped herself in her sealskin cloak and, smoothing down her hair, swathed a thick cashmere shawl about her head and shoulders. Slipping unseen out of the hotel, she waited for a streetcar to take her across the river to Buda. She felt the cold intensely, a foreboding of winter rather than of autumn, but she listened with pleasure to the Hungarian spoken by the people beside her.

She found the older town of Buda less altered. From the main square of Castle Hill, she wandered up the narrow cobbled streets where she had walked so many times as a girl. She paused and turned to look back down into the wide, sloping square: there was the same line of cabs waiting, the steaming horses patiently munching in their nosebags; there was the gaudily painted Church of St Matthew where the Emperor and Empress of Austria had been crowned King and Queen of Hungary, with the view across the wide grey river beyond where she had often stood with Rudi. Yet, after all, she did not experience the rush of nostalgia and remembrance she had expected. These stones and buildings were indifferent to her; there was no answering resonance of feeling. She could find little trace of herself here.

She walked on up the street and around the corner, past the pretty doorways and painted stucco fronts of the old, narrow houses. Around the back, beside the old city wall, was the familiar avenue of chestnut trees, their leaves already turning to the parched and vivid shades of autumn – yellow, brown and sunset-orange. A few empty conker husks lay on the ground, the creamy softness of the inner shells naked and fleshy against the glistening cobbles. In the gardens below, she could see the red berries of a rowan against the grey slate roofs.

At last she turned her face to the house where she was born, looking up at her bedroom window and the ornate wrought-iron balcony of the drawing room. It all looked much the same as she remembered it. Pulling her shawl more closely about her, she stood against the wall beneath the trees, out of the way of hurrying passers-by, and examined every window in turn, picturing the furnishings that had once stood inside, feeling the warmth of the old ceramic stove, recalling snatches of music, conversation or laughter. She remembered, painfully, Rudi's death. She had never so much as visited his grave, and wondered now where he lay buried – on the family estates, she supposed. She didn't even know precisely where they were. How little she knew of him after all! She sighed at the impossibility of ever comprehending her own life.

Drawn automatically to the familiar movements, she strolled back into the narrow streets to where the gateway and passage opened onto the central courtyard of the old house. She heard the slight echo of her light footsteps beneath the archway and her hand caressed the worn balustrade beside the wide stone steps that led upstairs. Dreamily, she almost reached out to pull the bell beside the half-glazed door before turning to leave, when she saw a figure come slowly down the stairs. Sylvie looked up, half expecting to find Kati there, smiling at her, but it was Racker.

'Welcome, Madame Lazar.' The little man greeted her with a polite bow. He was still dapper and compact, despite his advancing years. 'My master told me to expect you. Please enter.' He stood to one side, gesturing with his arm for her to precede him up the stairs.

Sylvie passed him silently and walked up to the gallery that overlooked the courtyard below.

'Mr Nye bought this house years ago, before we left Budapest,' Racker explained. 'Please,' he repeated his gesture as she paused outside the door to the salon. 'The house is empty. We have it to ourselves.'

Sylvie calmly pushed open the door to the old drawing room, while her rage burned up hard and clear inside her: how dare Nye be there in her father's house, treading on her memories, trespassing once more on her inner life! Yet there seemed a dreadful inevitability about his presence here. She looked curiously and apprehensively around the once familiar room, but it bore no resemblance to the salon where Rosa had held her famous gatherings. The subtle colours and patterns of her mother's era had given way to the heavy veneered and inlaid pieces so beloved in Eastern Europe.

With a shock, she turned and saw, on the wide wall beside the door, Will's huge painting of *The Angel.* For a moment, her own face seemed to leer down at her in the dim afternoon light, promising some impossible, unthinkable seduction. She looked angrily at Racker, but he stood, as he had always done, impassive and aloof, inspecting some insignificant spot on the floor. Then, as she stood in this familiar yet altered room, other voices drifted through her head: Rudi, skating with her – 'See! You can do it, you little angel. You can do anything!' – an old woman sitting on her bed upstairs in this house – 'Don't you ever let people tell you you're not as good as they are, or old Kati will have something to say about it!' – and Laura Falkirk – 'the great secret of that lovely painting is that it's the greatest love-letter that any artist could hope to write.' And there was Will, Will with his brown otter's hair and his sharp friendly eyes, Will who had always loved her, who would be here soon to hold her in his arms again and whom she now knew she wanted more than she had ever wanted anything. She lifted her head and smiled in complicity at the painting on the wall. She was no longer afraid to be the Angel.

But she hated Nye more intensely than ever for not leaving her alone, for being in this house, for owning *The Angel.* Suddenly she felt nauseous, as though the hand that seemed clenched about her life were squeezing at her internal organs. She turned to go.

'Wait. I have something for you.' Racker, instantly alert, walked over to a side-table and picked up a flat packet. Sylvie flung up her head and laughed in derision.

‘Not another diamond necklace?’

But the man’s face was blank as he put the packet into her hands.

Sylvie immediately opened the case. Inside was a single, enormous tear-drop diamond of such silver purity that even Sylvie gasped at its unequalled beauty. An ornate claw mount in the form of an oriental dragon held a fine gold chain that looped around the huge stone within the box.

‘There’s no message to accompany it?’ she asked contemptuously, as she snapped the box shut. Racker shook his head. Sylvie looked once more about the room, then left the house.

In the square, she took one of the waiting cabs, but ordered the driver to stop in the dead centre between the two stone bastions of the grey suspension bridge. It was almost dusk and the mist lay thickly about the hills of Buda; the slim onion-domed spire of the Taban parish church rose, green and wet, in the smoky air, while the lights of the fashionable cafés and hotels on the opposite bank beckoned. The horse dropped its head and waited patiently, balancing its weight on three legs as the heavy traffic of carts, carriages and cabs passed by, their drivers looking curiously as Sylvie got down from the cab and walked to the parapet. The smooth grey waters of the river reflected only the wide expanse of sky above.

Looking up, she saw the great chains of the bridge bowed above her, and the cab driver caught sight of her face, until then hidden by the cashmere shawl. It was a beautiful face, and, for an instant, he was about to leap from his high perch and save her, for the intensity of those large, grey eyes made him fear that she meant to jump. But, before he could move, with a sudden gesture, she took her hand from her muff and swiftly and contemptuously flung a long, flat packet as far from her as she could out into the space between the sky and the deep, fast-flowing river. As it fell, spiralling downwards, it opened, and, just for a moment, there was a glint of whiteness before the huge diamond hit the choppy water and disappeared. But Sylvie did not wait to see the trophy sink from sight; she calmly climbed back into the cab and waved the astonished driver to go on across the bridge to her hotel.

That night, she gave such a fiery, flawless performance on stage that those who watched her told themselves that this would be an evening they would recount to their grandchildren in years to come.

In the morning, Louisa brought in a telegram with her breakfast. 'Is it from Sir William?' she asked excitedly, for Louisa loved a romance, and thoroughly approved of Will.

'Yes,' confirmed Sylvie, as she read the printed lines. 'He arrives today with my mother, as we planned.' Louisa smiled, but was dumbfounded to see Sylvie's lips tighten and her hand, where it lay on the counterpane, clench into a fist. Then she swept out of bed and took the surprised woman by the shoulders. 'In the next few days, Louisa,' she said in a determined voice, looking into her eyes, 'I shall play the greatest part of my life!' Then she disappeared into the bathroom, leaving her dresser to look after her in confusion.

As she emerged later from her bedroom, dressed to go out, there was a knock at the door, and a bell-hop presented a card on a silver salver. Louisa took it, but then handed it to Sylvie. 'I can't pronounce it,' she apologized.

Sylvie read the elegant copperplate: 'The Countess Karatsonyi.' She turned wonderingly to the bell-hop.

'The Countess presents her compliments to Miss Lazar, and asks if she may come up?' he recited.

'Oh yes, yes,' answered Sylvie joyfully.

Rudi's sister's hair had turned an iron grey, but her

bearing remained regal. She paused on the threshold, examining Sylvie critically, looking hard into her eyes, then her face softened into a wide smile and she stepped forward, holding out her hands: 'My dear,' she said warmly.

Sylvie rushed to take her aunt's hands, and instantly found herself embracing the Countess and fighting back the tears. The quality of her skin and hair, the expression in her eyes, all reminded Sylvie sharply and painfully of her lost father. Somehow she even smelled like Rudi! 'How can I thank you for coming?' Sylvie said at last, as the two women seated themselves on the gilt hotel sofas in the salon of Sylvie's suite. 'This is so kind, and so unlooked for!'

'What nonsense!' answered Elizabeth. 'You're my brother's child! And how like him you are! I saw your performance last night. He would have been very, very proud of you.'

Sylvie felt as though she were in a dream. Of all the compliments she had ever received, this was the one she would treasure forever. To sit here and see such affection glow in eyes so like her father's! It was a dream come true.

'It was courageous of you to return to Budapest,' continued Elizabeth, looking directly at her. 'But I think I saw from your performance on stage that you have the true Lazar spirit, that you are not afraid to deal with the truth.'

Sylvie did not quite understand what the Countess meant by this firmly-stated opinion, but took it as a comment on her acting and smiled gratefully.

'You do know, don't you, how Rudi died, my dear?' Elizabeth pressed gently.

Sylvie nodded sadly. 'In a duel. Protecting my mother's honour,' she answered. Nye's words, spoken so long ago, were all that she actually knew of the affair. She hoped that now, at last, she would be told the full story of her father's honour, and waited expectantly. But as she raised her eyes, she saw with surprise and mounting alarm that her aunt's expression had changed, had become set and hard, and that her eyes glinted in anger.

'Your mother's honour!' The Countess almost spat out the words. 'Who told you that?' But before Sylvie, confused and afraid, could answer, the door burst open and in rustled Rosa, flushed with the urgency of her completed journey and followed by three porters carrying cases, bags and hat boxes.

'Sylvie, my darling!' cried Rosa, throwing open her arms in greeting. Immediately, Rudi's sister rose from her seat and walked determinedly past Rosa and the porters with never a backward glance at Sylvie's ashen face.

Shattered, and unable to face Rosa's gushing tales of her journey, Sylvie made her garbled excuses, left Louisa to help her mother unpack and ran to find Will. She found him in his room down the corridor, and she clung to him as he took her immediately in his arms.

'I know you've just got here, but will you come for a drive with me?' she asked him shyly at last, looking up from his embrace. Ten minutes later, piled with rugs against the cold, the hood of the carriage down, they set off up Andrassy-ut towards the Varosligeti To. Will sat quietly beside her, content for the moment to let her settle whatever troubles she obviously had in her own way. Understanding that it was always hard for Sylvie to greet her mother with equanimity, he merely drew her hand into his and held it warm under their wraps.

In the Varosliget park, the driver trotted them slowly between the avenues of trees, many already with yellowing leaves. 'My father used to bring me skating here when I was a little girl,' explained Sylvie, relaxing now and leaning back against the leather cushions as she looked about her. 'He used to call me his little angel, too,' she added wistfully, before lapsing back into silence. The pond was grey and choppy, but Sylvie could easily recall the fiery braziers and noisy excitement of midwinter.

Sulphurous steam hung over the Szeczenyi baths and mingled with the tang of autumn decay. An image came to her mind of some melting ice sculptures that she had once seen on the pavement outside a house in London where there had been a ball. They seemed suddenly meaningful – grotesque, evocative images of their age: once formed, but now formless or deformed, spoilt playthings discarded but not yet dissipated back into the element from which they came. Their sweet claim to pity lay in that hopeless promise that they might yet be redeemed, made good once more. She felt on the rim of an abyss. Again the wings of memory were beating at the door: like the half-melted ice sculpture of a once-proud swan, she felt that her memories were breaking down, melting and re-forming in her mind. She stood at the edge of some cruel knowledge that could either distort and maim, or render her life and her feelings whole and healthy once more.

At this moment, Will made up his mind that he should tell her now about her father's death. 'Sylvie,' he began, turning to her, and cupping her face with his free hand. She looked trustingly into his eyes, and his stomach lurched. He steeled himself: 'Sylvie, I . . . '

But she put a finger to his lips and smiled a sweet, sad smile. 'Please,' she said, shaking her head. 'Please let's not talk. It means so much to me just to be here, with you, remembering it all. I feel as though I'm pouring that little girl I once was into a new mould, finding the happiness and confidence my Papa gave me once again in you.' She put her face up for a kiss, and their lips met lingeringly. Then she sighed and, resting her head on his shoulder, looked about her once more with eager, poignant eyes. Defeated in his purpose, Will let her be, resolving to tell her the truth the minute they returned to the hotel. When he asked if she wanted the driver to make another circuit of the park, she merely gripped his hand tightly and nodded in assent.

Early that afternoon, while Will and Sylvie were in the park, Nye had called on her at her hotel. Having sent his card ahead of him, the bell-hop came to escort him upstairs. But the woman who greeted him was not Sylvie, but Rosa.

'My dear Jack!' she cooed, running to give him her hands, unable to hide her delight. 'How attentive you are. So kind, as always. Sylvie is not here, but when I received your card, I sent word for you to come up. What a happy coincidence that you should also be in Budapest.'

Rosa stood a little too close to him, and he could smell her perfume. She was dressed in the height of fashion, in a Paris gown that must have cost a small fortune, thanks, he was certain, to Sylvie's generosity, but her former robustness was finally fading. She was still attractive, he remarked to himself, but she had none of Sylvie's magnificence. He kissed her on both cheeks, and she moved closer to him, waiting for an embrace, wanting to touch the smooth fabric of his sleeve, but he turned and walked past her into the room.

'But it's no coincidence, my dear. Didn't Sylvie mention to you that she called on me yesterday?' he said deliberately, turning to smile at her, conscious of the full effect of his familiar charm upon her. 'She came to the old house yesterday. I own it now, you know.' He spoke with cruel relish. Rosa's own smile faded.

'She has so many visitors . . . ' she began uncertainly, aware that she must feel her way, and not wanting to insult him. She took a new tack: 'I haven't been in Budapest since we were here together. And Vienna, too! So lovely to see old haunts again. Do you remember those times? We went to the races at Freudenau. The Queen-Empress was there, and you won on almost every horse! You couldn't lose! You said I brought you luck.' She chattered desperately in the old way. 'And you bought me the most lovely parasol in the Graben, as I had left mine behind in the stands. Apricot-coloured silk, it was. I kept it for years.' She approached him once more, looking up into his eyes. She slipped her hand into his and squeezed it. 'We dined at the Hotel Sacher, and you could hardly wait to get me upstairs to bed,' she reminded him. 'You said I was the most lovely woman there.'

Nye politely disengaged his hand. 'Please, my dear. That was nearly fifteen years ago.' He walked towards the door. 'I'll leave a note for Sylvie downstairs at the desk.'

'Jack!' Rosa ran to him, desperation in her face. 'Oh Jack!' She clung to his arm, and he kindly took her hands in his, kissed her on the lips, and smiled as her eyelids fluttered and her mouth remained open, waiting. As she looked supplicatingly into his dark, familiar face, he spoke.

'No man enjoys shooting tame rabbits. You should remember that, my dear. Especially at your age.'

And he was gone.

When Sylvie returned from her drive, Rosa lay prostrate on the sofa while Louisa dabbed at her forehead with a cologne-soaked handkerchief. Sylvie had collected Nye's brief note from the desk, and had instantly divined that some kind of scene, some outburst of jealousy, would await her upstairs. As she and Will climbed the wide, ornate hotel staircase, all she could think was: 'I'm not ready for this. I'm not ready.' Will had anxiously tried to persuade her to go to his room, and let him deal with Rosa, but she had shaken her head and, taking a deep breath, opened the door.

Sylvie was grateful for Will beside her – it gave her unforeseen strength not to have to face her mother alone – but the actress in her automatically took control of the situation.

'Now, Mamma,' she addressed the invalid. 'Louisa, plump up that pillow behind Mamma's back, would you?' Louisa took the cushion from behind Rosa's head, causing her to pull herself up from her languishing position. 'How do you feel after your journey?' Sylvie continued. 'Would you like Louisa to fetch you something? A little wine? Or have you more of an appetite? Perhaps a light pancake, stuffed with paprika chicken like you used to adore?'

Rosa waved away Sylvie's suggestions with the hand that clutched her lace-edged handkerchief, but nevertheless sat up a little more. Sylvie signalled Louisa to withdraw into the bedroom, but remained standing, safe in the shelter of Will's presence close beside her.

'Did Mr Nye upset you, Mamma?' she asked casually. 'I believe he called on you while I was out?'

At that, Rosa shrieked aloud, clasping her hands to her bosom. 'How sharper than a serpent's tooth, to have a thankless child!' she exclaimed dramatically. Her hand shot out and she pointed one beringed finger at Sylvie. 'Hypocrite! Act like you're a little angel, but you're a whore!'

Will moved as if he would grasp the woman by the throat and throttle her words, but Sylvie reacted more rapidly.

'Stop it, Mamma!' She didn't shout, but with her practised voice, the sound of her command rang around the room. 'I won't put up with any more of your scenes. Stop it, or I shall call the manager and remove myself to another hotel.'

Rosa was genuinely shocked. She had never seen

such determination in her daughter's stance. Stopped in mid-flight, she gasped for breath. 'Don't bully me, Sylvie, please,' she said plaintively.

'I'm not bullying you, Mamma, but I won't listen to any more of your complaints against me either. I've done nothing to harm you.'

'Only go to Jack behind my back!' Rosa hissed venomously. 'Only take from me the only man I ever loved. But you have always been so selfish, always so uncaring.'

'No!' Sylvie flared into anger. 'It's you who've been uncaring. You always put your own gratification before me, even when I was a child.'

'How dare you blame me for anything! I am your mother!'

'Then behave like one!'

'Oh!' Rosa gasped as if winded. 'Oh, what monster did I give birth to? You're unnatural!'

Sylvie backed away. Will clasped her from behind, and she drew his encircling arms tight about her. In spite of her rage, she felt the familiar urgent pull of her unconscious to give in to her mother, to admit that all the faults lay with herself, that her mother was always right in everything, her shining, beautiful Mamma. The desire to say that black was white if that would mollify Rosa was uppermost in her mind, and she fought for clarity, struggled to remember once more all the events that had surrounded Sari Fodor's death. There was a word in German, the language she had grown up with, for what she felt for her mother – *Schadenfreude* – she loved her with horror, and hated her with an impossible longing. This was the woman, she told herself, who had withheld her love and, in its place, doled out nothing but pain and hurt; this was the woman who had lied and bullied and belittled her, yet her feelings for Rosa remained inexplicably shot through with love.

With the instincts of absolute selfishness, Rosa instantly sensed that Sylvie was weakening, and blindly pressed home her advantage. She had deliberately ignored Will's presence, familiar with his unyielding strength, but also knowing that it was only through Sylvie that she could weaken and hurt him too.

'Unnatural child! Cavorting with Jack Nye! You don't know what he is to you. If you did, you would cut off your hand, rather than caress his flesh with it,' she snarled, vicious and cold as she went in for the kill.

Will hugged Sylvie to him as hard as possible. With horror, he realized what Rosa was about to do. There was nothing he could do to avert it. He knew, in fact, that what had held him back until now had been the implacable emotional logic he now acknowledged – that it had to be Rosa who told Sylvie the truth. At least, he told himself, holding Sylvie as if he would never let her go, at least, now that the moment had come, he was here for her. It was not much, and yet he knew in his heart that to someone who, like Sylvie, had always been alone, it made a vital difference. He whispered words of love and encouragement in her ear, and felt her resolve strengthen once more.

'I do know, Mamma,' struggled Sylvie weakly. 'I do know what you did to me. I know that he killed Madame Fodor. Let's not quarrel about things that we cannot help. Please, Mamma, I beg of you. Let the past alone.'

'So you know that he's a killer. That excites you, does it? You, too, like to be mastered, to be held by a strong hand. But you don't know all.'

'Stop it, please, this is senseless.'

'You know that I loved Nye far more than I ever loved your father?'

'Please, Mamma,' Sylvie begged, holding up her hands and turning her head from side to side like a hart at bay. She felt that the atmosphere of hatred would overwhelm her and drive her mad. She sensed blindly that Rosa intended some unspeakable atrocity against her, that, this time, Rosa's jealousy had turned loose a ruthless psychological assassin.

With each statement, Rosa took a step towards where her daughter cowered against Will's sheltering body. 'How did Rudi die? Do you know?'

'In a duel.' Sylvie's voice was a whisper.

'In a duel. What was the duel about?'

'I don't know. Mamma, I don't want to know.'

'Over me,' declared Rosa triumphantly. 'They fought over me.'

'Please, Mamma.'

'Who fought for me? Who? Do you know that?'

Sylvie shook her head, her mind dulled with pain.

'Who killed your father?'

'I've no idea. I don't want to know!'

'Think, girl, think. Who loved me enough to fight for me? Who has loved only me? Who will never love you as he loved me, no matter what wiles you use to draw him to you, to steal him from me. He doesn't care for you!' Rosa's thin, cruel voice droned on and on, taunting and stabbing until the sense of what she was saying finally began to penetrate Sylvie's terrified mind. She felt as if a huge, roaring wind had blown up out of nowhere and was tearing its way through the room, taking Rosa's words with it so that she could not hear, so strong that the scream that she knew she must be screaming was blown back into her open mouth, silenced by the demonic force that had entered the quiet room. For a moment or two, she could not understand how the vases were not dashed to the floor, how the petals of the flowers were not hurled against the wall, how they themselves weren't sucked into the eye of the storm.

But then the wind died down, and Sylvie again noticed the soft crackling of the fire and heard the sound of people talking as they passed in the corridor outside. She felt her scream subside, and felt her mother staring at her. She began to shiver. The shivering turned to uncontrollable shaking. She saw Rosa's mouth open and close in front of her face, saw her mother's face pucker as she started to laugh uncontrollably. Her eyes, wild with unbelief, met Rosa's.

'Who do you think!' her mother screamed maniacally. 'Nye killed your father! You never knew! Never even suspected! He killed Count Rudi Lazar, and I loved him for it!' She triumphed over Sylvie at last. 'I loved him for murdering your father, and I love him still!'

All that Sylvie remembered before she fell unconscious was pleading for Will to take her mother away, but she could not drown out Rosa's crazy laughter.

CHAPTER TWENTY

Nye was waiting for Sylvie. He was certain that she would come to him, that his gift of the magnificent stone would entice her. All the women he had known had ultimately been seduced by diamonds, and it would be merely to Sylvie's credit, a sign of her true greatness, that it should take such a truly fabulous gem to bend her finally to his will. It was a stone that he had kept about him, treasured for its purity, for years.

Ever since their meeting in Will's studio, Nye's fantasies surrounding Sylvie had grown, and it was now beyond his comprehension that she would not ultimately match and return his desire. All the strands of his life had fitted together too neatly for him not to believe that it was pre-ordained that he should enjoy a woman like Sylvie Lazar, the only woman, in recent years, whom he had really desired, for the part he had played in her past life must be significant! Used to the pleasure of anticipation, he had savoured every day that passed, feeling his desire for her mount and stoking the fire so that it should burn ever more fiercely. His appetite for betrayal was aroused as it had never been before. What sweetness to kiss the soft eyelids that had wept so many childish tears because of his pleasures and desires. What pride to possess the woman whom the world now revered – beautiful, wealthy, independent, famed across two continents. It seemed to him impossible that such a state of passion could be accidental, and, gripped by the fantasies of betrayal that surrounded Sylvie like a cloud in his mind, he almost suspected that he might be possessed of some god-like power.

He had gone alone that evening to watch her, absorbing the mood of the audience into his own passion. As the gas-lights dimmed and the curtain whooshed up, he had looked slyly around at the faces of the men, immaculate in their evening dress, eyes shining, mouths apart in anticipation of her performance. Unseen, he had smiled obscenely to himself, imagining their eventual coupling in infinite detail.

After his return from the theatre, he had sat immobile in an armchair by the big ceramic stove in the corner of the salon of the old house on Buda, his hands resting in his lap, the tips of his fingers pressed lightly together, gazing up at *The Angel*, waiting for her to come to him. In repose, his expression was closed and unyielding, and the flesh of his cheeks was just beginning to drag with age. But the diamond studs in his shirt-front glittered and, as always, he looked at ease in his close-fitting evening clothes.

At last he heard a light knock and sprang up, smiling broadly, his eyes bright, the smooth finish of the man unusually perturbed. Racker showed Sylvie into the dimly lit room. Nye revelled in her beauty: the gold threadwork on her dress glittered in the gaslight and her pale skin had the soft sheen of some medieval ivory Madonna. She smiled vaguely at him as she brushed past him and walked to the centre of the room where she composed herself as she did on stage, controlling herself, concentrating on acting a part that would cocoon her and keep her safe from him. He came to stand beside her and Sylvie was aware of his eyes fastened on her face, of his closeness. They stood together in silence, both sensing each other's tension – his of sexual desire, hers of both fear and rage. She pulled off the shawl that swathed her head, shaking free her mane of hair. He looked at her in growing admiration, as if she exceeded even his estimation of her stature. His heart leapt, his judgement uniquely clouded by his passion.

'Sylvie! You look enchanting!' He took her lifeless hand and kissed it formally, then took her cloak from her shoulders and placed it over a chair by the door.

'Good evening, Jack,' she said calmly. She looked around the room, noticing that, to one side, a table spread with a white cloth bore heaped plates of smoked salmon, fruit and cheese as well as glasses and bottles of wine.

He followed her glance. 'Some champagne?' he asked. 'Or would you prefer some brandy? I have a fine old Armagnac.'

'Some brandy, please.'

Nye took a decanter from the table and poured some spirit into a heavy glass. He surveyed her from head to foot as he handed it to her. She stood rock-steady, never flinching at the obscenity of his gaze, but the sight of Rudi's emerald on his little finger made the icy rage that gripped her freeze her very thoughts. When her mind cleared again, she realized he was talking to her.

'You deserved the applause you received tonight, my dear,' he was saying. 'Your performance was unique. But then, I guessed the reason.' There was something crazy about the way he smiled at her.

'Tell me, then,' she said lightly, enthroning herself in a chair beside Will's painting of her, as if sheltering beneath its spirit of guardianship. He came to stand before her.

'You knew that I was there,' he explained triumphantly. 'Maybe without knowing it, you have anticipated this evening all your life, just as I have. Your performance was alight with the knowledge that I sat there in the darkness, wanting you, waiting for this moment.'

Sylvie nodded briefly, as if in agreement. A strange

smile played about her lips. Her tongue darted out to lick away the dryness, and Nye caught a tantalizing glimpse of her half-opened mouth.

'I admire you more than any woman I've ever known,' he went on. 'Elusive, unpredictable, alive! We shall be like the gods on Mount Olympus. Our mating will rock the world, for our children will be young princes; they shall inherit it all!'

'Africa,' sighed Sylvie in acknowledgement.

He grinned. 'As stockholders, we're already united. You've already taken my heart, out on the Rand, haven't you? I like your way of wooing a man! I admire astuteness in a woman. Now let's complete the union!'

It had never occurred to Sylvie that Nye might interpret her actions in this way, that he should believe her to have been courting him through her investments. But for now, his delusion suited her purposes. She meant somehow to disarm him, to get him at her mercy, even, if need be, by promising him sexual satisfaction, and then to kill him. The plan that had been hatched in Threadneedle Street for her to trap him into a confession of his murders had completely disappeared from her mind in the wake of Rosa's terrifying revelation that afternoon. Since then, her life seemed to have contracted to a single obsession; nothing else mattered – not Will, not her career, nothing but that Nye and the evil he represented should be removed from the face of the earth. She did not know how else to avenge herself for Rudi's death other than by Nye's own, although she did not feel it was revenge. The past was immutable. No present action of hers could restore a childhood or emotions that had never existed. But she believed that only with his death could she now free herself.

'You know I tried to match your compliment?' He was laughing now.

'What do you mean?' she asked sharply.

'Didn't Mr Abbey tell you that I tried to buy your contract from him?' Nye crowed with delight at his joke. Sylvie fought the wave of nausea that threatened to overwhelm her. 'But Abbey wouldn't sell you as easily as young MacKenzie did!' he laughed, looking up over her shoulder at *The Angel*.

Sylvie wanted to spring at him, to silence him, but with the actress's discipline over her emotions, she fought with herself to show him a relaxed ease of manner. 'You wouldn't have wanted so easy a victory, though, would you?' she taunted him, and he laughed again. He was exultant, ravished by her manner and unable to believe that something he wanted so much might be outside his reach.

'So,' she resumed carefully. 'Together, you and I could control the Rand?'

He grinned and nodded, seating himself opposite her where he could watch her.

'But there is more to your plans than profit?'

'Whoever owns the Rand will hold the world's economy in the palm of his hand,' agreed Nye. 'Cecil Rhodes is nearly ten years younger than me, yet he's successfully monopolized the diamond fields, now that I've moved my money to the Rand. You can be sure that Rhodes's ambitions are colonial. I wouldn't be surprised if he doesn't end up with a country named after him. Stranger things have happened. I want the same! Only I shall have gold, not diamonds.' An almost animal grimace passed fleetingly over his features, like the snarl of a wolf over his prey.

'Mine is no ordinary passion,' he went on, his voice thick with emotion. 'I meant it when I said I'll make you a queen! Consider it! You and I together could found a dynasty that could rule the world another day. You were made for such a role!'

Sylvie sipped at her brandy to stop the uncontrollable shivering that suddenly gripped her. She no longer knew what she was doing here. She had no gun, no poison, no knife. She was as insane as he was to imagine that she could extinguish a man's life as easily as she could just wish him dead. A sob rose in her throat. She realized she had never thought the thing through, that she could not physically endure it, for she had somehow imagined that the sheer force of her hatred would miraculously be enough to do the deed. And now she was afraid.

At this moment he rose and came towards her, holding out his hand to her. 'Come,' he said. 'The bed is ready for us upstairs.'

She looked up into his face, the face of her father's killer, like a small animal transfixed in the beam of a lantern.

Rosa's secret world of passion had closed in about her that afternoon in Sylvie's hotel when Nye had repudiated her so explicitly. Her own dreams of power as Nye's consort had been shattered, and her intense focus on her inner emotional world narrowed down to one hard point of pure hatred. Even Sylvie was excluded from the single-minded frenzy that gripped her. Her return to Budapest had reawakened so many memories, recollections that had thrown into painfully sharp relief the differences between her current future and the heady days of her past. She recalled how she had so willingly given herself up to the reckless impulse to accept Nye when he had reappeared in Budapest with his dramatic gift of the diamond necklace, how she had believed that, in giving herself to this violent, mysterious man, she had forged a unique destiny for them both. The crude realization that the images of her dreams had never formed themselves into the reality of her life was terrible to her.

All evening she had sat in her hotel room in a state of shock. Leaving Louisa with Sylvie, Will had held a whispered conference with Henry Abbey in the corridor outside Rosa's room. They had agreed that Rosa should not be left unguarded. Louisa could not be spared from her duties at the theatre with Sylvie, and Abbey had insisted that it should be Will who went with Sylvie to the theatre and accompanied her safely home, while Abbey remained at the hotel to keep an eye on Rosa and also to make arrangements for her to be escorted back to London the following day. With a wildness that both men had feared, Sylvie herself had insisted on appearing that night as planned. It had been Will who had overruled Abbey: 'She's safer on stage,' he had explained. 'Her performance will soothe and restore her as nothing else can, especially here in Budapest, among her father's people. Let her go on. She's laid many wounds before an audience, and come back healed.'

And Abbey had seen the wisdom of Will's words when Sylvie returned that night, white with exhaustion, but calm and sane once more. Both men had gone to bed hoping that the worst was now over.

But Will was woken from his sleep by someone shaking his shoulder.

'Wake up,' said a voice in his ear. 'Wake up. You must come with me. Quickly. I know where they've gone.'

As Will sat up, the figure moved across the room and turned up the gas. As he turned, he saw an unfamiliar elderly man standing before him.

'Get dressed, and I'll explain as we go,' he said. 'I'm Onslow Lapham. Rosa's husband. She's gone to follow Sylvie. I know where they're going, to the old house. I've followed her there in the past many a time. Come with me. Hurry!'

As Nye reached out his hand for her, Sylvie sprang up, throwing her glass to the floor, and ran from him and from her own foolishness. Just as she reached the door, it flew open, hitting her on the temple and temporarily stunning her. She stumbled backwards. She heard a rustle of skirts and a hissing breath. A shot rang out. She heard Nye start to scream, a high-pitched keening like a small animal caught in a trap. She could smell the cordite and also the foul stench of Nye's bowels opening helplessly. Another shot, and then a third, and the screaming changed to a gurgling rattle. She turned, clinging to the side of the open door, to see Rosa standing on the threshold, the gun smoking in her hand, her lips drawn back in a snarling grimace of victorious savagery. Certain that her daughter was going to Nye's bed, she had waited, giving them time alone together inside, waiting for the very instant of the consummation of his desire for Sylvie before she unloosed the lethal accuracy of her final arrogant act of jealousy.

Before Sylvie could take a step towards her mother, Rosa was seized from behind by two men. Sylvie's last sight of her was of Mr Lapham leading her away as she laughed dementedly. Then Will was at her side, shielding her from the sight of Nye's mutilated body, holding her to him.

'Thank God you're all right,' he repeated, looking into her face with terrified concern for signs of her distress. 'Thank God he didn't hurt you.'

Racker pushed past them through the door. He cried out as he saw his master's body sprawled on the floor, his guts spilling out onto the mess of faeces and blood that had been his chest and groin. He knelt beside Nye, helplessly stroking the hair back from the dead man's temples.

Sylvie turned away and walked shakily out into the familiar glazed-in passageway of her old home, from where the stone steps led up to her childhood bedroom. She looked about her and gave a shuddering sigh of relief. Despite the horror of the scene she had just witnessed, she felt a peace descend upon her. She turned and smiled at Will, then, reaching out for him, pulled him to her, and with the other hand reached up and ran her fingers through his thick hair. She looked into his anxious face and smiled.

'I'm all right,' she said. 'It's all over. I can start again now.'

Astonishment was mixed with solicitude upon his dear, familiar face.

'You see, I wasn't the Angel in the end, was I?' she went on. 'I couldn't take my revenge.'

With relief, he shook his head and met her smile. 'I'm glad,' he admitted.

'I never was very brave.'

He looked at her wonderingly. 'No,' he answered firmly. 'I've been the coward. But not now,' he cried, hugging her to him again. 'I'll just have to start on a new portrait, I guess,' he whispered, as he leant down to kiss her.